Freedom Never Rests

J-12

Freedom Never Rests

A Novel of Democracy in South Africa

James Kilgore

First published by Jacana Media (Pty) Ltd in 2011

10 Orange Street
Sunnyside
Auckland Park 2092
South Africa
+2711 628 3200
www.jacana.co.za

ISBN 978-1-4314-0119-2

Job No. 001505

Photos and design: Trevor Paul: www.behance.net/trevor_paul
Crowd photos: Boris Vahed

Set in Garamond 11/14pt
Printed and bound by CTP Printers, Cape Town

ISO 12647 compliant

See a complete list of Jacana titles at www.jacana.co.za

Che Guevara quote on page 329 used with permission
from Ocean Press.

Although you don't know us, we know ourselves: we are the movable ladders that take people up towards the skies, left out in the open for the rain, left with the memories of tear gas, panting for breath.
– Alfred Temba Qabula

Acknowledgements

Freedom Never Rests is the second of the novels I wrote during my six and a half years of incarceration in federal and state prisons in California. The inspiration for this book came one day in February of 2003, when I was climbing out of the shower stall at the Federal Detention Center in Dublin, California. In the stall next to mine a full flow of water, too hot for anyone to use, poured onto the tile floor and drained away. It would be almost a month before a plumber would bother to come to turn that water off. Every time I saw that steaming water shooting out I thought of communities in South Africa – Orange Farm, Odi, Queenstown, Madlebe and hundreds of other places – that had no such luck with their water supplies. In those communities officials and water profiteers tirelessly searched for ways to make sure someone paid for every drop, past and present. The perverse inequality of the global economy meant that I was fortunate in comparison not only to those in marginalised communities in South Africa but in relation to millions of people across the world. Their struggle for water continued. On the other hand, I had water security. As a federal prisoner I could take a hot shower and draw water for coffee with impunity.

Over the course of the next several years I wrote a number of drafts of this novel. In May 2009, as I exited High Desert State Prison in California, I carried a 243-page version of the text written on my most cherished prison possession, a Swintec electric typewriter. It took me more than a year to get

James Kilgore

the typescript onto computer and do the necessary research to make it complete.

The book would not have come to fruition without the efforts of a whole host of beloved comrades, friends and family.

I must start with the source of my inspiration: the people on the ground who have continued to battle for service delivery – organised communities, municipal workers, and thousands of other activists who carry on South Africa's grandest tradition, popular democracy and political determination. I extend a similar gratitude to those with whom I worked doing research on service delivery issues in the early days: Eddie Cottle, Hameda Deedat, Grace Khunou, Greg Ruiters and Mthetho Xhali.

But a novel cannot come to fruition via inspiration alone. A wide variety of people lent support in another form by sending books and materials that helped me to reconnect with my sense of the struggles for service delivery portrayed here. These include Mary Bassett, Patrick Bond, Moses Cloete, Laura Czerniewicz, Roger Dunscombe, Martin Hart-Landsberg, Stephen Morrow, Dan Pretorius, Tim Reagan and Laura Worby. Dianne Feeley was kind enough to read two different versions of the draft and provide wonderfully insightful and supportive comments. David McDonald, who first sparked my interest in water issues, also added his thoughtful observations on the manuscript. Rick De Satge read substantial portions of the story and sent me a systematic assessment of its strengths and weaknesses. At a later stage Ighsaan Schroeder lent assistance with the historical and political context and Mary Bassett provided medical advice on issues pertaining to HIV/Aids. Then there were the wonderful people from Jacana: Maggie Davey, whose instant enthusiasm and openness kept me going, and Lisa Compton, who provided incredibly helpful support on all levels, from correcting spelling errors to offering in-depth critiques of character development and plot. I also must express my appreciation to Lulu Mfazwe-Mojapelo for doing the editing of the Xhosa in the book.

Lastly, there was my immediate family – my heart and soul, my real emotional connection to southern Africa. Without my mother, Barbara Kilgore, sons Lewis and Lonnie, and my in-laws Pat Barnes-McConnell and Dave McConnell, I would never have maintained the frame of mind required to write while in prison. Pat deserves special praise here for tackling the Byzantine prison mail system to shunt the various drafts back and forth from me to readers.

And finally there was my partner, Terri Barnes, who held us all together through the dark days and then rose to the occasion repeatedly to review my feeble words and guide me to more appropriate prose. I am grateful for having such people around me. Perhaps the greatest thing about prison (and not much of it is great) is that I learned to fully appreciate what it means to be surrounded and supported, albeit at a distance, by those you love. I hope this book is a small return for all the help and support I have received. I also offer it as a gesture of solidarity with those for whom a hot shower remains a distant dream.

James Kilgore
Champaign, Illinois
February 2011

Part 1

Chapter 1
Johannesburg, 1993

THE FIRST FLOOR OF THE ageing Unified Bank Building vibrated with the footfalls. Since Unified's executives had moved their offices to the white suburbs, the old headquarters had turned into a hothouse of political activity. Rissik Street's Sunday window-shoppers were used to the rhythms. Freedom songs provided musical background as people admired the latest Toshiba boom boxes and knock-off running shoes on their way home from church. Today dozens of shop stewards were taking their turn in forging a new nation, a South Africa for the working class.

Monwabisi Radebe's feet flew above his head in this well-practised routine. Limber hotel waiters and plump, middle-aged female street sweepers handled the steps and sways with equal grace. The Movement was preparing to take a decision. They'd honed the process for more than two decades. Toyi-toyi and song provided the comforts of home, firing joyous bullets of inspiration to the heart of the enemy. A hand-lettered banner across the front wall reaffirmed the basic message of solidarity: 'An Injury to One is an Injury to All.'

The singing gradually wound down. Like thousands of South Africans, these shop stewards from the Congress of South African Trade Unions (COSATU) were examining the draft of the Reconstruction and Development Programme, or RDP, a 147-page bible for a new nation. This was their third session. Only one crucial topic remained – nationalisation.

1

Though his headache was getting worse, Monwabisi had to bring the house to consensus. This was democracy in action: discuss an issue for hours, sometimes days, until everyone agreed. They called it 'workers' control'.

'Nationalisation without compensation is the only answer,' argued the thick-chested Nathaniel Mda of the mineworkers' union. 'More than 69 000 miners have died in disasters over the years. It's time to reverse history, to claim the gold and diamonds on behalf of the working class.'

A cohort of several dozen showed their support for Mda with a song in Sesotho. 'The land of South Africa belongs to all the people,' their voices proclaimed, 'not just a greedy few.'

Once the quiet had returned, Monwabisi sought responses from the meeting.

'Nationalisation is premature,' said Tshepo Jiyane. The long-time shop steward for the food workers wore his usual attire – a black cap bearing the hammer and sickle of the South African Communist Party and a T-shirt with the smiling face of Madiba. 'We are in the democratic phase of our revolution,' he added, 'leading a broad front of all progressive classes, including the national bourgeoisie.'

'The comrade is proposing we jump in bed with the bosses!' shouted Mda as he leaped to his feet. 'The workers must speak with one voice. Sifuna inationalisation kuphela.'

Monwabisi's fist slammed down on the metal table at the front of the hall.

'Comrade Mda, we need order, not personal attacks,' said Monwabisi. 'Take a seat.'

Monwabisi's vision was starting to blur. The headaches did that sometimes. He got one almost every day now, and Panado didn't help. Plus those small lumps in his neck weren't going away. He just wanted to find somewhere to lie down in the darkness. That brought a little relief.

As Mda apologised for his outburst, suddenly the hall

shook. The deep-level gold mines under Joburg had made tremors a way of life. Then came the blast. The workers went silent for a second, waiting to see if the twelve storeys above them were going to collapse on their heads. A few of them dove under their chairs.

'That was no earthquake,' said Mda.

'Sounded like a thunderclap,' said Monwabisi, 'but there's not a cloud in the sky.' He sent Jiyane and two shop stewards outside to survey the street.

Members of POPCRU, the police union, took up positions at the door to the hall, guns drawn.

'No one must leave until we know what happened,' said Monwabisi.

'Bloody Boers,' said Mda.

Jiyane came running back inside.

'They bombed the ANC office up the road,' he said. 'Fire trucks are already there. It's serious.'

'We must find them where they sleep,' said Mda, holding a massive panga in the air.

'The POPCRU delegation will guard the building,' said Monwabisi.

'We must strike back,' said Johannes Mtsilo, regional secretary of the railway workers and a former boxer. He began the musical plea for machine guns: 'Awuleth'umshini wami, awuleth'umshini wami.' This time the lyrics weren't ceremonial. The song continued for fifteen minutes. As Monwabisi joined in the toyi-toyi he remembered that his cousin Mthetho, who had just returned to South Africa for the first time in fifteen years, was attending that ANC meeting. The joyous image of him kissing the tarmac at the Joburg airport when he arrived was vanishing from Monwabisi's mind. Instead, he saw his cousin's corpse lying under a pile of building rubble. The killing just never seemed to stop.

The singing wound down but the house was divided on

the next step. Mtsilo and others wanted to rush to the ANC office. 'We need to defend our comrades!' Mtsilo shouted, daring anyone to shy away from their duty.

'Rushing there will do no good,' said Jiyane. 'There are already hundreds of people in the streets.' He proposed an adjournment, arguing that the venue was no longer safe for their deliberations. 'We may be the next target,' Jiyane added.

The delegation shouted him down.

'The Boers can't halt the mission of the working class,' said Mda. 'We are COSATU. We don't run away.'

'POPCRU comrades to the front!' Monwabisi called out. 'Yizani phambili.'

Monwabisi ordered the six POPCRU delegates to set up a team of lookouts on Bree and Rissik streets to make sure no one who wasn't part of COSATU entered the building. At least it was a Sunday. The streets were quiet. Boers in their Land Rovers and Voortrekker gear would stick out like Gerrie Coetzee in a shebeen.

Before the POPCRU guards could take up their positions, twenty more black policemen arrived and closed the streets for two blocks in all directions. Meanwhile Police Sergeant Pheto dashed into the hall and assured the shop stewards the authorities had cut off the Boers at each and every point. He said that at least two comrades had perished in the explosion. 'But the workers will be protected,' he promised. Pheto rushed out of the room before Monwabisi even had a chance to ask him the names of the deceased. He'd catch them on the radio later. He had a meeting to chair.

'We've waited too long for this moment to be derailed by a few Boers,' Monwabisi told the crowd. 'We, the shop stewards of the Witwatersrand, must be heard.'

'No one needs to worry,' Mtsilo said, glaring at Jiyane. 'I will protect you.'

The railway worker swung his knobkerrie in a circle as the delegates rose to their feet with applause.

'We stand for the nationalisation of South Africa's mines, commercial farms and major industries,' read the meeting's final resolution. 'We stand for justice and workers' control.'

The delegates added a supplement that wasn't on the day's agenda: 'We stand for the prosecution of all apartheid war criminals and murderers.'

The result satisfied Monwabisi, though it wasn't enough to rid him of his headache. The pain was worse than ever. When he'd spoken on the phone to his wife Constantia, the previous week, she'd advised him to see a doctor. Maybe she was right.

After the workers closed the gathering with a moment of silence and the singing of 'Hamba Kahle' to commemorate those who died in the bomb blast, Monwabisi dashed up the road to look for his cousin. He found him standing next to one of the fire trucks wearing his usual grey suit. At least the Boers had spared Monwabisi's family this time around.

Though the shop stewards were convinced that nationalisation was the correct path, their resolution ultimately lost out. The Consultative Business Movement and the leading black commercial associations backed 'socially responsible entrepreneurship'. The final draft of the RDP advocated a 'thorough democratisation of South Africa', but made no promises about nationalisation.

Monwabisi and the other shop stewards were disappointed, but they accepted the decisions of the democratic movement. What was more important than the result was the process. People had given their lives for this democracy. In the new

South Africa everyone, including workers, would have their say before government took decisions on vital issues. The process of developing the RDP would be the model for the future government led by the ANC. For once the workers could say: 'The future is now.'

Chapter 2
Brooklyn, New York
27 May 1994

THE SOUNDS OF HUGH Masekela's 'Bring Him Back Home' echoed through the rafters of the enormous church basement. South Africa's famed jazz trumpeter had come to St Luke's to celebrate the downfall of apartheid. Just a month earlier millions of South Africans had gone to the polls. Not only had they brought Nelson Mandela back home, they'd elected him and his party, the African National Congress, to head their first democratic government.

With his quiet dignity and elbow-swinging, arthritic dance style, the world's most famous political prisoner had graciously received the sceptre of power from the National Party's F.W. de Klerk. The handover was not just a South African moment. Mandela and the black majority of his country had become global symbols of freedom.

Hundreds of well-wishers attended the event at St Luke's. They listened as keynote speaker Mthetho Jonasi, the ANC's Deputy Representative to the United Nations, claimed the night for the 'freedom fighters of North America, those who put their bodies on the line in solidarity with our cause'.

Joanna Ross and Peter Franklin fell in that category. Joanna looked much the same as she did that Thanksgiving Day in 1985 when she and Peter had chained themselves to the front door of a Buffalo bank that had invested in

7

South Africa. A crowd of three dozen chanted 'Freedom yes, apartheid no' while the police carted the couple away. Mthetho and his cousin Monwabisi Radebe, who was visiting from South Africa, led the lively chorus. Joanna and Peter spent the weekend in the Buffalo City Jail. Their romance blossomed in that brief interlude of shared martyrdom.

Joanna's straight brown hair was still neatly combed, reaching slightly below her ears. Her weepy brown eyes had just begun to sprout a tiny wrinkle or two around the edges. Unlike most of her friends, Joanna hadn't gained a pound over the years, maintaining her wiry, almost gaunt physique. In fact, her life hadn't really changed much at all. She remained the persistent conscience of the community, gently proselytising shoppers, pedestrians and neighbours about the latest human rights atrocity in the world. For the last seven years she'd spent a month of her summer vacation from her job as a school librarian doing counsellor work at a camp for, as the brochures called them, 'wayward inner-city youth'.

Nearly a year had passed since Peter and Joanna's break-up. Though she rarely talked about it, Joanna was still heartbroken. She blamed the separation on Peter's trip to Washington, DC. He'd been arrested there with Whoopi Goldberg and Stevie Wonder in a protest against US investments in South Africa. After that he started to belittle Joanna's penchant for second-hand clothes and what she called her 'vow of poverty'. He talked of becoming a 'role player' in the cause of social justice, not a screamer at the margins. His personal ambition disturbed Joanna. She'd always thought their love was based on a certain humility, a lifestyle in harmony with the poorest of the poor.

Though on this occasion Peter had jettisoned his now trademark suit and tie for a yellow ANC T-shirt, he'd long since abandoned any traces of his old activist appearance. The shoulder-length blondish locks which Joanna once loved to brush had morphed into an executive cut that would blend seamlessly into any corporate boardroom. His reddish Abe Lincoln-style beard had disappeared altogether, revealing his smooth, almost boyish cheeks.

As they met amid the sea of celebrants, the two exchanged tentative hugs, labouring to share the excitement of the occasion. They recalled the half-cooked instant mashed potatoes of the Buffalo City Jail and the three ants Peter found floating in his morning coffee.

'You told me you took them out and drank it anyway,' she said. They laughed.

'South Africa is a buzzy place,' he said. 'You have to visit, see the fruits of your labour.'

'It's not really my labour,' she replied. 'The South African people deserve the credit.'

'Of course,' he said, 'but we played our role. That's all I'm saying.'

Peter went on to tell Joanna how his company, Pellmar Corporation, saw lots of opportunities for greenfield investment and partnerships in South Africa. They'd been undertaking similar projects in Bulgaria, Romania and the Ukraine with great success.

'We are a small firm but we are a game-changer,' he said. 'It's a win-win situation. The needs in South Africa are endless – housing, water, education, electricity, management at all levels. Our people have been in dialogue with the ANC. The new rulers, especially Mandela, recognise their capacity problems.'

Peter handed Joanna his beige business card. His name and title, 'Investment Consultant', were embossed in gold letters. She didn't ask him what an investment consultant actually did. A few years earlier, investment consultants were among the kinds of people Peter referred to as 'money-grubbing parasites'. She never thought someone she once loved so much could shed his principles so easily.

She excused herself, saying she had to meet an old friend, and went to join the queue for food. The South African students had cooked a cow on a spit and slaughtered several goats. Joanna didn't normally eat meat. She asked one of the South African women serving the food about a 'vegetarian option'. The woman smiled.

'Sorry, my dear,' she told Joanna, 'but in Africa we can't celebrate our freedom with lettuce.' She handed Joanna a plate piled high with goat ribs, steak, collard greens and a fat sausage they reverently called 'wors'.

As she looked for a place to sit, Joanna spotted the frizzy black beard of Zoltan Steinberg. He'd been in the crowd that day outside the Buffalo bank. Zoltan was still a student, doing research on something he called 'alienation and worker self-organisation'. He'd explained his topic to her a couple times before, but Joanna couldn't wade through the academic jargon.

'I haven't eaten meat in six years,' Zoltan told her. 'But only once in our lifetime will we see apartheid fall.'

He chewed the wors delicately, as if gentle bites could keep the toxins from coming out.

'I'm getting into computers,' he told her. 'They've got great potential for working-class organisation at a global level. The South Africans are at the cutting edge.'

He took another bite of the wors. 'Not too bad,' he said. 'Better than Denny's anyway.'

'Have some more,' said Joanna as she stabbed her sausage with her plastic fork and plunked it onto Zoltan's plate. Zoltan buried it under a pile of collards.

'South Africa has the most advanced trade union movement in the world,' he said. 'They put the AFL-CIO to shame. Imagine workers who can shut down whole cities.'

'Sounds amazing,' said Joanna. The plastic knife broke as she tried to cut the steak. Hot grease seeped into her fingertips as she picked the meat up in her hands and took a bite.

'I've already visited Johannesburg and met with some leaders of the metalworkers,' he told her.

Zoltan also had business cards. 'I feel like a fool carrying these things around,' he said. 'But everyone over there has them, even the shop stewards.'

He opened his blue nylon billfold and shook out a handful of cards. Each bore the symbol of a different South African union – from the mineworkers' pick to the open-ended wrench of the metalworkers.

'I've got a collection going,' he said, 'but only from the unions. I don't trust the ANC. Too many intellectuals. I'm going to Brazil next. They've got a genuine workers' party there.'

Joanna decided not to touch the goat ribs. She wrapped the meat in a paper napkin and put it in her purse. She'd throw it away outside, when no one was watching. She was a little bit envious of Peter and Zoltan. She'd spent most of her life fighting for justice in the world but she rarely ever left New York City. Maybe one day she'd go and actually meet the people she was fighting for.

By night's end the cow and goats had shrivelled to gnarled bones. A few cases of beer remained but the South African students had plans for those. Their celebration was just beginning. After the crowd rendered a slightly drunken version of the new South African national anthem, a photographer gathered Peter, Joanna, Zoltan and Mthetho together for a picture.

By that time Joanna had covered her light grey blouse with the yellow T-shirt of the ANC. Pictures taken, Peter and Joanna embraced, the final cap to a joyous evening. He kissed her on both cheeks, then on the lips for a little too long. She wanted to pull back but the beer had gone to her head.

'We should have lunch sometime,' he said.

'Good idea,' she replied.

11

She doubted he would phone. She imagined that investment consultants were busy people.

○

Three weeks later, Angela Arness, the national director of Unitarian Vision (UV), rang Joanna. Angela was an old friend from the anti-nuclear power protests of the early eighties. She and Joanna had been arrested together in New England with the famous radical priests, the Berrigan brothers. Angela told Joanna the UV human rights project was hunting for a country representative in South Africa.

'The job involves living inside the country and reporting to Unitarian churches around the US about human rights in South Africa,' Angela explained. 'Later on there might be some project money. We need someone with a church affiliation and a background in the anti-apartheid movement, and we want you to apply.'

'I don't even have a passport,' Joanna replied, 'and I don't know much about South Africa. There's got to be more qualified people.'

'I don't want anyone going there who has a personal agenda,' said Angela. 'Mandela deserves better than that. So do our members.'

○

Joanna found the offer flattering but she worried about having to resign from her job at the school library. She was building up an impressive collection of titles on global issues. Some of the kids had started a study group on 'Solving World Poverty'. Who would help them? And then there was Misty. None of her friends had time to look after an ageing cat.

She spent a week mulling it all over, consulting with friends and rereading a collection of the speeches of Desmond Tutu that she found at a second-hand bookstore. What an inspiring man.

In the end Joanna submitted her résumé and went to Washington for the interview, though she still hadn't figured out what to do with her cat if she got the job.

The first question Angela and the other two people on the interview panel asked was why she was interested in the position.

Joanna told them the rest of the world had a lot to learn from South Africans, a people who'd been through so much yet were still willing to forgive. As she spoke, she pictured herself in the middle of one of those huge marches in Pretoria that she'd seen on the news. That collection of books in the school library felt a little less important.

The Unitarians didn't move fast. After a month, Joanna had almost forgotten about the job. A few days later Angela finally phoned to tell Joanna the position was hers if she wanted it. They expected her to be in Johannesburg in about three weeks. Joanna said she'd think about it for a couple of days. She said she was worried about her school. The next day she talked to her school principal, Bill Callaghan. He said if she took the UV job, he'd recommend a year's leave of absence. He said he envied her, that she was the luckiest woman in New York to have a chance to live in the world's newest democracy.

Callaghan's comments turned the tide for Joanna. She phoned Angela that afternoon and told her she'd take the job.

Shirley Bullock and her eight-year-old daughter Emily, who lived in the flat next door, agreed to take Misty. Joanna had only one remaining concern. She hoped she wouldn't bump into Peter Franklin – he brought up too many painful memories. Besides, she was afraid they might be on different sides of the fence.

Chapter 3
South Africa, 1995

'VIVA MABHOKOBHOKO, viva!' the taxi driver shouted out the window. The green-and-gold flag perched on the dashboard matched his Springbok jersey and cap. Two young boys herding goats across this desolate part of the former Ciskei gave him a thumbs up.

'Your mabhokobhoko are full of shit, my brother,' said Monwabisi. 'Keep your eye on the road.' Monwabisi wanted to remind the driver that the only black player on the Springboks was a coloured and he'd been a member of the security forces. He probably used to hunt down comrades in the townships.

'The Springboks are the champions of the world,' the radio announcer screeched. 'And that's our president, Nelson Mandela, presenting the trophy to team captain François Pienaar. Who could have ever dreamed this would happen? I'm so proud to be a South African today. So proud.'

'And what about two years ago, when your police were shooting us on the streets of Katlehong, when the impis were mowing people down at the train stations?' asked Monwabisi. 'Were you proud then? Bloody Boers will never change.'

'Halala, mabhokobhoko, halala!' the driver shouted. He took off his cap and waved it at two old women carrying buckets of water on their head. 'You must join the new South Africa, bhuti,' he said to Monwabisi. 'You are living in the past.'

The taxi driver cruised into Sivuyile township, passing through Section 4 where Monwabisi's mother used to live. Monwabisi ran these streets for cross-country during his school days. One time he almost beat the legendary Willie Mtolo, but just ten metres short of the finish line Monwabisi fell and knocked out his front tooth. He'd lived for years with that gap between his teeth, a lingering reminder of the defeat. He was thinking of using his provident fund money to get it fixed.

If the driver wasn't such a fool, Monwabisi would tell him to drive down his mother's street, where he could teach him a little history. It was on that street where the police kidnapped his brother Ishmael during the State of Emergency in 1987. A couple of weeks later, they left his brother's hands in a plastic bag outside their front door. His mother died of a broken heart a few months later.

'Just get me home safely,' said Monwabisi. 'That's all I ask from this new South Africa of yours.'

Monwabisi wanted to sleep. A month earlier, while the Springboks were crushing Romania, he and his eighty workmates had spent their final days at Metal Links in Johannesburg packing the machines from their shop into shipping crates bound for Jakarta. Their boss, Herbert Felton, was closing up his metal fabrication business after two decades.

Felton had found an Indonesian buyer for his drill presses, punches and the arc welder Monwabisi had operated for eight years. As the workers loaded the last pieces of equipment into the crates, the chubby shop manager, Allen Croeser, handed Monwabisi and the thirty-five other workers who'd been with the company for more than five years a gift certificate for R50 at Edgars department store.

'With this money you'll be dressing like Mandela,' Croeser said. Monwabisi gave his gift certificate to another worker in exchange for two cassettes by his favourite horn player, Kaya Mahlangu.

Two weeks later, with Felton safely tucked into his new house in Perth, Australia, Monwabisi received a notice that the R8 432.62 from his provident fund would be deposited in his account in three days. The letter also noted that the fund had suffered some 'adversities' in recent months. Therefore, the amount might be slightly less than anticipated. 'The company regrets any inconvenience this may cause,' the letter stated.

According to Monwabisi's previous statement, his provident fund held more than R30 000. This R8 000 of Felton's wouldn't keep him going for more than a few months. He'd planned to add a second storey to his family's four-room house in Sivuyile, maybe buy a few head of cattle. Now he doubted he could afford even a tiny extension to accommodate his wife's sickly mother. After more than eight years as a shop steward, he had nothing.

The taxi driver banged out the rhythm of 'Shosholoza' on the hooter as he cruised down Makana Boulevard, Sivuyile's main thoroughfare. While the radio blared interviews in Afrikaans with Joost van der Westhuizen and the star of the cup, Joel Stransky, the jubilant driver halted at the top of the dirt street where the Radebes lived, dropping Monwabisi a few metres from his house.

Musa and Fidel, Monwabisi's young sons, were kicking a soccer ball back and forth in the street. When they saw their father, they came running.

'Ufikile utata!' they shouted as they wrapped themselves around his legs. They'd grown since he'd last seen them. Fidel was four now, Musa three. They were almost strong enough to pull him down. He set his bags on the ground, took control of the soccer ball and dribbled around the two boys, easily dodging their challenges. He loved to hear their giggles.

After a couple of minutes, Monwabisi was battling to get his breath. It had been a long time since he'd played soccer, let alone run a marathon, but this was more than just being out of shape. It might be the virus taking over.

He walked the boys inside and told them their favourite stories. They especially loved to hear about the Eastern Cape's greatest boxer, Happy Boy Mgxaji. After telling them about Happy Boy's victory over a fighter called 'Pangaman', Monwabisi then delighted the wide-eyed pair with his account of the fiery speeches of the giant Joburg trade unionist Sam Shilowa.

'Sam is so tall he has to duck to pass through doorways,' Monwabisi told them. His breath came back when he saw the awestruck smiles on his sons' faces. Everything would turn out all right. The boys still loved his stories.

Chapter 4

'I'M WORKING FULL-TIME for the South African working class,' said Monwabisi as he took two beers and a Fanta out of the fridge.

After only two weeks in Sivuyile, the local ANC branch had elected him chair. His predecessor, Lungile Qobo, had been appointed to the Department of Labour in Pretoria. The branch had already given Monwabisi a nickname: Comrade RDP.

'You must be careful,' said his wife, Constantia, eyeing the cans of Amstel. She wanted to say more, but she couldn't mention the virus, especially not in front of the housekeeper. Portia was her cousin, but she was a radio, broadcasting to all who would listen.

Constantia didn't know how to discuss this virus with him. How could he have been so careless? He'd probably been seduced by some slim-bodied young thing. Women from Sivuyile still followed traditional notions of beauty. No woman with bird legs could carry water or hoe a field. At least Constantia had tested negative.

'We must celebrate,' Monwabisi said. 'Chiefs have won two–nil.' She heard him popping open the cans for Jeff Ntoni and Elvis Jim. Both were leaders in the Sivuyile ANC; Ntoni was the deputy chair. Ntoni was a little too old to play soccer but he still looked match fit. At least he didn't take beer.

Constantia handed Portia the tiny sharpening stone her mother had given her.

'Make sure that blade is razor sharp,' said Constantia. 'Otherwise some wool will remain.'

Portia dragged the blade of the long-handled knife along the stone for a few minutes.

Usually Constantia prepared the sheep's head herself, but she had some paperwork to do for the umgalelo. Sheep's head was Monwabisi's favourite dish. He claimed no one in Joburg could cook it properly, that it needed the hands of a Xhosa woman born and bred in the Eastern Cape.

Constantia had to make sure Portia got that skin extra smooth. Men could have tantrums over such things, though Monwabisi was generally level-headed about everything except soccer.

'Nkosi yam!' Elvis Jim shouted as Doctor Khumalo missed an easy chance.

'The Doctor is showing his age,' said Monwabisi.

Constantia hoped Elvis Jim would leave soon. During the years Monwabisi was in Joburg, the rotund Jim often dropped by unexpectedly, usually on his way home from Mama Patty's shebeen. His wife, Zandile, was a schoolteacher, but Jim liked to tell Constantia he was a traditionalist who couldn't stay with just one woman. Constantia would smile and nod until he left. The one time he tried to touch her with his sausage fingers she told him she was a Christian. He retreated.

'Doctor Khumalo is the greatest South African footballer in history,' the TV announcer said. 'The man can do it all.'

'Thetha, mhlobo wam,' Constantia heard Monwabisi say. 'Now you are talking sense.' She didn't like the beer in his voice. At least only five minutes of play remained. Hopefully the drinking was over.

As a cheer came out of the lounge at the final whistle, Portia asked Constantia to test the sheep's head. 'I want to make sure it's perfect for utata,' the young girl said.

Constantia rubbed her hand along the forehead. 'Feels like the bottom of a baby's foot,' she said.

As Monwabisi escorted the others out the door, they launched into a freedom song. It always happened when there was beer. Constantia hoped they wouldn't get as far as 'Kill the Boer, kill the farmer'. She'd heard it too many times.

'If only Lucas would come home,' she heard Ntoni say. 'And Shoes. Then Amakhosi would shine.'

'Lucas is earning three thousand pounds a week in the UK,' replied Monwabisi. 'He will never come home. Never, I tell you.'

'Always crying about this Lucas Radebe,' said Portia to Constantia. 'As if one man can make a team.'

Monwabisi came back inside after a few minutes. The TV had gone over to news. Mandela was visiting the Free State, speaking Afrikaans to some white farmers.

'Usofti,' said Monwabisi. 'We love that old man but he's a bit too kind-hearted.'

Portia put the sheep's head in the pot and reminded Constantia that she had to leave early to attend a baptism. 'I'm going to be a godmother,' she said as she grabbed her bag and left.

Monwabisi came to the kitchen for another beer.

'You need to think about your health,' Constantia said.

'I'm a man of the struggle,' he told her. 'My mind and body remain strong when I'm fighting oppression and exploitation. If I stay at home thinking about what that little virus is doing and letting my buttocks burn, I'll become sick after a few days.'

'I wasn't talking about politics,' she said. 'I mean those tins and little brown bottles that you love so much.'

Constantia was tempted to add that drinking was something their family could no longer afford, at least not until Monwabisi found work. When her husband first came home, she'd suggested he approach his cousin Mthetho. Surely a Provincial Deputy Minister of Local Government must have something to offer. Monwabisi said he intended to start his own welding business, making burglar bars and driveway gates. Since then he hadn't mentioned the idea. He did nothing but attend meetings, watch television and read old copies of the *Business Day* newspaper that people brought from Johannesburg.

Monwabisi went back to watching the news, laughing at Madiba and his Afrikaans. When he came to fetch another beer, he tried to convince Constantia she must start attending ANC meetings. She'd done that back in the early nineties, but the young comrades had told her Fidel lacked 'revolutionary discipline' because he cried too much. When she tried to explain that the baby had colic, they wouldn't listen. After that she took a back seat when it came to politics. Her duties as a mother came first.

'I will try,' she promised Monwabisi, though she had no real interest in the affairs of the branch. If she went, it would be for only one reason: to keep an eye on Comrade RDP. The chairman of the ANC branch would be a prize catch for one of those young female hyenas on the streets of Sivuyile.

☽

The following evening Monwabisi sat on a wooden chair in the front garden reading an old *Business Day*. Constantia had temporarily evicted him from the house. Her umgalelo was meeting in the lounge. Each of the eighteen women had been setting aside R50 a month for years. A banker was advising them on investment strategies.

As Monwabisi finished an editorial on the independence of the Reserve Bank, Ntoni and Jim came by, along with the

21

branch's most senior member, Cleophas Nobatana. The stocky old man had spent twenty years on Robben Island with Madiba.

'We have come with a proposition,' said Ntoni.

Monwabisi scrambled to find some stools for his visitors to sit on.

'The umgalelo has taken all our seats,' he said. 'Sorry, comrades.'

Then he remembered the new garden furniture his wife had bought. He led the three ANC cadres to the back garden.

They ducked under two blankets hanging on the line to arrive at the shiny new set of white plastic chairs. Ntoni helped Nobatana ease into his seat.

'We want you to be the party's candidate for councillor in the upcoming local elections,' said Ntoni. 'We need someone who can stand up for the community.' The deputy chairman folded his arms and waited for Comrade RDP's reply.

'I'm honoured,' said Monwabisi, 'but I'm not a politician. I can't put on a suit and tie.'

As he spoke, Mrs Sithethi from next door came out her back door and eased through a hole in the shrubs between her house and the Radebes'.

'Your throw-throw has already started, mama,' Monwabisi told her.

'Sorry, I'm late,' she said. 'The girl has burnt the samp. Nothing but smoke in there.'

'Shame,' said Ntoni.

Mrs Sithethi knocked once on the back door and went in. The irritating TV voice of the notorious Ntsiki Lukhele mixed with the consultant's sales pitch on emerging markets. The women always combined business with their favourite soap opera, *Generations*. Ntsiki was the husband stealer they all loved to hate.

'I can see your picture on the campaign posters now,' said Ntoni. 'A better life for all in Ukusa.'

'Where did they get this idea for Ukusa?' asked Nobatana. 'Why can't we remain Sivuyile?'

'It's from Pretoria,' said Monwabisi. 'They want us to join with the whites from Northridge. That way we can get some of their money. Bopape and Basil February townships will be part of Ukusa as well.'

'If it means getting some of the whites' money for the community, I support it,' said Nobatana. He licked his lips. 'With this diabetes,' the old man added, 'you are always thirsty.'

Monwabisi filled a silver cup with water from the tap and brought it to Nobatana.

'Comrade RDP, you are the obvious candidate,' said Elvis Jim.

The women inside the house unleashed a Xhosa hymn. When they started the second verse, Monwabisi suggested that the men take a walk. They couldn't hear each other over the chorus.

As the men moved into the street, two small, barefooted boys raced past pushing a bicycle wheel rim.

Nobatana reminded Monwabisi that the Movement was bigger than the wishes of any one individual, that a cadre must accept any post to which the organisation decided to deploy him. The former shop steward didn't budge. He told them he was merely exercising his 'democratic right to refuse'.

Nobatana informed Monwabisi that the councillor post came with a salary. 'You have to think about supporting your family,' said the old man.

'I'm going to start a welding business,' Monwabisi said. 'With all the tsotsis we have these days, people will need plenty of burglar bars.'

As the four walked up the road, Ntoni told Monwabisi they would return in a few days to see if he had 'changed his mind'.

'There is a better chance of the leopard changing its spots,' said Monwabisi as Ntoni and the others headed for home.

○

When news of Monwabisi refusing the nomination spread throughout the branch, the Sivuyile ANC Women's League called an emergency meeting. Attending ANC meetings was challenging enough for Constantia, but she avoided the League at all costs. There were too many petty quarrels among the women. But this time Monwabisi insisted that she go. She took along a jersey she was knitting for Fidel. At least she could do something useful for the two hours. Keeping her hands moving would also help her from getting cold. The brick walls and steel rafters of Sivuyile Hall offered little warmth on a winter night.

Chairwoman Nompumelelo Mpupa informed the audience that Elvis Jim had the support of many branch members. Constantia strained to hear. The chairwoman's roundish shape belied her tiny voice. She only became audible when she lost her temper.

Nompumelelo asked the women to comment on Jim as a candidate. Constantia kept on knitting while she requested that Jim's wife, Zandile, be excused.

'People might be shy to speak in her presence,' Constantia said without dropping a stitch. Zandile Jim pranced out of the hall without protest, the echo of her black stiletto heels a reminder of her husband's booming business. His construction firm had recently won a sizable contract from the Department of Trade and Industry.

Nompumelelo told the members the ANC needed a stronger person, one who could stand up to the white councillors. 'Besides,' she added, 'Jim has other problematic qualities.'

Constantia grinned. She wasn't the only one who'd had to fight off Jim's advances. If he was a councillor, what would be the consequences of refusing?

Nompumelelo asked if Constantia couldn't try to talk to Monwabisi. 'You must use your powers as a woman to convince your husband to stand,' the chairwoman said.

'You don't know my husband,' Constantia replied. 'He's as stubborn as a tired donkey. Nothing will change his mind.'

Mrs Mehlo, a middle-aged woman who sat next to Constantia in church every Sunday, took the floor. A yellow doek concealed her thinning hair.

'I have asked the Lord for guidance on this issue,' she said, holding her gilt-edged Bible aloft. 'I have waited for an answer and finally it has come.'

She looked heavenward for a moment, then checked on the bag of second-hand clothes she'd brought from her stall at the market. It was still sitting on the chair next to her.

'If we can't have Monwabisi,' said Mrs Mehlo, 'let us have the next best candidate, Constantia Radebe. She is a woman of God and the community.'

Constantia reached into her bag to look for another ball of wool. Anything to avoid showing her face. Mrs Mehlo's son Oupa had gotten caught with dagga at school. Maybe Mrs Mehlo had been smoking some herself. How else could she have come up with an idea as mad as Constantia Radebe running for council? Constantia wanted to remind the meeting that she was just a lowly aide at a nursery school. The only thing she'd ever organised was the Hand of God umgalelo. But collecting a few rands from a handful of women didn't qualify her for city council. A councillor had to be clever, had to know about politics, like her husband.

Four other women followed with support for Mrs Mehlo's proposal.

Nompumelelo asked Constantia for her response. Two

cries of 'Viva Councillor Radebe, viva!' came from the back of the hall. Constantia stood up, still holding Fidel's sweater and the knitting needles in her right hand.

'I am honoured that the League wants to put me forward,' she said, 'but I just don't think I'm the best person. I would like to respectfully decline.'

Nompumelelo shook her head and stood up.

'Comrades, freedom comes with responsibilities,' said the chairwoman. 'Now that freedom has dawned, we African women will be asked to do many things we never dreamed of doing, like running for city council.' Constantia stopped knitting, looked up and met Nompumelelo's fiery gaze.

'If we refuse responsibility, Comrade Radebe, we will remain oppressed. I think we must ask you to reconsider. We can't have two people from the same household refusing the mandate of the community, isn't it?' The applause and ululations didn't give Constantia a chance to answer. Once the community spoke, it was difficult to say no. She kept on knitting but her fingers were starting to shake. If only she hadn't let her husband talk her into coming to this meeting. After a few stitches, she stopped and gave a thumbs up to Nompumelelo. She didn't really have a choice. When she arrived at home and told her husband the news, he said she was the 'perfect candidate', that her nomination was in line with the ANC's policy of non-sexism.

'I'm not qualified for this job,' she said. 'I know nothing about politics. The League has made a terrible mistake.'

'The League is following the policy of the ANC. We are equals now,' he said. 'This is the new South Africa.'

○

'My wife has asked me to surrender the chair for this discussion,' Monwabisi told the meeting at Sivuyile Hall, 'and as a combatant in the struggle against sexism, I always follow her orders.' The branch members' eyes turned towards a blushing Constantia. She'd worn a green jersey Monwabisi had brought her from Joburg. Back when they first met, he used to tell her she looked beautiful in green.

As the two nominees exited, Jeff Ntoni took over the meeting. Monwabisi remained at the head table.

'We are all aware that Comrade Jim has served the community tirelessly,' Ntoni said, 'and he is level-headed. He won't become emotional or derelict in his duty because of the pressure of outside responsibilities. He is first and foremost a soldier of the ANC.'

Nompumelelo Mpupa's hand shot up. 'Because a woman has responsibilities in the home,' she said, 'does not mean she is not a loyal solider. If more men carried their load at home, we wouldn't even hear such comments.' A few women let loose ululations of support.

Mrs Mehlo rose to assure the branch that the good Lord would look favourably on the nomination of a loyal, churchgoing woman like Constantia Radebe. 'We need clear and sober thinking,' she told the meeting.

When several women applauded Mrs Mehlo's comments, Ntoni warned that a 'war of the sexes' seemed to be emerging. 'This is not a welcome development,' he added.

'This is not a war of the sexes,' retorted Nompumelelo. 'Just a few male comrades still living in the dark ages.'

Cleophas Nobatana called for calm. 'We all come from the same movement,' he reminded the crowd. 'Surely we can reach agreement.' He adjusted his dark glasses. He wore them almost all the time now. He complained that even the dim light inside Sivuyile Hall had become overpowering.

'Both our comrades are highly qualified,' said Nobatana. 'Both are seasoned in the struggle. To solve our problem, perhaps we need to go back to our history.'

Ntoni looked at his watch. Two young men got up and left through a side door.

Nobatana recalled the days more than a century ago when the amaXhosa men went to sleep and put their fate in the hands of a young girl named Nongqawuse who had plunged the nation into disaster.

Ntoni looked at his watch again, tapping loudly on the crystal. He put it up to his ear, as if he expected to hear something.

Nobatana abandoned the tale of Nongqawuse and the cattle killing and moved on to the glories of the 'heroic martyr Makana in whose very shadow I lived for eighteen years'. Three young women exited via the back door, dragging two small children with them. Two more men followed closely behind, one tucking a folded-up newspaper in his back pocket. Nobatana went on to remind people that 'Makana had united his people in the struggle against the British imperialists and finally died in 1819 trying to escape from Robben Island'.

'Point of order,' said Mrs Mehlo. 'Can the comrade bring us to the issue? We have dinner to prepare.'

'You just want to watch your *Bold* and *Days*,' said Youth League chair Sandile Veki. He was dressed in camouflage as usual, topped off with a black ANC cap. 'Our organisation must not be blackmailed by imperialist soap operas,' he added.

'Our youth have no respect for their mothers,' said Mrs Mehlo, 'calling me an imperialist because I want to go and cook. Even my dagga-smoking son doesn't talk such foolishness.'

Ntoni clapped his hands three times. 'We are not schoolboys who talk willy-nilly,' he said. 'Let us respect democracy here.'

When Nobatana resumed, the back door slammed. Five more people were on their way home.

'Some say that because of our history we can never trust a woman to lead,' said Nobatana. 'I disagree. I say we give them a second chance. This time, though, we men must be vigilant. I support the nomination of Comrade Radebe, though I might have preferred the husband.'

'For better and for worse!' shouted a Youth League member.

The Women's League rose to sing their Women's Day song 'Malibongwe'. Ntoni tried to call them to order, but Nompumelelo Mpupa ran to the front to assume the role of conductor and chief choreographer. After the final 'igama lamakhosikazi malibongwe', Ntoni reminded people they must consider the candidates 'objectively'.

'Point of order!' Mrs Mehlo shouted. 'It is time to vote. Let us appoint our Independent Electoral Commission and move.'

The two candidates were called back into the meeting room. The Youth League circulated among the crowd, handing ballots to every paid-up member.

When everyone had deposited their ballots in the cardboard box at the front, the members crowded around while Ntoni unfolded the papers and Nompumelelo shouted out the name written on the ballot. Sandile Veki took control of the chalkboard. He drew a white line down the middle, recording Constantia's votes on the left in blue chalk, Jim's on the right in yellow.

Constantia stayed in her seat and knitted. She felt like the waves of the Indian Ocean were crashing against the walls of her stomach. At least she was almost finished with Fidel's jersey. Only the collar remained.

The results seesawed back and forth. Cries of joy and alarm greeted Nompumelelo each time she shouted out one of the names. Gradually the supporters of Elvis Jim grew confident. By the time his total hit a hundred, the right side of the chalkboard was bursting with marks. Constantia's tally was a mere eighty-three.

Mrs Mehlo fell to her knees to pray that 'the Heavenly Father would turn the tide towards righteousness'.

Nompumelelo assured League members that prayers were not necessary. 'We were sitting at the front,' she said. 'All of our ballots are at the bottom. They are the last to be counted. Victory is certain.'

The deeper Jeff Ntoni's hand sunk into the box, the closer Constantia's total grew to Elvis Jim's. With just four ballot papers left, the woman they were now calling 'Mrs RDP' had surged ahead. She led by two votes. Out of the last four ballots, Constantia got just one vote. The election had ended in a draw.

The rules said the chairperson held the tie-breaking vote. Since Monwabisi had stood down, Ntoni had the final say. Once everyone had returned to their seats, he spoke.

'Everyone knows I have supported Comrade Jim for this position,' Ntoni said, 'but I must do what is best for the branch, what is best for the ANC.'

Constantia put her face in her hands. She just wanted Ntoni to get it over with. Maybe her stomach would finally settle.

'I am standing in for a man who has shown his respect for the people by recusing himself,' Ntoni continued, 'but I must not take advantage of my temporary position to sway the outcome. Though my heart is with Comrade Jim, in the interests of democracy, I cast my vote for Constantia Radebe.'

Constantia stuffed her knitting into her black cloth bag. She wanted to escape the celebrations and just go back to the nursery school on Monday as if nothing had happened. She was comfortable there. She cried as Nompumelelo Mpupa and three other women lifted her high on their shoulders and pranced around the room. The League women saw tears of joy, but life as Constantia had known it for more than ten years was over. How would she cope? None of those toyi-toying women understood her position and they didn't know about her husband's status. To make matters worse, she couldn't even think about mentioning her fears to Monwabisi. He would just tell her she had to carry out the mandate of the community. As usual, he was probably right. This was the new South Africa and people had to shoulder new responsibilities. She just wished the responsibilities of being a councillor were falling on someone else's shoulders. She was trapped.

Chapter 5

WITH ITS CALIFORNIA-STYLE freeways, skyscrapers and state-of-the-art shopping malls, Johannesburg carried the intensity of an American city, something Peter Franklin never expected in Africa. The excitement and high spirits of the new democracy were palpable everywhere. All the white businessmen he'd met on behalf of Pellmar accepted the new order. He never found one who claimed to have supported apartheid.

The black government officials he encountered breathed enthusiasm for the 'miracle of peaceful transition'. They reminded Peter of himself during the eighties, when he believed changing the world was straightforward and inevitable. Then he went to Washington and discovered the futility of shouting at the margins. Whoopi and Stevie had shown him that. To bring about change, a person needed power and resources. A touch of fame didn't hurt. The Reagan and Bush years ripped away any other illusions. Peter understood the economic realities now as well: competition and individual initiative were the kingmakers of modern societies. The sooner the leaders of South Africa discovered this, the better. The days of those noble anti-apartheid slogans were over.

This time Pellmar was sending Peter to a new destination: the Eastern Cape. He'd read the consultant's report on the province. It was the poorest region in the country, the greatest challenge possible for Pellmar in terms of greenfield investment and commercial development that would turn a profit. But for Peter this was about more than profit. He and Pellmar would be reversing years of poverty and oppression. Unlike many other corporations, Pellmar was a company with a heart.

The trip to the Eastern Cape would also give him a chance to see Mthetho Jonasi, his old ANC friend from the UN. Mthetho had introduced Peter to Whoopi in 1988. A life-changing event.

The day before the South African trip, Andrew Wesley, Pellmar's CEO, assigned Peter to attend a presentation by Willard Dubell of Metertronics, Inc. 'He has a new product that should interest you,' said Wesley. 'I want you to be there.' Peter wasn't eager to add another meeting to his diary, but he didn't say no to Wesley. The man had an eye for opportunity and a social conscience. He'd been a draft resister during the Vietnam War days. Peter saw him as a role model.

Dubell brought a PowerPoint presentation and a stack of brochures to the meeting. Peter had little patience for the man's pixilated photos and inconsistent paragraph indention. In the computer age there was no excuse for sloppiness.

The first slides were landscapes: the Great Lakes, the Mississippi River, a reservoir in Wisconsin.

'I'm not merely showing you pretty pictures,' Dubell said. 'I want you to understand that water is the new oil, the pivot around which countries will rise and fall in the future.'

Peter's mind started to drift to the report he had to edit before he left. Fifty pages on restructuring the steel industry in Romania. There was big money in Bucharest but the consultant hadn't done the research properly. Out-of-date statistics, tables that didn't make sense. Peter would have to correct it all before he got on the plane. It would be a long night.

'Across the world,' said Dubell, 'ageing pipes and

infrastructure endanger the continued availability of safe, cheap water. Like the white rhino and the spotted owl, water is under threat.'

When Peter lost interest in what a speaker was saying, he liked to think about repackaging the presenter's image. Dubell was easy. Start with a decent hairstyle instead of that crude comb-over. Even during his long-hair days Peter kept his hair neatly trimmed. And Joanna used to brush it constantly. She had a wonderful touch.

'The problem,' Dubell said, 'is that providers and consumers have always considered water to be free, like air. And we know what happens when we get something for free. It loses all value.'

Dubell paused for a minute and fumbled around with a ziplock bag in his briefcase.

'This, ladies and gentlemen, is the device that will transform water into something we value,' he continued. 'It will be the Big Mac of the water industry: the prepaid water meter.'

He held up a small grey metal box, then paused as if he was waiting for the jets to fly past.

'It functions like a vending machine,' he explained. 'You insert a plastic card or a key and the water flows. The consumer loads money onto the card before it will work. Water bills are history.'

Dubell predicted that one day water – or rather 'access to water' – would be sold everywhere: malls, 7-Elevens, service stations, maybe even at McDonald's restaurants.

The final slide showed the box connected to a water pipe, like a traditional meter.

'The prepaid allows the provider to adjust the price instantaneously to ensure cost recovery, like a service station varies the price of gas at the pump,' Dubell said.

The visual of the water meter brought Peter back from his efforts to project a five-year budget for steel production in Romania. An interesting device, he thought.

'The prepaid meter will open up water service to private industry,' Dubell continued. 'With a guaranteed client base, the capacity to set tariffs in line with profit maximisation, and an assured income stream, another sphere of government domination has been conquered. In the future, provision of water to homes and industry will be driven by entrepreneurs and shareholders, not clock-punching civil servants.'

Jake Moyer, an intern in the front row, asked Dubell why local government would want to entertain such a system.

Dubell smiled. 'Brilliant question,' he said, 'with an easy answer. Local government has many other things to do. Water is not their core business. Plus, they are civil servants. If they can do less work for the same money, they'll be happy.'

Dubell went on to note that there might be a few 'dinosaurs' who want to cling to municipal control over water. 'But like cassette players and floppy disks, their days are numbered,' he assured Moyer.

Peter took Dubell's business card and one of his brochures. He didn't have time to chat or let the implications of the presentation sink in. Still, despite his preoccupation with the upcoming trip and the tasks he had to complete before his departure, Peter understood why Wesley had sent him to the talk. Apartheid had left millions of South Africans without access to water. Prepaid meters were cutting-edge technology, something that always attracted Pellmar. Peter just had to figure out how these meters would fit into the company's mission.

Chapter 6

Mᴛʜᴇᴛʜᴏ's ᴅʀɪᴠᴇʀ, Hᴀɴɪғ, picked Peter up at East London airport in a white 3-Series BMW. He drove the Pellmar executive along a coastal route to the house in Bunkers Hill, carefully sidestepping the American's wish to get a peek of Mdantsane, South Africa's second largest township. The consultant's report had called Mdantsane a 'dysfunctional monstrosity where nearly a million people crowded into matchbox houses and unsteady lean-tos'. Peter couldn't wait to get a look. These were the places where Pellmar could make a difference, where his notions of justice and business sense could converge.

The Jonasis' two-storey five-bedroom house was far from the township. As Peter and Mthetho enjoyed a Heineken together in the lounge, the Deputy Minister described how the previous owner had fled 'in a panic' to England in 1993.

'The old guy sold us this lounge suite for R300,' he said. 'These sofas are not what our people call goma goma. They're real leather.'

The chair gently squeaked as Peter sat back to enjoy the view of the sea. He wished he could read the lettering on the ocean liner that was passing by. It looked big enough to be the *Queen Mary*.

A young woman with a baby strapped to her back brought them refills on their beer.

'Sisi is carrying is my first-born,' said Mthetho. 'We call him Nkululeko. It means "freedom" in our local language.' A trace of saliva ran down the sleeping Nkululeko's chin as the child's cheek pressed against the young woman's back.

Mthetho's wife, Letitia, was out of town on business. Her husband boasted that she was the first black woman accountant appointed by Dekker & Associates.

'One of East London's biggest firms,' he said. 'It's a win-win situation. She gets the experience and the company gets the inside word from government via their partner's husband.'

The following morning Peter launched his day with a swim in the Jonasis' kidney-shaped pool. He found a few dozen laps of backstroke far more invigorating than his before-dawn treadmill sessions at the gym in Manhattan. At midday, after he'd seen the coelacanth at the local museum and visited the grave of Black Consciousness leader Steve Biko, Peter met Mthetho and a friend he called 'Lungi' for lunch at the city's most exclusive venue, the London Towers Hotel. The rising columns in the lobby reminded Peter of the Waldorf Astoria. He felt right at home.

Lungi turned out to be the shiny-faced provincial Minister of Finance, Mlungisi Mgijima. Peter had seen Mgijima in photos of the ANC guerrilla camps in Angola. In those days they called him 'Bazooka Giant'. Back then he wore camouflage instead of a carefully tailored suit with a silk handkerchief in the pocket.

While Peter perused the assortment of seafood on the menu, Mthetho regaled Mgijima with tales of 'Peter the freedom fighter'.

'He was once arrested in DC with Stevie Wonder,' Mthetho said. 'Whoopi was there, along with many others.'

Peter gave the Minister of Finance some background about Pellmar, emphasising the company's capacity to plan as well as manage.

'Many of our local white business owners are reticent about working with African partners,' Mgijima said, 'but it is time for the majority to share in the wealth. Your company, I'm sure, would take an enlightened approach.'

'Absolutely,' said Peter.

The Finance Minister paused to tell the waiter to bring a round of Glenfiddich and lemonade for everyone.

'The Towers is one of the few places in the Eastern Cape where you can still find Glenfiddich,' he said.

'Their standards haven't fallen an iota,' said Mthetho.

When the drinks arrived, the Minister of Finance proposed a toast to Pellmar for sending a 'former freedom fighter' to head their ventures in the Eastern Cape.

'They have made a wonderful choice,' Mgijima added.

'Actually,' said Peter, 'it was Mthetho who introduced me to Stevie, plus other stars as well. He knew them all, even Harry Belafonte and Danny Glover.' Peter took a hesitant sip of his drink. What a horrible thing to do to a good single malt. At least they hadn't added real lemonade, just something that tasted like SevenUp.

'If you should ever need security,' said Mgijima, 'let me offer you the services of my brother's firm, Take Charge. They employ many former freedom fighters, yet they are still having difficulties securing loans from a bank. One of the holdovers from the bad old days which we are trying to cure.'

'I can assure you,' said Peter, 'when we have a need for security, we will give him a call.'

'Let's make that a deal,' said Mgijima, shaking Peter's hand, 'between one freedom fighter and another.' Mthetho ordered another round of drinks, telling the waiter to serve Peter's Glenfiddich 'neat'.

Though Mgijima and Mthetho advised against it, Peter ordered snoek. He said he wanted to try something different, something he'd never heard of.

His companions laughed when Peter spent more time spitting out bones than eating his fish.

'These days a freedom fighter must know how to navigate the menus at our hotels,' said Mthetho. 'If you keep ordering snoek, one day you will choke on those bones.'

Peter pushed his plate to the side. Half of the fish remained untouched. In the future, he would have more respect for local knowledge.

○

As Mthetho pulled out of the London Towers' underground car park, Peter closed his eyes for a moment. His mind was leaping ahead. With Mthetho's connections, there were no boundaries for Pellmar. It was just a matter of locating the correct niche.

'You're going to see a different side of South Africa now,' Mthetho said. 'Hold on to your watch.'

Half an hour later, Peter stood in front of a meeting of the Sivuyile Civic Association, the SCA for short. He didn't usually get nervous speaking to groups of people, but this was different. He was part of making history. These people had lived through soldiers shooting down their children and police throwing their comrades out of seventh-storey windows. His mouth was as dry as the sands of the Kalahari.

'We at Pellmar are looking for partners in development,' Peter told them. Three dozen pairs of eyes were trained on his face. He suddenly felt conspicuously white. He wished he hadn't worn a tie.

'Excuse me, Mr Franklin,' said Jeff Ntoni, the chair of the SCA. 'There is a question.'

Ntoni called on a young man named Slim Yanta in the front row.

'Mine is a comment,' said Slim. 'A reminder that we can never surrender the fruits of our struggle. Our oppressed masses are the rightful owners of those fruits, not the American imperialists.'

Like most of the members of the Sivuyile Civic Association, Slim wore unlaced leather shoes without socks. Mthetho told Peter it was township fashion. Going 'tubeless', they called it.

'No one is talking about surrendering anything,' said Mthetho. 'Let Pellmar come and invest in the community. You will benefit from the jobs and training opportunities. These days companies that exploited us in the past are working with government. Even Anglo American and Gencor.'

Peter tried to think how to convince Slim and other doubters that Pellmar was not an exploiter, an 'imperialist' as they put it. Mthetho had borrowed Mgijima's term 'freedom fighter' to introduce Peter, but it didn't seem to have helped.

Although he was already standing, Peter raised his hand to get Ntoni to call on him. Hand-raising seemed to be the custom here, but it would take some getting used to. Still, if Peter could adjust to men in Bulgaria kissing each other, he could learn to raise his hand. At least he didn't have to speak through interpreters. The 'comrades', as they called themselves, spoke good English – a curious blend of Marxist jargon and *Robert's Rules of Order*.

'You have shown the world how to transform a tyranny into a democracy,' Peter told them. 'We at Pellmar offer our services in support of your efforts to build a new society. We are not here to dictate.'

Peter couldn't think of what else to say. So much to communicate, so few words. He wished he'd prepared some slides on his laptop.

'I suggest you judge us by our actions,' Peter added, 'not by any flowery words we may offer you in a meeting.'

A young man in the front row interrupted his cigarette rolling to give a thumbs up.

'With all due respect,' said Comrade Slim as Peter sat down, 'you can't teach the old capitalist dog new tricks.'

'Out of order!' shouted Sandile Veki, the Youth League leader. 'We are tired of hearing Slim's opinions on every issue. Let him wait his turn like others.' The round-faced Veki stood up for a second and pointed his finger at Slim. Sandile had the body of a boxer, except for a tiny trace of softness around the middle.

'The chair must acknowledge you,' Ntoni told Slim. 'Do not undermine my authority.'

The meeting moved to a new agenda item while Peter wondered how many others had this same mistrust of 'capitalists'.

'The test for Pellmar,' he thought, 'is whether we can win these doubters over to our side.' South Africa was so different from the former Soviet-bloc countries. In Bulgaria and the Ukraine, people saw capitalism as a breath of fresh air in a society polluted by the socialist system. In South Africa, the perpetrators of apartheid claimed to be capitalists, part of the war against communism. That didn't help. Even Ntoni wore a T-shirt emblazoned across the front with a hammer and sickle and the letters S-A-C-P for South African Communist Party. At times this country seemed to be a throwback to discredited ideas of the past. A young man wearing that same red SACP T-shirt gave a 'report back' on a conference he attended in Port Elizabeth on educational transformation. Peter counted. In two minutes, the young man used the word 'comrade', or 'com' for short, sixteen times. Even the bus driver was a 'comrade'.

As someone at the back of the room asked a question about 'outcomes-based education', Peter could see Mthetho fidgeting. After eyeing his watch a few times, the Deputy

Minister informed the meeting that he and Peter had another 'urgent appointment'.

'On behalf of the civic association,' said Ntoni, 'let me thank Comrade Deputy Minister for bringing Comrade Franklin here today. Comrade Franklin must know that he is always welcome in Sivuyile.'

The chairman stood up to shake the hands of the departing guests. For the first time Peter got a look at the slogan under the hammer and sickle on Ntoni's shirt: 'People Before Profits'.

Peter did a quick headcount, then peeled off thirty-seven business cards, one for each person in the hall. Ntoni passed the cards to a young man in the front row to distribute.

'Feel free to contact me anytime,' said Peter. 'My cell number is there, and my address.'

Comrade Slim said something in Xhosa which prompted lots of giggles. Peter thanked Ntoni and headed for the door. As he walked past Comrade Slim, the young man was rubbing his finger across the raised gold lettering on the card.

Peter rushed outside to catch up with Mthetho. 'Where to next?' Peter asked.

'I can only take so much of those community meetings,' said Mthetho as the two got into the back seat of the BMW. 'They take forever to get anything done with all those report backs and mandates. What good is a leader with no power?'

As Hanif pulled out of the parking lot, three young men blocked their path.

'Gun it,' said Mthetho.

Hanif put the pedal to the floor. The young men dove out of the way as the car flew past.

'You can never be too careful,' said Mthetho. 'So many hijackers these days.'

Peter kept quiet as the BMW bounced along the dirt roads of Sivuyile. Lots of young children played in the street.

Hanif had to stop once while a herd of goats crossed the road.

'How many of those civic guys are communists?' Peter asked.

Mthetho grinned. 'Plenty,' he said.

'But what percentage?' asked Peter. 'Ninety, thirty?'

'Hard to know,' Mthetho replied. 'I'm also a member of the Communist Party. Gives me credibility in the community. I don't go to the meetings, though. I've had my fill of Karl Marx.'

'It's a dead end,' said Peter. He'd flirted with left-wing ideas in the early anti-apartheid days but he quickly realised they led nowhere. That was a big part of why he and Joanna broke up. She had no business acumen, no sense of reality. He'd heard she was in South Africa, working for some church group with a very earnest-sounding name. Perhaps a dose of reality would wake her up.

A taxi passed Mthetho's car, hooting half a dozen times to make sure no one got in its way. 'Stupid asshole,' said Mthetho.

'Those taxis seem to have rules of their own,' said Peter. Mthetho and Hanif laughed.

'We're slowly bringing our people to understand that nationalisation and expropriation are self-defeating,' said Mthetho.

A taxi squealed to a stop a metre short of a woman walking her three-year-old across the street. 'For God's sake,' said Peter, his eyes closed.

'The SACP members are some of our strongest supporters,' said Mthetho. 'They're far more reasonable than those shop stewards from COSATU. Those ones are real radicals.'

Though it didn't quite make sense, Peter liked this idea of communists who opposed communistic policies.

James Kilgore

'You must remember our past,' said Mthetho. 'When we fought the Boers, the Soviets gave us weapons. Reagan supplied arms to our enemies.'

'That's ancient history now,' said Peter.

'For you maybe,' said Mthetho. 'Our people can't forget so easily.'

Hanif slowed down as he landed on Champion Boulevard, the main street of OR Tambo informal settlement. The houses here were jumbles of corrugated zinc, scrap wood and old road signs. Peter knew only massive injections of capital would turn this place around, not hammers and sickles. He saw nothing but opportunity for Pellmar in the Eastern Cape.

As they drove further down Champion a group of women standing around a water tap waved at Mthetho.

'My aunties,' he said. 'They all know me here.'

Some shacks had old car tyres on the roof to keep the tin sheets from blowing away. A collection of various wires passed from backyards to a power pole.

'The people of OR Tambo have their own power company,' said Mthetho.

'Eskom Sivuyile, they call it,' said Hanif.

'These houses will blow away in a storm,' said Peter.

'And the people will put them right back up again as soon as the ground dries,' said Mthetho. 'There are master builders here.'

Peter had lots of other questions he was afraid to ask. How did people manage to smile, to sleep or to have sex in a shack in OR Tambo? He couldn't imagine a life without privacy. He'd spent a couple of nights in jail in Buffalo and DC. It drove him crazy always having someone watching him whether he was sleeping or just peeing into a steel toilet.

After a few minutes Hanif drove past a sign that read 'Houghton East'. The shacks disappeared.

'These are Sivuyile's suburbs,' said Mthetho. 'Only they are out of fashion. Now people want the real thing.'

Hanif turned up the volume on the CD player. 'How do you like Hotstix?' Mthetho asked. 'This is "Jive Soweto", an oldie but a goodie.'

The lively horns pacified a few of Peter's worries, though he wasn't sure which of South Africa's eleven official languages this Hotstix was singing in. Peter tried his best to feel the rhythm, but he kept seeing those hammer and sickle emblems on the T-shirts of the comrades. How could he get these people to shed these futile illusions? Sivuyile was a long way from Bulgaria.

Chapter 7

CONSTANTIA SAT IN THE Parliament gallery with dozens of other new councillors from around the country. Now she was someone important. She'd won 92 per cent of the vote in Sivuyile. Monwabisi said she had a 'powerful mandate' from the people. She was beginning to feel the weight of responsibility. Though she'd only been a councillor for two weeks, her job at the nursery school felt like ancient history.

This was her first trip to Cape Town. She'd never dreamed she'd be in such a place. The Parliament floor was wall-to-wall with heroes of the struggle seated in high-backed leather chairs. She spotted Thabo Mbeki, Ronnie Kasrils and Winnie Mandela. Madiba himself sat in the front row. The enormous South African flags on the poles behind the podium brought a sliver of new life to the colonial decor.

They had gathered to hear the Minister of Reconstruction and Development, Carl Prince, deliver what the media had called a 'major address'. As Prince strode to the podium, the audience rose and applauded for several minutes. Constantia remembered the Minister when he worked with Monwabisi in the union. In those days, Prince wore nothing but jeans and T-shirts and was always on his way to a workshop or meeting. He looked strangely awkward standing behind the podium in his charcoal suit, like a man not quite used to power. Still, she knew she had to listen carefully to every word he said.

'Let all South Africans come together in a spirit of forgiving the transgressions of the past,' Prince began, 'to create a new South Africa, a Rainbow Nation of which we can all be proud.' He paused briefly, waiting for the trickle of applause to die. His gold cufflinks glimmered as he gripped the edges of the oak podium.

Prince's words excited Constantia, but Monwabisi was teaching her to temper her emotions, to view such occasions in a new way. When he'd bid farewell at the airport, he reminded her that 'the devil is in the details. Where there is a carrot, later comes a stick.'

'Masakhane,' said Prince, 'is an Nguni word meaning "let's build together". Let masakhane be our guiding light.'

While the people on the floor cheered for Prince, Constantia sat back in her seat and tried to reflect. She was hunting for details the way she used to survey the sandpit at the nursery school for toys. Anyone could spot the plastic motorcycles the four-year-olds rode. But only a trained eye could locate the tiny corner of a Lego peeking out from the sand. Other times a handful of beads would be completely buried. The searcher had to know the habits of certain children, their favourite hiding places.

Besides masakhane, the Minister also spoke of 'cash-strapped municipalities'. He went on to describe the R200 million owed by local authorities across the country.

'Much of this debt was incurred during the apartheid days,' he said, 'when our people boycotted payments to illegitimate local governments. Those debts we can forget. But we must tread carefully. We have been a global pariah once. Let it never happen again.'

Constantia didn't know what the word 'pariah' meant – she wasn't even sure how to spell it. She would ask Monwabisi when she got home.

The Minister went on to explain South Africa's 'difficult

position in the world'. Though his voice blasted through the microphone, Prince looked tiny from Constantia's vantage point near the back of the chamber. The room felt big enough for Kaizer Chiefs to play a match.

'If we cancel all debts of the past we might incur the wrath of Washington and Geneva,' said Prince. 'They may deny us the loans we so desperately need for development.'

Constantia had never thought of such connections before. What did Washington or Geneva have to do with implementing the RDP in Sivuyile? She had her own problems without thinking of people thousands of kilometres away, like getting a new light bulb in her office.

She'd had to wait two weeks for the maintenance people to change the bulb. Nothing would ever have happened if one of the white councillors, Mr Kelly, hadn't told her she had to 'walk the work order through'.

'Take it from one desk to another until everyone has signed,' he said. 'Or better yet, get one of the boys to do it. Petrus is very good at that sort of thing. Otherwise you'll be waiting until the cows come home.'

She'd followed the white councillor's instructions, though she felt like she was making a pact with the devil even talking to Kelly. Maybe this is what the Minister meant by 'masakhane'. If Madiba could speak Afrikaans to farmers in the Free State, Constantia could endure a white councillor who referred to Petrus Mthimkulu, a black man with grandchildren, as a 'boy'.

Prince continued. Constantia could hear his voice change. The stick was on the way.

'While we are determined to provide services to all historically disadvantaged communities,' Prince said, 'we need to remain realistic. We must think of our municipalities as if they are families whose monthly bills are more than what they earn. Such a family must learn to spend less or earn more. Or both.'

Constantia understood the example. Prince was talking about families like hers. They'd lost Monwabisi's income and she had new expenses to think about. A councillor made no more than a nursery school aide. But at the nursery school her image was prepackaged. The blue smock covered her clothes, the doek concealed her hair. A councillor needed matching shoes and handbag, visits to the hairdresser. She'd even begun to think of jewellery, perfume and watches befitting an elected official. She'd never thought anyone could need more than one watch. Monwabisi now said she looked like a 'real little bourgeois' when she went off to work. But his provident fund was almost gone. Where would she find the money to maintain her councillor's image if her husband kept living the life of a revolutionary? Anyway, he'd just say that a councillor's image didn't matter; what mattered was whether or not the councillor served the people. He was probably right, but she'd still need a new dress every now and again. She'd borrowed money from Mthetho when Monwabisi was still in Joburg, but she'd never told her husband. He wouldn't approve.

'Economics contains some brutal lessons,' Prince said. 'One of those is that as government we must earn more money. There are those who would choose the easy route – tax the wealthy, make them pay for the inequalities of the past. This is short-sighted. In the long run such a choice would be shooting the nation in the foot.'

Constantia could already hear Monwabisi's arguments against what the Minister was saying. Her husband always said that the bosses had profited for too long, that now it was time for the workers to get their fair share.

'Our goal is not to bankrupt the wealthy or drive them away,' said Prince. 'We say to them 'masakhane'. We need their resources and expertise to benefit all South Africans.'

The Minister's words made Constantia think. Perhaps

49

some of the dreams of the past were unrealistic. She wished it could be different – that, as the Bible promised, the meek would inherit the earth.

'Apart from taxes,' said the Minister, 'our other source of revenue is payment for municipal services. We have a problem here: a culture of non-payment.'

'Now we have democratically elected local governments,' he continued, raising his hand towards the gallery where Constantia and the others sat. The parliamentarians on the floor rose to their feet and turned in Constantia's direction. She'd never forget this moment. Even Madiba was joining in the standing ovation.

'There is no longer any excuse for someone not to pay,' Prince said. 'Anyone who wilfully avoids payment is undermining the progress of our nation. Everyone must carry their own weight.'

What the Minister said made perfect sense to Constantia. But she wasn't quite clear. Did he mean that households must pay all those old debts? Even her family couldn't afford that. And what about the people in Sivuyile who only survived off granny's pension, the nkam-nkam as they called it, and a few piece jobs? The Minister and his aides had surely thought of such cases. There were still so many things she didn't understand.

She also wondered how the Minister could preach this sermon of frugality while putting all the councillors up in a posh hotel. At the reception the night before, they'd been served lobster and deep-fried prawns. A huge ice sculpture of an elephant marked the centre of the room. How much did it cost to make an elephant out of ice? By the end of the reception it had melted down to a calf.

The Minister closed his speech by offering a 'hand of solidarity' to all the newly elected councillors. 'We shall work together to make South Africa ring with democracy and development, from the most remote rural village of the Transkei to the heart of industrial Johannesburg,' he concluded. The audience stood and applauded Minister Prince for a full five minutes. By the end of it, Constantia's hands were beginning to sting.

○

After her day in Parliament, the newly elected councillor from Sivuyile did a bit of window-shopping. A couple of the other councillors had cautioned her not to walk around downtown, that it was full of tsotsis. She ignored their warnings, but she'd taken out all her cash before she left the Parliament Building and slipped it into her bra for safe keeping. She waded through the densely packed pavement along Adderley Street, clinging tightly to her suede bag.

She could feel that life had a different pace here. Taxi drivers were yelling everywhere, the roads were filled with new BMWs. She'd never seen so many white people at once. Those huge mountains that surrounded the place made her feel almost like she was at the bottom of a hole somewhere. And the coloureds spoke a special kind of Afrikaans she couldn't understand. In the window of one store she saw a pair of jeans that cost R500. How could anyone pay that much for a pair of trousers? She'd heard things were even more dear at a place called the Waterfront, but she didn't have time to get there. Maybe next time.

When she got back to the hotel room she indulged herself in a long, lavender-scented bubble bath. The complexity of the Minister's message began to sink in. It all made Constantia long for the simplicity of the past. At the nursery school she had a clear set of tasks: make porridge, serve breakfast, sweep the floor, read a story to the children. A councillor had to think about everything: delivering services to the community,

James Kilgore

getting reports to Mayor Siziba, satisfying the wishes of people in Washington.

At least she solved one problem when she got back home to Sivuyile. She looked up the word 'pariah' in the dictionary. In fact, she felt like she was becoming a pariah herself. She no longer had time for the meetings of the umgalelo and she couldn't remember the last time she'd watched *Bold* or *Generations*. She didn't even watch the reruns on weekend mornings. Everyone wanted something from their councillor. She wondered if life would ever return to normal.

Chapter 8

JOANNA RENTED A TINY one-room office for UV in the Eden Building, a twelve-storey office block in Braamfontein, the bustling hub of international development organisations in Johannesburg. Many of her neighbours in the Eden wielded annual budgets well into eight figures. The corridors of the building echoed with the latest rumours about the new South Africa in Danish, French, German and Zulu. It was all a little overwhelming for Joanna but she was learning. The best part was meeting the heroes of the struggle, people like Walter Sisulu, Sam Shilowa and Terror Lekota. On one occasion she even shook the hand of the resplendent Winnie Mandela, who had come to meet some Danish government officials about a project for women in Soweto.

Not long after she settled into the Eden, Lelina Bergman, a project officer for German government programmes, invited Joanna to lunch. Generally Joanna turned down such invitations. She couldn't afford fancy lunches on her salary; besides, she was in South Africa to connect to the grassroots, not to sip French wine at five-star hotels.

'We'll be meeting with Carl Prince,' Lelina told her. 'He's looking for partners for water projects in the rural areas.'

Joanna immediately perked up. Carl Prince was a captivating figure, a tall, thin man with a wispy beard. A former trade union leader, he now had the noblest task of all – making the dreams of the people come true. Joanna accepted the invitation.

The venue for the lunch was the Parktonian, a hotel with the kind of glitzy opulence that typically turned Joanna's stomach. But this time she ignored the subservience of the top-hatted black valets and the gleaming brass fixtures in the ladies' room. Lelina had given her a seat right next to Carl Prince. She figured he'd probably ignore her. There were three men in the party who had millions to spend. Instead, Prince immediately turned to her and asked her what brought her to South Africa.

'I was part of a small church group in New York,' Joanna said as she fumbled with the buttons on her sweater. 'Now I'm here with Unitarian Vision. We call ourselves UV.'

Prince smiled his approval. He didn't look a day over thirty. 'And what work does UV do here?' he asked.

The other people at the table retreated to their private conversations. Joanna couldn't believe he was talking only to her.

'We report to our members on what's happening in South Africa,' said Joanna. 'Plus we'll be funding a few projects in the future. Not a lot of money.'

She'd run out of words. The Minister held his proud smile, like a teacher looking at a star pupil. Joanna felt like she'd earned an A+.

A couple of weeks later she attended a reception for the Danish ambassador at nearby Wits University. She munched on a tiny samoosa in a high-ceilinged conference room as she tried to find someone to talk to. All she saw were a lot of dressed-up people with fat Filofaxes. She'd only come because UV's office was next door to Danish Aid Abroad.

'How's my friend Joanna today?' she heard someone ask. She didn't have to turn around to know who it was. Out of all the thousands of people Carl Prince met, he remembered her name.

He spoke to her about water projects. He told her they were connecting millions of people who'd never had access to a tap.

'What a country,' he added as the two settled into a corner of the room. 'We can produce BMWs and computers, yet our people are still getting water from cholera-infested rivers. The Boers have a lot to answer for.'

As she fished for an intelligent reply, Joanna heard a familiar American accent just behind her. She turned and saw the back of Peter Franklin's neatly coiffed head. In his navy-blue pinstripe suit, he was commiserating with two programme officers from the Swedish Development Agency about the complexities of importing a car for their organisation.

Joanna hoped to duck away before he saw her. But she didn't want to abandon Carl Prince. Eight thousand miles away and Peter Franklin was disrupting her little infatuation.

'We're focusing on rural communities,' said Prince. 'Then we'll tackle the informal settlements. Technical problems are less vexing in the urban areas, but the political process is always complicated, especially where the ANC's hegemony is contested.'

She'd never heard anyone use the word 'hegemony' in a conversation before. She wasn't quite sure what Prince meant.

The Swedes told Peter they had to pay 40 per cent duty on a Toyota Hilux they imported for one of their projects.

'And the vehicle sat in the Durban port for nine weeks until it cleared customs,' one of them said.

'My God,' said Peter, 'that's outrageous.' She could detect the feigned sympathy in his voice. He often grew impatient with people who couldn't solve their own problems.

'In which areas is the ANC's hegemony contested?' Joanna asked Prince.

Peter's conversation froze the minute she spoke. He was like that. He could eavesdrop on two or three discussions in a crowd while still carrying on his own. He turned around, shouted Joanna's name and reached out to give her a hug. Joanna mustered the required enthusiasm, then excused her and Peter's interruption to the Minister.

'We're old friends from the anti-apartheid struggle in the States,' she said, making a slip. She'd discovered the correct way to pronounce 'apartheid' since she got to Joburg, but in her uneasiness she'd reverted back to the American 'apartide'. So embarrassing.

'I can see you two have a lot to catch up on,' said Prince. Joanna tried to think of a reason the Minister shouldn't leave. Peter already had his right hand extended while he searched in his jacket pocket for a business card with his left.

'I'm from Pellmar,' he said. 'We're looking for investment opportunities in line with the RDP.'

'We welcome investors with a pedigree in the struggle,' said Prince, glancing briefly at Peter's card. 'Give my secretary a ring. We can talk. I hope you'll excuse me, though. I have another appointment. Freedom never rests in South Africa.'

Peter detained Prince for another minute to get the name of his secretary and his direct phone number.

'I'll be in touch,' Peter promised the Minister.

Joanna had gone from ecstasy to the agony of being stuck in this isolated corner with Peter. She could tell he'd been drinking. His voice rose in volume after two or three whiskys.

He told her about his meeting with Mthetho, and watching the ocean liner passing from his lounge window. 'His house is amazing,' he said, 'and his wife is a marvellously ambitious woman. I'm told she's beautiful to boot. Pellmar will be doing business with both of them soon. I'm just putting together a business plan.'

Their conversation turned to Carl Prince. At first she thought Peter was probing her personal connection to the

Minister. Men's jealousy could continue after love faded.

'I don't know him that well,' she said. 'I'm surprised he remembered my name.'

'At least he knows your name,' said Peter. 'It's a start.'

Joanna knew it was a start and nothing more. She was a quiet church woman, hardly material for a stylish Minister.

A waitress in a black skirt and white blouse circulated with a tray of drinks. Peter took a glass of red wine for Joanna. She tried to decline but he was insistent.

'Enjoy yourself,' he said. 'No one is watching. You only live in the honeymoon of South African freedom once.'

She sipped slowly on the wine. 'I ordered a Merlot,' Peter said. 'I know it's your favourite.'

She smiled. Suddenly a few of the good moments of their time together came back. Little things, like how Peter would often come home with gifts for her. Thoughtful things most men wouldn't think about, like dangly earrings or a book of poetry by Denise Levertov. One time he bought her an original painting by some artist from Soweto. They'd seen it at an exhibit and she told him how much she loved it. She never expected to see it again. It was on the wall in the school library. Since she and Peter broke up, no one bought her gifts.

'I'm thrilled about getting my business card to the Minister,' he said. 'It's a real windfall.'

As they talked, Joanna realised she missed making casual repartee with another American. She didn't have to curb her vocabulary to suit the limited English of some Swede or German. Nor did she have to endure the condescending derision of her Americanisms by the Brits and Aussies.

As the glasses of Merlot kept coming into Joanna's hand, the two wound their way backwards, glossing over those nights when they repelled each other in New York as their political paths diverged. Suddenly there was nothing but the comfort of familiarity, their shared ideas of the time before they'd grown apart. Loneliness and alcohol wrote their own version of history. Eventually Peter invited her to his hotel for dinner.

'It's just up the road,' he said. They laughed as he caught himself using the South African version of 'down the street'.

Though she rarely mixed her drinks, Joanna enjoyed the Chardonnay with dinner. Peter remarked that the wine's 'butteriness was almost reminiscent of a Meursault'. The Cape hake which he recommended reminded her of New England whiting.

They left the dining room arm in arm. South Africa was exhilarating, yet she felt curiously odd here, unable to connect. She was always 'the foreigner'. In Peter's company she could at least be herself, and that felt like enough for the moment.

○

'We probably shouldn't have done this,' he told her in the morning, 'but it was nice.'

Joanna resented the remark. He was right, but she'd always been the first to speak when something felt amiss in their relationship. She was out of practice, had spent too much time alone in her little two-room flat in Joburg. This time with Peter was different, however. She'd thought the whole time about Carl Prince, wished it was his goatee tickling her stomach instead of Peter's tanned fingers. Silent revenge but it wasn't enough. She felt slightly sick, and not from mixing the Chardonnay with the Merlot.

She stayed just long enough for room-service coffee. Lounging around the hotel room in last night's clothes didn't suit her and she wasn't about to put on Peter's robe like she used to.

They didn't kiss goodbye or promise to meet again. They left things bittersweet, with a touch more of the bitter for Joanna. Hit-and-run was always easier for a man.

Chapter 9

CONSTANTIA DROPPED HER bag on the floor by her office door and rushed to get the phone. She was running a bit late. The taxi driver had stopped to curse some fat old man in a Benz for cutting him off. Fidelis Fakude, the ANC councillor from Bopape, had told her she should get a car, but that would also mean driving lessons. Where would she find the time or the money?

Anyway, she wasn't thinking about finances for the moment. The previous night the Sivuyile ANC, under provocation from Monwabisi, had decided to protest against Prince's masakhane speech. They called masakhane appeasing the Boers. The branch planned a demonstration at the municipal offices in two days. Constantia stayed awake most of the night trying to figure out how the ANC councillors should respond.

She got the phone on the sixth ring. It was Mthetho. He'd already heard about the branch's decision.

'I tried to explain that it was premature, bhuti,' she said, 'but there are a few young lions there who won't listen.'

'Who are those?'

'I don't know all the names,' she said.

'I have heard that one is called Slim, and then there is the one we both know well.'

'Slim, yes,' she said. 'I think he is one of them. Slim Yanta.'

'And you will rein in our friend?' he asked.

'I will do what I can,' she promised. 'You know him, bhuti.'

'Remind him that this is the era of development, not destruction,' said Mthetho. 'We must use the proper channels. When the ANC needs a demonstration, we will let you know.'

Constantia put down the phone and straightened the framed map of Africa on the wall. She picked her suede bag up off the floor and brushed away some white specs of dust. She should never have bought black. A lighter colour wouldn't show the dirt.

She hunted for the baking soda in her desk drawer. She'd left it at home. The heartburn was starting early today.

She dashed down the hall to Fakude's office but he wasn't in. His secretary, Nandipha, a former Miss Duncan Village, was busy on the computer laying a seven of spades on top of an eight of diamonds. She said one of Fakude's taxis had a wreck and he had to go arrange the repair.

'It might be a write-off,' Nandipha said, stopping to pluck an Eet-Sum-Mor from the packet on her desk. She'd put on a few kgs since winning her last beauty contest.

Constantia checked with Richard Jacobs and Johnson Phakhathi, the other two ANC councillors. They'd gone to a conference in Bhisho.

The demonstrators would be there the following afternoon. She and the other ANC councillors couldn't run away and hide like the Bantu Administration Board used to do. Mthetho seemed to want her to stop the whole thing in its tracks. That was impossible. Monwabisi had made up his mind. He always told her the working class must be decisive. To her that sounded like being as aggressive as three angry bulls.

As she rushed back to her office, she bumped into Fakude in the hall.

'This fool of a driver I've got has crashed again,' he said. 'This time it's major – blood everywhere. It will cost me thousands, I tell you.'

Constantia informed Fakude that the Sivuyile branch had voted unanimously for a demonstration. 'They are organising in Bopape and in Basil February as well,' she said. 'They are protesting this masakhane thing about paying past debts.'

'Who is behind this?' he asked.

'A few of the hotheads in the branch.'

'Tell your husband to stop them,' said Fakude.

'It's not that simple,' said Constantia.

'I can imagine,' said Fakude. 'Those former shop stewards are real loose cannons.'

She told him about the phone call from Mthetho in the morning. 'He was angry,' she said.

'Let them march,' said Fakude. 'They can blow off some steam.' He excused himself to go for a 'conference' with his mechanic. 'The problems of the taxi business never stop,' he said as he strode down the hall.

That night Constantia asked Monwabisi what she should do about the demonstration. She didn't mention the phone call from Mthetho.

'I can't run away, but if I join there may also be problems from Bhisho, maybe even Pretoria,' she said.

'It's your decision,' he replied. 'I can't dictate to my councillor how she should respond. She is a member of the ANC. The principles of the organisation will guide her.'

She wasn't sure which principles he was referring to. The ANC was many things to many people. Before she had time to question him further, he told her he had to rush off to meet a friend who'd arrived from Joburg with a pile of newspapers.

'He's brought my *Business Day*,' said Monwabisi. Constantia saw the look in his eye – like a starving man who's just seen a T-bone steak land on his empty plate. How could he get so excited over a newspaper?

○

The ANC councillors mingled with the crowd of two hundred marchers assembled in front of their offices. Constantia and the ageing Councillor Phakhathi chatted with Cleophas Nobatana. A bouncing group of municipal workers sliced through the crowd in their direction. 'iR-D-P, iR-D-P, abantu bayayifuna iR-D-P,' they chanted.

Constantia pulled Nobatana out of the way.

'Even a friendly train can run over a blind old horse,' said Nobatana as he relocated himself away from the line of fire. He told Constantia this demonstration reminded him of the Defiance Campaign of the 1950s. 'Only then,' added the old man, 'we were dealing with an oppressor government.'

Slim Yanta trailed at the end of the municipal workers' group. He offered Constantia a placard with the slogan 'A Better Life for All – Now'. She declined, saying she had her hands full with 'the old man'. Then Councillor Fakude addressed the people from the back of a flatbed truck.

'As councillors,' said the short, thick-fingered Fakude, 'we remain your servants. Your issues are our issues; your problems, our problems.' The demonstrators strained to hear his high-pitched voice. During his time on Robben Island he had gained fame as a superstar in the prison's soccer league. One season he scored a record six goals. He preferred to talk with his feet.

'The key to success is that we work together,' added Fakude. 'We remain accountable to you as we build a better Ukusa for all.' He finished with the usual string of 'vivas'.

Two black policemen in their blue uniforms monitored the activity. They stopped to shake hands with Nobatana.

One of them said it was an honour to meet a real freedom fighter. Nobatana gave them a thumbs up.

'Don't worry about those,' one of the police said, pointing to the cameras mounted on the brick facade of the building. 'We disconnected them the day after the ANC won.' Constantia thanked the police for their 'service to the people'. Then she stared for a few seconds at the chain-link fence topped with razor wire that surrounded the building. She'd bring a motion to council to have it torn down. The police were on the side of the people now; there was no need to make their headquarters look like a prison.

As Monwabisi took the mike the chant resumed: 'iR-D-P, iR-D-P, abantu bayayifuna iR-D-P'.

'The non-payers,' Monwabisi said, 'are the whites who lived off the exploitation of blacks for so many years. Let government worry about them, not those who have boycotted in order to gain our freedom.'

The crowd changed its tune to 'Umshini Wam'. Though Monwabisi had never touched a machine gun in his life, it remained one of his favourite freedom songs. As his kicks began to fly higher and higher, a white BMW slowly cut a path through the crowd until it stood just next to the flatbed. Two men in suits got out, followed by Mthetho, then the broad-shouldered Mayor Siziba with the gold key to the city dangling around his neck. The pair of bodyguards jumped up onto the back of the truck, then pulled up the Deputy Minister and the Mayor. They stood next to Fakude. Monwabisi ignored them and kept on singing. As the crowd wound down, Mthetho took his cousin's hand and raised it in the air. 'We are so grateful that the Deputy Minister has made himself available,' said Monwabisi.

While the League women ululated, a few men let loose staccatos of whistle fire. Mthetho reached for the mike. He told the crowd that government would always respect their democratic right to speak out.

'Yet we don't encourage such gatherings, comrades,' said Mthetho. 'You have proper channels now. Your councillors are here, your Mayor. Speak to them. We don't need to go into the streets.'

'We will always need to go into the streets,' shouted Slim. Constantia excused herself to Nobatana and pushed towards the young man. She wouldn't have this lightie disrupting the Deputy Minister. By the time she reached Slim, Sandile Veki and two other Youth Leaguers had surrounded him. Veki was in full battle dress, his usual camouflage rounded off by well-polished combat boots.

'We don't want to hear another word out of you,' Veki told Slim. 'You can speak at our meetings. Here you must respect our leaders.' Constantia heard Slim mumble a reply. The Youth League had it under control. She headed back to Nobatana.

Mthetho grabbed the hand of the Mayor, who latched onto Fakude. The bodyguards motioned for the ANC councillors to join them. After a couple of minutes an ANC wall of unity formed a new tailgate for the flatbed. Fists raised high in the air, the crowd sang the national anthem, leaving out the verses in Afrikaans.

Mthetho's cordial facade at the demonstration disappeared at a meeting of the councillors and the branch executive in the Mayor's office half an hour later. He told them he didn't want such actions to be repeated.

'You have embarrassed me in my home area,' he said. 'This must not happen again.'

Monwabisi tried to say that even a people's government needed wake-up calls, but the Mayor said he was out of order.

'The Deputy Minister has travelled all this way to be with us,' said the Mayor. 'Let us give him our undivided support.'

Mthetho thanked the Mayor and said he hoped he had made himself abundantly clear. 'Demonstrations are a thing of the past,' he added.

Before Monwabisi had a chance to respond, the Deputy Minister's bodyguards had whisked Mthetho out of the building and into his waiting BMW. He had an appointment in King William's Town.

Chapter 10

THERE WAS ONLY ONE seat left in the taxi – in the back row next to three young men. Not a good choice but what could Joanna do? The trains and luxury coaches were full and she had to get back to Joburg. Her church meeting in East London had already kept her away too long.

The young men slid over. At least she wouldn't have to push past them. The slender man nearest her introduced himself as 'Thabo from Sivuyile'. They shook hands. His stocky partner with a gold earring was named Corleone; next to him sat the long-legged Cosmas.

'Don't worry about Corleone,' said Thabo. 'He's not really a gangster. It's the name his parents gave him.'

Joanna smiled and took out her copy of the RDP. She wanted to read the section on democratisation again. She loved the notion that 'democracy is not confined to periodic elections. It is rather an active process.' If only people in the US could understand this.

'I see you are reading our bible,' said Thabo.

'It's an amazing document,' she said.

'I'm doubting whether it will ever be implemented,' said Thabo.

'Thabo is worrying himself over nothing,' said Corleone. 'Everyone, even the president himself, remains accountable to our structures.' He spoke with a rhythmic cadence Joanna found hard to follow.

'You've never called me Thabo before,' the slender man said.

'It's true,' Corleone said to Joanna. 'Usually we call him Slim.'

Joanna glanced at Thabo's long neck, then went back to reading. She didn't want him to think she was staring.

'My nickname has a double meaning,' said Thabo. 'Slim means "clever" in Afrikaans.'

Cosmas reached across to offer Joanna a hard-boiled egg.

'I can peel it for you if you like,' he said.

'I prefer not to eat things that come from animals,' she said. 'But thank you.'

'You are a vegetarian?' asked Thabo.

'I try to be. Sometimes I fail.'

The driver slowed down and two women in the seat by the door got out. Joanna thought of moving up but two men got in and took the seats before she had a chance.

She continued reading the RDP document. She also liked the part about 'participation by forces outside of government'. Ordinary people seemed to have gained so much power in South Africa.

'You see, Joanna,' said Thabo, 'I don't like this idea of National Democratic Revolution, the NDR. Have you read Comrade Lenin's *State and Revolution*?'

'I'm a Christian,' said Joanna.

'Comrade Lenin is also good for Christians,' he said. 'We need to smash the bourgeois state apparatus, not simply install black faces.'

'It seems you are doing quite well,' said Joanna. 'You have so much to be proud of – electing Mandela, the RDP. There's peace in your country at long last.'

Cosmas sprinkled some salt on the egg, took a bite, then gave the other half to Corleone.

'But we haven't yet reached true democracy,' said Slim. 'That comes with socialism.'

Joanna thought perhaps the young man was baiting her. Socialism and democracy were, as the South Africans liked to say, chalk and cheese.

'We are studying Comrade Slovo's "Has Socialism Failed?"' said Thabo. 'We don't want to repeat the mistakes of the Soviet Union. Our civics and our unions are like soviets.'

'It seems you are from America,' said Corleone.

Joanna nodded.

Corleone told Joanna how heartbroken he was when President Clinton's health-care bill didn't pass. 'It was a great defeat for the working class,' he said.

'Yes,' said Joanna, 'I guess it was.' She had followed the debate in the media but she'd never thought about it quite like that.

'Do you think it failed because his wife was behind it, that if he himself had been in the driver's seat it might have succeeded?' asked Corleone.

'He's trying to ask you if America is still sexist,' said Thabo.

'Hard to say,' said Joanna. 'Maybe.'

Thabo then talked a little about his disappointment with the British Labour Party. He spoke of his admiration for 'Comrade Tony Benn'.

Joanna went back to reading the RDP. She'd never heard of Tony Benn.

As the taxi pulled to a stop, Thabo wrote down his details on a piece of newspaper and gave it to Joanna.

'One day you must come and visit here in Sivuyile,' he said. He pointed out the window at a wooden shack with a hand-lettered sign: Rocky's Five Star Cafe. 'Just go to the spaza there and ask for Comrade Slim,' he said. 'The old man will direct you.'

Joanna gave all of them one of her UV business cards. They seemed pleased.

The taxi waited at Rocky's for about ten minutes. The driver had gone next door to Bra Curly's Tailor Shop while the conductor bought some cool drinks and chatted with three men sitting at a metal table. One of them passed him a cigarette.

The driver emerged from Bra Curly's in a new brown shirt. As the conductor started yelling something about leaving, a man in a blue floppy hat and a sweaty friend came through the sliding door of the kombi and headed towards Joanna. She scooted over against the window to give them room to sit down. They smelled of beer. They asked where she came from and why she travelled by taxi. She gave curt replies, then pulled out her King James Bible. She didn't feel like talking.

As the taxi left Sivuyile, she flipped through the pages of Ecclesiastes, looking for a passage about friendship. Something like 'Woe unto the person who falls alone'.

'The madam doesn't want to talk to us,' said the man in the floppy hat. 'She's very rude.' He had two scars on his cheek.

There were empty seats towards the front, but to get to them Joanna would have to climb over the men. She clutched her brown bag tightly. She was glad she'd put her passport and traveller's cheques in a cloth pouch and tucked them in the waistband of her panties.

Suddenly the man in the floppy hat grabbed her thigh. She looked down in disbelief and saw the blood pumping under his fingernails. She stared out the window. Screaming wouldn't work. The man could deny everything. His grip dug deeper. The beer smell was too close.

'I know you like it,' he whispered to her. She grunted, as ugly a noise as she could produce. He didn't stop. She'd have a bruise the next morning.

She was about to shriek when the driver cranked up the

volume on the cassette – a Lucky Dube song about being a prisoner drowned out Joanna's options for attracting attention. She'd have to fight the battle alone.

Two large, middle-aged women sat in the front row. They'd gotten into the taxi carrying a host of plastic shopping bags from the OK. Joanna figured they were thinking about what to cook for dinner or how far they had to tote all those bags. What was happening to a foreign white woman two rows behind them belonged to another universe.

The taxi stopped to drop off a passenger. Two more young men got in, taking the seat right in front of Joanna. One carried a Bible. She thought about alerting him but he might just join in the fun. Carrying a Bible didn't mean a person couldn't be talked into evil deeds.

The Lucky Dube song finished. She could hear the driver rustling through the cassettes looking for a sequel.

'Get your hands off me!' screamed Joanna. 'Let go of my leg!'

The high pitch and force of her voice surprised her. The two women turned around but said nothing. Joanna tried to wriggle away. The man pressed down on her shoulder with his other hand, then slammed her forward, banging her head against the back of the seat in front of her. He slid his hand up under her top, pulling it back like a straitjacket. Her arms flapped helplessly at her sides as her bag fell to the floor. She should have known better than to travel by taxi. His partner picked up the bag and riffled through it. The women weren't looking any more. Lucky Dube had given away to Brenda Fassie's Siyajola. The men next to Joanna had different ideas about what it meant to jol.

The man's left hand slid down inside her underpants. He grabbed a handful of buttock while she tried once again to wrench free. She felt like he'd tied her up with a hundred yards of rope. The man with the Bible glared around at them. For a moment he looked confused. Then he jumped up, turned around and knelt on his seat facing backwards. A wooden cross hung at his chest. 'Let her go,' he said.

'Voetsek,' said Joanna's assailant as he pulled his hand out from her pants and eased the hold on her jacket. It was a stand-off. The man with the Bible reached into his belt, pulled out a long-barrelled .45 and pointed it at the head of the man in the floppy hat. He yelled in Zulu at the women with the shopping bags. One of them leaned forward and shouted through the wire grill that separated the driver from the passengers. One of the words she used was 'medem'.

'Get down,' the man with the Bible told the two drunken men, 'before I become angry.' The van began to slow down. Joanna had never been that close to a pointed gun before. If the man in the floppy hat decided to fight, anything could happen. Maybe the drunken men had weapons of their own. As the driver pulled to a halt, Joanna's assailant and his partner got up and scurried out. They left Joanna's bag, minus R27, on the floor.

'I'm sorry, m'am,' said the man with the Bible. 'I hope you are all right.'

'I'll be okay,' Joanna managed to say. But she felt weak and shaky.

She still smelled the beer, felt the man's fingers on her thigh. She was lucky that the man hadn't gotten her passport and traveller's cheques, but how long would it last, this sensation of her body being violated? It could have been worse, but she didn't want to know worse, didn't want to think about worse. Young black women probably faced this sort of danger all the time. Joanna knew they were tougher, smarter than her. They never sat in the back of a taxi next to two drunken men. South Africa wasn't all fairy tales. The two women in front ignored her for a reason. A man could carry a Bible and a .45 in this country. They did that in America too, only not in kombis.

When Joanna got home, she took a hot bath. She tried to read a few passages from Ecclesiastes but she couldn't concentrate. She lay there into the night. The bath hadn't washed away that man's fingers gripping her thigh, the smell of his beer breath. When she finally fell asleep, she didn't wake up until late in the afternoon. She needed to talk to someone. She thought of calling Peter. He used to be supportive in situations like this. She remembered how he'd spent days in the hospital with Sandra Oliver, a friend in the anti-apartheid movement, when Sandy fractured her skull in a car accident. He'd even cooked her pots of lentil soup. But that was the old Peter, the long-haired activist. She wasn't sure he'd be so sympathetic now. He was an investment consultant. He might just scold her for being foolish enough to travel in a taxi. She wasn't in the mood for a sermon.

〇

Instead of calling Peter, she spoke with Angela by phone two days later. Joanna described the incident in detail, the blue in the man's fingernails, how terrified she felt when the man pulled the .45.

'I still love what's happening here,' Joanna told her, 'but not every South African is a Nelson Mandela or Desmond Tutu.'

'Do you want to come home for a while?' Angela asked. 'You can recover, recharge your batteries. I can arrange something.'

Joanna refused the offer, but she felt vindicated, that she wasn't weak or silly to take such an assault seriously. Thousands died to overthrow apartheid and thousands more would be the target of criminals. Exposing and attacking evil in South Africa was complicated.

Chapter 11

First she'd gone to Parliament and now Constantia was sitting in a conference room at the Eastern Cape's most famous hotel. 'London Towers' was embroidered in blue on the linen napkins and tablecloths. She took care not to spill her coffee. A stain on those tablecloths would be a sacrilege.

At the podium stood Petrus Morūdu, the youngest director in the Department of Local Government in Pretoria.

'This chart,' said Morudu, 'shows the increasing debt of municipalities over the last decade.' According to the Mayor's introduction, Morudu graduated from the MBA programme at Wits after completing his degree in accountancy at Cambridge. He had to shake his laser pointer a few times to make it work.

'You can see the trend here,' he said as the tiny beam traced a steadily upward-sloping red line on the screen.

After three scones with jam and cream at the tea break, Constantia was starting to doze. She got Morudu's point, even if she missed some of the figures. He talked just like the trainers at the workshops she'd attended for the umgalelo. Balance sheets, financial plans, expenditure projections.

That R200 million in municipal debt kept coming back. She rubbed her eyes and tried to tune out the thin, fast-talking presenter's message of impending doom. She reached for the ring binder Morudu had handed out to each of the new councillors in attendance.

She read a summary of how Atlanta in America and Brisbane in Australia had rebounded from monstrous debts. She twisted her wedding ring around her finger as she read.

'Today these are global issues,' said the introduction to the material. 'All municipalities face similar dilemmas.' Constantia wondered how the situation in America or Australia could be similar to that of Sivuyile. Had this Morudu forgotten Sivuyile was in Africa?

After Morudu's battery of graphs came the ageing treasurer of Ukusa, Andries van Huis from the National Party. The thin-moustached bureaucrat projected a deficit of R7 million for Ukusa by the end of the financial year.

'As we extend service provision,' said Van Huis, 'debt will increase. We are painting ourselves into a corner. I cannot guarantee we will be able to pay the salaries of our municipal employees for the entire financial year.'

Constantia closed the binder. Atlanta could wait. What would happen to her family if the council actually ran out of money? They'd spent nearly all of Monwabisi's provident fund to add on another bedroom. Then her mother refused to move in, said she had to remain in a place where she could grow her vegetables. When Constantia suggested they put a lodger in the room, Monwabisi said he could never be a 'capitalist landlord'.

The last resort would be borrowing from Mthetho again. She didn't want to think about it.

A middle-aged woman in jeans wearing a 'No to Privatisation' cap interrupted Van Huis. 'We refuse to be blackmailed by the bosses,' she said.

'I'm doing nothing of the sort,' Van Huis replied. 'You people always plead for transparency. Now I'm giving you the facts. When you don't like them, you accuse me of something else. Remember, if you are not paid, I am not paid.'

'From Northridge to OR Tambo,' said the woman, 'without the municipal workers of Ukusa you would be wallowing in rubbish, sitting in the dark with no water. We don't take threats to our wages lightly.'

'We still remember how to strike,' added a woman sitting next to her.

Van Huis assured them that cutting anyone's pay would be the 'very last resort, that the union would be fully informed before drastic measures were taken'.

'We don't want to be informed,' the middle-aged woman said. 'We want to be consulted, to be part of the decision-making bodies.'

'That's out of my hands,' said Van Huis. 'All of that is up to the politicians.' He turned off the overhead projector and took his seat.

The next speaker was an American named Peter Franklin. He talked about the anti-apartheid movement in New York, about how he'd been arrested in some protests about banks. Constantia had already seen quite a few of these well-wishers from overseas. They'd come, enjoy the coastline, sample the seafood, then make a token trip to Ukusa. After that they could go home and tell people they'd been to the 'land of Mandela'.

Henry Winston, head of the Northridge Ratepayers' Association, spoke after Franklin. This grey-haired white man in a dark blue suit said his organisation was heartened by the spirit of masakhane.

'Apparently this means government does not intend to tax the residents of Northridge out of existence nor force us to bear the burden of carrying citizens who contribute nothing to the tax base of this country. We are totally on board with this new government thinking,' he added.

Constantia wanted to point out to Winston that Northridge represented a small white minority of Ukusa, but Van Huis's figures were starting to get into her head. Pie charts, bar graphs, images of empty dinner plates in front of her children. There must be some way the municipality could invest taxpayers' money and keep afloat. The consultant who visited their umgalelo said the emerging markets were paying an annual rate of return of up to 25 per cent. Surely the municipality could benefit from this.

That night, when she told Monwabisi the municipality might not have money for salaries, he responded by saying government remained 'a site of struggle'. 'We can't deny the masses housing and water to pay for the guns the SADF used to shoot us,' he added.

Constantia was starting to worry that her husband's head was permanently buried in the sands of the 1980s. People in government didn't use terms like 'the masses' any more. Or 'site of struggle'. Just that morning she'd received a copy of the Mayor's draft mission statement for Ukusa. It spoke of 'world-class governance models' and 'financial sustainability'. Once her husband read it, he'd probably be urging the branch to take to the streets again. If she couldn't talk Monwabisi out of such wild ideas, Mthetho would be ringing her night and day. No matter how hard she tried, she couldn't seem to find this 'win-win' formula the leaders kept talking about, especially not at home. Things just moved too fast in this new South Africa. Freedom never seemed to rest.

Chapter 12

AFTER A WEEK'S REST, Joanna sat down at her laptop with a cup of rooibos tea and a rusk to write her first UV report. Rooibos was supposed to calm the nerves.

'The soul of South Africa has captured me,' she wrote. 'I have travelled across the country, felt the vibrancy of a liberated people. Black South Africans young and old have repeatedly expressed their determination to deepen democracy. Many whites have embraced the spirit of reconciliation.'

As she wrote she could feel the man in the floppy hat gradually ease his grip.

'Although Nelson Mandela spent twenty-seven years in prison and enjoys universal respect,' she continued, 'one youth from a remote Eastern Cape town told me the president remains accountable to the people and their structures. Indeed, "structures" is a magic word in South African communities. People organise everywhere. Even primary school students have their structures and can bring an irresponsible principal to his or her knees.'

She went on to describe how just that week a transport workers' strike had halted all the trains and buses in Johannesburg. She realised Americans might not understand why such things continued even with Mandela in power. But she had to write about them, to speak the truth.

'Yet all this struggle is done with great joy and a spirit of forgiveness that has to impress any Christian. There is no desire to exact revenge on whites. Such vindictiveness would violate the very essence of the democratic movement. With such a spirit it is difficult not to believe in this country's ultimate success, hard not to be swept away by the tide of optimism and hope.'

Joanna had second thoughts as she saved the document and prepared to email it to Angela. Was this a true picture? She'd left out the event that probably stuck in her mind more than any other: the men attacking her in the taxi. She didn't want to overplay it, but by omitting it she was hiding part of the truth. She now felt 'accountable' to UV members. Concealing painful facts wouldn't help. She reopened the report and added a final paragraph.

'However, there are a few worrying trends. One is the scourge of violent crime. While riding in one of the vans that serve as taxis here, I experienced a taste of this scourge. A man accosted me in the back of the van. He grabbed me forcefully and tried to touch my private parts.'

Joanna wrote this account almost as if it had happened to someone else, as if she had already moved beyond this incident. Sometimes in her dreams the man with the Bible's .45 was pointed at her. Then she'd wake up. She was accepting that those memories were her cross to bear. But did she really need to include this event in the report? She wasn't sure and didn't know how to find out. She had no one to talk to.

'Both the attack and the rescue terrified me,' she added. 'And my experience was only a mild dose of the multitude of rapes, carjackings and murders that take place here regularly.'

She stopped for a moment to reread her words. They sounded so self-serving. She tried for perspective, not pity, in her conclusion:

'The solution is to provide jobs for the millions of unemployed who form the pool of perpetrators. The ANC must make good on its promise of "A Better Life for All" or run the risk of a quiet civil war between have-not outlaws and the rest of society.'

Joanna feared some people would take her tale as a betrayal, like revealing long-held family secrets to gossipy neighbours. Yet without honesty, freedom could lapse into tyranny.

Three weeks later Joanna received a copy of UV's newsletter in the mail. The centre spread contained her report plus a photo of the smiling Mandela in his Springbok jersey as he handed over the World Cup trophy to François Pienaar. The two paragraphs about her assault had been edited out.

She emailed Angela to find out what happened.

'We ran out of space,' Angela replied. 'We had to fit it all on two pages.'

'That part was critical,' Joanna wrote back. 'There is danger. We can't hide it.'

The next day Angela phoned her.

'I understand your feelings,' she said to Joanna. 'But some people might get the wrong idea.'

'The wrong idea?'

'Lots of people think Africa is nothing but a continent of violence – never-ending coups and wars,' said Angela. 'We have to give a different picture. Destroy the stereotype.'

'By hiding the truth?'

'There's already a mountain of criticism out there, so many who want South Africa to fail.'

'Nothing breeds failure like mindless supporters,' said Joanna. 'How do we deny hatred and bitterness when we see it?'

'Okay,' said Angela, 'we'll put something about crime in the next newsletter. I'll send you a brief in a few days.'

A week later Angela emailed Joanna, saying she'd discussed the crime issue and the omitted text with the UV advisory board. The board members all supported Angela's decision to cut the offending copy.

'Their view is that at the moment we should focus not on crime, but on the successes of the Mandela government,' read the email. 'He already has enough enemies. I trust you will accept the board's decision.'

Joanna's structures had her trapped. She was accountable to Angela who was accountable to the board. The UV members had no real say. In fact, they'd never find out. It was all upside down. Accountability wasn't an issue only in South Africa.

Part 2

Chapter 13

BRIAN MURPHY, ONE OF the Movement's leading town-planning experts, poured another round of the Nederburg. His faded T-shirt and well-worn jeans highlighted his proletarian pretension. Pellmar had employed Murphy to write a report on urban problems in South Africa. When he'd found out that Peter was a former anti-apartheid activist, Murphy had invited him to dinner at Marta's Restaurant in the trendy Joburg suburb of Yeoville. Peter felt at home, enjoying the conversation with Murphy and half a dozen other white veterans of the political struggle, though the weak-bodied red wouldn't have been his first choice to accompany chicken vindaloo.

'The problem with the white left,' Murphy told the group as he opened their third bottle of wine, 'is that they lack faith in black leaders. Our civics are the most democratic organisations in the world.'

Susan Vickers, professor of urban planning at Wits, sipped her wine while she waited for Murphy to finish. Peter looked forward to her response.

'That's a lot of kak,' said Susan. 'If we're going to succeed in South Africa, you need to come down from those left-wing clouds.'

Susan's wavy blonde hair fell into a perfect frame for her high cheekbones. Peter could count the freckles on her face. There were just five – clear and precious.

'We need investment,' she said, 'not higher taxes. The community structures can't do it alone. They need partners, partners with money,' she added, looking at Peter.

She made so much sense, looked so graceful in verbal combat while holding her wine glass casually aloft. Peter appreciated the fact that Susan wasn't oblivious to her appearance, unlike so many activist women. Joanna was the perfect example. When Joanna wanted to dress up, she would buy a new T-shirt with 'No Nukes' or 'Save the Earth' screen-printed on the front. Susan had a carefully constructed elegance: gold posts in her ears, a pastel striped woven top. Not mainstream fashion, but crisp and distinctive. She knew how to use an iron, understood what a little lipstick could add.

Debates between the likes of Susan and Murphy were part of the nightly fare at Marta's. The restaurant was a social centre in Yeoville, the self-proclaimed heart of progressive Joburg. Long before the 1994 elections, residents had defied apartheid laws and declared Yeoville a 'grey area' – neither white nor black. Returning ANC exiles, student activists, plus freelance intellectuals like Murphy mingled amid Yeoville's variegated landscape of half-century-old houses and modern blocks of flats.

Susan's reaction didn't stop Murphy from continuing his discourse on the centrality of breaking down the apartheid city.

'The north of Joburg is wealthy, white and planned. Pure petty bourgeois,' he said. 'The south is poor, black, chaotic and proletarian. We must overthrow it all.'

Murphy explained that his research had shown there was enough unused land in the northern areas of Joburg to accommodate a million blacks.

'It's the perfect opportunity to destroy spatial apartheid,' he concluded.

He poured himself and Peter another glass of wine. The others were lagging behind.

'Our newly elected council members are going to turn Joburg upside down with democracy and development,' Murphy said.

'None of these castles in the sky are possible without raising taxes,' said Susan. Peter found her voice pleasant but forceful. She didn't sound like an Afrikaner.

'Precisely,' said Murphy. 'The whites must pay. It's about time.' He took a few seconds to light a small cigar. Peter fanned the smoke away with his menu.

'If we raise taxes, people with skills and capital will flee,' said Susan. 'Without them we are lost.'

'That's what I mean about the white left,' said Murphy. 'No faith in black leadership.' He flicked the ash from his cigar into an empty beer bottle. Peter could see that Pellmar had hired the wrong man. A corporation was hardly part of the left. He'd have to check and find out who'd referred Murphy to his boss.

'Blind faith never helps anything,' said Susan,

Murphy ordered a shot of Jameson's with ice and nibbled on the white plastic tip of his cigar. He told Susan she was sounding 'like Roelf Meyer', the National Party's chief negotiator in the country's political settlement process.

'So if I don't believe in your fairy tales I'm a bloody Nat, eh?' she replied.

The ice cubes clinked lightly as Murphy swirled his glass. 'Nothing like a shot of Jameson's to cap off a rigorous debate,' he said.

'Answer me,' said Susan.

Peter enjoyed watching Murphy squirm. Joanna used to be smug like that as well, but at least she wasn't loud and arrogant. The left could be so self-righteous, even when they got it totally wrong.

'Of course not,' said Murphy. 'I'm just saying we need to be careful how we react to this transition. There are lots of dangerous ideas out there.'

'Finish your Jameson's,' said Susan. 'It's time you went home to bed before you dig yourself into a bigger hole. Ag, shame, Brian, you're a hopeless dreamer.'

The rest of the dinner guests excused themselves. They had to catch the first flight to Cape Town the following morning to attend a workshop on the post-apartheid city. An architect from Amsterdam was giving the keynote speech on 'cooperative living design'.

Murphy ordered another Jameson's and then went to the gents. Peter was trying to read the chemistry. Intense argument could mask forces of attraction. Maybe Murphy and Susan were using an American as a pawn in a jealous tug of war. Still, she kept touching Peter's arm when she wanted to make a point. That was a good sign, but why had Murphy ordered another whisky?

'He's living in the dark ages,' Peter said to Susan. 'I didn't know people still used words like "bourgeois" and "proletarian".'

'He's missed the bus,' said Susan. 'The problem is, he's not alone.' She finished her wine. 'I can give you a lift to your hotel,' she told Peter.

Murphy came back and chugged his Jameson's without sitting down. He then fumbled with the notes folded up in his pocket to cover his share of the bill.

'A revolutionary doesn't use credit cards,' he said.

'A revolutionary's got no credit,' said Susan.

'Could be that too,' said Murphy. He stuffed several crumpled R10 notes into her hand, then headed for the door. A minute later, he was back. He'd left his car keys on the table.

'He's totally deurmekaar and still thinks he can run a city,' she said once Murphy was out of earshot. 'What a joke.'

Peter laughed while Susan ordered a final brandy.

'He's not the only one living in the past,' she said. 'There are many others, especially in the unions. They're still talking about the dictatorship of the proletariat. It's laughable.'

Her face was closer to Peter now, their shoulders nearly touching. She wore clear polish on her nails. Joanna chewed hers.

'I've had my days of airy visions,' she said. 'How about you?'

'I worked that out one weekend while I sat in the Buffalo City Jail,' he said. 'We got arrested for chaining ourselves to a bank that invested in apartheid. That's when I realised petty little groups don't have any impact. You end up alone, talking to a few other like-minded people.'

'Impact is what it's about,' said Susan. 'Too many people in this country want to destroy what we already have rather than build on our strengths. I'm tired of posturing.'

She laid her hand on top of his for a few seconds. 'Why don't we have a nightcap at my place?' she asked. 'Then I'll take you to your hotel.'

○

The balcony off Susan's lounge overlooked Yeoville Park. As she and Peter sipped port, they followed the trail of a man pushing a shopping trolley along a concrete walkway. He stopped and walked over to the wading pool to scoop some water into his mouth for a drink.

'In the daytime the bergies flock to one corner of the park,' Susan said. 'The police chase them away if they bother the few respectable people who still pass through here. Most have fled to the north. Even the synagogues are closing down.'

Peter didn't want to say it, but he felt like he was looking at a budding Washington Square Park, one of New York's dens of drug dealers and unsavoury elements of all races. Susan probably wouldn't understand his cynicism. This was not a night to accentuate differences.

They found more common ground in Susan's bedroom, making love in the company of wall posters of toyi-toying ANC martyr Chris Hani and fallen white trade unionist Neil Aggett. Susan fell asleep almost immediately afterwards. For a while Peter lay awake, trying to hold on to the moment. But in the turbulent transition of South Africa nothing, least of all a first sexual encounter, felt permanent. Still, his night with Susan confirmed one thing: he'd never go back to the likes of Joanna. Why drink a bodiless table red when the world holds finely aged Bordeaux?

○

Peter had to catch his flight back to New York right after breakfast. Susan apologised for not going to the airport to see him off, but she had to chair a meeting of the municipal land-use committee.

He promised to keep in touch and told her the night held a 'special place' in his life. Her preoccupied 'thank you' left him a little disappointed. She managed a peck on the cheek in between jotting down notes from a proposal for a sewage treatment plant on the West Rand.

Peter thought about Susan all the way from Joburg to Heathrow, then across the Atlantic until his flight touched down at LaGuardia. He'd never been so enchanted by a woman's freckles or her political sense.

Two weeks later Peter presented a 73-page report to top management at Pellmar. He assessed South Africa as a country 'rife with opportunities, perhaps the equivalent of the wealthier former Soviet republics'.

He cautioned, however, that a considerable element within the ANC, centred in the South African Communist Party and the unions, still clung to 'socialist, statist and redistributive economic models of a bygone era'.

'If this group is not marginalised,' he continued, 'investors will face a nightmare of strikes, taxes and outlandish demands for "sharing of wealth". Even nationalisation could be a possibility.'

The report proposed that Pellmar build partnerships with local stakeholders and role players to 'gain the inside track for opportunities to facilitate the restructuring of state-owned enterprises in transport, electricity, tourism and water provision'.

Top management complimented Peter on an excellent effort and urged him to create a plan of action in the suggested areas. A memo from Wesley promised that 'South Africa was definitely part of Pellmar's future'.

Peter faxed Susan the good news. He said he hoped to 'continue their relationship in the not-too-distant future'. He followed up the message by sending her a dozen red roses via an international florist that advertised on television. He hoped the flowers would arrive.

All he got in response was a form letter via fax two days later telling him that the Deputy Minister for Local Government in Pretoria had resigned due to health reasons and that the president had appointed Susan Vickers as the replacement. She had already begun winding down at the university and moved into her office in Pretoria. Pellmar now had a connection at the highest level.

Chapter 14

FOR THE THIRD STRAIGHT night, Susan woke up at 3 a.m. Had her secretary remembered to book the teleconference with the Danes? Were the remarks she made at the departmental meeting about 'inefficient systems' potentially offensive to the Minister? She tried to go back to sleep, but eventually she got up, wrapped her dressing gown around her and booted up the computer. There could be an email from those USAID people in Washington. With a seven-hour time difference, messages from the Americans came at all hours.

She put on the kettle and dropped some tea leaves in the pot. At least at this hour she had time to let it steep. Except for her computer, her bed and those wilting red roses from Peter Franklin, everything was either in boxes or wrapped in plastic. She'd be moving to a new house atop a hill in Kensington at the weekend. The security people said a Deputy Minister couldn't be properly protected in a flat. Besides, her job came with a housing allowance. She might as well put it to use.

Her driver arrived at seven. By that time she had finished her second pot of tea, edited two reports and shed the dressing gown for the black suit and flats that had become her work uniform. She missed the relaxed atmosphere of the university, where she sometimes even wore jeans.

She had to do some editing of a consultant's report on water roll-outs in the Eastern Cape before a ten o'clock meeting. The writer had forgotten to include the former Ciskei area in his budget projections. The Ciskei had been plundered by homeland leader Brigadier Oupa Gqozo. Susan had to make sure the area didn't get neglected again. Besides, the new municipality of Ukusa, one of the area's biggest, couldn't be overlooked. The Deputy Minister of Local Government for the province, Mthetho Jonasi, came from there. Susan was learning to pay attention to fiefdoms.

As Susan came out of the lift, her secretary, Mrs Kruger, hurried towards her. She was a well-dressed woman in her mid-fifties who took great pride in her precision management of Susan's diary.

'The Minister phoned just now,' Mrs Kruger said. 'He says you can catch him in the next five minutes.'

Susan dug in her purse for her cellphone and dialled through to Minister Tumahole. He just wanted to tell her about the change of venue for the management team's weekend retreat. His secretary could have done that, but Susan appreciated the personal touch.

When she tried to open the consultant's report on her computer, the folder where she'd saved it was empty. She went to File Manager and hunted for the document. Nothing. She was sure she'd saved it to her hard drive the night before. She checked the plastic case of disks on the bookshelf. She backed up every day before leaving work. But her latest backup disk was gone. She called Mrs Kruger into her office.

Mrs Kruger told her that Mr Molefe had been in the office twice when Susan was out. 'He said he had forgotten something on your desk,' she said. 'He's a skelm,' she added lowering her voice as if someone might hear.

The short, balding Molefe was a Deputy Director, though he was still taking evening classes to complete his Bachelor's degree. Susan remembered him from the UDF days, when he wore threadbare struggle T-shirts. She sometimes gave him money for taxi fare home from late-night meetings. 'Tell Molefe to come and see me immediately,' she told Mrs Kruger.

The Deputy Director arrived five minutes later. Susan invited him to take a seat.

'She's lying,' said Molefe when Susan told him Mrs Kruger mentioned he'd been in her office. 'I was never here.'

Susan called in Mrs Kruger. The secretary took a seat by Susan's desk, leaving an empty chair between her and Molefe.

'Mr Molefe says he was never in my office,' Susan said.

'He was here twice,' said Mrs Kruger. 'Last week Wednesday afternoon and last week Friday morning.'

'Why are you making this up?' said Molefe. 'I was never here. What is the problem?'

'It's my mistake,' said Susan. 'Let's just forget this ever happened. I misplaced something and I made some wrong conclusions.'

'Wrong conclusions?' said Molefe. 'Like what – that I'm a thief? So you can take the man out of the township but you can't take the township out of the man, is that it? Better hide your ballpoints and staplers too. The natives are running loose now in government buildings.'

'Please, Comrade Molefe,' said Susan. 'I made a mistake.'

'So it's comrade now, is it?' Molefe stood up and left.

'He was here,' said Mrs Kruger. 'I don't know what he's covering up.'

'You can leave now,' said Susan. 'I'll sort this out myself.'

Susan could get the consultant to email her another copy of the report. She wouldn't get the budget fixed before the ten o'clock meeting, but she had bigger problems now. She went to Frances Mmusi, the Deputy Director of Finance, and explained what had happened. Mmusi had studied finance in the US after her husband died of malaria in an ANC camp in Tanzania. Susan felt she had a more mature perspective on things than did most people in the department.

'Once I had Molefe in my office,' Susan told her, 'I remembered that only Mrs Kruger had the password to my computer. She deleted that document, then stole the disk. The sabotage of the old guard.'

'But you can't prove it,' said Mmusi, 'and now you've got Molefe accusing you of racism. Welcome to government. Now go and talk to the Minister before Molefe does.'

'I'm still left with the problem of Mrs Kruger,' said Susan.

'Sack her immediately.'

'There's procedures, regulations.'

'Find a way,' said Mmusi.

Twenty minutes later, Susan was in Tumahole's office. The Minister had been a town planner in Glasgow for ten years before he returned to join Mandela's Cabinet. He'd already won international awards for his department's roll-out of water service to rural areas.

'Let us not make mountains out of molehills,' Tumahole said to Susan. 'We have enough mountains already.'

Susan wanted clarification on what she had to do to sack Mrs Kruger. 'I don't want to do it wrong and have it end up in the headlines: "ANC Minister Illegally Sacks Ageing Afrikaner",' she said.

'We can't sack her,' said Tumahole. 'We place her on paid administrative leave and make her an offer she can't refuse. It might cost two or three hundred thousand rands, but it's nothing compared to the chaos she can cause. Nothing.'

'So she gets rewarded for sabotage?' said Susan.

Tumahole smiled. 'Susan, we have millions of people clamouring for water, dozens of companies banging on our door with investment offers,' he said. 'We don't have time to fight one administrative assistant. Send her home right now. I'll take care of Molefe.'

Three days later Susan had a new administrative assistant,

Dipuo Mothopeng. She wasn't quite as meticulous with Susan's diary as Mrs Kruger was, but she could learn. By the end of Dipuo's second day, Susan had finalised the water roll-out budget for the Eastern Cape. Water was on the way, or at least the money for water. How they'd manage to lay all those pipes and install all those taps was another question. The department would be looking for business partners.

After work Susan drove to Peter's. She needed an escape. Pellmar had rented him a three-bedroom house just five minutes down the hill from her new place.

By the time she was walking up the front steps, Peter was already at the door.

'I'd know the sound of that Jetta anywhere,' he said. Peter called it her 'minimum mobile'. A Deputy Minister's allowance was sufficient to buy any car on the road. Susan chose a Jetta to set an example of 'frugality and discipline'. The only compromises she made were central locking and air conditioning. The car didn't even have a CD player.

Peter boasted that he'd been studying the RDP all day and that his boeuf bourguignon was simmering on the stove. 'I was lucky enough to find some decent mushrooms,' he said.

Susan could smell the wine seeping into the bright red meat. Peter would have found the freshest stewing beef Joburg had to offer. He didn't compromise on such issues.

He held up the brightly coloured volume entitled *Reconstruction and Development Programme*. 'I can recite some passages verbatim,' he said. 'People will be impressed. Listen.'

Peter began to shout as if he were speaking to a filled stadium: 'The RDP seeks to mobilise our people and our country's resources towards the final eradication of apartheid and the building of a democratic, non-racial and non-sexist future.'

He put the book down. 'How was that?' he asked.

'I've got a little skinner for you,' she said. 'The RDP will soon be a thing of the past.'

'But it was the election platform of the ANC,' said Peter. 'Everyone loves it, even the white businessmen. It's a wonderful document. Something for everyone. What the hell's a skinner?'

'It means gossip in Afrikaans,' she said. 'Anyway as we speak, a team of World Bank economists is drafting a new economic policy more in line with global trends. The RDP is scaring away investors.'

'It doesn't scare me,' said Peter, 'but with the Bank, you can't go wrong.'

'Why don't you open this?' said Susan. She brought out a bottle of a local Cabernet. Peter was thinking of the Chateau La Clotte 1994 he had in the rack in the kitchen. Not the best, but far superior to anything South Africa produced. He only used local brew for cooking. He took Susan's wine into the kitchen, then eyed the La Clotte. He opened her Cabernet and filled Susan's glass. Then he turned to the Chateau. He eased the cork about halfway out, then wrapped a tea towel around it to make sure Susan wouldn't hear the final pop. He poured himself the Chateau, then held the two glasses up to the light. The colour was close enough. She'd know the difference.

After a candlelit dinner, which Susan labelled 'exquisite', they snuggled on the sofa and watched an idiotic video, *The Bridges of Madison County*, a Clint Eastwood film about some woman who had an affair and kept it a secret for thirty years. Peter fell asleep. Susan said the movie had a 'distinctly male perspective, trying to separate romantic love from the love women express every day with their labour'.

'Jesus,' he said. 'You South Africans make a political issue out of everything.'

'And you Americans try to pretend you don't,' she said.

Peter woke up at four o'clock with a faint taste of Chateau on his tongue and those passages of the RDP running through his head. 'The RDP integrates growth, development, reconstruction and redistribution into a unified programme...' He couldn't block it out. Why couldn't these South Africans make up their minds?

Chapter 15
June 1996

'THE BOY FROM D Village makes good,' shouted Fakude, 'UWorld Champ weth'.'

The councillor didn't come to the shebeen that often but he had to celebrate. The Eastern Cape's finest, Duncan Village native Mbulelo Botile, had knocked out the Filipino boy the night before. Mama Patty had been up the whole night preparing the golden brown smileys that welcomed the guests. She'd taped the fight and kept playing it over and over again. As long as they could watch Mbulelo's left jabs and right hooks, the men would keep drinking. There seemed to be no end to it. Just to be sure, the four space heaters were cranked up all the way. Mama Patty hoped they wouldn't blow the electricity but she couldn't let the cold of an Eastern Cape winter scare away the customers. She loved the Eastern Cape boxers. Not that men beating each other up delighted her, but she'd sold more beer and whisky on the night Vuyani Bungu won the world title than on New Year's Eve. Now another Xhosa boy was mining gold for her shebeen.

'First there was Happy Boy, then The Beast, now we have Mbulelo,' said Monwabisi, pointing with pride at the posters of great local boxers of the past on the wall. 'The Eastern Cape is the boxing capital of the world.'

'We are a factory of champions,' said Fakude, handing Monwabisi another Amstel. 'Let the beer flow like Mbulelo's uppercuts.'

Jeff Ntoni didn't take beer, not even to toast another home boy winning a world title, but he joined Monwabisi in the mini toyi-toyi to celebrate. It was also a good way to keep warm.

'Ndifuna inews,' said Monwabisi. He hadn't even listened to the radio that day. He had to know what was happening in the world.

'Ah, no,' said Mama Patty. 'People don't come to the shebeen to hear the bad news. They come here to enjoy.'

'Just for a minute,' said Monwabisi as he edged closer to the TV. 'To catch the headlines.' He strained for the channel button but it was just out of reach. He slid a chair over from one of the tables and climbed on it.

'I'll give you thirty seconds,' said Mama Patty, looking at her watch. 'Otherwise mna I'll have a riot on my hands.'

The channel change left Mbulelo walking back to his corner after round five. Instead of Botile's rippling midsection, the screen now held a balding man standing behind a podium reading from a paper.

'In Cape Town today,' the announcer said, 'the Minister of Finance, Trevor Manuel, unveiled a new economic policy called Growth, Employment and Redistribution. The Minister said this policy would bring South Africa "in line with the rest of the world".'

'Asiyifuni!' someone shouted from the back. 'Sifuna uchamp weth'. Put back our boxing.'

Monwabisi strained to hear more details. He caught something about 'fiscal discipline' and 'favourable climates for investment'.

'Time up,' said Mama Patty. 'Back to mkhaya, the champion of the world.' Her gold earrings bounced gently as she moved towards the TV.

'This is crucial,' said Monwabisi. 'Just another minute.'

'What's crucial in a shebeen is selling beer, bhuti. No one

buys beer to watch news, in Xhosa, English or Afrikaans.'

'That's where you're wrong, Mama,' replied Monwabisi, digging into his pants pocket. 'I'll buy five beers if you let me watch for five more minutes. That's one beer a minute.'

'We want Mbulelo!' came another shout from the back.

'I can't take any chances,' said Mama Patty. She lifted a remote from her pocket and switched back to the VCR.

Monwabisi returned his money to his wallet. 'I'm going to organise a boycott,' he said. 'We'll be picketing outside your door tomorrow morning.'

'I can buy those boycotters of yours with less than a crate,' she replied. She brought out a fresh Amstel from behind the bar and handed it to Monwabisi. 'To make up for your pain and suffering because of not seeing news,' she said.

'Boycott cancelled,' said Monwabisi. 'I'm going home.' He gave the bottle of Amstel to Fakude, then said his goodbyes. He'd already had four beers, more than someone with the virus should be drinking. Besides, beer cost money. He'd talked to a couple of people about making burglar bars but no one had cash. They all wanted to pay him later.

The sight of Trevor Manuel had sobered him up. He remembered Manuel from the UDF days. He had long, wild hair then, not this polished dome and professor's glasses he'd donned since he became Minister of Finance.

Monwabisi got home in time to hear the English news. He didn't learn much more, other than that the policy was drafted by a team of economists linked to the World Bank.

For the next three days, Monwabisi scrambled to find out exactly what Manuel was talking about. At moments like this he hated being in Sivuyile. In Joburg he'd have five different newspapers to read, plus comrades would have their own sources. Here he was lucky to get the *Dispatch*, which only had two paragraphs on what they were now referring to as GEAR.

James Kilgore

Monwabisi didn't know what gear this policy was shifting South Africa into. He finally convinced Constantia to put a call through to the metalworkers' union office via her work phone.

He spoke to Comrade Blast, a former shop steward at Metal Links who had become a regional organiser.

'The RDP is dead,' said Blast. 'We are in a state of shock. They never told us this was coming. Even at COSATU head office, they first learned about this from the radio.'

Comrade Blast said the unions were planning a march to protest the policy and the government's lack of consultation.

'It's a slap in the face of the working class,' Comrade Blast said. Then their connection went sour. Monwabisi felt his headaches returning. What was the government thinking? The unions would have to bring them to their senses before it was too late. He wished he'd remembered to ask Comrade Blast what was meant by 'fiscal discipline'.

Chapter 16

'IT'S ALL RIGHT,' MONWABISI SAID to the bellman. 'We'll carry our own bags. We are comrades.' The gold revolving door of the London Towers whirled automatically and brought them in out of the cold. Mrs Mehlo stopped to unbutton one of her jerseys and the door clipped her heels. Monwabisi reminded her to keep moving.

As their feet sunk into the rich brown carpet of the lobby, Monwabisi recalled that his father used to work at this hotel before he went to Joburg.

'He stayed in the gents all day to brush the dust off white men's coats and hand them towels.'

'I once applied for a job here,' said Mrs Mehlo, 'but I used the rear entrance.' She stopped to pull off her top layer. The London Towers didn't cut corners when it came to keeping their guests toasty warm.

People had come from all over the province for the briefing on GEAR. The Department of Local Government had allocated four seats to Ukusa. Jeff Ntoni travelled with Monwabisi and Mrs Mehlo in the taxi, but he had gone off to talk to some Communist Party comrades from PE. The other delegate, Henry Winston from Northridge, apologised. He had to attend his son's championship rugby match.

Mrs Mehlo edged her way across the lobby, gazing up at the crystal chandeliers that hung over the reception desk. Monwabisi pointed to a huge fish mounted inside a glass case.

Mrs Mehlo turned her head and let out a shriek, grabbing Monwabisi's arm.'Nkosi yam!' she said. 'What the hell?' She let go of his arm when she realised the coelacanth was dead. Once Monwabisi explained it to her, she recalled hearing about a fish that was here 'before the Bushmen'.

'Abelungu put strange things in their houses,' she said.

Mrs Mehlo and Monwabisi checked in at the registration table and pinned their printed name badges onto their shirts.

'We are in the Protea Room,' a woman in a dark blue suit said and directed them down the hall.

The Protea Room had a very high ceiling with a sliding divider down the middle. Monwabisi could hear a white man talking about insurance premiums on the other side. He and Mrs Mehlo found their seats. The former shop steward removed his 'Workers' Power' cap. It was a memento from the 1987 miners' strike, when he'd just started working for Felton. He still remembered his first pay packet – the fattest envelope he'd ever seen.

A yellow banner covered the front wall: 'Growth, Employment and Redistribution: The RDP in Action.' Madiba's picture was underneath.

Mrs Mehlo busied herself with a big glass of ice water and several red-and-white peppermint sweets while the other participants straggled in. A group from Cradock shone in their green 'Viva RDP' T-shirts. One of them looked young enough to be in high school. A woman from Qunu dressed in traditional Xhosa attire, including a long pipe, walked over to greet Mrs Mehlo. They knew each other from church meetings. While everyone quietly waited for the proceedings to start, three men from the Butterworth branch distributed the black 'GEAR Consultation Conference' carrier bags. All those who attended would have a souvenir.

Mthetho arrived late. Two men in suits tried to head off

Monwabisi as he approached his cousin. Mthetho waved away his security. Monwabisi asked the Deputy Minister if he minded being in the 'hot seat'.

'By the end of the day,' Mthetho replied, 'you'll be singing the praises of GEAR.'

'And Bafana Bafana will have won the World Cup,' said Monwabisi.

The Deputy Minister began his presentation by suggesting that the government did have other alternatives.

'We could carry out a full-scale revolution,' he said, 'and nationalise all the mines, industries and farms.'

Monwabisi sat back. His cousin had tricks. Those years at the UN had made him into a master orator.

'For a few days,' said Mthetho, 'maybe even a few weeks, we would celebrate while we chased the owners away, put our feet up on their desks and emptied all their bottles of whisky.'

'Imported whisky,' interjected one of the people from Cradock.

'Yes, imported whisky,' said Mthetho. 'But recognise, comrades, from the moment we took that action, we would have gone backwards into the world of outcasts, just like in the days of Botha. We may have the strongest army on the continent, but we are no match for the power of the dollar and the US armed forces. Iraq couldn't last three weeks during Desert Storm. How long could we hold out? Government has made the correct choice – a tough choice but a prudent one. In the long run you will not regret the course on which we have embarked. That I promise you.'

When the Deputy Minister finished, it was time for tea. Monwabisi guided Mrs Mehlo down the serving line, assuring her that she could take as many shortbread and ginger biscuits as she wanted. He chatted to a young delegate from Cradock. They called him 'Khayelitsha'.

'Why are they spending so much money for a hotel?' the young man said. 'Are there no government schools in East London with classrooms?'

Jeff Ntoni overheard the conversation. Before Monwabisi could respond, Ntoni stepped in to tell Khayelitsha that because the ANC had booked on very short notice, nothing else was available. Monwabisi left the pair and walked back to Mrs Mehlo. They all knew it was Saturday. Schools in Mdantsane weren't occupied on the weekends.

Mrs Mehlo was spooning sugar into her second cup of tea. 'I'm enjoying the biscuits,' she said. Just three Romany Creams remained on the round silver tray in front of them. Monwabisi picked them up and set them on Mrs Mehlo's saucer.

When the group reconvened, Mthetho introduced their visitor from the Ministry of Finance, Mr Petrus Morudu. The financial expert turned on the overhead projector.

'He is going to explain the technical details of GEAR,' said Mthetho. 'We have assembled a world-class team of economists to put this together.'

'We still have comments from your input,' said Monwabisi. 'We are disappointed.'

Mthetho eyed Morudu.

'If you don't mind, Mr Morudu, we will steal a few minutes of your time,' said Mthetho. 'We want to be as transparent as possible.'

Morudu switched off the projector and sat down.

'You were disappointed, my brother?' said Mthetho, pointing towards his cousin.

'Your pessimism is very troublesome,' Monwabisi said. 'You have forgotten the achievements of the Cuban Revolution. Under Comrade Fidel Castro everyone has running water and education. Their health-care system is superior to that of the Americans. They even export doctors to Africa.'

'We are friendly with the Cubans,' said Mthetho. 'They have indeed achieved some remarkable things. And they helped us in Angola.'

Monwabisi was surveying the crowd. He knew most of them from the ANC or the unions. In the past, they would have rallied behind him, defended the Cuban Revolution and Comrade Fidel Castro. But people were changing. One day they were on the side of the working class, the next day they were wearing suits and calling themselves entrepreneurs or consultants. He didn't know who to trust.

'Cuba survived because the Soviet Union bought their sugar at inflated prices,' Mthetho added, 'but the USSR is gone, comrades. Now the Cubans are begging for US tourist dollars. We admire the Cubans and we cheer for their boxers when they fight the Americans, but we are an African nation of forty million people. We produce cars and computers. We are nothing like Cuba. Nothing at all.'

Quiet comments percolated through the room. Jeff Ntoni reminded the house that South Africa couldn't go it alone. Monwabisi accepted the reality. He was a lone wolf howling in the night.

Morudu switched the projector back on, turned out the lights and delivered the audience promises of economic growth rates of six per cent and the creation of 409 000 jobs in five years. By the time he finished, just three minutes before lunch, Khayelitsha was snoring loudly, his head bobbing up and down like a buoy in a storm.

Mrs Mehlo led the charge to the lunch queue. She asked the chef to slice off three pieces from the roast beef, two from the roast pork and four from the lamb. She refused the mashed potatoes and gravy. She hesitated at the bread rolls, but when Monwabisi explained that the poppy seeds on top were just for decoration she took four. He left her to her food while he tracked down Mzimande Matswele, the regional secretary of COSATU. Mzimande had shaved his head since Monwabisi had seen him last, a sure sign that he was losing his hair. The new South Africa did that to a trade unionist. Mzimande and Monwabisi vowed to 'hijack' the agenda for the afternoon.

'Though the die is already cast,' said Mzimande, 'we must make sure the participants have their say. The masses learn from their failures as much as their successes.'

'We can still go the way of Cuba,' said Monwabisi.

'That point is past,' said Mzimande. 'We have no Fidel Castro and they've killed Chris. He was our Che Guevara.'

As the delegates regrouped after lunch, the Cradock group began to remind the Deputy Minister about the working class with the we-work-hard-song 'Sisebenza kanzima'. Mthetho rushed over to stop them.

'Comrades, comrades, we must remain orderly,' he said. 'The management of this hotel has given us this conference room on very short notice. They have been promised an orderly session. Please.'

'The people have been promised a better life for all,' said Khayelitsha. 'Instead we've gotten GEAR. Phantsi nayo.'

'Comrades, let us respect each other's views,' said Mthetho.

'Phantsi nayo,' said Khayelitsha, bringing his arm down for emphasis. A few people echoed his cry.

'Excuse us,' came a voice from the other side of the divider. 'Can we ask you to keep it down, please? We can't hear ourselves think.'

Mrs Mehlo used the break in the discussion to rewrap the white cloth napkin around her pieces of roast pork and lamb. She'd eaten the beef. Monwabisi poured some ice water and sat down.

'It's a problem,' said Khayelitsha. 'We are meeting in the hotels, yet many of us live in little hokkies.'

Mthetho walked back towards the podium at the front of the room.

'These meetings are a joke,' said Khayelitsha.

'Let us have one meeting and one chair,' said Jeff Ntoni.

Khayelitsha sat down, crossed his arms momentarily, then got up and left the room. Mthetho looked at some notes while the three remaining Cradock delegates talked among themselves. One of them got up and left; the others stayed.

'Your concerns are valid,' said Mthetho. 'Important, in fact. That is why we are here. At the same time we must realise there is no alternative. The Russians are selling off everything to the West. The Chinese run a dictatorship where sweatshop workers produce consumer goods for the Americans. On the African continent, socialism has brought famine, poverty and war. Who is South Africa to resist the tide of history?'

'There is always an alternative,' said Monwabisi. 'We will find it through our struggles, just like we found the unions and the civics.'

'We have moved to the next stage,' said Mthetho.

'Government has been empowered to make these decisions by your votes. We have made our choice.'

'We fully understand government's dilemma,' Jeff Ntoni added. 'At the same time, it is important that government acknowledge it made an error in failing to consult before acting.'

As Ntoni spoke, Mthetho left the podium and moved to the centre of the floor. He took a quick glance at his watch before replying to Ntoni.

'We are consulting,' said Mthetho. 'Other leaders are speaking at meetings like this across the country.'

'It is too late,' said one of the remaining Cradock comrades.

'It can never be too late,' said Mthetho.

'For us it is too late,' said one of the Cradock delegates. 'We have a taxi to catch back to our mukukus.' They both gathered their things and left.

The meeting continued for another two hours. Mrs Mehlo only spoke at the end. She said she ate too much, that the meat for lunch was 'very difficult' for her to chew.

'Even an old woman with few teeth can tell the difference between roast beef and neck bones,' she said. 'At the workshops we are getting roast beef but in the community we are fortunate when we have neck bones. And often they have been chewed on before.'

Mthetho laughed and said something about the amusing but insightful wisdom of the elderly. Before he adjourned the proceedings, he said the ANC would circulate a summary of the comments at all the meetings and schedule follow-ups where required.

'We want your continued input,' he added.

Monwabisi helped Mrs Mehlo put her papers together.

'Your cousin thought I was joking,' she said. 'Was I trying to be funny? Ah no, these leaders of ours are becoming too big for their boots.'

One of Mthetho's bodyguards tapped Monwabisi on the shoulder and told him the Deputy Minister wanted him. The former shop steward followed the bodyguard to the hotel lounge. Mthetho sat in a grey armchair, talking on his cellphone. He closed the phone and warned Monwabisi about fighting uphill battles.

'Clinging to that struggle mentality of yours is a nonstarter,' said Mthetho. 'Think of the future of your family.'

'I don't work for the bourgeoisie,' Monwabisi said with a smile. 'The ANC seems to be moving in that direction.'

'This is the only way forward for the working class,' Mthetho replied.

'This GEAR of yours will bring a better life for some and a worse life for the majority,' said Monwabisi.

'In three months you'll be with us,' said Mthetho. 'I'll make you an offer you can't refuse.'

'I can't be bought.'

'This is not about buying,' said Mthetho. 'It's about common sense.'

'I must go,' said Monwabisi. 'Auntie Mehlo is waiting.'

He walked back to the Protea Room. Mrs Mehlo had her black conference bag around her neck. She was packing a handful of mints into the pocket of her jersey. Once the bowl was empty, she and Monwabisi headed for the taxi rank. He couldn't wait to get in the taxi and close his eyes. The headache was coming again. He needed some darkness.

By the time he reached his house, his head was clear. He stayed up past midnight drawing up a plan for Sivuyile's campaign against GEAR. When he woke up in the morning, his headache was back. Looking into the light felt like the hot end of a welding rod had pierced his temple. After a few minutes, he went back to bed and quickly fell asleep.

As he dreamed of leading a procession of workers down Rissik Street in Joburg, he heard a knock on the door, then the voices of Nobatana and Ntoni. He'd forgotten they were meeting this morning. He scrambled out of bed and pulled on his trousers.

'I'm coming,' said Monwabisi. He put on three vests. It was his way of hiding the weight loss. He looked around for the paper with the plans on it. Must have left it in the lounge. The two men had let themselves in.

'Amakhosi were devastating yesterday,' said Ntoni. 'They are regaining the Coca-Cola Cup form.'

Monwabisi hadn't heard the result. He went to the kitchen and switched on the kettle, then paused to remember where the sugar was. 'Just a minute, comrades,' he said. 'I'm bringing coffee. There are newspapers there from Joburg.'

Nobatana picked up a copy of *Business Day*. He read the headline: 'Anglo to Move Offshore.'

'These Boërs are taking their companies out of South Africa,' said Nobatana, squinting to read the story about Anglo American. He gave up, took off his sunglasses and pulled a magnifying glass out from his shirt pocket. 'This diabetes is like termites eating your house,' he said. 'One day it all just collapses.'

'You're a long way from that day, tata,' said Ntoni. 'You're still on the front lines.'

Monwabisi brought a tray with the coffee. He wished he had some biscuits to offer but it was the middle of the month. They were lucky to still have coffee.

The three men sipped while Monwabisi told them he needed to take a leave of absence from the branch.

'I've got this ulcer,' he said. 'They say it is about to perforate. When I eat it's like pouring mineral spirits on an open wound. I need time to recover. I don't want to let down the branch.' He gave them the plan he'd drawn up for the mobilisation. 'I hope you can use it,' he added.

'The comrades will appreciate your honesty,' said Ntoni.

'They have all noticed that Comrade RDP has not been feeling well.' He folded the paper and put it in his pocket.

'Honesty,' said Nobatana. 'It's in short supply these days.' He flipped through the sports section. 'Baby Jake is going to fight another Englishman,' he said. 'That one is a keg of dynamite.'

'A mini-keg,' said Monwabisi.

The three drank their coffee and bemoaned the lack of attendance at recent branch meetings.

'Some people say they are tired,' said Ntoni, 'that they want to spend time with their families instead of in the structures.'

'That's no excuse,' said Monwabisi. He held his stomach and put down his cup. 'I can't take coffee,' he said. 'It's like swallowing razor blades.'

Nobatana folded up the newspaper. 'Comrade RDP,' he said, 'your eyes are telling us a sad story.'

Monwabisi tried to think of a joke. If people thought his supposed ulcer was too serious, they'd start to talk about other diseases. These days conversations like that led in only one direction, the direction Monwabisi wanted to avoid.

'We must fight this GEAR,' said Monwabisi.

'It's a problem,' said Ntoni. 'We should have been consulted.'

'I think we need T-shirts,' said Monwabisi. '"ANC Yes, GEAR No." Something like that.'

'You must rest,' said Ntoni. 'Recharge your batteries. Then we can discuss this issue.'

Monwabisi mumbled something about the class struggle not allowing for time off, but after Nobatana and Ntoni left he went back to bed. He didn't wake up until Constantia brought him a plate of pap and vegetables when it was almost dark. She sat on the bed while he ate.

'If you don't go to the doctor, I will file for divorce,' she said.

He made an appointment the following day.

Chapter 17

PETER RANG THROUGH to Mthetho's office. Three o'clock in the afternoon and no one answered. What a country. A taxi had collided with a bus on the road to Bhisho and they blocked all traffic for nearly half an hour. Peter wanted to tell the Deputy Minister he'd be late. He was still twenty minutes from Bhisho.

He tried the phone again as a sea of almost modern-looking buildings came into view. This was his first visit to the former capital of the Ciskei. It looked like an industrial park plunked down in the middle of the Mojave Desert. Why would anyone put a capital in a desolate place like this when the Eastern Cape had some of the most beautiful coastline in the world?

Apartheid planning rarely made sense.

When Peter finally pulled up to the Social Services building that housed Mthetho's department, a picket line blocked the driveway. Peter got as far as the entrance to the car park before two young male strikers stood in his way. Hooting the horn brought no reaction.

'I have a meeting with the Deputy Minister,' Peter shouted out the window. 'I'm already late.'

'We are on strike,' said one of the men. He approached the car window and handed Peter a leaflet. 'We Demand a Living Wage,' the heading read.

'You're expecting a raise?' said Peter.

'It's obvious,' the young man replied. 'We've been suffering for too long.'

The young man didn't look so underpaid to Peter. He wore a nicely pressed blue shirt and a matching tie. 'We are asking for 40 per cent over three years,' the striker said.

'Forty per cent? You're out of your mind,' said Peter. 'Your province is broke. Read your financials. It's not a pretty picture.'

'Government can find the money,' said the young man.

'Who are you people?'

'We are from COSATU,' he said. 'This is not America, my friend. Here workers have rights.'

Peter threw the leaflet on the passenger seat and jammed the car into reverse. Driving through the picket line would create unnecessary ripples. One of the strikers might break a window. The young man walked alongside the car as Peter reversed.

'You need to reduce your workforce,' Peter said. 'Try working instead of striking.'

'Hiring and firing is not the business of the union,' the young man replied.

'Je-sus,' said Peter. 'You people landed on the wrong planet.'

He found a parking space three blocks away. He tried Mthetho's office phone again. The answering machine replied. Peter ducked through the picket line and finally tracked down Mthetho on the fourth floor. The Deputy Minister was alone in his office.

'Where the hell's your secretary?' Peter asked. 'I've been phoning.' He sat down in an old Dralon armchair.

'Good afternoon, my brother,' said Mthetho. 'You must relax. Remember, you are in Africa, not New York. Here we greet one another.'

'I was telling those strikers that if they don't reduce the

workforce, there'll be no money for anyone,' Peter replied. 'It's like talking to a brick wall.'

'My secretary is with them,' Mthetho said. 'Probably leading the chants of "Down with the bosses".'

Peter opened up his laptop and searched for the consultant's report on the Eastern Cape.

'You must clean house,' said Peter. 'No government can function spending 65 per cent of its budget on salaries. That's way beyond the international standard.' He clicked to the consultant's footnote. It said that anything beyond 55 per cent was in the danger zone. 'And you've got thousands of ghost workers,' he added.

Mthetho walked to the corner of the room and switched on the kettle. He took a minute to find the tea bags. The long-life milk was almost empty. He left his black.

'It will take time to calm the situation,' said Mthetho. 'We have our own unique history.'

'You haven't got the time.'

'We will find the time. We are not in such a hurry in Africa.' He emptied the milk into Peter's tea.

Peter closed his laptop. If only a sense of urgency could accompany all this political goodwill. He looked at the picture of Mandela above Mthetho's desk. How could a man who spent twenty-seven years in prison not feel that urgency, the desire to make up for lost time? He couldn't blame Mandela, though; the man was a saint.

'The municipal workers are the biggest problem,' said Mthetho. 'Many of them reject the ANC because we are not socialist.'

'This is the Wild West,' said Peter. He stirred his tea a few times, trying to dissolve the curdled milk.

'The union's only concern is to get more members and keep their own jobs,' said Mthetho. 'What happens to the province or the local authorities is not their problem.'

'You have to be ruthless,' said Peter. 'These people are obstructing progress.'

Mthetho launched into one of those silences that told Peter he had overstepped his boundaries again. South Africans could be so sensitive. He wanted to shake Mthetho, warn him of the stakes. At Pellmar they'd seen first-hand the disasters of state-run economies in Eastern Europe. All initiative stifled, consumers waiting in line for hours to buy a loaf of bread. The people of South Africa deserved so much better. They were a beacon of hope for the world.

'To make matters worse,' said Mthetho, 'our people are accustomed to not paying.'

'Force them.'

'They will refuse.'

'You have to cut their services until they pay. Otherwise, the debt just grows.'

'If we cut people off,' said Mthetho, 'they will march to the municipality. Things can happen. You've heard of the necklace?'

'You are in power now,' said Peter. 'Use that power.'

Mthetho was making excuses for not acting. Weak excuses. Peter hoped other people in government had more spine. Mandela had the courage, but tough love against your own people required a different toughness from enduring decades in prison.

At least there was the Finance Minister, Trevor Manuel, a perfect role model for South African leaders. He had those stand-up qualities. Competitiveness was in his blood. He was sticking by this GEAR, calling it 'non-negotiable'. Manuel understood that a leader must lead. Then there was Susan, another shining example of someone ready for plunging South Africa into a globalising world.

Peter hadn't given up on Mthetho. But if his friend didn't change soon, he'd be taking his province down a dismal road. The joy of overthrowing apartheid couldn't sustain this country forever.

Peter stayed with Mthetho for another hour, promising him that Pellmar would put the Eastern Cape on the map if the province could start to run a tighter ship. The Deputy Minister seemed to offer only more excuses about the problems of the past.

'You should visit Bulgaria,' said Peter as he left. 'No workers there can hold the government to ransom. You need to think about that.'

Mthetho didn't reply to that comment but told Peter that when his secretary got back he'd have her let him know when he'd be in Joburg again.

'There's still lots to talk about,' said Mthetho. 'You must be patient.'

Peter waved to Mthetho and started running down the hallway. His plane for Joburg left in an hour. If there weren't any more taxis smashing into people he could make it.

○

By the evening Peter was safely tucked away with Susan in a corner table at Romero's, a quiet little family restaurant in Kensington. They were feasting on prawns. Susan preferred hers Portuguese style – lots of butter and garlic, with a smattering of peri-peri and lemon. She was on her second glass of port.

'Our movement operated on consensus,' said Susan. 'Individuals didn't take decisions without a mandate from their organisations, even if you were the leader.'

Peter could see that wistful look in her eye. Such nostalgia could be dangerous. That's why he tried to put Joanna and his own activist days behind him. This was a new era. Everyone should have grown up by now. 'Unbelievable,' he said. 'How did you get anything done?'

'I can't explain it,' said Susan. 'Everyone was equal, from the cleaner to the general secretary. We accepted that.'

'We did that sort of thing when I was a student but you can't run a country that way,' said Peter. 'Not even a baseball team.'

'We're learning that,' she said, 'but not everyone agrees. The unions and community structures want to be part of every decision. It's just not practical.' She shook a little bit of hot sauce onto her plate. 'I wish they'd put the peri-peri right in the butter,' she said. 'It actually brings out the garlic.'

'You can't wait for everyone to agree,' said Peter. 'The world will leave you behind.'

A flan followed the prawns. A bit too rich for Peter, but Susan said it was her favourite. She asked for a little heavy cream to mix with the caramel sauce.

'Today is an anniversary for me,' she said as she scooped the rest of Peter's flan onto her plate.

'Anniversary?'

'Maybe that's the wrong word. Twelve years ago today my good friend Graeme Temple died in detention. He was twenty-four.'

'I'm sorry,' said Peter. 'You were close?' He hoped she wouldn't think he was prying. This was obviously a sensitive issue. He was amazed she was sharing it with him.

'You could call him my mentor,' said Susan. 'Politically, I mean.'

Susan had never mentioned any previous relationships to him. Maybe Graeme was the reason. Peter could understand that it was hard to talk about someone you loved if they'd died like that. The only experience he'd had with death was at his grandmother's bedside when she passed away. He still didn't like to think about her hand just going limp on the bed and the nurse pulling grandma's eyelids down.

'The police claimed he had a heart attack,' Susan said. Peter tried to think of the perfect reply. Her opening up like this was a breakthrough in their relationship. He had to capitalise on it, show he was sensitive to her grief.

'It must have been so painful,' said Peter. 'I don't know if I could cope with anything like that.'

'You find a way,' she said.

She put down her fork and fumbled for something in her bag, finally pulling out a pack of cigarettes and setting them on the table.

'I shouldn't eat so much flan,' she said. 'I'm putting on weight.' She patted her stomach.

'Still looks as flat as the top of Table Mountain,' said Peter. She lit up a cigarette, then ordered an espresso and two cognacs. He reached out and grasped her hand. She squeezed his fingers and he got chills all over.

'When did you start smoking?' he asked. As soon as the words came out, he realised he'd spoiled the mood. 'Never mind,' he said. 'Let's drink a toast to Graeme. That is, if it would be appropriate.'

'Wonderful,' she said. 'I appreciate that you're trying to understand. It means a lot.' She squeezed his hand again.

They hoisted the snifters but took meagre sips. Cognac was awkward for toasting a fallen martyr. Peter waved away the cigarette smoke with his hand.

'I wonder what Graeme would think of all this,' said Susan.

'He'd have to be as shocked as everyone else,' said Peter. 'No one dreamed apartheid would fall so soon, so peacefully.'

'I think he'd be frustrated,' she said. 'He was a man of ideas.'

'We all were back then,' said Peter.

'A movement must have a long-term vision, he used to say, a dream.'

'What a tragedy that he didn't get to see his dream come true,' said Peter.

'It's one of the saddest things about our democracy,' she said, 'that so many wonderful people never got to see it become a reality.' She took another drag on her cigarette, then slid her hand away from his.

'I hope this isn't going to become a regular habit,' said Peter.

'Talking about Graeme?'

'No, smoking.'

'I have one a year,' she said. She looked like she was about to have a teary meltdown. He'd never seen her do that before. He hoped he could handle it. When Joanna used to cry Peter never knew what to do. He'd usually hold her until the tears stopped, but it never quite felt right. But that was Joanna.

Susan put the cigarette out in the ashtray.

'Ag, man, enough of that,' she said and ate the last of the flan.

Chapter 18

'YOUR T-CELL COUNT IS under two hundred,' Dr Clausen told Monwabisi. 'Well below normal.' He fingered his stethoscope while he waited for a response from the former shop steward and his wife. The doctor's eyes looked like they'd never blink again.

'I know what below two hundred means,' said Monwabisi. 'What can we do?' Constantia could hear that her husband had slid into his negotiator's voice. The issue on the table was his survival. What was on offer? What demands could he put forward?

Clausen scribbled in a file, touched his pen to his mouth, then scribbled some more.

Three years ago the Northridge Medical Centre would have chased the Radebes out the door. Where was this Dr Clausen in those days? Tending to the wounds of police injured in the townships? Making up lies about political prisoners dying of heart attacks and falling from tenth-storey windows?

The doctor told Monwabisi all about safe sex, healthy eating, exercise. He spoke as if he was giving a tourist directions on how to get to a museum. For the doctor, lifestyle change seemed to be just a few right turns and waiting for traffic at some four-way intersections.

Constantia wasn't listening. She blamed herself. If she'd kept an eye on her husband he wouldn't have deteriorated so fast. But then, if he hadn't gotten the virus in the first place she could be thinking of other problems.

'There is also a new anti-retroviral medication,' Dr Clausen said, 'but it's very pricey. They call it Nevirapine. It combines with another drug called AZT.'

Monwabisi didn't reply.

'We can discuss that in a minute,' said Clausen. 'First I need to examine you. Take off your shirt and get up on the table, please.'

Monwabisi slid off the NUM jersey and the three T-shirts underneath. The thin paper on the table crinkled as he sat down. Constantia glanced at her husband's chest. He was all ribs, like those Ethiopians she used to see on television back in the eighties. He breathed deeply so Clausen could listen to his lungs through the stethoscope. If someone didn't do something fast, flies would be landing on Monwabisi's lips and he wouldn't have the strength to chase them away. For years Constantia worried that Monwabisi would become one of those absentee husbands, the walking hats who disappeared into the arms of women in Nyanga or Alex. Now at last he was home, yet maybe about to depart again, this time for good.

'Your lungs are clear,' said Clausen. 'Just stay away from anyone with a cold or, even worse, TB.'

Constantia read the carefully framed certificates on the doctor's wall. They came from the London School of Medicine. He had no idea about life in the township. How could her husband tell if someone in a taxi had a cold, if the vegetable seller had TB? In Sivuyile people didn't hide behind their vibracrete walls and Dobermans. 'Involuntary sharing' is what Monwabisi used to call it when their neighbours would fight late at night. If he shouted a couple times, they might lower their voices. She couldn't expect the doctor to know these things.

'And the anti-retrovirals,' Monwabisi asked, 'how pricey are they?' A tiny drop of saliva flew off his lip as he pronounced the 'p'.

'About R1 700 a month,' said Clausen, 'though we expect they'll come down. Government is also talking about provision but I don't know how soon that will happen. In your case, the sooner the better.'

'And there is nothing cheaper?' asked Monwabisi. 'Seventeen hundred a month is for the Oppenheimers, not the Radebes.'

Clausen sat down at his desk and wrote some notes. 'If you are ever in a position to want the ARVs,' he said, 'just let me know. I have a connection. Sometimes they are difficult to find.'

'Government will sort this out,' said Constantia. 'It can't take long. There's a commission looking into it now.'

Monwabisi put his shirts back on and thanked the doctor for a very clear explanation.

Clausen then explained that it would help if Monwabisi changed his diet. 'Less red meat, no alcohol, and cut down on the processed foods,' the doctor advised. 'The more vegetables, the better.'

'What is life without meat and beer?' asked Monwabisi.

'Much better than the alternative, Mr Radebe. Think about it.'

Monwabisi and Constantia left and walked towards a place they could catch a taxi. After two blocks he had to stop and lean on his wife's shoulder for a minute to catch his breath. Constantia remembered her husband as a long-distance runner, not someone ready to collapse after a walk to the taxi rank.

'The doctor says they are a bit "pricey",' he said, mimicking Clausen's through-the-nose style. He got the doctor's accent perfectly. Constantia laughed so hard the tears welled up in her eyes.

A taxi drove past. Then another. All full up.

'Those pills might as well cost R1 million,' said Constantia. 'Even borrowing from the umgalelo will only pay for a month's supply. And it would be like putting it out on the SABC.'

'Tell them it's for a surgery on your mother's heart,' he said.

'But how will we pay them back?' she asked.

'Andazi,' he replied. 'No clue.'

'There is always the possibility of a lodger.'

'Ironing an old shirt doesn't make it new,' he replied. 'A shop steward can't become a landlord.'

Two women standing next to them talked about a sale on bedroom suites at Morkels. They spoke of the problem of queen-size versus king-size beds and whether a two-year guarantee was long enough. Constantia wished she and Monwabisi had such worries.

'I should probably become a vegetarian,' said Monwabisi.

'You?' she said. 'Eating beans and broccoli?'

'It may be my only chance,' he said.

On the way home they stopped at the Checkers. Monwabisi strolled through the vegetable section and bought two cauliflowers, a stalk of broccoli, some spinach, a head of lettuce and a kilo of green beans. He looked delighted when he found a packet of bean sprouts. Constantia said they looked like 'something you'd find under a rock'.

'Some of the white comrades in the union used to eat them,' said Monwabisi. 'They're very healthy.'

That night, for the first time in Constantia's memory, Monwabisi had a salad for dinner – nothing else. He bragged to his boys how healthy this food was. He offered some bean sprouts to Fidel.

'Yuk!' the boy screeched. 'You're eating worms.'

Monwabisi told his family he was a lucky man because

everyone else refused to eat the bean sprouts so he got them all for himself. 'One day,' he said, 'when you see how healthy I am, you'll all be begging me for these sprouts.'

Constantia spooned a couple more small pieces of meat and gravy next to her rice. She hoped she'd never have to be eating those sprouts. Besides, she didn't see how bean sprouts would put any meat back on Monwabisi's bones. It just didn't make sense.

Chapter 19

CouNCILLOR FAKUDE READ the proposal just after midnight. The measure called for an increase in the monthly 'stipend' for councillors from R1 000 to R4 500; the Mayor's would rise from R1 500 to R7 000.

Historical differences didn't polarise black and white council members on this issue. The Mayor and three ANC councillors favoured the motion, as did Koosman and Kelly. Just a few minutes earlier, these same council members had fought like starving Alsatians grappling over a titbit of meat. In the end, the council voted four to two to erect a monument to the late Chris Hani in the main town square. Consideration of the ANC councillors' proposal to change the name of George Grey Boulevard to Moses Kotane Avenue was rolled over to the next meeting. The delay didn't matter much to most people in Ukusa. They'd been calling it Kotane for years.

Constantia Radebe had remained quiet on the monument issue. Fidelis Fakude and Richard Jacobs represented her views quite well.

'Fellow councillors,' she began when the Mayor called for discussion of the stipend increase, 'we live in a city where the majority suffers from dire poverty. Half our youth have no jobs. How do I convince my community I am looking after their interests and not my own if we pass this measure?'

Constantia's high-pitched voice echoed through the empty council chambers. Earlier in the evening hundreds of bodies absorbed the sound. They'd left after the vote on the monument. They'd had a good laugh in response to Koosman's proposal for a statue of Hani shaking hands with F.W. de Klerk. When Fakude followed with a suggestion to carry out a 'final cleansing of all Afrikaans names from our streets, parks and monuments', Koosman threatened to resign. This brought even more cries of delight from the legions of ANC members who'd come to speak on behalf of recognising Chris Hani's memory.

Only three spectators remained for the debate on remuneration. One was the frustrated cleaner, poised for action with her cart of tools. Steam from the water in her mop bucket wafted towards the ceiling.

'In the past,' said the Mayor, 'being a member of council was a part-time affair for people who had other sources of income. Today we are full-time. More than full-time, in fact. We have no family fortunes to support us. We black councillors are expected to provide for a host of relatives as well.' The Mayor loosened his tie. His neck seemed to be growing thicker as the night wore on.

'Every aunt, uncle and distant cousin assumes we are rich,' said Fakude.

'Plus every Tom, Dick and Lungile in the township,' added Phakhathi.

The Mayor urged the council to expedite the matter. 'I'm moving house tomorrow,' he said. 'It will be a long day.'

'I understand we'll be neighbours,' said Koosman. 'Northridge is a lovely place to raise your children.' He reached out to shake the Mayor's hand.

'I have a suggestion for Mrs Radebe,' said Koosman. 'If she so desperately wants to serve the poor, she can donate her pay rise to them directly. There are a number of charitable organisations. I'm sure no one among us would oppose such a thing. I can provide a list of potential recipients.'

Constantia didn't smile. A pain shot through her chest and she was all out of Eno. Thinking about grabbing Koosman by the throat didn't do anything to ease the heartburn. She'd never had urges like this when she worked at the nursery school.

'I think we should announce it at the next council meeting so the people of Ukusa know just how generous Councillor Radebe is,' said Fakude.

Constantia sat up straight and shot her hand in the air. The Mayor didn't look her way.

'Perhaps a press release would be in order,' added Mr Kelly.

'Apparently there is no further response to your suggestion,' said the Mayor to Koosman. 'It's late. Let's vote.'

Constantia couldn't believe the Mayor was joining forces with this Boer. Koosman once played lock for the Springboks. He claimed to have broken the colour barrier back in the 1950s by playing against the legendary Eric Majola, though no one could recall such a match.

'I want to object to Councillor Koosman's belittling of the poor,' she said. She hadn't lost that calm in her voice but she was getting close. 'Poverty is a serious issue in our communities, though maybe not in Northridge, where some members of the council live.'

'Where people live has nothing to do with this issue,' said the Mayor with a slight grin. 'Let's vote.'

'I demand an apology on behalf of the struggling masses of Ukusa,' said Constantia.

'Thank you, Councillor Radebe,' the Mayor replied. 'Given the hour and the complexity of your request, I suggest we postpone discussion until our next meeting and proceed to a vote. There is a proposal on the table concerning remuneration.'

'Agreed,' came the chorus of five male voices. Constantia's objection had the wrong pitch. She was becoming a pariah on the council.

Constantia wondered if moving these meetings to Sivuyile Hall would help. Sitting inside those cold concrete walls might bring these men to their senses, help them remember who their constituency was. They wouldn't have the courage to pass huge stipends for themselves in Sivuyile Hall. The voters could wait for them in the car park.

The motion passed five to one. Constantia concealed her tears as she left the chamber. Was this the only way for her husband to get his medicine?

○

She woke up Monwabisi when she got home. She hadn't told him about the motion on remuneration before the meeting. Councillors giving themselves an increase would have agitated him, but she had to tell him now. He threw the blankets back and jumped out of bed when he heard the news.

'So councillors are already filling their pockets before a single house has been built in Sivuyile?' he said. He was pacing the floor, lost in his own frustrations.

'We must make the best of the situation,' Constantia said. She waited for him to slow down, to at least look her way. He kept pacing, pulling gently on his goatee. He had no shirt on. Constantia couldn't stand to look at his ribs.

'We will spend the extra money on medicine,' she said. 'When the government begins to provide the medication, we can donate some money to build a crèche in Sivuyile.' She couldn't see another option for her family. How could she just let the father of her children die when the money was there?

Monwabisi stopped and turned toward Constantia. His eyes drooped, like those of an old man ready to make his final testament.

'I'm the most fortunate man in all of South Africa,' he

said as he sat down next to Constantia on the bed. 'Most women would have thrown a husband in my condition out of the house.'

A fit of coughing overtook him. Constantia fetched him a glass of water.

When the coughing stopped, Constantia told him buying the medication was a temporary measure, that government was bound to move quickly on the issue of HIV.

'It's a national crisis,' she said. 'They just need to finalise their policy.'

'These days everything needs a policy,' said Monwabisi. 'When people are sick, a tablet of policy cannot make them better.'

'You are recovering already,' said Constantia. 'When you are criticising government it means your strength is coming back. The only problem you have is that the government sleeps in your bed. You mustn't forget that.'

The following morning Constantia and Monwabisi went back to Dr Clausen and got a prescription for the anti-retrovirals. Within two weeks, his T-cell count had climbed back up to five hundred. He told his wife that with this medication he once again felt strong enough to lead the working class to victory.

Chapter 20

PETER HAD FOUND THE magic bullet for South Africa: Dubell's prepaid water meter. Prepaids would convey the fundamental principle of a market economy: no pay, no service. The meter would make water affordable for all. And if Pellmar could become the sole agent for connecting the nation to a prepaid system, profits could reach the eight-figure range. This was the real win-win.

The first step was to persuade Mthetho to set up a pilot. What better place to begin than the Eastern Cape, South Africa's poorest province and home of Nelson Mandela? Once the councils saw how the prepaids grew their revenue while diminishing debt, every local authority would want to change over. Pellmar could offer the technology, write and negotiate the contracts, then monitor delivery and maintenance – the complete package. They would work hand in hand with the new government, show South Africa just what a socially responsible company could do. If they handled it right, South Africa would become the launching pad for other international deals. Peter could end up running workshops in Buenos Aires and presenting papers to World Bank commissions in Geneva, billing himself and his company as pioneers in global water service technology.

Dubell sent Peter a portfolio of documentation on the meters – photos, brochures, colour-laser graphs and pie charts. Prepaids had turned around balance sheets in

Birmingham, England, and Lambaré, Paraguay. The city treasurer of Birmingham claimed the prepaids had increased water revenues by 15 per cent while decreasing usage by a tenth.

'The meters are not only a financial tool,' the treasurer wrote, 'they promote conservation as well.'

Peter hadn't thought of it that way before. It was perfect. South Africa had limited water resources. Johannesburg got most of its water from a dam in Lesotho, more than three hundred kilometres away. The prepaids would teach consumers to ration or pay a penalty.

Peter arranged a dinner meeting with Mthetho at the London Towers. Some things couldn't be handled properly over the phone. Besides, he got tired of looking out his window at Africa's tallest building, the fifty-one-storey Carlton Hotel. The Carlton was decaying from the bottom up. Peter couldn't even take a walk without being accosted by a sea of 'micro-entrepreneurs' selling everything from boom boxes to tomatoes. And those were the legal businesses, self-starters who didn't pack weapons or home-made knives. In the Eastern Cape, Peter could relax.

○

Before Peter had a chance to sample the appetiser, Mthetho told him they'd ruled out prepaids 'a long time ago'. Peter pushed aside the crab cakes and laid out laminated copies of the line graphs he'd created on his laptop.

'After five years,' said Peter, 'the meters will be paid for. You have to look at this from a long-term financial perspective.' He pointed to the intersection of the black cumulative surplus line with the horizontal graph of initial capital costs. A Quattro spreadsheet could work wonders. 'In the meantime,' he continued, 'consumers will have been educated to conserve and to budget for water as a monthly expense.'

Peter let the ideas sink in. He'd learned the role of a pregnant pause with a client, just long enough to let them absorb what he'd said but not sufficient time to formulate alternative conclusions.

'I can negotiate greatly reduced installation and capital costs for the first pilot,' said Peter. 'We have the utmost confidence in this product.'

Mthetho squeezed a little lemon over his marlin, then took a sip of the Riesling Peter had ordered for them.

'This is the closest thing to meat you can find in the sea,' said the Deputy Minister.

'With the prepaids,' said Peter, 'consumers will think twice about watering their lawns or washing their cars. They'll learn the virtues of grey water, the water that's already been through washing machines and dishwashers.'

'I'm familiar with the concept,' said Mthetho.

As Peter prepared to launch into the next phase of his presentation, an ageing white man rolled his wheelchair past their table. Mthetho told Peter he was Mr Connolly, the manager of the Towers restaurant.

'He lost his legs in Angola, fighting for the SADF,' said Mthetho, 'but we're best friends now.'

'Time heals all wounds,' said Peter as he laid another pair of laminated graphs on the table.

'Not quite,' said Mthetho. 'He still can't walk.'

'Well, you know what I mean,' said Peter, rubbing a slight smear of grease off the lamination with his serviette. 'Time does usually help a little.' Susan's friend Graeme popped into Peter's mind. Her wounds were healing but it was a long process.

'Anyway,' said Mthetho, 'I get the point about grey water. But remember, our consumers don't have lawns, they travel by taxi and they wash their clothes in big plastic buckets. And I've never seen a dishwasher in South Africa. Definitely not in Sivuyile.'

'I'm still learning about this country,' said Peter. 'Fortunately, I have a lot of good teachers.'

Mthetho gave Peter a thumbs up and took a small sip of the Riesling.

'Even when they cook and clean,' said Peter, 'they'll use less. And they're working on a way to link electricity and water on the same card. If consumers haven't paid their electricity bills, they won't get water and vice versa. Corrals all the freeloaders in one fell swoop.'

Mthetho wiped his hands on the serviette before picking up Peter's documents.

'The beauty of the prepaid,' said Mthetho, 'is that it does the cut-off for us.'

'Exactly,' said Peter.

'We have such a problem with municipal workers and these cut-offs,' said Mthetho. 'Sometimes the people chase the workers away. Other times the workers shut off the water in the afternoon, then come back at night. For a beer or two they reconnect the very same household.'

'That's criminal,' said Peter. 'They must be charged.' He was determined not to let Mthetho deliver more excuses for inaction. A leader had to be decisive.

Mthetho's cellphone began playing 'Mary Had a Little Lamb'. He looked at the screen and cut off the call. 'Some people think these phones are toys,' he said.

The phone rang again. Mthetho reached in his pocket and turned it off.

'To make matters worse,' said Mthetho, 'at their last congress the municipal workers passed a resolution opposing all cut-offs of water and electricity. They're more loyal to the union than they are to their employer.'

James Kilgore

'That's bullshit,' said Peter. 'They won't even cut off those who just don't feel like paying?'

'Right.'

'And they're not fired?'

'It's difficult. Workers will say a Doberman was guarding the meter.'

'Service delivery is a circus in this country,' said Peter. 'Labour relations are worse.'

'I'm not sure our communities will accept these prepaids,' said Mthetho.

'Give them a carrot,' said Peter, 'to go with the stick of the cut-off. Maybe raffle a new car. Everyone who buys R50 of water gets a free raffle ticket.'

'I might join myself,' said Mthetho.

The London Towers specialty sweet was lemon cheesecake. Peter judged it the best he'd ever tasted outside New York.

'My friend Lungi calls this the "young girlfriend",' said Mthetho. 'Too sweet to resist but a killer if you enjoy it too much.' He patted his stomach. 'Maybe none for me tonight.'

The crust wasn't quite as sweet as the graham crackers Peter was used to, but he still didn't leave a crumb.

'How secure are these meters?' Mthetho asked.

'What do you mean?'

'We've got people's plumbers. They can bypass anything,' said Mthetho.

Peter didn't quite understand the question so he reviewed the highlights of the prepaids one more time, taking care not to mention lawn mowers and dishwashers. He'd save that part for the white ratepayers if he got that far.

Mthetho used an after-dinner shot of whisky as an opportunity to tell a long story about a German aid worker named Gunther.

'This man had big plans for rural toilets,' said the Deputy Minister. 'He convinced every household in one of our villages to donate R20 to dig the hole for the latrine. They built five hundred toilets. The Minister came for the launch of the project. A local band played. Then when the first rains came, all the toilets collapsed into those R20 holes.'

Peter wasn't quite certain why Mthetho told him this tale of woe. He was also annoyed that the Deputy Minister hadn't even finished his glass of Riesling before ordering the Laphroaig. That was an authentic Riesling from the German Rhineland – the most expensive white on the list.

'Now the people of the community have a new word for anything that doesn't work properly,' Mthetho continued. 'It's called iguntheri. A child who fails in school is called umguntheri. You get the picture?'

'You're afraid the prepaids will fail and every piece of junk in the province will be called iJonasi.'

'You're learning fast,' said Mthetho as he finished his whisky.

'But remember the other possibility,' said Peter. 'The more likely scenario. The project is a brilliant child and all the credit goes to the father, Deputy Minister Mthetho Jonasi. No one ever succeeded without taking chances. This isn't even a chance, it's a well-calculated risk. A slam dunk really.'

'I haven't given up on the idea,' said Mthetho, 'but I have to talk to some people. In South Africa, no one takes decisions alone.'

Peter packed his graphs back into his briefcase and tried to pretend he was satisfied with the Deputy Minister's indecision. No one moved slower than a government bureaucrat in South Africa. Why didn't they give people authority in this country?

Chapter 21

'THE BOYS NEED SHOES for school,' said Constantia. 'Where can we find this money? Your payout is now less than R100.'

Monwabisi continued reading a two-week-old *Business Day*. 'This new Labour Relations Act is going to do nothing for workers,' he said.

Constantia grabbed the newspaper off the table. 'Our boys' shoes,' she said. 'Where do we get the money?'

'Thula, thula, thula,' he said. 'Finish the provident fund. We have fought bigger struggles than this one of yours for shoes.' He looked down at his feet. The soles of his loafers were beginning to tear away.

'And for a rainy day?' Constantia asked.

Monwabisi craned his neck to look out the window. 'The sun is shining brightly mhlobo wam',' he said. 'Sizowina.'

Constantia headed off to work. She'd phone Mthetho again in the afternoon and borrow the money for the boys' shoes. If her husband found out she was getting money from his cousin he'd throw a fit. She was also thinking of asking Mthetho for a loan to buy a second-hand car.

That night Constantia came home carrying a chicken and a packet of rice. Monwabisi was reading the newspaper. At least he was looking healthier now. The broccoli he boiled every night seemed to be having some effect, or maybe it was those little worm-like bean sprouts that he sprinkled on top of the raw spinach. Now he just needed to get that welding business going. She wondered if he'd been reading about the Labour Relations Act all day.

'You have forgotten something,' she said.

He didn't look up. 'Ntoni?' he said.

'What day is it today?' she asked.

He glanced along the top edge of the page of the newspaper looking for the date.

'Was this the day they hanged Solomon Mahlangu?' he asked.

'Let's go,' she said, grabbing him by the arm. 'You will now give me my birthday present. The best one ever.'

The couple went into the kitchen. Constantia took the chicken and rice out of the plastic bag and held them out for Monwabisi.

'This year you will honour your wife by learning how to help her in the kitchen,' she said. 'It is part of the ANC's policy of non-sexism.'

Monwabisi sat down at the kitchen table. 'Happy birthday,' he said without looking her way.

Constantia waited to see if her husband would dare to sing to her. Instead, she got the celebratory tones of Fidel from the backyard. Apparently he'd just scored a try in a make-believe World Cup rugby match with Musa.

'I won't be treated like a small boy in my own house,' Monwabisi said.

'Cooking is not for small boys,' she said. 'I am at work all day long. Then, even though Portia is on leave, I'm expected to cook. Men and women must carry an equal load.'

'I've carried my load for the working class for years.'

Constantia began chopping an onion.

'Bring me a tomato,' she said. 'Even the working class needs tomatoes for cooking chicken.'

He got up slowly, walked to the fridge and pulled a

tomato out of the vegetable tray. Constantia handed him a small knife.

'Chop the tomato, please,' she said with an exaggerated smile.

He hesitated, then set the tomato down on the table and tried to slice it. The blade wouldn't cut through the peel. He pressed harder and the juice squirted out, splashing on his shirt.

'You should have peeled it first,' she said.

Monwabisi put down the knife and wiped the tomato juice off his shirt with a tea towel. 'The peels will disappear when they cook,' he said.

'Where will they go?' she asked.

Constantia put some oil in the frying pan and switched the ring onto one. It was the only setting that worked. Monwabisi finished chopping and put the tomato into a small plastic bowl.

'Now what?' he asked.

Constantia dropped a piece of onion into the oil. A perfect sizzle. She added the rest of the onions and watched them cook for a few seconds, then dumped in the tomatoes.

'Now you must cut up the chicken,' she said. 'I'm going to rest.' She switched on the kettle.

Monwabisi wrestled with the chicken, finally managing to get it out of the plastic wrapper without spilling any of the blood. Once the kettle boiled, Constantia poured a little of the water on the onions and tomatoes, then used the rest to make some tea in her husband's favourite Amakhosi cup. She sat down at the kitchen table and spooned some sugar into the tea. She wanted this one to be extra sweet. 'This is the best present of all,' she said. 'Drinking tea and watching my husband prepare dinner. This is the new South Africa.'

'You think I don't know how to cook?' he asked. 'How

do you think I survived all those years in Joburg?'

'Umasihlalisane,' she said and laughed.

'I never had a live-in,' he said. 'You know I'm not that kind of husband.'

'When the cat is away,' she said.

'I am the mouse,' he said. 'Look at me. I'm cooking and you are seated.'

'Now I just need you to sing me happy birthday,' she said.

The smell of the simmering onions and tomatoes floated across the kitchen as Constantia finished her tea. The aroma was even better after Monwabisi added some curry powder. She went into the lounge, returned with the *Business Day* and opened it to page three to read the article on the LRA that Monwabisi had quoted to her earlier.

'They are allowing flexibility now,' said Monwabisi. 'The bosses can make you work forty-eight hours without paying overtime. And they're excluding farm workers.'

Constantia continued reading.

'Where is the Bisto?' Monwabisi asked.

'Bisto is finished,' she said. 'You must use Oxo and some cornflour.'

She went back to the *Business Day* while Monwabisi spooned some cornflour into the pot. Two hours later, after the boys were asleep, Monwabisi laid the enamel bowls of rice, chicken and broccoli on the table in front of Constantia.

She scooped a ball of rice from the bowl. It stuck together like pap.

'I forgot I must boil the water first before adding the rice,' he said. She giggled.

'Also, the next time I must cook the chicken a bit longer,' he said.

'It's perfect,' she said, wiping her hands on a serviette. 'The best birthday present ever. And you don't have to wait until my next birthday to do an encore.'

She leaned across the table and kissed him on the cheek. She decided not to say anything about the lumps in the gravy.

○

The following night Constantia and Monwabisi celebrated again. Mthetho had invited the couple to the London Towers for dinner. This was not a second birthday party. The Deputy Minister said he had some 'important business' to discuss. Constantia told Monwabisi he must wear his suit. She thought more about such things now. During dull moments in meetings, she often sketched her ideas for a new top or dress.

For this dinner she'd bought a special black outfit with puffed-up shoulders and gold buttons down the front. It went perfectly with her patent leather stiletto heels, the shoes that made her a little taller than her husband. He seemed to be shrinking. His suit coat hung on his shoulders like a mealie sack; his bell-bottom trousers dragged on the carpet. When the couple stood together in the foyer of the Towers, Constantia slouched slightly. She wouldn't abandon those stilettos, though, especially now that she could walk steadily in them. A female friend told her they made her legs look 'luscious'.

The hat brought her the most pride. The saleswoman promised her it was a 'photocopy' of the one Madiba's daughter wore at her father's inauguration. When Constantia put it on for Monwabisi, he told her she looked beautiful. He hadn't said that to her in years.

Constantia could feel the gaze of the white clientele in the restaurant as the maître d' delivered this odd pairing of chic and shop floor to Mthetho's table.

'How can you bring this young girl here, my brother?' Mthetho asked his cousin. 'What will I tell your wife about this "weekend special" of yours?'

The maître d' pulled out Constantia's chair as Mthetho complained further about the 'awkward situation' in which Monwabisi had put him. After two quick Johnnie Walker Reds, Monwabisi started to relax. He decided he could live without his broccoli for a night. It was time for meat. When the T-bone steak arrived, the former shop steward called it a 'wall-to-wall carpet, big enough to cover two rooms'.

'The first time I came here,' said Mthetho, 'the place went quiet as a church at midnight. Every head turned in my direction. These are English people, though. They whisper.'

He leaned over the table and lowered his voice as Monwabisi doused his potatoes au gratin with more salt. 'After a few minutes of their staring and comments,' said Mthetho, 'I shouted, "Long live Comrade President Nelson Rolihlahla Mandela, long live!" The abelungu, their mouths fell open so wide I could see the half-chewed pieces of meat inside. Then they went back to whispering and the waiter brought me free drinks for the rest of the night.'

'It's not so bad now,' said Constantia, looking at a painting of a seascape on the wall. She loved the gold-leaf frame. Such class.

'Watch this,' said Mthetho. The Deputy Minister waved to Mr Connolly as the manager sped across the room in his wheelchair.

'I'll be by to check on you just now, Deputy Minister,' Connolly promised Mthetho with a smile.

Constantia found it difficult to eat with her hat on, yet she couldn't take it off. Her hair was hastily plaited, too ordinary a style for the Towers. She had an appointment with the hairdresser the following morning. Mthetho should have given them more notice.

'I haven't brought you here to tell stories over big pieces of meat,' said Mthetho. 'I have a proposal. Together we will put Ukusa on the map.'

Mthetho wound his way through lots of figures about deficits, explaining how debt was the major obstacle slowing down the progress towards 'A Better Life for All'. He reached under the table and pulled his black briefcase onto his lap. He spun the tumblers and out came the colour copies of Peter's graphs. Mthetho's fingers travelled along the x axis, then headed north as he detailed impending financial gloom. Suddenly Constantia's roast lamb went tart. She was tiring of this tale.

'We are now part of the global economy,' said the Deputy Minister. 'If we want to survive, we need to become competitive. Our municipalities face the same challenges.'

'My bosses spoke of this competitiveness right before they closed down and retrenched all the workers,' said Monwabisi. Constantia could feel her husband gearing up for a fight. He always told her how intellectuals could mislead the working class, especially those who had studied overseas. Mthetho was his cousin but she knew Monwabisi still saw him as part of something he called the petit bourgeoisie.

'That was different,' said Mthetho. 'We are restructuring so our historically disadvantaged communities can enjoy the benefits of the global economy, eventually become world-class themselves.'

Monwabisi was surprising Constantia. He was actually listening.

Mthetho promised that Ukusa could become an example for the whole country, that people would look up to 'this tiny town of ours'.

'This is the heart of it all,' he said, holding up a key ring with a small plastic card attached. 'A consumer loads money onto this card. No more bills, no begging the municipality for an extension on payments.'

Mthetho brought out another stack of graphs covered in plastic. 'We want Ukusa to be the first pilot for the prepaid water system in South Africa,' he said. 'National government will pay the set-up costs. Within five years your council can eliminate all debts.' Mthetho's forefinger glided across the graph, stopping where the black and red lines crossed.

'The bosses use graphs to bamboozle the workers,' said Monwabisi as he swallowed the last sliver of his steak. Now Constantia was certain a confrontation was on its way. She hoped her husband wouldn't make a scene. The London Towers was not the streets of Sivuyile. A councillor had a reputation to protect.

'After seven years the surplus will have reached a million,' said Mthetho, looking directly at Constantia. 'Enough to build several crèches in Sivuyile,' he added. 'I know that's your dream, Councillor.'

Constantia zeroed in on the graphs, looking for that surplus. Monwabisi's cousin talked like someone from the Department of Finance.

'You two will be the spearheads of this project in Ukusa,' said Mthetho. 'My sister here will become the advocate on council. We will bring you to workshops in Cape Town, then to the Kruger Park. You can see the Big Five, watch the lions eat a kudu for breakfast. You just need to get all the councillors on board.'

'I can't see why they would oppose,' said Constantia, 'if the surplus goes to the community.' She put her hand on her husband's thigh. If she could just keep him calm long enough to listen to the whole story.

Monwabisi took a matchstick out of his jacket pocket and broke off a couple of splinters.

'You can find the real thing there,' said Mthetho, gesturing towards a small crystal cylinder on the table.

Monwabisi put the match back in his pocket and grabbed half a dozen of the neatly packaged toothpicks. Constantia was glad to see Mthetho teaching his cousin a little bit about how to act in a place like the London Towers. Monwabisi would never listen if she told him. He'd just dismiss it as bourgeois formality.

'I know your finger is on the pulse of all the community structures,' Mthetho told his cousin. 'Our partners at Pellmar have a high regard for your experience.'

'A private company is behind this?' asked Monwabisi.

'They are our partners,' replied Mthetho. 'And they are prepared to pay you R4 000 a month as a community liaison officer. Plus a car.'

'Nkosi yam. It's time for champagne,' said Constantia. That was almost twice as much as her husband earned in Joburg. With their two salaries, they could live like royalty. Their boys would wear real Nikes, not those R15 Fong Kongs from China. Private schools were even a possibility.

'I've always been on the side of the working class,' said Monwabisi.

'It's the working class who benefits here,' said Mthetho. 'Especially those who've never had a tap at their house, the poorest workers of all.'

'No business operates without making profit,' said Monwabisi. 'Where there is profit, there is exploitation.'

'You must stop taking us backwards,' said Mthetho. 'In the old days it was win or lose. In the new South Africa we have win-win. Business profits, the workers gain. But we must move quickly. Freedom never rests.'

Monwabisi reached into his mouth with his fingers to dislodge a piece of toothpick stuck between his teeth. Constantia hoped no one was watching. 'I'll think about it,' he said.

'It's a big step,' said Constantia.

'No problem,' said Mthetho. 'But remember, like the Americans say, opportunity only knocks once.'

Constantia put her arm around her husband. Before she could say anything, Mthetho's cellphone rang.

'My baby is crying,' said the Deputy Minister as he

unhooked the phone from his belt. 'Sorry.'

Mthetho kept telling the other party he was 'breaking up'. As he closed the phone, he reached for his tumbler of whisky. 'To a new partnership – or to rebuilding an old one,' he said.

The three touched glasses over the centre of the table. Constantia thought about her husband. If he took this job, he would be around to kick the soccer ball with Fidel and Musa, right up to the day when they went to the bush. Their family's future would finally be secure.

The two men then told stories about the 'holy terror' – Miss Giyose, their grade seven teacher. She used to drag students in front of the class by their ear lobes if she caught them speaking Xhosa. She only allowed English in her class – the 'Queen's English', as she called it.

'One day she made me dig a hole as big as a grave,' said Mthetho, 'only to fill it up again. She said I was "too cheeky".'

Constantia enjoyed the two men's reminiscing. It gave her more time to daydream about how the family budget would look with an extra R4 000 a month. It wasn't just the medication; she could wear some of those clothes she'd seen in the shop windows in Cape Town. She'd start to look like a real councillor.

As the couple bid goodnight to Mthetho, the Deputy Minister reminded Monwabisi that there were dozens of people willing to take the offer from Pellmar.

'The ship of history will sail regardless of who is on board,' Mthetho added.

'I will convince him,' said Constantia, looking at her husband. He was busy taking the wrapper off another toothpick.

'There is nothing like the power of a woman,' she added as the couple made their exit arm in arm.

Chapter 22

IT TOOK MONWABISI A few minutes to find the red plastic bucket. His wife was in Pretoria so he couldn't ask her why she had put it there, hidden behind the arm of the sofa. Besides, he had other things to worry about, like washing clothes. There was no one else to do the job. Portia had gone to the rural areas for her sister's wedding.

By the time Ntoni and Nobatana knocked on the front door, Monwabisi's arms were covered in No Name soap suds. His wife preferred Omo but they were economising. Monwabisi held out a limp wrist to greet the two comrades. They had come to discuss the decreasing attendance at branch meetings.

'We didn't know you would be busy adding brightness to whiteness,' said Ntoni. He and the old man bellowed with laughter.

'Because my wife has gone to Pretoria for the weekend, must my sons and I wear dirty clothes?'

'I intend to follow your heroic example, Comrade RDP,' said Ntoni. 'When I get home I'll be polishing the kitchen floor.'

'The day you polish a floor is the day the horse grows horns,' said Nobatana.

The old man lurched to his left, almost falling down with amusement. Ntoni grabbed him before he toppled over.

'We can't have a chairman spending his day washing

clothes,' the old man said. 'We have business to discuss.'

'Our discussion can wait,' said Ntoni. 'We'll come back after you've hung the washing on the line.'

As the two men exited through the front gate, Monwabisi reminded them that non-sexism was a policy of their organisation.

'We know the policies of the ANC,' said Ntoni.

By the time Monwabisi asked them if a man had a right to 'exploit his wife', the two were out of earshot.

A few minutes later Mrs Sithethi knocked at the back door.

'I'll be bringing some hot porridge now-now,' she said.

'We appreciate your offer, mama,' he told her, 'but we have just eaten.'

'The boys need porridge to grow strong,' she said.

'Thank you, mama,' he said, 'but we are fine.'

He closed the door and went back to the laundry. Just three shirts remained. As he squeezed the rinse water out of the last one, Mrs Mehlo arrived. She offered to take the children to church with her the following morning.

'They can come home afterwards,' she promised Monwabisi. 'That will give you time to rest.' She handed Monwabisi a pack of Smarties. 'We are praying for you,' she added.

'I'm the last person you need to pray for,' he said. 'My God is the proletariat.'

'We all need the hand of the Lord to guide us,' she said.

'The boys will be grateful for the sweets,' he said as he stuffed the Smarties into his pocket and escorted Mrs Mehlo to the gate. He thanked her and assured her that a shop steward could handle every kind of crisis known to the working class, including the absence of a woman for a weekend.

He went back inside, grabbed the red plastic bucket full of clothes and started to drape them over the washing line in the front garden. Portia and his wife always used pegs. He preferred just to lay them over the wire. Pegs were a waste of time. Just as he pulled out the last shirt, the wind blew a pair of Musa's shorts off the line into the dirt. He dusted them off, threw them over the line and went to look for the pegs. He wasn't about to wash those shorts again.

After searching every drawer and cupboard in the house, he found a tin full of plastic pegs by the back door. He got all the wet clothes attached before the wind gusted again. Now he was ready to consider the offer from Mthetho.

He sat on the bed with a yellow notepad and drew a line down the middle of the top sheet. He scribbled 'Plus' on one side, 'Minus' on the other. He'd learned that in the union.

He wrote 'R4 000 a month' in the plus column, then added 'No more washing clothes'.

'Mna!' shouted Fidel from the lounge. 'I was the first to have it.'

'You are lying, you. I was reading, then I went to the toilet.'

'Hey, go outside, boys,' Monwabisi yelled. 'I'm trying to think here.'

'But, tata, it's raining.'

'It's just a few sprinkles,' said Monwabisi. 'You must keep quiet or I'll take the magazine away.' The boys stayed inside.

Monwabisi wrote 'Not sure about prepaids' and 'Don't know about Pellmar' on the minus side. He added 'Lose ties to community'. The rain was now beating a steady rhythm on the roof. Monwabisi grabbed the bucket and went out to rescue the laundry. If he waited too long he'd have to squeeze everything out again.

He left the bucket of balled-up wet clothes by the front door and went back to his plus/minus chart.

He drew a picture of a car on the plus side, then added a bottle of pills.

'Tata, amanzi!' shrieked Fidel.

'Get it yourself,' said Monwabisi. 'Why are you asking me for water? I'm busy here.'

'Amanzi, tata,' said Musa. 'It's leaking.'

'Leaking what?' said Monwabisi, putting down his pen.

He walked into the lounge. Water was coming through the ceiling in sheets. Fidel and Musa were huddled in the lone dry corner of the room.

Monwabisi dumped the wet clothes onto the floor and put the bucket right back where Constantia had left it, under the biggest leak. He found two more buckets in the boys' wardrobe, plus a wedding pot in the kitchen. By the time he got them all in place and rearranged the furniture, the cover photo of Shoes Moshoeu on *Soccer Today* was soaked almost as badly as the brown rug on the floor. He'd bought that rug at a Boer's shop on the East Rand three years ago for R150. It smelled of a white person's house back then.

Luckily the leaks had only hit one arm of the sofa. He could dry that later with an iron. He gave the boys the pack of Smarties and sent them to play at Mrs Sithethi's house while he cleaned. Once they were gone he rolled up the rug, then emptied one of the buckets he'd used to catch the leaks. He needed to scrub the floor. He filled the bucket with hot water and added some Dettol. It still didn't look strong. He poured in a few drops of methylated spirits, hoping it wouldn't turn the floor purple.

An hour later the rain had stopped and the boys were back, dragging muddy footprints across the lounge floor.

'Now you must clean up your mess,' said Monwabisi. 'And wash your shoes.' He filled the bucket again and carried it into the lounge.

'An older brother must lead,' said Monwabisi, handing the mop to Fidel. 'Qalani, you two. Get going.'

As Fidel slowly swished the mop across the floor,

Monwabisi lifted the rolled-up carpet onto his shoulder and carried it to the front yard. He slowly unravelled it over the top of the washing line. The fringed end of the rug hovered just a few centimetres above the ground. As he picked up the bucket, the laundry pole closest to the house began to waver. Monwabisi snatched the pole and held it with one hand. He dropped the bucket and with a two-handed grip tried to shove the pole deeper into the ground, but it wouldn't budge. If he let go of the pole, the rug would plunge into the dirt and he'd have to start over again. He held the pole with one hand and tried to lift the rug with the other. No luck.

'Ndizokunceda,' said Mrs Sithethi from her bedroom window. 'Just hang on.' A few seconds later she came trudging out her front door in her slip-slops.

'You can't hang a carpet on your line,' she told him. 'Your poles are not strong.'

She brushed a little bit of mud off the edge of the rug and rolled it up. Before she could get it on her head Monwabisi snatched it away.

He thanked her for the help, carried the rug inside and laid it down against the lounge wall where it was before. He didn't need any more advice from Mrs Sithethi. After a few hours, the rug would dry even if it was rolled up. Fidel and Musa were still mopping. Monwabisi went back to his list.

He wrote 'Working for a foreign company' in the minus column. He added a star to that entry.

'Stop, you!' shouted Musa from the lounge. 'It's your turn.' A few cries of protest came from Fidel. Then there was the sound of small bodies rolling on the floor. Just as Monwabisi got to the lounge, Fidel rolled out from under Musa and kicked over the bucket of mop water, instantly flooding the room.

Monwabisi sent them to the spare room and locked the door. It took him almost an hour to clean the mess. The water had drenched three *Business Days* that he hadn't even had a chance to read.

He told the boys they could come out if they agreed to polish the lounge floor.

'We are on strike,' said Fidel. 'This is unfair labour practice.'

'You are not workers,' said Monwabisi. 'You are children.'

'We are being exploited,' said Musa.

Monwabisi took fifteen minutes to negotiate an end to the boys' labour stoppage.

Halfway through the polishing, Musa put down his brush. 'I'm not doing any more girls' work,' he said.

'Do you see any girls here?' asked Monwabisi. He was tired. Traditional Xhosa families didn't have these problems. Children did as they were told. Though Monwabisi had grown up alone with his mother, he knew better than to refuse to do what she said. She was small but could punish like a school headmaster.

Nowadays it was all more complicated. Monwabisi wanted sons who would question authority, demand their rights. That's what made a democratic movement. It would just be easier if they demanded their rights somewhere besides in their own home.

By the afternoon the lounge was clean and the boys had settled in front of the TV. Monwabisi was back to pondering his employment future.

He scribbled 'Pride' in the plus column. Though he hated to admit it, he felt shame at not having a job. Marxism explained it all. Unemployment was not the fault of the individual worker. It was part of the laws of motion of capitalism. Unemployed workers constituted what Marx called a 'reserve army of labour', a contingent large enough to make sure any workers who wanted too much money could be easily replaced. Still, Monwabisi felt humiliated relying on

153

a woman's salary. And how would his sons view their father in the long run? They might never recall that he was a man who once worked as a welder, was a leading shop steward and a proud member of the workers' movement, not just a body around the house who filled in for an absent working mother.

He cooked boerewors, gravy and pap for dinner. He mixed the flour into the water carefully to avoid lumps in the gravy. The boys ate everything and washed their own plates.

When Constantia came home the next day, he told her he'd take that job from Mthetho, that with the extra money they'd be able to buy his medicine and still afford clothing for the boys.

'Plus, we'll be able to pay Portia a living wage,' he added. 'I can't have exploitation of workers happening in my own house.'

Constantia laced her fingers together as if she was thanking God. Then she threw her arms around him.

Monwabisi was shocked not only by the hug but by the bright red varnish on his wife's fingernails. He'd been with her for more than a decade and she'd never done this. Why was she starting now?

'Just something different,' she said when he asked. 'By the way,' she added, 'why is the rug rolled up in the lounge?'

'We were polishing the floor,' said Monwabisi. 'I'll put it back in the morning.'

'I never expected you to be polishing the floor,' she said. 'Is there something wrong?'

'A man can also do a woman's job,' said Monwabisi. 'Isn't that what freedom is all about?'

Chapter 23

CONSTANTIA SMILED AS Monwabisi walked across the lounge, modelling his new navy-blue pin-stripe suit for her. Mthetho had taken him to his personal tailor in East London, Mr. Makan. The Deputy Minister said he couldn't have his cousin dressing like the Jackson Five or lumbering around in struggle T-shirts. Makan had made Monwabisi a charcoal three-piece as well, double-breasted with a gentle flare on the trousers.

'You look very smart,' she said. 'Now you must do something with that front tooth. It doesn't look right when you smile.'

'I'll think about it,' he said, 'but let me not spend my first pay cheque before it is in my hand.'

With the seed planted, Monwabisi grew self-conscious. Sometimes he caught himself in mid-laugh and quickly closed his mouth. He needed that tooth to make sure he was the one for whom Constantia was varnishing her nails. He made an appointment with Dr Jacobs, the brother of the councillor for Basil February.

Things were coming together. The next day he'd be meeting Mthetho again at the London Towers. He was looking forward to another wall-to-wall carpet.

○

'I'll take you there personally,' Mr Connolly told Monwabisi when he arrived for his lunch date. 'The Deputy Minister is one of our prize customers.' The wheels of Connolly's chair left a light-coloured trail in the dark brown carpet as he wove his way through the tables of white patrons. Monwabisi felt more at home now. This time he had a proper suit. He'd chosen the navy blue, complemented by a yellow shirt and dark tie.

Mthetho introduced his guest to Monwabisi. The former shop steward didn't recall the name Peter Franklin or the face. Only when his cousin spoke of the bank in Buffalo did Monwabisi make the connection. Monwabisi remembered standing on the sidewalk with a group of demonstrators while the police put Peter and a woman in handcuffs. It was so cold his goatee had grown icicles.

'Peter is the point man for Pellmar,' said Mthetho, 'our partners on the prepaids in Ukusa. He'll be your boss.'

Monwabisi forced out a smile. The blonde-haired Franklin looked almost like a teenager. Only his carefully tailored suit hinted that he might be a man of responsibility.

'We're calling our project Water for Freedom,' Peter said. 'We anticipate suspicion at first, so your main task is to establish the bona fides of Pellmar. Our business model is inclusive – everyone must be on board. We are trying to follow the South African way.'

Monwabisi glanced at Mthetho. He figured this phrase 'bona fides' was French. The white comrades did that, threw academic jargon into ordinary conversations, as if a worker could easily understand everything in his third or fourth language. Once in a while Monwabisi used to reply in Xhosa or Sesotho just to level the playing field.

While the trio outlined a series of meetings with community structures, Peter tried to persuade his colleagues of the virtues of red wine.

'Two glasses a day cleans your arteries like a Roto-

Rooter,' he said. 'Perfect insurance against heart attacks. We're reaching that stage in life.'

Peter inhaled the fumes before he drank the wine. Monwabisi imagined walking around a metalworkers' congress carrying one of those long-stemmed glasses. He decided it was easier to take it all in one gulp. As soon as he set down his glass, Peter poured him a refill. Monwabisi reached for the ice water. Cold water always helped wash away lingering bad tastes.

'I have visited the Sivuyile Civic Association with Mthetho,' said Peter. 'There is apprehension about foreign investors. We need you to quell such doubts. We want the people on our side. Our project is for them.'

'It's not a problem,' said Monwabisi. 'If the community is to get water, they will come on board. People have been walking too far for too long just to fill a bucket for washing clothes.'

Mr Connolly wheeled up to the table holding a bottle of red wine. He covered the cork with a white towel and gently eased it open. 'Compliments of the manager,' he said. 'A delightful Shiraz from our own vineyards in Stellenbosch. The finest wine in Africa. You can almost taste the plums.'

A waiter arrived with three wine glasses on a tray. Connolly handed one of them to Mthetho and poured a little for the Deputy Minister.

Mthetho swirled the red liquid around in the glass. 'I'm testing the body and legs,' he said to his cousin. He held the glass out to Monwabisi. 'Smell the bouquet,' he said.

Monwabisi took a quick whiff. 'It has the odour of wine,' said the former shop steward.

Mthetho ran the glass under his own nose. 'Very fruity,' said the Deputy Minister, taking a tiny taste.

'How about that one kid who claimed the government was selling the country to the imperialists?' said Peter as the waiter filled the other two glasses.

'Slim Yanta,' said Mthetho.

'What planet is he living on?' asked Peter.

'Those who always have a grievance are easy to handle,' said Monwabisi. 'Just give them responsibility. Either they will use their energy positively or they will learn to keep quiet.'

'Let my cousin spend ten minutes with Slim,' said Mthetho, 'and the youngster will be begging to wear a T-shirt for our project. No one has the respect of the community like Monwabisi Radebe. They call him Comrade RDP.'

'We would like to offer you a permanent position,' Peter told Monwabisi, 'but at present we are operating on a year-to-year basis. We will start with a renewable one-year contract. We hope that will be acceptable.'

Monwabisi's mentor in the metalworkers' union, Boots Mohale, had taught him the power of a drink of water. A pause could derail a boss's concentration. Monwabisi took a long sip.

'I'm thinking R5 000 a month would be more appropriate,' said Monwabisi. 'I have no job security or benefits.'

'We think our offer is more than generous,' said Peter. 'Remember, a Corolla is included.'

'A Corolla fails to present a correct image for the project,' said Monwabisi. 'And will Pellmar cover the costs of petrol? There may be a lot of travel involved.'

Mthetho flagged the waiter and asked for another jug of water. 'With lots of ice blocks,' he added, looking at his two companions. 'These negotiations are becoming far too hot.'

'I don't think we can offer more than four thousand, though we could consider an upgrade on the car,' said Peter.

Monwabisi took the frosted glass jug from the waiter and refilled his glass. 'And petrol?' he asked.

'This is more trouble than I expected,' said Peter. 'Quite frankly, I think our offer is sufficient to attract a range of candidates. Based on the recommendation of the Deputy

Minister, you were our first choice. But if our terms are not adequate, we can find someone else.'

Peter looked at Mthetho for a few seconds, then excused himself to 'go see a man about a horse'.

'This is no time to play your trade union games,' said Mthetho. 'Take what is on offer. Peter doesn't have time to waste here.'

Monwabisi reached for his water.

'Leave that water trick alone,' said Mthetho. 'The offer is R4 000. End of story.'

'Whose side are you on?' asked Monwabisi.

'I'm on your family's side,' said Mthetho. 'Enough of this class struggle foolishness.'

When Peter came back, Monwabisi left his water alone and agreed to the R4 000 a month. Peter said he'd still consider a car upgrade and a petrol allowance. 'I'll need to clear those with head office,' he said.

Monwabisi shook Peter's hand and the three drank a Shiraz toast to what Peter called their 'glorious PPP – public-private partnership.'

Monwabisi still thought he could have bargained for R4 500. At least he got to order a Johnnie Walker Black and soda for the road. Even plain tap water tasted better than Shiraz.

○

A week later Monwabisi's Audi A4 arrived. It was lapis blue with air conditioning and a six-CD changer bolted into the boot. Two boxes on the front seat labelled 'His' and 'Hers' held a pair of brand-new Nokia cellphones. Constantia would be delighted.

Within a few days the bass thump of the car stereo became Comrade RDP's signature sound. When his comrades heard the horns of Kaya Mahlangu, Bra Hugh or the piano of Johnny Dyani's 'Blame It on the Boers', Monwabisi and his food for the ear were on the way. When he arrived at a house, he switched over to 'Whispers in the Deep' by Stimela. Monwabisi would power down his window and turn up the volume while he sang along to Ray Phiri's refrain.

At last the days of being a tributary of that great river of pain were receding for Monwabisi and his family. Heads would turn when he got out of the car, walked a few steps, then pushed the alarm remote. His car would make two beeping sounds and the lights would flash. The vehicle seemed to have a mind of its own.

Just two days after the car arrived, Monwabisi, wearing his charcoal suit, stopped at Mrs Mehlo's house to take her for a spin around the block.

'God has finally blessed your family,' she told him, 'and you deserve it all.' She reached over to touch the cloth of his suit jacket. 'Intle,' she said. 'So perfect.'

Her son Oupa was standing in front of the house when Monwabisi dropped Mrs Mehlo back home.

'Maybe you can talk to your wife,' Mrs Mehlo said. 'My boy failed his matric and now he is just idling. Look at him there, loitering with his friend Mzi, doing nothing all day. They're probably smoking dagga when I'm not around.'

Monwabisi glanced at the two young men in their baggy trousers and American-style baseball caps. Oupa's T-shirt had a big red heart on the front, with 'I Love New York' in cursive written below.

'I'm sure the boy will be all right,' said Monwabisi.

'If there is something at the council,' Mrs Mehlo said. 'Even a training programme can do.'

As she got out of the car, Oupa and Mzi came to the driver's window. Monwabisi had turned on the radio for news but he changed the station. The DJ was playing Boom Shaka's 'It's About Time' – music for Oupa's generation.

'I see you've joined the bourgeoisie,' said Oupa. 'Soon you'll be moving to Houghton and just come to see us on Christmas.'

'He'll be one of the "ooscuse-me brigade",' said Mzi.

'Never,' said Monwabisi. 'I was born a worker and I'll die a worker.' These were lighties, too young to even remember what apartheid meant. One day he'd come back and give them a few lessons.

'Workers only wear suits to funerals and weddings,' said Mzi. 'Who is getting married today?'

Monwabisi didn't reply. Besides being young, they were jealous. These two had no idea about the Water for Freedom project or how Monwabisi would help make the RDP a reality in the township. He closed his car window, switched the CD back to Ray Phiri, and left Oupa and Mzi and their smug smiles by the side of the road. One day they'd appreciate what Monwabisi was doing for Sivuyile.

☽

A week later, Monwabisi had his final appointment with Dr Jacobs. The dentist spent two hours anchoring the false tooth. When Monwabisi got home he told Constantia that he now had a 'million-dollar smile'.

'Sometimes it gets in the way when I try to talk,' he said. 'It's like speaking into a wall.'

'You'll get used to it,' she said, laughing.

Monwabisi had finally started to relax. He had a job, a new car, and he didn't have to worry about embarrassing his wife with a smile. He had begun to taste that better life the ANC had promised.

Chapter 24

'OUR COMMUNITIES ARE payers,' Councillor Kelly said. 'The culture of non-payment is in the townships.'

Peter kept staring at the kudu head mounted on the office wall behind the desk. Kelly looked up from his papers, took off his reading glasses and faced his prize hunting trophy.

'One hundred and seventeen centimetres,' said the councillor. 'I bagged it in Tanzania. Ours here in the Eastern Cape are a bit smaller.'

'The way the antlers twist is very impressive,' said Peter. Kelly pointed out the 'full third curl' as Peter reached for his smartphone. He'd downloaded some stats from Van Huis's financial reports. Plus, he didn't want to hear anything more about this revolting animal head on the wall. Just the idea of looking into the eyes of a living thing and pulling the trigger made him sick.

Kelly put his reading glasses back on and said that installing prepaids in Northridge would be a 'waste of resources'. 'We've always run a surplus,' the councillor added.

Peter quickly reviewed Van Huis's list of delinquent service accounts. Kelly was correct in one sense. Most of those owing money were from the townships. In Sivuyile, everyone from Andile to Zola had arrears, most of them only a few hundred rand. The ten biggest overdue accounts, on the other hand, belonged to white-owned businesses. Freeman Mansions, a commercial block housing several prestigious

162

law firms, including one where Kelly was a partner, owed nearly half a million in back payments for water, electricity and sewage. Two other firms had more than R300 000 outstanding.

'The prepaids are better for everyone,' said Peter. He read the dates on Kelly's framed UCT law degree on the wall. With a quick subtraction he figured the man was fifty-seven. A little late in life to be playing silly games.

'The problem isn't just water,' said Kelly. 'It's a question of attitude. My constituents sometimes feel under attack, as if they're somehow supposed to right all the wrongs of the past from their own wallets.'

Peter felt the urge to tell Kelly what a charmed life he and his white compatriots lived. The blacks could have killed half of them and probably justified it to the rest of the world. After all, the United Nations had called apartheid a crime against humanity. Usually criminals at least ended up in prison.

'I don't quite see it like that,' said Peter. 'Mr Mandela and his government have been incredibly magnanimous.'

'You don't have to live here,' said Kelly, 'have your car hijacked, everything you've worked for go up in a cloud of smoke. We are all in favour of democracy, but democracy on a level playing field.'

'I couldn't agree more,' said Peter as he put his smartphone back in his briefcase. He'd miscalculated. He would leave before he got angry. That wouldn't help. This ignorant fool of a councillor wouldn't be persuaded to accept the prepaids by a few statistics. He needed a serious reality check. He and his kudu with the full third curl would have to learn this lesson the hard way. Peter thanked Kelly for the meeting and weighed up his options for bringing more pressure to bear. For Pellmar, this was not just a racial issue. The whites had the money to provide the firm with a guaranteed income stream.

The next day Peter met with Constantia and Monwabisi at her office. The Radebes would seal the deal. Peter began with his list of the major debtors, then moved on to explain the inequalities in service charges.

'Blacks pay more per unit of water than whites,' Peter told them. 'I like to think of it like this: it costs almost as much to wash a baby's nappies in Sivuyile as it does to fill a swimming pool in Northridge.'

'This is the best-kept secret in Ukusa,' said Constantia.

'It's virtually the same with electricity,' Peter added.

'Apartheid lives on,' said Monwabisi, 'but not for long. This campaign can't wait.'

Within two days posters with the ANC logo spread throughout the townships. They urged the citizens of Ukusa to attend the next city council meeting if they wanted to 'stop apartheid water tariffs'.

Once the posters appeared, Peter got phone calls from Kelly on his cell. In twenty-four hours the councillor left seven messages. Peter only listened to the first one. Kelly was speaking of a 'racist campaign', arguing that the ANC had violated the 'spirit of the Constitution'. Peter didn't return the calls. He would let the man sweat.

The morning of the council meeting Kelly wandered into Constantia's office.

'I hear you are promising to bring a big crowd to the meeting tonight,' she said. He told her it wasn't too serious.

'You just must be seen to be doing something,' he said. 'Showing them that you're not dead wood.'

She pretended to read a report for a few seconds while Kelly stood there. She loved to see him squirm. It didn't happen very often.

'Actually, Koosman and myself would like to talk to you,' Kelly said, 'along with the other ANC councillors.'

'I thought you had just come to say hello,' said Constantia.

'This is politics,' he said. 'No one ever comes just to say hello.'

Two hours before the council meeting, Constantia and her three ANC colleagues met with Kelly and Koosman in an anteroom just outside the chambers. Constantia opened the gathering by expressing a hope for 'some kind of reconciliation'.

A cleaner served tea and shortbread while Constantia explained that the people of Ukusa had now 'embraced the spirit of Simunye'.

'We are one,' said Koosman.

'Something like that,' said Fakude.

'We wanted to have this discussion before the meeting,' said Constantia, 'so we don't end up fighting like angry hyenas.'

The white councillors both gave a thumbs up. She wondered if they had any idea what was coming. There was always a chance for leaks in the municipality.

'Much of our constituency believes that whites should pay more in service charges to compensate for the past,' said Constantia. Kelly and Koosman looked disinterested. For them, this was old news.

'We've been doing our best to dissuade them,' said Fakude, 'pressing for equity.'

'That's why we support the installation of prepaids in all households in the municipality,' said Constantia. 'The meter can't discriminate.'

Koosman read from a printout, noting that there were arrears of less than 1 per cent among the Northridge residents.

'The installation of the meters will cost far more than the 1 per cent we will recover,' he said. 'The municipality doesn't have money to waste.'

'We take your point, Councillor,' said Constantia as she flipped through a grey ring binder until she came to the list of the biggest debtors. She slid the binder in front of the two white councillors.

'While thousands of people in the townships do owe money,' she said, 'it is in your constituency where the biggest debtors reside. Look at the figure for Freeman Mansions: R473 237.54. Truly a staggering amount.'

'And there are others almost as large,' added Fakude.

'How could debts like this accrue without some extraordinary arrangement?' Constantia asked. 'It seems there were certain "favoured customers" in the old municipal offices.'

'Thank goodness those days are gone,' said Fakude.

Kelly mumbled something in Afrikaans about Golden Acres, a nursing home owned by Koosman. Their bill stood at R127 000, number nine on the list.

'As ANC councillors,' said Constantia, 'we have taken a decision not to make these bills public if you will agree to the prepaids in Northridge.' She folded her hands in front of her and rested them on the table. The fluorescent lighting highlighted the fresh red varnish on her nails. She'd had her first professional manicure that afternoon.

'If we are compelled to reveal all of this information to the people in Sivuyile and Bopape,' said Fakude, 'I shudder at the possible outcome.'

While Kelly and Koosman perused the figures in greater depth, a busload of ANC supporters arrived in front of the building. Constantia suspected some divine intervention. Who else could have engineered such perfect timing?

The ANC contingent was singing an old freedom song Fakude translated the lyrics of the song for Kelly and Koosman: 'Khawuleth'umshini wami' – 'Bring Me My Machine Gun'. Constantia could see the confidence of these two white men draining away. This was part of what democracy was meant to do: level the playing field.

As the music wound down, Councillor Jacobs asked to speak. Even in their ANC caucus meetings he rarely said a word. He was the only member of the ANC council who could be described as 'thin', or soft-spoken. For the first time, Constantia noticed how striking his nearly green eyes were. His glasses always covered them up.

'The needs of black people, both Africans and coloureds, are paramount,' he said. 'In Basil February we have backlogs in every area, housing and electricity as well as water. Justice must prevail.'

The white councillors asked for some time alone to consider their options.

'No problem,' said Constantia. 'You still have a few minutes. I do want to point out, though, that if the township residents were to learn that certain municipal officials owed arrears into the hundreds of thousands while they themselves have no water, their response might be difficult to predict.' She could feel her power now. The ANC councillors were beginning to act like they actually were the ruling party.

A little less than an hour later, the council meeting achieved an easy consensus. Kelly and Koosman remained silent during the debate about prepaids in Northridge. Constantia had promised that if they didn't contest the motion, she wouldn't release the data on delinquent accounts.

When the measure passed 6–0, the toyi-toying began. The pounding on the linoleum floor of the chambers shifted to a muffled roar as the celebrants moved into the carpeted foyer. They cleared the platters of finger food the kitchen staff had prepared for the council members. A last chorus of 'Umshini wami' accompanied the devouring of sausage rolls, samoosas and shortbread.

In the front of the building, Monwabisi addressed the jubilant crowd. He'd shed the suits for his old union tracksuit and cap. Amid cries of 'Viva Comrade RDP!' few heard the challenge he posed: 'Now we must make sure that when the prepaids are implemented, no one in Ukusa will ever be without water again.'

Only Comrade Slim and a few of his friends at the back of the crowd failed to join in Monwabisi's final slogan of the evening: 'Viva prepaids, viva!'

Chapter 25

MTHETHO AND PETER sat with Monwabisi under the marquee. Susan, wearing a bright blue African-print dress, stood nearby chatting with a local church minister. She'd be delivering the keynote.

Peter surveyed the scene. The rough-hewn Sivuyile High soccer ground was bursting with the excitement of the occasion. The lively sax of Kaya Mahlangu serenaded the crowd. Peter didn't normally listen to jazz but this was upbeat. Maybe it was just the feeling of being solidly on the road to success.

'Who ever heard of famous artists coming to small towns in the Eastern Cape?' said Monwabisi. 'This is the greatest day ever.' He went on to recall how the tapes of Mahlangu's band Sakhile used to echo through COSATU House in Joburg during the State of Emergency. 'Those were our darkest days,' said the former shop steward.

Peter recognised that wistful tone in Monwabisi's voice. He sounded just like Susan when she talked about the past. He was beginning to realise how important history was in South Africa. Any company that wanted to succeed here had to recognise that. While Monwabisi reminisced, Peter took in the aroma of the freshly slaughtered meat sizzling on the oil-drum braais, the perfect complement to the sounds of South Africa's greatest sax player. This launching of Pellmar's Water for Freedom Project was history in the making.

South African Breweries had added to the joy with a subsidised beer garden. A draught was just fifty cents. Next to the beer garden a huge truck replica of a Coca-Cola can dispensed free cool drinks to youngsters and teetotallers. Winding its way across the field, a queue of grandmothers and delighted screaming kids waited to refill their plastic cups with Coke and Fanta.

Susan surprised Peter by delivering most of her address in isiXhosa. He had no idea she was so fluent. He'd managed to learn a few phrases, but the clicks were a real challenge. What better message could there be for a new South Africa than a blonde woman in an African dress speaking the local language? In the English portion of her speech she praised the 'remarkable job' the municipality of Ukusa had done in bringing formerly disparate local authorities under one umbrella, calling the first public-private partnership in prepaid meters 'the kind of unity that will drive our nation forward'.

The formalities closed with singing by the Bopape Methodist Choir. Their conductor, Mr Xoseni, dedicated their final number, 'Wade in the Water', to the 'mastermind behind this project, Mr Peter Franklin'.

When the choir concluded, Susan, Peter, Mayor Siziba and a host of local dignitaries walked through the school gate down the dirt road to house number 483D, where a red ribbon stretched across the front garden of the four-room house of the Damane family.

The TV crew and flashing news cameras moved in as Susan and the Mayor cut the ribbon with a metre-long pair of cardboard scissors. Then Susan stepped forward and turned on a shiny brass tap just a few feet from the front door. The water splashed in the concrete drain below.

To complete the occasion, the portly Reverend P.X. Mncube offered a blessing, asking God to 'continue the flow of democracy and water into the community'. The preacher reserved a special word for Peter, who had 'come all the way from America to provide water for the people in this township. We shall never forget him.'

As Peter smiled and looked around, he caught Joanna's face in the crowd. He hadn't seen her for months. They lived in different worlds. She held her usual stoop-shouldered posture, standing next to some young girls doing traditional dances in the road. She'd always pontificated about serving the poor. But it was Pellmar that was bringing water to thousands of poor South Africans, not her noble church people. She smiled at him. He half-heartedly waved back.

Mncube drew a glass of water from the tap and raised a toast.

'To the government of the people,' he said. He took a sip, then passed the glass to Mr and Mrs Damane.

'God bless everyone,' said Mr Damane. 'This is a miracle.' He poured the water in the cup over his head, letting it run down his cheeks onto the collar of his faded brown sports coat. The cameras flashed again.

As Peter walked back to the school, Joanna caught up with him and tapped him on the shoulder. He stopped and they looked at each other, unsure of the next move.

'I just wanted to congratulate you on your success,' said Joanna. 'This is a great day for this community.'

Peter thanked her and reached out for a hug. He felt a little pity for Joanna. History seemed to be passing her by. Maybe this day would be her wake-up call.

'I'm so surprised to see you here in Ukusa,' Peter said.

Joanna explained that she'd come from a conference in East London and that a young man from Sivuyile had invited her to come and visit him in his home area.

'Just for a day,' she said. 'I'll be flying back to Joburg tomorrow.'

'I'm glad you've met someone,' said Peter.

'It's not like that,' Joanna said. 'We're friends. He's almost young enough to be my son. He has a lot of problems.'

'South Africa is a country with many problems,' said Peter, 'but the beauty of the place is that there's a chance to solve them.'

Just then Mthetho called out to Peter. He wanted to introduce him to some local businessmen. Peter promised Joanna they'd talk later.

○

While a local band covered 'Last Night a DJ Saved My Life', Joanna chatted to Slim by the soccer goal. He was telling her how his parents had died in a road accident.

'They were coming back in a taxi from PE,' he said. 'The driver fell asleep. That was five years back. Ever since then I've been living with my uncle here in Sivuyile. We are many in that house.'

'I like your scarf,' said Joanna, fingering the red-and-white checked cloth wrapped around Slim's neck. She saw Peter approaching out of the corner of her eye, but she ignored him.

'They call it a kafiyyeh,' he told her. 'They are worn by Palestinian freedom fighters. There's still a lot of freedom to fight for in South Africa.'

As Slim held the scarf out in front of him, Joanna saw Peter off in the distance, dancing gleefully to the music with a couple of hefty men in suits. Though she wasn't much of a dancer, they'd had great times at some of the anti-apartheid fundraisers. She loved Hugh Masekela and Miriam Makeba.

Slim told Joanna he often felt 'very weak'. He rolled up his sleeve. A line of sores covered his arm.

'Maybe you need to go to a hospital,' she said.

'I've been to Makiwane,' he told her. 'They gave me vitamins, and said government is still working on its policy.'

Joanna's first impulse was to take Slim to a supermarket and buy ten bags of groceries. This was the wrong instinct. Individual charity wasn't the answer. The gospel of UV always held that the key was to attack the root of the problem through organisation of communities.

She found it hard to look at him. He had gone beyond slim. Maybe new clothes would help. The yellow sport shirt under the kafiyyeh looked like it belonged to an older brother.

'The government is still developing its policy as we become thin like sticks,' he said. 'Talk shops are sprouting like weeds after a rainstorm.'

'They must do something,' said Joanna. 'People are dying.' She fingered the kafiyyeh again.

Slim said standing up hurt his back, so they found two empty chairs near the beer garden.

'I'm doubting this project,' said Slim. 'These meters could be problematic.'

'Who can oppose people getting water?' asked Joanna.

'There are rumours some may be cut off,' said Slim.

'There are always rumours in South Africa,' said Joanna. 'This country runs on rumours.'

'Like a taxi runs on diesel.'

Joanna was trying to think of some way she could help Slim, at least lift his spirits. He had that youthful impatience, wanted everything to change overnight. He needed to calm down. She was certain Carl Prince and the others had everything under control.

'If there are cut-offs,' said Slim, 'things could get worse. Previously the communal taps were free.'

Slim's voice came back to life as he launched into a long tirade against 'privatisation'. 'People must come before profits,' he said.

'Of course,' said Joanna. She went quiet. She'd seen the joy of the Damanes. Poor people were benefiting in Sivuyile. Slim was getting carried away again.

As Slim talked about how multinational corporations were dragging Africa into the dust, Peter came walking past. Joanna caught his attention. Peter approached and shook Slim's hand.

'We've already met,' said Peter, 'at the SCA meeting.'

'Comrade Franklin has a good memory,' said Slim as he wrapped the kafiyyeh around his neck.

Peter excused himself, saying he had to talk to the caterers. Joanna walked part of the way back to the marquee with him. They promised to have lunch one day in Joburg.

Joanna and Slim chatted until sunset. She could see he was exhausted but he had a lot of things on his mind. If she could just find a way to get him to the right doctor, she was sure he'd calm down. She imagined that when a person was afflicted with HIV, it was difficult not to lose perspective.

○

As Joanna read Isabel Allende's *House of Spirits* while waiting for the plane to take off, Peter and Susan came down the aisle carrying their bags. Their seats were just across the aisle. Joanna told Susan how much she enjoyed her speech.

'At least the part I understood,' Joanna said. 'You seem to be quite fluent in the local language.' She resisted using the word 'Xhosa'. It had one of those click sounds that were hard to do.

'I grew up on a farm,' Susan said, 'and played with the workers' children. Xhosa was almost like my first language, though I wouldn't say that in front of my parents.'

'How can they not approve of you? You are a Deputy Minister.'

'For an enemy government. They're verkrampte. They voted for the Conservative Party.'

As Susan spoke she reached across the aisle and touched Joanna lightly on the shoulder. The Deputy Minister definitely didn't look like a farm girl.

'Peter's told me a lot about your work,' Susan said. 'Without people like you we could never have overthrown apartheid.'

'We did what we could,' said Joanna. She didn't know what else to say. Susan talked a little more about solidarity, then apologised because she had to crack open her laptop and finish a policy paper.

While Susan's fingers flashed across the keyboard, Joanna told Peter about Slim's HIV.

'The government is developing a policy on that,' said Peter. 'I'm sure a large-scale treatment programme is on the way.'

'It's top priority,' said Susan without taking her eyes off the computer screen.

'She would know,' said Peter, giving Susan a light peck on the forehead.

'But he needs treatment urgently,' said Joanna. 'Yesterday he could barely stand.'

'Give me a few days,' said Peter. 'I'll make some calls. There's always a way to get these things done.'

Joanna thanked him and went back to Isabel Allende.

○

Once she was safely tucked into her flat in Yeoville, Joanna began to write another monthly report for UV. The morning newspaper had inspired her. A front-page picture showed a smiling Mr Damane pouring water over his head. 'Masakhane Comes to the Eastern Cape,' read the headline. 'Government and Private Industry Join Hands.'

'We in the United States take water for granted,' Joanna's report began. 'We turn on the tap and out it comes. A monthly water bill probably doesn't equal the cost of a meal in a restaurant. In South Africa, water is a struggle. Women may walk three miles to fill a bucket from a contaminated well or polluted river just to wash clothes or cook some vegetables.'

She went on to tell the story of the partnership between Pellmar and government. She hesitated when it came to mentioning Peter by name. Some readers might be interested if she recalled his anti-apartheid days, his arrests in DC with the rich and famous. But she reminded herself that this report was not about any one individual. It was about rebuilding communities and a whole country.

'I saw girls dancing in celebration,' she wrote, 'as people filled the first glass from a tap in their garden. Children told me they could go to school with pride now because they would have water to wash themselves before leaving the house in the morning. A miracle can take a small, simple form. So it is with the miraculous arrival of piped water in Ukusa.'

A few days later, a card came in the post. The cover had a photo of Nelson Mandela standing in his prison cell on the occasion of his first visit to Robben Island since his release. 'It was nice to see you,' Peter had written inside. 'If your friend ever needs any help, don't hesitate to ask.'

Part 3

Chapter 26

'IT'S NOT MY JOB,' SAID Monwabisi. 'I've got a meeting in Bopape in the morning. Peter is here in the afternoon. We're going for dinner.'

'You didn't hear me,' said Constantia. 'The Mayor wants us this morning – all the ANC councillors. It's mandatory.'

Monwabisi had already knotted his tie. He was feeling in his pockets for the car keys.

'One of the neighbour girls can look after them,' he said. 'I must go.'

Portia's mother had gone to the hospital in the night. That left Fidel and Musa with no one to care for them. Constantia had already tried the two girls up the road. They were going for a matric exam workshop. Mrs Sithethi's worker, Nonceba, was a little too partial to daytime beer drinking to be trusted.

Constantia heard Monwabisi start the car. She'd be late now. She phoned the office, left a message on the machine. The Mayor called tardiness part of the 'struggle mentality' they needed to destroy. Why did men always think their commitments were more important? She'd heard all Monwabisi's speeches on anti-sexism and what he called 'the woman question'. He could have at least waited and given them all a lift.

Fidel was almost dressed by the time his brother sat up and rubbed his eyes. They both hated spending the day at Constantia's office.

She couldn't believe Monwabisi had told her it wasn't

his job, as if the community had elected her to look after children.

Constantia packed bags for the boys – apples, a few books, some coloured pencils and scrap paper. She quickly slapped some butter and jam on four slices of bread. If she brought her sons into the meeting with the Mayor, who would take her seriously? She'd heard of day-care centres in council buildings overseas – not in South Africa.

Musa was still groggy when they scrambled into the middle seat of the taxi. He sat on Constantia's lap. Fidel read a picture book about the activist Lilian Ngoyi.

'I hate the office,' said Musa. 'Why must we go there?'

'It's only for one day,' said Constantia.

By the time the taxi stopped at the council buildings, Musa had fallen back asleep. Constantia tried to pacify her sons by buying koeksisters from a café across the street from her office. The boys ate the syrupy breakfast gifts without a smile.

Luckily Mrs Abrahams, a distant aunt of Councillor Jacobs, was at the front desk. She wore her usual flower-patterned cotton dress.

'I know how to keep them occupied,' she told Constantia. 'And if they get out of line, they'll wish they hadn't.' Constantia brought two chairs and sat the boys down next to the reception desk.

When Constantia went to collect the boys at lunchtime, Fidel boasted that he'd helped one of the maintenance workers, Mama Ophelia, mop a conference room. He showed her two sweets still in their wrappers.

'That's my pay packet,' he said. 'Strawberry flavoured. One is for Fidel.'

'It's good to share with your brother,' Constantia told him.

Mrs Abrahams had a doctor's appointment in the after-noon. Constantia had nowhere to leave the two boys.

She rang Monwabisi on his cell. He was driving to the Methodist church in Sivuyile.

'I must explain Water for Freedom to your church ladies,' he said.

'How long will it take?' she asked.

'Maybe an hour. Why?'

'Just wondering.'

She hung up and summoned one of the council drivers. She told him she needed him and his vehicle for half an hour. She and the two boys jumped into a council Camry and headed for Sivuyile Methodist.

○

Monwabisi stood at the pulpit in the front, a large gold crucifix looming above him on the wall. He used to call religion the 'mandrax of the masses'. Now he was preaching his own gospel.

Constantia sat down in the last pew, next to Mrs Mokoena, the elderly church organist. They hadn't seen each other since Constantia's election. A councillor had no time for church choirs.

'And this device will not only help you to budget,' said Monwabisi, 'it will help you conserve water. This is important for the future of our country and community.'

Constantia whispered to Mrs Mokoena about how she had business with the Mayor, that her husband would take the children as soon as he was finished speaking.

'He can drive them home,' Constantia said, 'if you could just keep an eye on them until he's done.'

'It would be an honour, Councillor Radebe,' said Mrs Mokoena.

Constantia heard Monwabisi say something about grey water as she went out the door.

181

An SMS from her husband arrived during her meeting: 'What r u doing?' She didn't reply. The next SMS said: 'Boys gone with Mrs Mokoena. U pick them at hr place.'

She didn't hear from Monwabisi again until nine o'clock that night, when Bra Hugh playing 'Stimela' screamed in front of the house. By that time Constantia was in bed, reading a very long report on bulk service delivery. She was having a hard time staying awake. Monwabisi's key rattled in the door, followed by his uneven footfalls.

'Why must you humiliate me?' he shouted from the lounge.

She kept reading.

'Why?' He was shouting even louder.

She stayed in bed. Monwabisi appeared at the door, his tie loosened, the top three buttons of his shirt undone. He'd slung his suit coat over his shoulder.

'What does it mean to say "It's not my job"?' Constantia asked.

'What are you talking about?' he said. 'You left these boys with a stranger. What kind of a mother does that?' He threw his coat over the back of a chair. His gait was a little unsteady.

'She's not a stranger,' said Constantia, 'and that's not the point. It's not just my job.' She put the report on the nightstand. She hoped to get back to it later.

'What you did was wrong, irresponsible,' he said.

She wouldn't take his bait and get into debating his definition of irresponsible. Her husband was in no mood to reason. He came and sat on the bed. She couldn't tell if he smelled of beer or Bols.

'Why do you want to argue?' he asked. 'You used to listen to me.'

'Things have changed,' she said.

'Now you seem to have your own opinions on everything,' he said. 'My ideas no longer count. You are listening to other people. To other men.'

She flopped her head back on the pillow, staring up at the ceiling. A water stain was coming through. They'd have to do something soon before the rains came.

'It's not about listening to other people,' she said. 'And it's definitely not about another man. Forget that, Tata ka Fidel. Think about your family.'

Monwabisi began to get undressed.

'In the future,' he said, 'we must make arrangements about these boys, not just dump them. There are plenty of young girls in the township.'

'What about young boys?' said Constantia.

'You are mad.'

'It's not their job?'

'I didn't mean it like that,' he said. 'These boys are still backward. They think of children as women's work.'

Constantia rolled over and closed her eyes. Monwabisi could always say the right thing. But he probably thought she was spending all those late nights with another man. Even if she was, he had no right to complain. He was the one who'd been irresponsible, who'd contracted the virus that was sucking thousands from the family's future. He had no right to judge her – none at all. There wouldn't be time to get back to that report. She just closed her eyes and went to sleep.

Chapter 27

THE COOL OF THE SUMMER evening was just settling in as Monwabisi pulled the car up to the front of his house. He leaned back against the headrest. A brief respite before he got inside. These days he never quite knew what Constantia had in store for him. At least they hadn't fought over childcare for awhile. Portia was working extra hours now. They could even afford to pay her overtime.

He turned up the volume on the Sipho Gumede CD as he took the letter from Peter out of the cubbyhole. He'd been meaning to read it since morning but it had been a day like all the others, packed with meetings and non-stop talk about Water for Freedom; never a moment to spare. He tore off the end of the envelope meticulously, not wanting to rip the paper inside. He treated written documents with care. A good shop steward knew that any time your boss put something in writing you had to hang onto it. Keeping the paper trail alive they called it in the union.

Sipho's rifts perfectly punctuated Monwabisi's joy as he read the words of praise from Peter.

'We want to congratulate you on the magnificent work you've done getting the project off the ground,' the letter began. Peter went on to summarise how critical someone with a 'cosmic connection' to the community was to Water for Freedom.

'At the end of the year, renewing your contract should

be just a formality,' the letter concluded. 'The ball is rolling full speed ahead and you are central to our team. My only concern is that there may be some restructuring at Pellmar, which may delay the renewal and your rise in pay. We are also exploring the possibility of getting you an office in Freeman Mansions. We trust you will be comfortable there.'

Monwabisi tucked the letter into a pocket of his briefcase. Freeman Mansions was old-style luxury, a red-brick façade, hulking white pillars across the front. No metalworker had ever darkened the door of Northridge's most prestigious office block.

He pulled the letter out one more time just to make sure he had read it right. None of his previous employers had ever sent him a letter like this. He was used to threats and warnings, not commendation. But Peter was right, the ball was rolling. Engineers, plumbers and a mass of labourers were busy installing taps all across Ukusa. The smiles of the Damanes on the day of the launch were multiplying across faces from OR Tambo to the remote corners of Sivuyile and Bopape. The shiny new taps were a concrete assurance to the community that the promised 'better life for all' was on the way.

To top it all off, Monwabisi could feel his career star rising. He was making himself indispensable to Pellmar. They'd even given him a team of three young facilitators to spread the gospel of Water for Freedom throughout Ukusa. One day he might end up in Pellmar's Joburg office or even at headquarters in New York. As long as the medication kept working, the sky was the limit. That word 'restructuring' in Peter's letter troubled him a little, though. In the metal industry, restructuring always meant retrenchments. This, however, was water, a very different world.

He grabbed his briefcase and went inside. Constantia was already asleep on the sofa, the TV blaring the sirens of some cops closing in on their prey on the streets of New York. He switched off the televison, hoping the sudden silence might wake her up so he could give her the good news. No chance. She was gently snoring. He left her alone and went to bed. Maybe he'd get around to showing her the letter in the morning.

For the moment he was focused on what was on his plate for the following day. He'd be heading to Northridge High School for a showdown with the white ratepayers. They were the only ones not going along with the project. They'd insulted one of his facilitators the last time she went there. He was kind of looking forward to reminding these arrogant Boers that they no longer held the power.

○

Monwabisi had never been inside the Northridge High hall. The walls held banners and bronze plaques of past glories on the rugby and cricket pitches of the Eastern Cape. It seems Northridge had won the provincial rugby title in 1987, the year his brother Ishmael disappeared.

Monwabisi found a chair on the stage as the facilitator, Nombuso, was about to start. She set her papers on the podium and greeted the audience. She was a Rhodes University grad, spoke that Tumi Makgabo English that the whites liked so much. Nearly a hundred of them had shown up. Monwabisi didn't know they cared that much about water. A few of them replied to Nombuso with a half-hearted 'good morning'.

The young woman began by reading from the script Monwabisi had prepared, describing the technical side of Water for Freedom, how the meters were calibrated so that everyone would get a certain amount of water for free, but when someone used extra water, like what was required to fill a swimming pool or water a garden, they paid a higher rate. The extra money would be used to subsidise water for the 'historically disadvantaged'.

'This system will help to right the wrongs of history,' Nombuso emphasised. She left out the line about the increased water rates being an 'apartheid tax'. That was only for people in the townships.

The ratepayers' leader, Henry Winston, jumped up and shook a finger at Nombuso.

'We don't want to end up paying an arm and a leg for our water just because we're white,' he shouted. 'Government wants to penalise us for the past.'

'This is not about retribution,' said Nombuso. 'We are trying to conserve our resources and guarantee water for everyone.'

She turned one of the pages over and started to talk about grey water.

'We don't need a sermon from some young girl fresh out of varsity,' said Winston as he sat back down. 'We need assurances.'

'I'm not here to provide insurance,' said Nombuso. A rash of chuckles broke out.

'And Jesus wept,' said a woman at the back.

Monwabisi stood up and sped down the stairs from the stage to the main floor. He wanted to get close to these people, make them feel his presence. He wouldn't have his facilitator degraded by those who had voted for the National Party ever since 1948. They probably celebrated the day Steve Biko died.

'As the leader of your community,' Monwabisi said to Winston, 'you are displaying a lack of respect for a woman who represents the duly elected government of South Africa. You cannot treat her like she's your servant girl.'

'We will not be insulted,' said Winston. 'The Mayor will

hear about this. Why is everything a racial issue? We have agreed to work with you people.'

Monwabisi held the prepaid card aloft.

'This device does not see colour,' he said.

Winston and a dozen others moved to the back-door exit. Monwabisi quickly made his way towards them. 'If you are watering your lawn all day or washing your six cars with a hosepipe,' the former shop steward said, 'this device will penalise you whether you are Smith, Van der Merwe or Nongqawuse. It is how much water you use that matters, not what colour you are. That reactionary, racist thinking has no place in a democratic South Africa.'

The door slammed. Winston and his colleagues were gone.

Monwabisi hiked back up to the stage while Nombuso asked for questions.

'Why were we not consulted on this?' asked a red-haired woman in the middle of the crowd. She had more to say, but a baby in a pram next to her started to cry.

A hefty black domestic worker raced from the back of the hall and plucked the child out of the pram, providing her red-headed madam with the quiet she needed to continue.

'We are being used as guinea pigs,' the red-haired woman added.

'Our system is transparent,' said Nombuso. 'One size fits all. This government no longer holds secrets.'

'But the decision has already been taken,' said the redhead. The baby cooed a little bit, then let out a screech of delight.

'Your duly elected council members, Mr Kelly and Mr Koosman, voted for it,' said Nombuso.

'Then let us tie them to a bakkie and drag them down the road. We have always paid our bills. This is the thanks we get.'

Nombuso laughed derisively. She was learning fast.

Monwabisi had shown her the fearlessness of a shop steward and now she was following suit, standing down these whites on their home turf. Beautiful girls didn't always pick things up so quickly.

A grey-haired man in a Springbok cap stood up. 'These people are making good sense,' he said. He reached into a lawyer-sized briefcase and pulled out what looked like a piece of pipe. 'We need to save our water,' he said.

'Shut up, Garth,' said the red-haired woman. 'There is a gadfly in every meeting. Why must it always be you?'

'This is a variable-flow shower head,' said Garth, holding up the pipe. 'It can reduce your usage by up to 50 per cent. Just nine ninety-five. Great value for money, good people. Who wants one? They won't last long.'

'This isn't a sales convention,' said the red-haired woman.

'The gentleman has the floor,' said a grinning Nombuso. 'Everyone has the same democratic rights.'

She winked at Monwabisi. Her pencil-thin eyebrows reminded him of Kosi, a girlfriend he had from Thokoza. That was eleven years ago. He heard she had passed away a couple years back.

'And when we just urinate,' said Garth, 'there is no need for a full flush. This has half-flush capacity.' He held up a colour poster of a shining white commode.

'You're turning this into toilet training,' said the red-haired woman. 'I'm gatvol of this water.'

'I'll take one of those shower heads,' said Monwabisi, reaching for his wallet. He walked towards Garth. 'I assume the price includes VAT.'

'Yes, sir, Mr Radebe. VAT included. I wouldn't have it any other way.'

'We have more issues,' said the red-haired woman. The residents around her began to collect their things.

'People seem to be voting with their feet,' said Nombuso.

'I thank you all for your attendance.'

A handful of the people huddled around Monwabisi, asking him how to load their cards. One man heard that he could transfer money onto the card via his computer.

'We don't have that capacity yet,' said Monwabisi. 'We are busy working to develop it in the future.'

As he finished his explanation, Nombuso pulled up to Monwabisi's side and put her arm around his waist.

'Enkosi, bhuti,' she said. 'You saved me.'

'You didn't need saving,' he said. 'A veteran of campus struggles can handle this crowd.'

She squeezed him gently. She was young enough to be his daughter, but he still felt an unwelcome urge. He was used to letting such things pass. This time he squeezed back.

Her perfume reminded him of Joburg even more than her eyebrows.

'I'll see you next time,' he said, 'but I doubt you'll need me again.'

'I hope there'll be a next time,' she said, passing him a slip of paper with her new cellphone number. 'Give me a ring,' she said with a little girl smile.

He could feel her watching him as he walked towards the back of the hall and through the exit. His dreamy infatuation didn't last long. Winston and the others had gathered under a shade tree near Monwabisi's car. The former shop steward took his key ring out of his pocket and locked it inside his fist, leaving the ignition key protruding between his index and middle fingers.

'I demand an apology,' said Winston, as the former shop steward came down the steps from the hall. 'I won't be insulted like this. I'm not a racist.' Winston and his followers were moving in on Monwabisi. They almost had him surrounded.

'I'm the one who needs the apology,' said Monwabisi. 'You lived off the exploitation of the black working class for years.' He tried to move past Winston but the old white man stepped over to block his way. Monwabisi clenched his fist tighter. That key could slash Winston's pale cheek in a split second. It would be such a pleasure.

'Now get out of my way. I have to be somewhere,' Monwabisi said. Winston stepped aside. 'I'll sort you out later,' he told the former shop steward.

'You won't sort out anybody,' said Monwabisi. 'You and your heroes Botha and Verwoerd are finished. Go and live in the dustbin of racist history where you belong.'

He got in the car and turned on the radio. 'Shosholoza' boomed out of the speakers. He quickly switched over to the CD and rolled down the windows. The baritone of Mzwakhe Mbuli reminded Winston and his cohort that the tradition of no surrender was the name of the game.

Monwabisi figured Mzwakhe should scare the hell out of them. When he got a couple of blocks away, he switched to a Sakhile CD and started to calm down. Maybe he shouldn't have been quite so aggressive but he had to admit that he enjoyed making these whites squirm. They had it coming.

Chapter 28

As MONWABISI TURNED onto Kotane Road, his cellphone rang. It was Nombuso. He'd only left her five minutes ago and already she was calling. He had a hard time hearing her voice. Talking on the cell while the car stereo boomed was difficult. But he wasn't about to shut the music off. For the time being the old Sakhile tunes excited him more than the voice of a beautiful young woman.

As he drove past Market Square, Mrs Mehlo waved him down. Nowadays she saved the famous brands for him: Lacoste, Gap, Wrangler. She probably had a new shipment. He once bought a beautiful pair of Levis in Constantia's size, but she told him that jeans made her look 'cheap'.

Monwabisi said his goodbyes to Nombuso as he pulled over. He'd call her back later when he was alone, get her thoughts on the meeting. Maybe they should get together for a post-mortem.

As he powered down the driver's side window, Mrs Mehlo scurried around the back of the car waving some papers.

'How are you, my brother?' she said.

Monwabisi asked about her son, and about her family back in the Transkei. She said Oupa was still looking for a job and that he was drinking far too much.

'I don't know where he gets the money,' she said. She held the papers up so Monwabisi could see the Ukusa Municipality logo on the letterhead.

'These people are refusing to turn on my water,' she said. 'They say I am owing R3 712 from the days of the Boers.'

She handed him the papers. 'It's Tyibelo who gave me this,' she said. 'I told him the ANC would make him suffer.'

'Tyibelo?'

'Cheeky young fellow at the municipal offices. He said he could give me an extra ticket to win a Kia, but no water. A Kia, what is that?'

'It's a car, mama. We are offering it as an incentive for people to pay.'

'Mama Mehlo wants her water,' she said. 'How can a car wash my family's clothes?'

Monwabisi reviewed the papers. Five pages of billing, dating back to 1991. He was certain some Boer like Winston was behind this Tyibelo, trying to sabotage the project. That was all they had left.

'They tell me I must get a letter from my church minister,' she said, 'showing that I cannot afford. Then they will turn on my taps. Just like what the Boers were doing.'

'I will sort this out, mama,' said Monwabisi. 'It's a clerical error. These debts are supposed to be written off.'

'We fought for taps, not more jerrycans,' said Mrs Mehlo. She gazed back towards her clothing stall. 'Tyibelo is a tsotsi,' she added. 'Why must I pay three rands in taxi fares just to get to the municipality and be insulted? You must talk to these people.'

'No problem,' said Monwabisi.

Mrs Mehlo scurried back to her clothes.

○

The next morning Monwabisi found Tyibelo collecting the post from his pigeonhole in the hallway. Monwabisi introduced himself as the Water for Freedom project leader.

Tyibelo was a happy man. Someone had left a copy of Arthur's latest CD, *Oyi Oyi*, in with his mail. 'I've been waiting for this,' he said, reading off the list of tunes on the cover.

Monwabisi showed Tyibelo the bills for Mrs Mehlo.

'There's a mistake here,' said Monwabisi. 'This woman owes from the past. She must be reconnected.'

Tyibelo took the papers from Monwabisi. He pointed to the 'balance due' box. 'More than R3 000,' Tyibelo said. 'Such people must pay a deposit.'

He handed the papers back and admired the cover of the CD.

'No, mhlobo wam',' said Monwabisi. 'Government has written off these apartheid debts. We don't pay them.'

'I never got that memo,' said Tyibelo. 'And I don't make the rules. I just do as I'm told. It's safer that way.'

'Even when it means cutting off an old woman's water?' asked Monwabisi.

Tyibelo shrugged. 'I don't remember her,' he said. He nodded towards a long queue of people waiting to pay their bills. 'I must get to work. Talk to Ntsele, my supervisor.'

Monwabisi found Ntsele in his office. He was a plump man in a dark suit wearing a big smile. 'I've been promoted,' Ntsele said after Monwabisi told him the story of Mrs Mehlo. Ntsele leaned back in his chair and surveyed his tiny office. The grey metal shelves were teeming with box files.

'I've got to pack up,' he said. 'I'll be starting tomorrow as chief accountant. To be honest, I couldn't care less about your Mrs Mehlo. She's no longer my concern.'

Monwabisi reminded him that Water for Freedom was a project driven by powerful people in Pretoria. The possibility of a phone call from an irate bureaucrat in Gauteng at least got Ntsele to tilt his chair forward and flip through the papers in his out tray. After a few seconds he found the memorandum from the Mayor to the accounts department that said that those who owed arrears in excess of R1 000 had to pay off at least 30 per cent before being reconnected. 'Our hands are tied, bhuti,' said Ntsele.

'Our hands are often tied because we tie them ourselves,' said Monwabisi. He left Ntsele dreaming about his new job and phoned Mthetho. One memo from the Mayor with some crazy declaration about debts from the days of the Boers couldn't destroy Water for Freedom. Mthetho had contacts all the all the way to Washington, DC. The Mayor was no match for that.

His cousin advised Monwabisi not to wake a sleeping Alsatian.

'Our municipalities are under pressure to balance their accounts,' said the Deputy Minister. 'The Mayor is doing his level best.'

'Level best isn't good enough,' said Monwabisi. 'If we don't give people their water, this project will become a disaster. People are already talking.'

'Let them talk,' said Mthetho. 'You must keep an eye on your own neck, your family, not worry about everyone else. Peter has already received a complaint about you from Winston.'

'That old Boer can go to hell,' said Monwabisi. He remembered the scene in the car park. Maybe he should have let 'Shosholoza' play.

'He's well connected,' said Mthetho. 'Be careful.'

'So what do we tell people who've been refused a connection?' asked Monwabisi.

As Mthetho prepared to answer, Monwabisi heard another call ring through.

'Tell them to be patient,' said Mthetho. 'Water is coming.' He excused himself to take the other call, then came back on the line.

'The Danes want to talk,' said the Deputy Minister.

'Where there's a Dane, there is a *krone*, maybe a trip to Copenhagen. I must go.'

A few minutes later Peter phoned Monwabisi and said that he understood how frustrating it could be working with these 'recalcitrant whites' but that Monwabisi had to learn to control his 'outbursts'.

'We can't afford to make unnecessary enemies,' said Peter.

'Winston is not an unnecessary enemy, he's a racist old fool,' said Monwabisi. 'I have no time for such people.' He cut the call and headed for Mrs Mehlo's spot in the market.

Someone had to tell her the truth.

○

Monwabisi found Mrs Mehlo at her stall. She was unravelling a new bundle of clothes from overseas. The packing tape bore the imprint, 'St John's Center for Peace and Mercy, Baltimore, Maryland.' Monwabisi explained that the Mayor had written a 'useless memo' and Tyibelo was just following orders.

'Then the Mayor must unwrite that memo,' she said. 'We didn't vote for the ANC to buy water from vendors.'

Monwabisi promised her he'd pursue the matter as far as he could, though he had no idea what to do next. His cousin didn't seem as if he was going to lift a finger. Mrs Mehlo picked out the best shirts, draped them over clothes hangers and placed them on the piece of rope she used as a display rail.

'How am I supposed to live without water?' she asked as she buttoned the collar on a bright yellow Van Heusen. 'Maybe we will have to march again,' she added.

'It won't get to that stage,' said Monwabisi. 'People will get their water.' He grabbed four of the shirts Mrs Mehlo had just put on the hangers.

'I'll take these,' he said.

Mrs Mehlo eyed Monwabisi's selection.

'Those are too small,' she said, 'I'll find you something better.' She rummaged around in the bundle tossing aside some jeans and a pair of blue pyjamas.

'They're not for me,' he said, 'don't worry. How much?'

'Twenty rands each,' she said, 'but we can negotiate.'

Monwabisi handed over four twenty-rand notes and took his leave, promising once again to do something about Mrs Mehlo's water.

'You must sort out that Tyibelo,' she said, 'he's too cheeky.'

A few minutes later Monwabisi was stopped at a traffic light still wondering why his cousin was more worried about pleasing those Danes than getting Mrs Mehlo her water. A young boy interrupted his thoughts by knocking on the window. He was carrying a squeegee and a paint container full of well-used water. Monwabisi was too preoccupied to chase him away.

The youngster dipped the squeegee in his makeshift bucket and slapped it against the windscreen. The rubber blade squeaked loudly as the boy smeared the dirty water across the glass. By the time the light changed the boy had done both sides of the windscreen and had started on the driver's side window. Monwabisi rolled down the window and handed the boy the four shirts he'd bought from Mrs Mehlo. The youngster gave a thumbs up, set down his bucket and slipped on the long-sleeved yellow Van Heusen. The tail almost reached the ground as the boy trotted away. Monwabisi sped off with Ray Phiri serenading the township at full blast. This walk to freedom was even longer than Madiba himself ever dreamed.

◯

A few days later, Monwabisi got a call from a secretary at the municipal offices informing him that a fax marked 'urgent' had arrived. She told him it came from Peter.

Monwabisi rushed to collect it. He was hoping there would be some news about his office. The cover sheet said: 'Personal: Note of Commendation from P. Franklin, Esq.' The text began by lauding Monwabisi on his 'marvellously successful efforts in facilitating popular acceptance and support for the pilot program'. Peter added that as a 'token of appreciation' he had deposited R1 000 into Monwabisi's bank account. Monwabisi sent Constantia an SMS to give her the news. He promised her a dinner at the London Towers to celebrate. As he left the municipal offices, he rang Nombuso. They'd have lunch the next day. No harm in rewarding the young woman's hard work. He couldn't wait to smell that Joburg-style perfume.

After his phone calls, he finished reading the fax. The last paragraph told a different story:

'Unfortunately, I regret that our executive board has decided that we will no longer have need of your services. I wish it could have turned out differently but circumstances have arisen which make it impossible to extend your contract. We thank you once again for your magnificent efforts. If you should ever need a reference, feel free to call on me.'

The fax had one more piece of bad news: 'Kindly leave your vehicle in the municipal office car park and inform us of the location. We will arrange collection.' A former shop steward should have seen this coming. Suits and state-of-the-art CD players had dulled his senses. He rang Mthetho. The secretary said the Deputy Minister was in a meeting.

'It's a family emergency,' said Monwabisi. 'Please inform him I'm on the line.'

She put him on hold and promised to tell the Deputy Minister about his call. 'He may have to ring back,' she said.

'I need to speak with him ASAP,' said Monwabisi. 'I'll wait on the line.'

He stayed on hold, listening to a recording of Kenny G provided by the department. There were so many great South African musicians, why did he have to listen to this long-haired white American? While Monwabisi waited for his cousin, he got into his car. He'd take it for a few last spins before handing it over. What were they going to do – arrest him for driving his own vehicle?

After a full ten minutes, his cousin's voice came on the line. He didn't give Monwabisi a chance to explain. 'I tried to tell Peter that complaints by Winston would add credibility to Pellmar among blacks,' said Mthetho. 'He didn'tagree, said they couldn't afford to alienate the ratepayers.' Mthetho went on to say that Henry Winston had been talking to people all the way to Pretoria about being called a 'racist' by Monwabisi.

'So the American freedom fighter has spoken,' said Monwabisi, 'and the Deputy Minister remains quiet.' He pulled out of the municipality's car park but he didn't know where to go. Peter Franklin had made him afraid to show his face. Retrenched again. He couldn't even impress a young girl like Nombuso any more.

'The board of Pellmar has taken a decision,' said Mthetho. 'My hands are tied.'

Monwabisi wanted to repeat his quip about tying your own hands but it didn't apply to a Deputy Minister. Instead of tying anyone's hands, Mthetho had helped wrap the noose around Monwabisi's neck.

'What have you sold me for?' asked Monwabisi. 'A trip to America? One of those big V8s of theirs? What was your price, comrade?' He rubbed his tongue against his shining front tooth. He wanted to rip it out, go back to his old proletarian, gap-toothed self. The real Monwabisi Radebe. He'd never gotten comfortable in those Florsheims. Imported shoes weren't everything he thought they'd be.

'I begged Peter to give you that job,' said Mthetho, 'and bought you suits so you wouldn't look like the Jackson Five and still you managed to create one disaster after another with that struggle mentality of yours. You have shot yourself in the foot time and again.'

'Awuleth'umshini wami, mfowethu, then we will see some real shooting,' said Monwabisi. 'And it won't be my foot I'll be hitting.' He closed his phone, yanked off his tie and threw it in the back seat. He might keep the car for a week. Maybe he could drive to East London and visit some of his old union comrades. He cranked up the music and drove to Mama Patty's. Once again he was flowing back into those tributaries that Ray Phiri sang about, that great river of pain was swallowing him up. The R1 000 Peter had deposited wouldn't buy a month's worth of medication.

○

Monwabisi waited until the following night to tell Constantia. By the time she got home, he'd finished cooking chicken and rice. He couldn't think of any other way to soften the blow. He hoped she wouldn't cry.

'I misjudged that American so-called freedom fighter,' he told her as he dished some rice onto her plate.

'Peter?'

'I've been retrenched.'

Constantia grabbed a chicken wing and munched it quietly.

'I knew it was too good to be true,' she said.

'It wasn't my fault,' he said. 'It was Henry Winston. You know how those Boers can be.'

'I know,' she said. 'They don't change.'

'I tried to play this game but I'm a worker. A worker is

not meant for suits and ties.' He thought she was going to cry but she ate in silence, taking very small bites and looking down at her plate as she chewed. She almost looked as if she didn't care.

'So what are you thinking?' he asked as she stood up to clear the plates.

'That happiness was not made for the Radebes,' she said. 'We were born to suffer.'

'We have overcome greater obstacles,' said Monwabisi, 'This job was nothing.'

'This job was everything,' she said. 'Our children's future. Your medication. Everything. Others are moving forward but the clock is turning backwards for us. We are lost.'

As she put the plates in the sink, he heard her praying under her breath. He thought she'd given up on this mandrax of the masses. Religion could be so debilitating. He'd wait until the next day to tell her he'd given back the car.

Chapter 29

'OUR LEADERS HAVE told us the ANC opposes cut-offs,' said Mrs Mehlo. 'So why have they brought us these cards we cannot use?' She yanked the card to her water meter from her bra and threw it on the floor.

Monwabisi hadn't been to a branch meeting in months. He didn't remember anything quite like this. His wife now sat at the front table with Jeff Ntoni. They'd added her to the branch exec as a 'member without portfolio'. She was recording her observations in a fat Filofax with daisies on the cover.

'I will leave the card here for the Mayor,' said Mrs Mehlo. 'It's of no use to me. Where will I find R3 000?'

'You must buy more tickets for Ithuba,' said Corleone. 'Water is only for those who win the lottery.'

Ntoni shouted for order.

'It is the council that needs to be called to order,' said Mrs Mehlo, 'not the people of Sivuyile.'

Before Ntoni could call on anyone else, Mrs Mehlo's neighbour Mama Bhurhu had struggled to her feet. 'I have something I want to read,' she said.

Monwabisi remembered her from the umgalelo. She seemed to be losing weight, though she still had plenty to spare. She read from a green paper. 'The municipality has the legal right to seize equivalent property of the signee in lieu of arrears,' she said.

She put the paper down. 'I'm not a lawyer or an Englishman,' she said, 'but others have told me this means the council can take my furniture if I fall behind in payments.'

Monwabisi had never heard about the repossession of furniture. So this was what that American was really about.

'The council is oppressing us!' shouted Slim. 'Soon we'll be selling the clothes off our back for a glass of water.'

Ntoni smashed his palm on the metal table to silence the chatter. Monwabisi was already getting a headache. 'Phantsi ngeprivatisation, phantsi!' shouted Slim.

Ntoni pounded his palm on the table again, but the clamour continued until Corleone began a song. The young man's voice cracked while the members tried to pick up the words.

'Iprivatisation asiyifuni,' sang Corleone, 'sifuna amanzi.'

Back in 1994, Monwabisi and the comrades used to sing 'uDe Klerk asimfuni, sifuna uMandela'. Lyrics, like politics, could change with time. To Slim and company, privatisation was the new De Klerk. They had a lot to learn.

'We don't want privatisation, we want water!' Slim shouted, as if somehow the leaders couldn't understand the words in the vernac.

Ntoni had given up trying to stop them. He and Constantia stared from the front table like parents waiting for a child to halt a temper tantrum.

Sandile Veki, the newly elected sergeant-at-arms, burst through the back door in a T-shirt with the famous picture of Che Guevara on the front. Veki fired one round through the roof from his .45. The singing stopped. Monwabisi ran toward Veki. He'd been attending meetings of the Movement for more than a decade and no one had ever fired a gun before. He never minded risking his life facing down the SADF in Katlehong, but gazing down the barrel of a .45 held by a comrade of the ANC was a new experience.

'We must respect our leaders!' Veki shouted to the quiet crowd.

'You must respect the masses,' shouted Monwabisi, stopping a few feet away from Veki. 'Put the gun away.'

Veki ignored Monwabisi and turned towards Ntoni, then slid his .45 into its holster. 'Comrade Chair, the floor is yours,' Veki said.

The Youth League leader's back was towards Monwabisi. Fist fighting wasn't the way of the workers' movement, but Monwabisi still wanted to klap Veki, knock some sense into him. Instead, the former shop steward went back to his seat and raised his hand to make a motion to discipline Veki. Ntoni ignored Monwabisi's hand.

'Phantsi ngabelungu abamnyama!' Slim shouted. Two people whispered a response.

Veki's eyes combed the crowd trying to discover who had let loose the slogan about 'black Europeans'.

'Com chair,' Monwabisi shouted, 'I request that the sergeant-at-arms take a seat. He is intimidating people.'

'I'm intimidating no one,' said Veki. 'Just maintaining the peace.'

'Let us not have personal quarrels,' said Ntoni. 'We have a meeting to conduct.'

'He must be disciplined,' Monwabisi said.

'I agree,' said Constantia softly. Ntoni pretended not to hear.

'Let us proceed,' said Ntoni. 'The first item on the agenda is the printing of posters for Freedom Day.'

'People have come about their water,' Monwabisi replied without raising his hand. 'The other items will wait.'

'I can agree to that,' said Ntoni, 'if we can conduct the discussion in an orderly manner. If people choose to ignore the chair again, they will be escorted from the room.'

'We will be happy to do the escorting, Com Chair,' said

Veki. 'Democracy and order go hand in hand.' He walked to the front of the room and took up a post to the right of the front table. When he crossed his arms, Corleone giggled.

'Am I clear?' asked Ntoni, looking directly at Slim.

'Yes, you are very clear, Com Chair,' said Constantia, 'but Comrade Veki must take a seat. We will call him if we need him.'

Ntoni asked Veki to find an empty chair. The youth leader put his hand on his .45, walked to the back of the hall and sat down.

'We want the Mayor,' said Mrs Mehlo. 'The great Fikile Siziba must come and speak to us.'

'He is a busy man,' said Ntoni.

'It's only a twenty-minute drive from Northridge to Sivuyile,' said Monwabisi.

'We hope he hasn't forgotten the way,' said Corleone.

'One more such outburst,' Ntoni told Corleone, 'and the sergeant-at-arms will remove you from the meeting.'

Veki looked around for his other comrades. Three of them huddled together near the back door, sharing a cigarette. The meeting finally agreed to Mrs Mehlo's proposal to invite the Mayor to their next meeting.

○

The Mayor arrived at the meeting a week later in a grey suit, no tie. Nompumelelo Mpupa welcomed him on behalf of the branch by draping a ribbon of ANC colours around his neck. Attached to the ribbon was what she called the 'key to the township', though actually Mrs Mehlo had found the key in the pocket of a pair of second-hand jeans from America.

Ntoni reminded everyone of Mayor Siziba's eight years on Robben Island and that no Mayor had ever made the journey to Sivuyile before.

'This is historic,' said Ntoni.

The theme of the Mayor's informal address was 'patience'.

'Rome was not built in a day,' he observed 'We must still iron out the kinks in the system. Every child experiences the pains of growing.'

Monwabisi had heard these words a hundred times before. The leaders of the ANC seemed to have become experts on the history of ancient Rome.

'We are tired of this talk about patience,' said Corleone.

The Mayor ignored the youngster and kept talking. Monwabisi raised his hand. The Mayor paused, then recognised the former shop steward.

'Comrade Mayor,' said Monwabisi, 'we need concrete answers. Hundreds of people in Sivuyile are without water. The prepaids are failing us. As a person who once promoted the system, I am heartbroken.'

Mrs Mehlo stood up and pulled the water card from her bosom just like she had at the previous meeting. She cast it across the floor like she was skimming a stone across a pond.

'The card is useless,' Mrs Mehlo said. 'At least in a dry river you can dig down and find enough water to fill half a bucket.'

A woman sitting behind Mrs Mehlo held up an empty baby bottle. 'Our children are thirsty,' she said.

Cleophas Nobatana leveraged himself to his feet with his cane.

'Sivuyile is ANC through and through,' the old man said. 'We have suffered at the hands of the Boers. Some of us met our children for the first time when we were still in prison. Yet in those days we paid Botha R10 for taps in our houses. For those with no taps, communal water was free. On a hot day, children used to splash in the mud there by the standpipe.'

Nobatana paused, then asked for a drink.

'A diabetic is always thirsty,' he said, 'but one day I won't

206

have money on my card and I will just have to suffer quietly.' Constantia filled a glass from the jug at the front table and brought it to Nobatana.

'Now we don't have to walk to the taps,' he said. 'We all have them. Or nearly all of us. We owe this to the new government. Yet some of the taps are not working. They are very beautiful but we are sending our daughters to the river again. This is a problem.'

Nobatana drank more water and waited for the Mayor's reply.

'We in government are facing many difficulties, many demands,' said the Mayor. 'We are doing our level best but sometimes we know it's not good enough.' He fingered the tiny key that hung around his neck. Monwabisi figured the Mayor would start talking about Rome again.

'Comrade Mayor,' said Nobatana, 'we are not asking for BMWs. Water is not a T-bone steak or even oxtail stew. Hayi. I remember when you first came to the Island, spouting Black Consciousness and saying that politics was about hating the white man. We schooled you on the Freedom Charter, comrade. You must not forget that Charter. "There shall be houses, security and comfort." How can we be comfortable without water? You must bring water to all the taps in Sivuyile. Do what you must do, but bring us water.'

As the old man sat down, his sunglasses slid to the end of his nose. He pushed them back into place and cleared his throat. Monwabisi was the first to clap hands. Then the rest of the meeting, including the Mayor, joined in the applause.

'Comrade Mayor,' said Ntoni once the crowd had settled, 'allow me to make an intervention. What most people are complaining about is not receiving the free lifeline of water with the meters, the sixty kilolitres promised by the RDP.'

'The lifeline,' said the Mayor, 'is a technical problem. I

can tend to that straight away. Just give me the details of the people affected.'

Constantia tore two blank sheets of paper from her black book, passed them around and asked people to write down their name and address.

'I will look into each and every case as soon as possible,' said the Mayor. 'By next week you will have a report.'

He looked briefly towards Constantia. 'We will constantly be in touch,' he said to her. She smiled back politely. Monwabisi hoped she wasn't falling for these politicians' tricks.

○

When branch meeting day came around the following week, the Mayor sent an apology, noting that he was in Pretoria with the Deputy Minister of Local Government, Susan Vickers.

The next week, an assistant to the Mayor, Martin Williams, arrived at Sivuyile to report that the his boss had 'stomach flu'. When Monwabisi asked about the list, the assistant said he didn't know anything but would check into it. Three days later the Mayor phoned Constantia at home. She was out so Monwabisi picked up the phone. The Mayor asked him to give Constantia the message that he was going to New Zealand for a study tour for ten days.

'We have a lot to learn from the Kiwis,' said the Mayor.

'I hope you'll find time to see some rugby there,' said Monwabisi.

'That you can be sure of,' said the Mayor. 'You know I used to be a prop for the Busy Bees in Cape Town. We looked up to the All Blacks, plus we loved their name.'

'And what should I tell my wife about our water?' Monwabisi asked. 'I want to learn their *haka*,' said the Mayor.

'The water, Comrade Mayor.'

'We'll be in touch on that matter,' said the Mayor. 'There

is so much to talk about and so little time. These days it seems I'm always rushing.'

'Freedom never rests,' replied Monwabisi, 'especially in New Zealand.'

The Mayor laughed and said he had another call coming through.

○

At the ANC meeting two nights later, Monwabisi explained that the Mayor was out of the country, that he had gone to learn the *haka*.

'How can the *haka* help us get our water?' asked Slim. 'I propose a march to the Mayor's house,' said Corleone. 'We can go for a swim in his pool.' A handful of people shouted in agreement, though no one launched into any songs. 'We have proper channels,' said Ntoni. 'We no longer have to go to the streets.'

'We must always go to the streets,' said Slim. 'Our power is there.'

Monwabisi argued that a demonstration at the Mayor's house was premature. 'We must meet with him first,' he said, 'and hear exactly what he has to say.'

Monwabisi knew Ntoni would go for this. The acting chair would support anything that kept the comrades off the streets. Monwabisi feared that a demonstration would provide fodder for the Mayor's cannon. Siziba would claim that no one had even consulted him before protesting, a damning criticism in the eyes of the leaders and the press.

The meeting agreed to send Monwabisi along with Nobatana, Ntoni and Constantia to speak with the Mayor. Monwabisi hoped they could bring Siziba to his senses before it was too late.

Chapter 30

MONWABISI'S HEADACHE HAD LASTED for three days. He was worried that he might have a brain tumour. He thought of going to the doctor, but that would cost money they didn't have. On the morning of day number four, with his head clear, he decided he'd cure himself with his own style of traditional therapy: long-distance running.

He used to feel so powerful at the end of a run, but he'd let all that strength seep away over the years. Running could give him the power to fight off anything. He couldn't justify draining half the family income for his little bottles of pills.

He went to the wardrobe and pulled out the black carry bag he'd gotten at the 1993 COSATU Congress, the days when an injury to one was still an injury to all. His red nylon shorts, New Balance cross trainers and Adidas tracksuit were all neatly folded inside. Putting them on felt like going to visit an old friend.

Musa and Fidel sat next to Monwabisi on the lounge floor as he began his warm-up routine. He grabbed his right foot, trying to bring his head down to his knee. He couldn't reach it. He used to be able to sit with his legs spread and touch his nose to the floor. He had a long way to go.

Musa stood up and pushed on his father's back, forcing Monwabisi's nose within a few centimetres of his knee.

'A little bit more,' his father said.

Musa threw his shoulder behind the push and something crunched in Monwabisi's spine.

'Take it easy on me, kwedini,' his father told the boy.

'You'll break me in half.'

Monwabisi moved to the front garden with his two boys in tow. He leaned against the facade of the house, stretching his calves. They'd never felt this stiff.

He started off with a slow jog. Musa stayed at his side for a few hundred metres. With his long, loping strides, the boy had potential. As Monwabisi doubled back towards the house, Musa dropped off.

Monwabisi stepped up the pace, felt his throat burning. When he ran in Joburg, the smog cut into his lungs. Sivuyile had clean air. This pain came from being unfit.

He caught Makana Boulevard, dodging the hooting taxis as he moved towards Market Square. He wanted to find Mrs Mehlo, but a string of buses from the terminus chased him onto the dirt side roads. Besides, dirt roads were easier on the knees.

Gliding down the street brought back memories of less complicated days, a time when he dreamed of trips to the famed races in Boston, London and Tokyo. For years he told his friends he would become the black Bruce Fordyce, the wispy little iron man who'd won the Comrades Marathon nine times. Monwabisi always joked that he'd be the first 'real comrade' to win the race. Those running days were also a time of romance. Long before Fidel and Musa were born, Constantia used to massage his legs after a training run. He'd never felt so relaxed. Her massages were a fingertip harbinger of the love to come.

As he cruised past Jeff Ntoni's house, the acting chairman asked if Monwabisi was 'running away from the ANC'.

'I'm just trying to become more long-winded,' Monwabisi answered, 'so I can keep up with the leaders.'

He wove his way to the ring road that circled Northridge and took off. He ran about fifteen minutes before he turned around. When he got within a few blocks of his house, he stopped to walk. His legs were flat. He was no threat to Fordyce's records, but he'd taken the first step.

Three weeks later, on May Day, Monwabisi ran his first race in thirteen years. Buttons from past campaigns dotted his vest: 'Fight for a Living Wage', 'Stop the LRA', 'No to VAT'. He was a mobile advert for the struggles of old.

He finished twenty-first out of 152 runners, sprinting past three fading high-schoolers in the last hundred metres. The best part was the kiss on the cheek from Constantia at the finish line.

'I'm back,' he told her. 'I'm cured. The medication has performed miracles.'

The next week, on payday, Constantia went through what had become the normal routine, cashing her cheque and giving Monwabisi what he needed for his medication. He stuffed the money into his sock. They always did it this way. He had a special arrangement. Mongezi, the chemist, lived in Sivuyile. He brought the pills home, then Monwabisi collected them from there – a way to keep anyone from finding out what medication he was buying.

Monwabisi told Constantia he'd stop at Mongezi's house during his training run and pick up the pills. He cruised past Mongezi's without stopping. He'd phone the chemist the next day and make up some story about how the doctor had changed the pharmaceutical cocktail.

The following morning Monwabisi carted his sweat-soaked money to Mr Koen, the stout manager at the local First National Bank. Koen was one of the few whites who'd jumped from the National Party. He was vice-chair of the Northridge ANC branch.

'Our branch is very busy,' said Koen. 'We are collecting books for the children of our members.'

'That's a wonderful idea,' said Monwabisi. 'I have a book or two I could contribute.' He had three copies of Marx's *Wages, Price and Profit*. He hoped they'd be interested but he'd worry about that later. He had his own economic issues to think about. He reached down and plucked the money out of his sock. 'I want to open an account,' he said.

'We would be proud to open an account for the person who has brought Water for Freedom to Ukusa,' said Koen. 'My branch members have told me how they now have taps on their property.' He took the still-damp notes from Monwabisi.

'This is our rainy-day money,' said Monwabisi.

'Seems like it's already been out in the rain,' Koen said.

Koen tried to talk Monwabisi into an investment account, promising him that 'emerging markets' would bring a very good return.

'I'm not an investor,' said Monwabisi. 'I just want a simple savings account.'

'ATM card or passbook?' Koen asked.

'A passbook will do,' said Monwabisi.

'An ATM card is much safer,' said Koen, 'and more convenient.'

'Passbooks have memories,' said Monwabisi. 'I still remember my mother stuffing hers inside her blouse when we travelled to the city.'

'The customer is always right,' said Koen.

Monwabisi's new green passbook came in a clear plastic sleeve. If his mother had a sleeve like that when he was growing up, her passbook wouldn't have looked like a twenty-year-old newspaper.

As he walked out of the bank, Monwabisi's mind raced with calculations. Three months without medication would give him a bank balance of more than R5 000. If he kept running, Constantia wouldn't notice a thing. At last they'd have money for a genuine rainy day. In South Africa one never knew when the rain might come.

After opening his account, Monwabisi returned home.

A new instalment of *Business Day* was waiting. Just as he sat down to read, Ntoni dropped by with a copy of a paper written by a 'Comrade Jit' from Mmabatho for the magazine of the South African Communist Party. The author claimed that people dying in Uganda, Zambia and South Africa were 'victims of poverty, not this incurable three letters'. Jit argued that poor nutrition, coupled with inadequate hygiene and water, made millions of Africans susceptible to diseases virtually extinct in the West.

'Conditions like TB and smallpox have become pandemic in parts of Africa,' the article added. 'Often these are wrongly diagnosed as Aids. In fact there may be no virus at all.'

The argument made sense to Monwabisi. No one ever really died from Aids anyway. They passed away from infections that took over when the immune system became weak. What could make an immune system weaker than lack of proper food and water?

'Aids is part of an imperialist conspiracy,' said Ntoni. 'A grand plan of genocide against the African people.'

Ntoni's words heartened Monwabisi. Comrade Jit had helped him see Aids in the bigger picture. The only mystery was why those R1 700 pills made him feel so much better. Maybe it was all in his head. Imperialism affected the mind of the oppressed in many ways. For the moment he was testing Comrade Jit's theories in practice. Monwabisi could feel the strength returning to his legs with each day's run. And the burning in his throat and lungs was disappearing. He would drive that virus into the ground and bring his family out of debt with a systematic training programme like he used to follow in his shop-steward days. It would be a blow against imperialism.

Chapter 31

CONSTANTIA WAS IMPRESSED. The Mayor's staff had covered the round oak table in his office with a linen tablecloth and a white tea service bearing the shield of the old Northridge Municipality. He didn't even do that when he met the councillors. Silver platters overflowed with crème donuts, vetkoek and slices of Madeira cake with half cherries inside. This meeting with the Sivuyile branch delegation was serious business.

The Mayor apologised for the Northridge shield on the cups and saucers. 'We have ordered the new china but there is a delay,' the Mayor told them. 'A signature was missing from the purchase order. It has been rectified.'

Nobatana said he once had a dream on the Island in which someone placed a plate holding a dozen crème donuts in front of him. 'That dream has almost come true today,' he said. 'The platter there holds eleven. My doctor will not be happy.' The old man put three of the donuts on his plate and sat down on the sofa with the others.

'We are following the national framework,' the Mayor said. 'We must provide lifelines, but those with debts must pay. Otherwise, there is no money for development.'

The Mayor paused to refill his tea, pulling out a small plastic bottle of NutraSweet from his coat pocket and adding three of the tiny pills to his cup. 'BP,' said the Mayor. 'Better to take away the sugar from my tea than the Johnnie Walker from my weekends.'

'You must watch your pressure, Comrade Mayor,' said Nobatana as he licked some crème from his fingers.

Constantia reminded the Mayor that forgiveness of past debts was part of the ANC's election platform.

'Non-payment was a political act,' added Monwabisi, 'essential to the collapse of the Boers.' Constantia reached for a piece of Madeira cake as her husband spoke. A little sugar seemed to calm her fears, though she was worried about her weight. She'd never been concerned about gaining a few kgs before, but she couldn't afford to buy a new wardrobe just to accommodate a growing waistline.

'Times are different now,' said the Mayor. 'We didn't understand certain things when we weren't in power. National tells us we must practise fiscal discipline. It is out of our hands.'

'Practise what?' asked Nobatana. 'Physical discipline? We had enough of that on the Island. All those years of breaking up stones.' The old man sized up the three donuts on his plate and finally grabbed the one with the most crème.

'No, comrade,' said the Mayor. 'Fiscal. It means we must spend our money more carefully.'

'Common sense,' said Nobatana. 'Why does it need a confusing name? If we were as good at bringing water to people as we are at inventing new words, we wouldn't need this meeting.'

Constantia bit into one of the cherries in the Madeira cake. She sucked on it for a moment. She loved the syrupy flavour.

'Fiscal discipline is part of GEAR,' said Monwabisi. 'The World Bank doesn't want government to spend too much on the people. That way they can lower taxes for the rich.'

Constantia could feel her husband getting ready for one of his tirades. The Mayor would have no patience for such talk. He liked to call it 'excessive verbiage'.

'The crème on this one is a little bit sour, Comrade Mayor,' said Nobatana. 'A crème donut is not amasi.' He wiped his fingers on a serviette, then licked the crème off the paper.

'The baker is a holdover from the days of the whites,' said the Mayor. 'We'll do better next time.' He wrote something in a small notebook, then went back to his tea.

'If the government doesn't pay off what Botha borrowed,' said Ntoni, 'the Western countries will strangle us, just like what they did to the apartheid regime.'

'The capitalists want their money,' said Monwabisi, 'even if it was used to pay the salaries of the troops that occupied our townships.'

'We can't afford to once again become a pariah among nations,' said Constantia. She rose to get the teapot and refill the cups.

'Please, Lord,' she thought as she filled Nobatana's cup, 'don't let my husband make one of those long speeches in the Mayor's office.'

'We are here about water,' said the Mayor. 'Let us stick to the agenda.'

'I agree,' said Monwabisi, 'but I want to remind Comrade Ntoni that sometimes our leaders are a little too quick to agree to the demands of the West.'

Constantia kept circulating with the tea, trying to ignore her husband's words. Surely someone would silence him before he humiliated their delegation. 'Water,' she said. 'Let us talk about water as Comrade Mayor has asked.'

'It's all connected,' said Monwabisi. He held up his cup to indicate he wanted more tea. 'You have missed me,' he said.

'Shame,' she said and moved slowly towards his seat to pour the refill.

'Actually,' said the Mayor, 'I have found a solution. We can exempt people by order of council. We will need to do it on a monthly basis.'

One of his aides had told him there was a process by which people could be declared 'indigent' – unable to pay.

'It's from the days of the Boers,' added the Mayor. 'To become indigent a family must fill out some forms plus submit a statement of income or show they are unemployed or pensioners.'

'We have illiterate people in our community,' said Constantia, 'especially among the elderly.' She put the teapot down and went back to her chair. Sometimes the Mayor's solutions weren't really solutions at all. Not everyone who spent time on Robben Island was a Madiba.

'We don't need a bureaucratic solution,' said Monwabisi. 'What of the people who just sell mealies or do piece jobs?'

'A letter from a pastor or social worker will do as proof of unemployment,' said the Mayor. 'We are prepared to be flexible.' The Mayor told his secretary through the intercom that he wanted the boxes delivered.

A minute later a messenger in a beige uniform brought two boxes of yellow indigent forms and set them next to the half-empty platter of donuts. The Mayor gave a form to each of his visitors.

'As easy as eating pap,' said the Mayor.

Monwabisi began to read the form. 'Why must the council know the birthdates of the applicant's parents?' he asked.

'We can waive certain non-essential information,' said the Mayor. 'We need only basic details.'

'We will make it work,' said Constantia. 'Our people need water.'

'It says "Republic of Ciskei Form 366A" at the top of each page,' said Monwabisi.

'I told you the forms were old,' said the Mayor, 'but they will do. Just like the teacups. They say Northridge but they still hold tea.'

'No need to reinvent the wheel,' said Ntoni.

Monwabisi laid his copy of the form down on the table and reached for a piece of cake. 'It's time to go,' he said.

'I agree,' said Nobatana, taking a last look at the three remaining donuts.

'We can get you a bag,' the Mayor told the old man.

'Maybe better to leave them,' said Nobatana. 'I must watch my blood sugar. My doctor will scold me until the cows come home.'

The Mayor winked at Nobatana as he called his secretary on the intercom again and asked her to bring a bag for takeaways.

'I'm counting on you to see that the paperwork is done properly,' said the Mayor, turning towards Constantia. 'I wish there was an easier way, comrades, but there isn't. We have to follow procedures.'

Constantia picked up one box of the forms and put it on her head. She asked Monwabisi to take the other one.

'I won't dirty my hands with the paperwork of the Boers,' he said. 'Let me carry the old man's donuts.'

'I hope you're not planning another demonstration,' said Constantia. 'We've had enough of those for awhile. It's time to roll up our sleeves.'

Monwabisi unbuttoned his shirt sleeves and began to roll them up. 'Now what?' he asked.

'Roll them back down,' she said, 'and stop mocking me.' The Mayor told the messenger to carry the other box of forms.

While Nobatana stopped to make sure they hadn't left the donuts behind, Monwabisi raced off towards the car park. Constantia figured he was already thinking of slogans for the next march on the municipal offices. He had a one-track mind.

Chapter 32

MONWABISI DECIDED TO WALK to the market and find out if they'd turned on Mrs Mehlo's water. Before he made it to her stall, Oupa and his friend Mzi intercepted him. Monwabisi readied himself for some disparaging comments. The last time they'd seen him he was driving the A4 and wearing his navy blue suit. Walking through the dusty township streets in his ten-year-old Batas with the wind whipping in his face carved a different image.

'Comrade RDP,' said Mzi, 'we are asking for a favour.'

'A big one,' said Oupa. The two boys were wearing matching tracksuits, shiny enough to be brand new. Mrs Mehlo must have gotten in a new shipment from overseas.

'You two are looking so smart,' said Monwabisi. A dust cloud rushed past the trio. Monwabisi wiped some dirt from his eyes and led the two boys behind a bus waiting to take people to Umtata. When the wind blew in Sivuyile, any shelter would do.

'I have had some luck,' said Mzi.

Monwabisi wondered what kind of luck could strike these two aimless school leavers.

'He has won the lottery,' said Oupa. 'Two big ones.'

'Two hundred rand?' asked Monwabisi.

'Two grand,' said Mzi. 'We want to throw a party.'

'Why not save some for a rainy day?' asked Monwabisi.

'A small party,' said Oupa.

Mzi explained that his mother had agreed to the party at their house but that they must find a responsible adult to act as security. His mother said she couldn't stand loud music or any of the other nonsense that might come with a party. And she didn't want any strangers sleeping in the house. Everyone had to be gone by morning.

'So Comrade RDP,' said Mzi, 'we are asking you to be our security guard. All the beer you can drink and plenty of meat.'

'I don't take beer any more,' said Monwabisi. 'It's bad for my stomach.'

'Okay, all the Fanta you can drink,' said Mzi.

After a few minutes, Monwabisi agreed. It would be a chance to see what the lighties were thinking, though he wasn't sure he wanted to know.

O

Monwabisi felt like a grandfather as TKZee blasted from the boom box in Mzi's lounge. All he could think of was sleep. Three bottles of Fanta lay empty by his feet on the floor. The party was winding down. A few people were still dancing.

It had been a remarkably calm affair – only Oupa had lost control. At one point he'd threatened to rattle another boy's teeth but Monwabisi intervened. Then Oupa passed out on the floor for a couple of hours. Now he was getting his second wind.

Mzi brought another Fanta, but Monwabisi refused. 'A man can only take so much orange,' he said.

'Maybe you should escort Oupa home,' said Mzi, 'before he checks out again.'

Monwabisi agreed and began a campaign to convince Oupa it was time to go. After a few minutes Oupa gave in to Monwabisi's urgings and tucked five beers in a neat row inside his belt.

'Five for the road,' said Oupa, patting the tins of Amstel. 'Masihambe,' said Monwabisi.

As he and Oupa went out the door, Brenda Fassie came on the box with 'Vul'indlela'. Oupa howled the refrain as Monwabisi guided him to the street. Monwabisi's warning that the tsotsis of Sivuyile were becoming more like Mdantsane's every day did nothing to silence the youngster's singing.

The sound of the young man opening the first Amstel added the background music to his off-key repeat of that Vul'indlela chorus. At the age of twenty-one, he had the slurred singing voice of a shebeen veteran.

Half a block from Mzi's, Monwabisi finally got him to quiet down.

'Forward to Mama Patty's, forward,' said Oupa, staggering towards the shebeen. Monwabisi grabbed him by the arm and redirected him homeward.

Oupa went back to his Brenda Fassie tune again, then paused for reflection. 'One day my mother will sing this song about me,' he told Monwabisi. 'She thinks I'm a loafer. I am a loafer but I'll succeed in life, mfowethu. You'll see. I'll have a beautiful wife and a house in the suburbs.'

After a few minutes they arrived at the Mehlos' house.

'We must have a nightcap, mfo,' said Oupa.

'All right,' said Monwabisi, 'but just one.' He wanted to make sure Oupa didn't rush off to Mama Patty's as soon as he lost his escort.

'I knew you hadn't joined the bourgeoisie,' said Oupa.

Monwabisi just smiled. He hadn't been up this late since his days as a young shop steward. He had staying power then. During those factory occupations they used to sing songs and debate politics all night. They called them siyalalas, or sleep-ins, but it was the wrong name. No one ever slept.

Monwabisi got into the lounge. He thought about lying

down on the sofa, but he didn't dare. Imagine if Mrs Mehlo found him asleep there in the morning. His hand knocked a doily onto the floor as he sat down in a green armchair. He picked it up and carefully draped it over the back cushion.

Oupa switched on Channel O.

'Ah, kwassa-kwassa,' said Oupa, trying to imitate the movements of Kanda Bongo Man. The singer was paired off with one of his backup girls.

'Can you kwassa-kwassa, bhuti?' Oupa asked.

Monwabisi didn't reply. The young man tossed him one of the beers from his belt.

'I can't drink alone,' Oupa said. He lit a cigarette and walked into the kitchen, then came back carrying a shoebox full of papers and photos.

'I want to show you something,' he said. He rummaged through a stack of yellowed black-and-white photos.

'Let me see that one,' said Monwabisi. He'd caught a glimpse of Mrs Mehlo's wedding picture. She wore a flowing white gown with a veil. She looked almost like Miriam Makeba as a young woman. So beautiful. Age wasn't kind to the working class. He set the photo on the coffee table as Oupa handed him several others.

'This is my grandmother,' said Oupa, pointing to a much thinner version of Mrs Mehlo. 'She came from Lesotho.' The young man set the photo on the floor, then kept rummaging through the box.

Monwabisi checked the time. Three thirty. If Oupa started telling family stories, going through these photos could take hours. Constantia would be getting all kinds of ideas by now. He took a healthy sip from the beer.

'Nkosi yam,' said Oupa, looking up from the photos at the TV. 'That's Angelique Kidjo. She's a goddess, bhuti. Even without hair.'

Angelique sang about giving out the water while Oupa started to work on beer number three and the last of his Barclay's.

'You need some coffee,' said Monwabisi.

'Beer is the only drink that mixes with kwassa-kwassa,' Oupa replied.

Monwabisi took one last look at Mrs Mehlo's wedding photo. She really was beautiful back then. It was time to leave. He bid his farewell to Oupa, declining the offer of the last Amstel.

Monwabisi decided to run home. The cool night air against his face washed away the effect of the beer. When he was in the union he used to drink a whole crate and still go to work the next day. Now a single can went straight to his head. He picked up his stride, passing a pair of lovers locked in deep passion at the taxi rank. The wind dried the sweat on Monwabisi's forehead as he found his running rhythm. He forgot about the late-night dangers like tsotsis and drunken drivers. He'd read an article in an American magazine that talked about getting into the 'zone'. He was sure he'd found that place. It all felt so good he took a detour. Another kilometre or two wouldn't hurt.

Near the market a pack of dogs charged after him. He pulled to a stop and shouted 'Voetsek!' The hounds froze, then slowly beat a retreat.

For the rest of the way home he was in full stride. He pictured a row of fading runners in front of him and stepped up his pace to reach that imaginary finish line.

When he turned the corner into his street, he could see a light was still on in their house. These days his wife usually fell asleep on the couch with some big report lying next to her. At least he couldn't be jealous of a report.

Constantia was putting on a dress while she talked to someone on speaker phone.

'I'm coming,' she said. 'I'm ringing the fire fighters straight away.' She closed the phone and hurriedly put on her jacket.

'There's a fire at the Mehlos' place,' she said. 'That was one of their neighbours on the phone.'

'I was just there,' said Monwabisi. 'There's no fire. I left Oupa dancing to kwassa-kwassa.'

'They say he fell asleep,' said Constantia. 'Mama Mehlo rang the fire fighters, no one picked up.'

'So why are they phoning here?'

'A councillor must take care of everything, even fires.'

Constantia got the fire chief on her cell. He promised her his men would be there within fifteen minutes. The sweat from Monwabisi's run hadn't even dried and here he was rushing through the night again. After a few metres, Constantia started panting. He tried to explain how she must pace herself but she ignored him. This wasn't just about the fire. She was proving that a councillor cared about her constituency even in the middle of the night. Her panting turned to agonising wheezes but she kept on until the fire came into view.

They found Oupa sitting in the dirt across the street from his house, tears streaming down his face. Bolts of flame shot into the sky from the burning residence.

'There is no water,' said Oupa. 'The card is dry.' The shoebox full of pictures rested next to him on the ground. Monwabisi saw a photo of a very young Oupa on top of the pile. His front teeth hadn't even grown in yet.

Mrs Mehlo came walking quickly up the street balancing a white plastic bucket on her head. Two young girls carrying jerrycans trotted right behind her. They all emptied their containers onto the blazing house. A bit of the flame calmed for a few seconds, then shot back into the air. Three other women came with buckets of water. Their efforts brought the same result. They were attacking an elephant with a slingshot.

Mr Ximiya, the Mehlos' neighbour, yanked his hosepipe out of his yard and tried to make it stretch far enough to reach the blaze. The water from the nozzle shot up in the air and landed in a puddle several metres short of the flames.

'I need another hosepipe, people!' he shouted. 'Khawulezani.'

With sirens sounding in the distance, Mrs Mehlo charged towards Monwabisi. As she drew near, she lunged, grabbing him around the throat. He pulled her hands off him.

'Because of you I've lost everything!' she screamed. 'Only Mama Ximiya has extra water. Others are dry.'

She clapped Monwabisi in the chest. Another blow caught him across the cheek. Monwabisi stepped back and gently blocked Mrs Mehlo's flailing arms. He'd allowed himself to be carried away by R4000, a car and some new suits. He should have seen that the prepaids would lead to this. But Mthetho and Peter never spoke of cut-offs or fires at the London Towers.

'Thixo ongunaphakade, bawo wasezulwini!' Mrs Mehlo screamed as she fell to the ground. 'Eternal God, our heavenly father, we bless thy holy name.'

Mrs Mehlo's entreaties faded to a whisper once the fire truck turned the corner. The flashing lights brought a red glimmer to the tiny windows of the nearby houses.

Constantia moved the people away from the front garden to make space for the fire truck. The force of the water conquered the flames while it spread the family's possessions across the burnt-out dirt. A melted enamel bowl full of blackened umngqusho skidded into what used to be the back garden. Within minutes the plot had been reduced to a lake of ash and scalded memorabilia of a once proud family.

Constantia, Monwabisi and a few neighbours stayed with the Mehlos until dawn, helping them sift through the remains.

Just after sunrise Mrs Mehlo apologised to Monwabisi, assuring him she knew he wasn't really to blame. He shrugged off her apology.

'We are thinking only of you and your family,' he said. He could still feel the sting of that clap to the chest, those rough hands gripping his neck. No one from the working class had ever assaulted him before.

'I just lost my senses,' she said, 'wanting to blame someone.'

'It's time now for you to rest, mama,' Monwabisi replied.

'At least I haven't lost my inventory,' she said. 'I store my clothes at Mama Patty's. I pay her R10 a month.'

'You are fortunate, mama,' said Monwabisi.

Mrs Mehlo went back to the shoebox. She flipped through the birth certificates and a few photos of Oupa when he was in school.

'My wedding picture is gone,' she said, 'and the last photo of my mother.'

At the bottom was the yellow indigent form Constantia had given her to fill out. She tore it to shreds, threw the pieces down and ground them into the ashes of her house with her foot.

'Never again will I fall for politicians' tricks,' she said. She put everything back in the box and wrapped a rubber band around the outside to keep the top on.

'I warned that boy about drinking,' she told Monwabisi, 'so many times. But youngsters today don't listen to elders. They think we are silly old fools.'

Mrs Mehlo and Monwabisi picked through the remains of the house one more time, managing to salvage a few pieces of cutlery and some pots. One metal bed frame could probably be scrubbed clean.

'Children these days have too much freedom,' said Mrs Mehlo.

She knelt in the ashes of her bedroom. 'Let the Lord work in his mysterious ways,' she said. 'Praise God maybe umntwana wam' will learn from this, will grow up now. At least we are alive. Praise the Lord.'

'It's not the boy's fault,' said Monwabisi. 'In the old days we had hosepipes. We would have put it out with water from your tap.'

'Children these days,' said Mrs Mehlo. 'I just don't understand them. Too much freedom is a dangerous thing.'

Chapter 33

Two days after the fire Monwabisi was looking for Mrs Mehlo at the market. Before he got to her stall he ran into Slim and Corleone. They were handing out leaflets.

'Comrade Monwabisi, check what our printing press has done,' said Slim. He handed Monwabisi one of the green leaflets. Splotches of black ink surrounded the hand-scribbled heading: 'Government has Abandoned the RDP: Houses Burning in Sivuyile'.

'It's an old Gestetner, bhuti,' said Slim. 'A church was throwing it away.'

A man in blue overalls walked past. When Slim offered him a leaflet he raised his hand in refusal.

'People still don't see how the ANC has sold them,' said Slim.

'Maybe they are busy with other things,' said Monwabisi.

'What can be more important than the council selling our water to the imperialists?'

'Putting food on the table, getting to work, taking a sick child to hospital,' said Monwabisi. 'Maybe even buying a lottery ticket.'

'We've got a plan to help you, mama,' said Slim. 'The council has sold our water to the imperialists. Ngabathengisi, mama.' He handed a leaflet to a woman carrying a can of baked beans on her head. She looked at the heading and after three steps dropped the paper on the ground.

'You see,' said Slim, 'people are growing complacent.'

'Your time will come,' said Monwabisi. 'You must remain patient.'

Monwabisi found Mrs Mehlo holding up a yellow dress shirt for two older women to inspect.

'It's an Arrow, mama,' said Mrs Mehlo. 'The best from America. Just R10. Those thieves in the shops will charge you a hundred.'

One of the women fingered the sleeve. 'There is a spot,' she said.

Mrs Mehlo glanced at it briefly. 'It will wash out, mama,' she said. 'Besides, if he wears a jersey or a jacket, who will ever notice?'

The woman offered Mrs Mehlo eight rands.

Mrs Mehlo said she'd rather cut the shirt up with a pair of scissors than sell it for eight rands. They agreed on nine. As the woman carried her shirt off in a yellow Checkers bag, Monwabisi approached Mrs Mehlo.

'Nine rands is too cheap,' she told Monwabisi, 'but what can I do? At least the branch has given me money. I am grateful.' She looked around, then pulled a roll of notes from inside her sock. 'R360,' she said, 'collected by Comrade Jeff and some others. The exec has sent a resolution to the Mayor, asking for help in finding us alternative accommodation.'

'Let us hope for the best,' said Monwabisi. 'If there is anything you need, mama...'

'We are staying with my sister for the moment,' she said. 'We are fine. Mrs Ximiya is keeping the tsotsis away from the remains of our house. There are jackals in the township these days.'

'I need a pair of trousers, mama,' said Monwabisi. 'Eighty-four extra long.'

Mrs Mehlo found three pairs in Monwabisi's size. He bought a pair of brown corduroys for R15 and some grey polyester slacks that looked like they should be part of a school uniform. He didn't try to bargain. She put the trousers in another yellow plastic bag.

Monwabisi sauntered back towards Slim and Corleone. As the two youngsters came into view, a taxi stopped near them. Sandile Veki and two of his comrades stepped out. As always, the .45 was tucked into Sandile's belt for everyone to see.

The three surrounded Slim and Corleone.

'Yintoni le?' Monwabisi heard Veki cry out. 'What in the hell is this?'

'The government has abandoned the RDP,' said Slim. 'It's the truth.'

Veki slapped the leaflets out of Slim's hand onto the dirt. 'This is ANC territory,' he said. 'Don't come here again with your rubbish.'

'I am exercising my democratic right,' said Slim.

'We will exercise our democratic right to silence you if you come back,' said Veki. He pushed Slim in the chest, knocking him backwards into a table where a woman was selling tomatoes.

'Watch what you're doing, kwedini!' shouted the woman. 'I have my business here.'

Veki apologised to the vegetable seller. 'We will have him out of your way in a few seconds,' he said. 'You don't want his preaching around here.'

'Enkosi,' said the woman as she inspected the plastic bags of tomatoes that had fallen to the ground.

'We have the right to preach wherever we want,' said Corleone. 'You and your troops in the township won't stop us.'

Sandile strode towards Corleone and kicked him in the kneecap. One of Veki's partners followed up with a fist to the back of Corleone's neck. Slim's partner toppled to the ground, landing on the pile of the green leaflets mourning the abandonment of the RDP.

'These tomatoes are split open,' the vegetable seller said to Veki. She showed him a hole in the bag. Some flesh from the tomato dripped onto the ground.

'Pay the woman for the tomatoes,' Veki told Slim.

'You pushed me, you pay,' said Slim.

Monwabisi caught Slim from behind as he started to charge Veki. The Youth League leader's two comrades had moved in front of him and raised their hands in combat position.

'Pay the woman,' said Veki.

'Never,' said Slim.

'How much are the tomatoes, mama?' asked Monwabisi.

'Two rand.'

Monwabisi released Slim and gave two rands to the woman.

'Time to go,' said Monwabisi.

'I still have more leaflets to hand out,' said Slim. As a woman and her young child passed by, Slim shouted, 'The government has abandoned the RDP! We must defeat them!'

Monwabisi took the leaflets from Slim's hand.

'For today, ziphelile,' he said. 'Tomorrow is another day.'

Veki kept an eye on Monwabisi and Slim as they walked past Mrs Mehlo's stall and stood at the window of Jimmy's Chicken Shack to buy a soda. The smell of wings on Jimmy's braai tempted Monwabisi. He hadn't eaten meat since those dinners at the London Towers. A young woman in a very short denim skirt kept the wings moving on the grill.

'We will have our revenge,' said Slim. 'Comrade Peanut is going to save this community.'

'How can a peanut save a community?' Monwabisi asked.

'He's a plumber. He's going to show us how to reconnect

people's water. We will do it at night, when no one is watching. He has all the tools.'

'In the township someone is always watching,' said Monwabisi.

He paid the young girl three rands for five wings. He took one and gave the others to Slim and Corleone. The young comrades devoured the chicken in less time than it took to say 'the government has abandoned the RDP'.

○

When Constantia arrived home from work that evening, Monwabisi told her how Sandile and the others had beaten Slim and Corleone. 'The Youth League are acting like thugs as usual,' he said.

'uSandile, he is a problem,' she said. She set her bag down on the sofa, then flopped into an armchair. 'We are falling behind again,' she said.

'What can we do with this Sandile?' said Monwabisi. 'Apparently he is a relative of Ntoni.'

'You didn't hear me,' said Constantia. 'We are falling behind. Everything is high these days. There are uniforms, books. Food has become unbearable.'

She bowed her head, examining her fingernails. 'Look,' she said, showing him the chips on the varnish. 'I can't even afford to do my nails once a month.'

Monwabisi looked away. He remembered when she didn't worry about such things, when she wore doeks and smocks. She had proletarian beauty then. Now it was about make-up and appointments at the hair salon.

'So this unemployed loafer of a husband of yours is embarrassing you?' he said.

'No one ever said you were a loafer,' she said.

'Look at you,' he said, 'worrying about your nails when

people's water is being cut. There is a class struggle out there.'

He glanced at the *Cosmo* magazine on the coffee table. It had a teaser on the cover: 'What Men Really Want: Five Bedroom Secrets.' Constantia couldn't have been reading that to uncover the desires of her HIV-positive husband. The Radebes' bedroom no longer held any secrets at all, or surprises. Once in a while when Monwabisi rolled over his foot might brush against Constantia's bare leg. That was about as far as it went.

He looked again at his wife. 'But a man who can't support his family is a loafer, andithi?' he said.

She didn't reply but he knew what she was thinking. He was an embarrassment to her. The whole situation was the fault of the bosses. If they'd never sacked him, all of this wouldn't have happened. In those Joburg days he could live for the class struggle, fight for the workers. That wasn't enough for her any more. He was so proud to have a son named after his greatest hero: Fidel Castro. Now he was afraid the bourgeois ideas of his wife would infect his sons. She once talked of a house in Houghton-by-the-Sea. Monwabisi Radebe would stay in Sivuyile until the day he died.

'Answer me. I'm a loafer, isn't it?' he said.

'You're missing the point, mhlobo wam',' she said. 'No one is pointing fingers here.'

'You think I don't want to work?' he asked. 'I'm pure proletarian.' He never thought he'd have to explain this to his wife, this issue of the working class. Even in the darkest days he always knew the working class would triumph in the end. That's what he and his comrades dreamed of in those siyalalas. Now his wife was moving to the other side. One of his favourite slogans was 'Victory is certain'. It brought confidence to the working class. Now nothing was certain. Nothing at all.

'You're too stubborn,' said Constantia. She reached out for a hug. It had been a long time.

'Because I don't fall for the tricks of the bourgeoisie,' he said, 'you call me stubborn?'

'You don't want to listen. This is not about bourgeoisie or working class. It's about our children. Their future.'

He felt a little better. She never held him any more. Maybe that was the problem. And she was too soft in the heart. A political leader had to be strong to stand up to the bosses and their stooges.

'I will never get a job,' he said. 'Not a proper one. I'm blacklisted. There is no alternative.'

'There is always an alternative,' she said. 'What about that business of yours?'

'No one is interested in paying for welding,' he said. 'They are all asking for credit.'

'What about other businesses?' she said. 'There are many things you could do.'

'So you want me to push a wheelbarrow around the townships, carrying jerrycans for fifty cents a trip?'

'I never said that.'

'I could join the strandlopers and scavenge the beach for little bits of fish.'

'Stop it.'

A metalworker didn't become a 'yes, baas' waiter in a hotel either. Especially not a former chairperson of the Witwatersrand Shop Stewards' Council. They had the bosses on the run when he was the chair. Now there was nothing but retreat. Retrenchment packages, downsizing, outsourcing. Everything was squeezing the working class. The few new labour laws hadn't helped much.

The previous May Day the Minister of Labour urged workers to tone down their wage demands to keep South Africa 'competitive'. As if when the companies earned more profits the money ended up in the pockets of the workers. These days the bosses took their profits overseas.

He had to teach all this to Musa and Fidel. There was more to manhood than going to the bush. A revolutionary son had to be initiated into the ideas and practice of the working class.

'You'll promise me, then,' she said, 'that you'll look a little harder. Leave some of that politics until we get back on our feet. First things first.'

'The working class comes first,' he said.

'Stop it,' she replied, playfully digging a finger in between his ribs. He giggled just like a little boy. Constantia knew exactly where all his weak spots were.

Chapter 34

'I SUPPORT THE IDEA,' SAID Councillor Fakude, 'but better to treat it as a roll-on.' Councillor Phakhathi, standing in the doorway, laughed a little too loud and made a motion like he was applying Shield to his underarm. 'We don't need to pass a resolution,' added Fakude as he slid his chair backwards and put his feet up on his desk next to a pile of unopened letters.

Constantia didn't appreciate Fakude's terminology or Phakhathi's sympathetic laughs. Though his wife was a school principal, Fakude had several of those secret girlfriends that township men called 'roll-ons', including a secretary at the municipal offices. He said it was part of African tradition.

'I have a better idea,' said Phakhathi. 'Print leaflets explaining how the system works in isiXhosa. The unemployed youth will distribute. We can pay them R20 a day. Job creation.'

'Once the people understand the system,' said Fakude, 'there won't be a problem. They will pay. This is all new to them. A few agitators are stirring the pot.' He took his feet off the desk and started to look through the pile of letters. He threw the first three in the bin without even opening them. 'A councillor gets too much junk mail,' he said as he tossed two more envelopes away.

Constantia was exhausted. Fidel had an ear infection and she'd been up most of the night.

'It's not a question of information,' she said. 'We can't

cut off people's water. Not even Gqozo used to do that.'

Fakude put down the stack of letters and flipped through his worn-out Filofax. A tattered receipt from Edgars fell out onto the floor. He didn't bother picking it up. 'I can't find that bloody phone number,' he said.

'No one will confuse us with Gqozo,' said Phakhathi. 'He was just a puppet of the Boers.'

'A thirsty person quickly forgets the water you gave her yesterday when you refuse her today,' Constantia said.

'You're talking like a feminist now,' said Fakude, looking up for a second. 'Ah, there's the number.' He reached for the phone, holding the Filofax open with his other hand.

'We need a grace period of half a year,' said Constantia. 'It will give us time to straighten things out with national. We can set up a better plan for the indigent. Something long term.'

Constantia handed the two councillors a copy of the resolution she'd written to suspend all water cut-offs for six months. She'd never written a resolution before. She hadn't even asked Monwabisi for help.

'Engaged,' said Fakude putting down the receiver. The two men looked at the paper for a long time.

'It's just a draft,' she said. 'We can make amendments.'

'We must run it past the Deputy Minister,' said Fakude. 'We can't afford to alienate leadership.'

'We can't afford to alienate the community,' said Constantia. 'There is lots of talk about sell-out councillors.'

'Talk is cheap,' said Fakude. He started hunting in his Filofax for another phone number.

'You should load them into your cell,' said Phakhathi. 'Filofaxes are from yesterday.'

'Where there is smoke, there is fire,' replied Constantia. She took the paper back from Fakude. 'I'll make copies for you,' she said. 'I must go and chat with the Boers on the same issue.'

'I still favour the roll-on approach,' said Fakude as Constantia stood up to leave.

'I get the point,' she said. She headed down the hallway to Koosman's office. He and Councillor Kelly were enjoying koeksisters with their coffee. She slid the draft resolution in front of them.

'This has nothing to do with our constituencies,' said Kelly.

'Cost recovery is the policy of national government,' said Koosman. 'We wouldn't want to go against the policy of our people's government, would we, Councillor Radebe?'

The two displayed matching smirks. Constantia took back the paper. Nothing got her heartburn going like Boers who pretended they never voted for Botha or Vorster. She left the two white councillors and walked down the hallway to meet with Van Huis about a car loan. The voice of a young man talking through a bullhorn wafted through a hallway window. Slim Yanta.

'Our leaders must hear us like they used to before they boarded this gravy train,' he screeched.

Constantia paused to look. A crowd of a dozen people had gathered in front of the building. Three security guards had gone outside to handle the situation. 'As much as we admire this madala we have for president,' said the young man, 'he may be getting too old to think clearly.'

Her heartburn was really going now. Who was this lightie Slim Yanta to be calling Madiba an old man? What had this youngster ever done for freedom in South Africa besides make a lot of useless noise? Constantia smiled as people walked past the youth and his cohort in the same way they would pass a vendor selling rotten tomatoes. No one was interested in their politics.

A man in a suit stopped in front of Slim.

'Why should I work and pay taxes so some loafers can

climb on my back?' the man asked. He walked away before Slim had a chance to answer.

'Some of our community still have very reactionary ideas,' Constantia heard Slim tell a young woman standing next to him. He got back on the bullhorn.

'There is only one councillor who serves the people,' he said. 'Councillor Radebe. She is at least trying. She is the one who works for the indigent. That's what they now like to call us. Not long ago we were comrades, we were the oppressed masses. Now we are the indigents.'

Constantia had no idea where Slim had gotten this impression. All she needed was to be praised by someone who called the president 'madala'. These youngsters were always crying about something.

Van Huis's secretary said he wasn't available. At least by the time Constantia headed back to her office, Slim and his cohort had departed.

○

An hour later Constantia's stomach had calmed down. She'd taken a teaspoon of baking soda in water and had a cup of Rooibos. The combination had worked wonders. She spent a few minutes straightening her desk drawers. She hated it when she was in a hurry and had to waste time hunting for a paper clip or a rubber band. As she was sharpening some pencils, Fakude shoved open the door and stood right in front of her with his arms crossed. He looked like someone had just stolen half of his taxis.

'Twenty-four houses in Sivuyile have had their water reconnected,' he said. 'Illegally. Apparently they are getting help from somewhere.' The councillor sat down and clenched his fists in front of his chest as if he was ready to explode across the desk.

'I don't follow,' she said.

'Apparently there is a team of so-called people's plumbers,' said Fakude. 'They even have a woman among them. We can't allow this. Plus, there is a rumour that someone in the council is supporting them,' he said.

'We can't respond to every rumour.'

'Where there is smoke, there is fire, Councillor,' said Fakude and left without waiting for a reply.

○

The next morning, Constantia's cellphone rang before dawn. The screen told her it was the Deputy Minister. She couldn't just roll over and go back to sleep.

'There's no going back on the prepaids' were his first words. Constantia was still a little groggy. He'd never phoned her this early.

'It's part of a national policy,' he continued. 'Sivuyile cannot go its own way.'

'We need a safety valve for the elderly, the unemployed, those who are ill,' said Constantia. She was starting to wake up. Who had been talking to the Deputy Minister?

'A safety valve must produce only a tiny leak,' he said, 'not open the floodgates. Those who are dodging must be dealt with severely. I want an end to those plumbers.'

Monwabisi was wide awake, listening to every word.

Constantia threw off the blankets and went out to the lounge.

'I can't stop them,' she said. 'I don't even know who they are.'

'Find out.'

'If we had delayed cutting off people's water,' she said, 'this wouldn't be happening.'

'Remember, Constantia, anyone from the ANC who

undermines the programmes of government will face the full wrath of the party,' he said.

'Of course,' she said. 'It's the only way.'

She hung up and scrambled to get dressed. Today would be a day for her black-and-white checked suit with the imitation fur collar. Constantia knew what it meant when powerful people began telling her things she already knew. Maybe this Comrade Slim and his friends meant well, but as Reverend Mncube used to say in his Sunday sermons, 'The road to hell is paved with good intentions.' Slim's good intentions could land Constantia in a hell of her own.

When she got to work she went straight to Fakude's office and told him about the early-morning phone call.

'He seems to think I have ties to the plumbers,' she said.

'I don't know where he could have gotten such an idea,' said Fakude.

He flipped through his Filofax, running his finger down the page. She wanted to tear it out of his hands. Him and his roll-ons.

'I'm sorry, Councillor,' said Fakude. 'I've got a meeting with some businessmen. They want to fund training programmes for local entrepreneurs. We can talk later at the Mayor's press conference.'

'We must work together as ANC councillors,' said Constantia. 'Otherwise we will go nowhere.'

'Tell that to your husband and his young friends,' said Fakude. He slipped on his suit coat and grabbed his briefcase. 'It must be difficult trying to explain all this to your sons.'

'All what?'

'We can talk about it later. I have my businessmen waiting.'

Fakude stood at the door and waited for Constantia to leave. She walked out slowly. The man had no right to talk about her children, let alone make up lies for the Deputy Minister. She brushed against his ever-growing stomach as she slipped through the door and dashed back to her office. She had several phone calls to make before the Mayor's press conference.

○

Constantia sat in the press room waiting for the Mayor. A reporter from East London complemented her on the fur collar. She'd never told anyone that she bought the outfit at the 'Elegantly Broken In', an upmarket second-hand clothes shop in Pretoria. A councilwoman wasn't supposed to wear used clothes.

She hoped the Mayor wouldn't speak for too long. She had two letters to write before her evening meetings. She'd forgotten to ask the topic of the Mayor's speech.

Finally Mayor Siziba strode toward the podium, a stack of papers in his hand. He didn't bother to look at the half-dozen reporters or smile for the flashing cameras.

'In a time of crisis, the chief executive must act,' the Mayor said as he laid the papers on the lectern. 'This is just such a crisis moment. I am acting in the interests of peace and development in Ukusa.'

'Illegal water connections now threaten to destroy the financial viability of this municipality,' he continued. 'Not only are they costing thousands of rands in lost revenue, they also send a message to investors that our communities are not ready to assume responsibility for our own welfare. We are fortunate in Ukusa to host the country's first public-private partnership for prepaid water meters. I cannot allow this project to fail because of the actions of a few misguided missiles.'

The Mayor went on to explain that the municipality was facing certain challenges in implementing its policy of cost recovery. 'To facilitate more effective measures in this regard, we have entered into a contract with Take Charge Security. Their first task will be to permanently remove all illegal water connections.' The Mayor went on to point out that Take Charge was a black-owned company, so the municipality's contract with them was 'totally in line with the notion of black economic empowerment'.

The Mayor finished by announcing a 'declaration of war against any and all who dare to undermine the financial stability of my city'. When a couple of reporters pressed him for details, he pleaded a prior engagement.

'I'm already late,' he said, ducking back to his office. Constantia was right on his tail. She waited until he closed the door.

'How can you do this without even informing the ANC council members?' she said. 'You have made us look like ignorant fools.'

Fakude and Phakhathi charged through the door next, along with Councillor Jacobs.

'We must be consulted on such decisions,' said Fakude. 'You have made a mockery of our structures.'

'Just a minute,' said the Mayor. 'I have to take my pills.' He rummaged through the drawers of his desk, found a brown plastic bottle and shook two tablets into his palm. 'I must remain vigilant about my BP,' he said.

'Why didn't you at least inform us?' said Fakude. 'We have been made to look like ignoramuses. We are your front line, Comrade Mayor.'

'I needed to act quickly, resolutely,' he said.

'We salute you for putting an end to illegal connections once and for all,' said Fakude. 'But you must trust us in the future. Inform us.'

'What about the cut-offs?' asked Constantia. 'The indigent programme is still not functioning properly.'

The office phone rang. The Minister of Labour in

Pretoria wanted to talk football. Moroka Swallows had beaten Orlando Pirates the previous day to win the Coca-Cola Cup. The game went to penalty kicks. The Mayor winked at Fakude as he spoke. The Bopape councillor was a Pirates supporter. When the Mayor put down the phone, Fakude promised that Pirates would annihilate Swallows next time.

'It will be ugly,' Fakude added. 'Very, very ugly.'

The Mayor remained adamant. His Swallows would prevail in the future as well.

'They have begun to evict people from council homes in our area,' said Jacobs. 'All of Basil Feb is talking about it. I phoned you yesterday. They kept saying you were in meetings.' He took off his glasses and wiped the lenses with a handkerchief.

'I am always in meetings,' the Mayor replied. 'Everyone wants to talk to me. As to this kleurling politics in Basil Feb, I'll never get it. When will our coloured comrades learn where their interests lie?'

Jacobs checked the lenses by holding them up to the light from the chandelier hanging over the Mayor's desk. 'Some have even deserted to the Nats,' Jacobs said. 'Others say this is a government only for Africans.' He finally put his glasses back on, then reached into his pocket, pulled out a yellow sheet of paper and handed it to the Mayor. Constantia could see the lettering across the top: 'Not White Enough for the Nats, Not Black Enough for the ANC.' The Mayor tossed the flyer onto the floor. Fakude picked it up and had a look.

'Bloody rubbish,' Fakude said. 'They must realise by now that the ANC is a non-racial organisation.'

'I will come to address them,' said the Mayor. 'Talk to my secretary to set a date. I want the biggest venue in Basil Feb. School kids, choirs, whatever you have over there.'

'Some people owe huge arrears,' said Jacobs.

'We can handle them,' he said. 'Just like my Swallows

handled Okpara and company yesterday. We have a powerful defence now that Take Charge is part of our squad.'

'A meeting is not enough,' said Jacobs. The Mayor slid his chair back from his desk, stood up and reached toward the ceiling with both arms. 'The doctor tells me I must stretch at least three times a day,' said the Mayor, 'otherwise I'll end up with this RSI. A body like mine wasn't built to be behind a desk all day.' The Mayor reached down to try to touch his toes. He grunted with the effort but he couldn't get much past his knees.

'I hope we are finished here, gentlemen and lady,' the Mayor said. 'I have a plane to catch. They're expecting me in Durban.'

'Don't forget your pills,' said Fakude.

Constantia waited until the Mayor finished putting his pill bottle into his briefcase.

'Bringing in security won't solve this problem,' said Constantia. 'This is not a soccer match. We need to discuss it at a proper meeting.'

The Mayor was looking for something in the bottom drawer of his desk.

'I agree with Councillor Radebe,' said Jacobs. 'This is not just about not being informed. It is far more complicated.'

The Mayor pulled a pair of soccer boots and a pair of shiny gold shorts from the drawer. 'I still have a touch like velvet,' he said, 'even though I'm a little short on speed.'

Fakude laughed.

'It's as if we are putting troops back into our communities,' said Constantia.

'A black-owned private security company is not the SADF,' said the Mayor, trying to press his briefcase closed over the top of the soccer boots. He gave it one last thrust and clicked the latches shut.

'They are also not soldiers of the ANC,' Constantia

replied. 'We need to meet further on this. At least can we have an assurance that Take Charge won't make any moves until you return from Durban?'

'Calm down, Councillor,' said the Mayor, putting on his sunglasses. 'There'll be plenty of time when I come back. I doubt these people can move that quickly.'

He exited with Fakude and Phakhathi.

'Cut-offs are killing our people and he's boasting about the Swallows,' said Constantia. She found an Eno's packet in her purse. 'We now have night watchmen policing our communities,' said Jacobs. 'It's a farce.'

She'd never really talked to Jacobs before. He was a quiet man. Monwabisi had told her he was a hero in Basil Feb, that he'd been tortured by the police when he was just seventeen. Maybe he could help her bring the Mayor to his senses.

The two adjourned their discussion to a small restaurant nearby. Jacobs pulled out her chair when they got to the table. Monwabisi called such things 'bourgeois formalities'.

Jacobs told Constantia how unsettled things were in Basil Feb. 'The NP and the DP are stirring things up,' he said. 'The Mayor is not interested.'

He explained that a few bureaucrats from the old regime still controlled housing allocation. 'They are evicting ANC supporters,' he said, 'coming up with all sorts of excuses. People are saying if you want a house you must join the NP.'

'It's all back to front,' said Constantia. She reached into her bag and switched off her cellphone. She was expecting a call from Monwabisi. They could talk later.

'The Mayor must sack those people,' said Jacobs.

Constantia liked how soft his voice was. She'd never even been to Basil February, never had a reason to go there. Monwabisi said most of the coloureds had been bought off by the Boers. He liked to point out that their schools had cricket pitches, something you'd never find in an African school.

'Your husband is very famous in Joburg,' said Jacobs. 'One of the great shop stewards of the metalworkers.'

Constantia tried to hide her face in her teacup. She didn't consider Monwabisi famous. Maybe in Sivuyile, but in Joburg there was Sam Shilowa, Cyril and the Mayekiso brothers. How could a former worker from Sivuyile match up? That was just it. Former worker. She was tired of living in the past. The struggle was over, or at least had moved to a different terrain. She could never convince Monwabisi of this. He was like a taxi with only one gear.

Jacobs told her he was divorced but had custody of his children. His wife had left him for another man, 'a rich one with diamond rings and Benzes. They live now in Bishopscourt.'

Jacobs surprised Constantia when he told her he was a Kaizer Chiefs supporter.

'You have a lot in common with my husband,' she said. 'Doctor Khumalo is his favourite.'

Constantia finished a whole pot of tea by herself. It tasted extra sweet. She and Jacobs shook hands when they left. Councillor Jacobs, who had asked her to call him 'Richard', had the hands of a clerk, soft and gentle. She wondered if he'd ever held a hammer or a hoe. When she looked at their hands together, she got a shock. His skin was darker than hers. Apartheid played strange tricks.

She thought about him all afternoon while she prepared her list of indigent households for the next council meeting just in case she could use it. His knuckles were smooth, not a single knot.

The last thing she saw that night before she fell asleep was Richard's face. For a moment she thought she felt him touching her cheek. Monwabisi was already snoring.

Chapter 35

MONWABISI WAS UP AT dawn. He liked to start his day with a run before the summer heat set in. He looped around the high school twice, then behind the market. He dodged women carrying their boxes of tomatoes, bananas and onions about to begin another day's business. Mrs Mehlo wasn't in her usual spot. Instead, her young niece was unpacking a weathered brown suitcase and laying out clothes on top of sheets spread on the ground. He saw a brilliant yellow T-shirt which would fit Fidel. He would come back and buy it later.

After leaving the market behind, he took a detour past Mrs Mehlo's sister's house. Mrs Mehlo and Oupa were still staying there. As he turned the corner into the unpaved street, two blue vans bearing the Take Charge lightning-bolt logo pulled up in front of the sister's house. Monwabisi stopped and jogged in place.

Two men in bright blue overalls jumped out of the back of one of the vans and posted themselves on either side of the wire gate. Each held a twelve-gauge shotgun and wore a camouflage flak jacket over his uniform.

Like armoured-car drivers guarding a bank, they surveyed the neighbourhood for anything suspicious. A couple of small boys were chasing each other two doors down. A young girl across the street was sweeping the yard. One of the men in overalls looked towards Monwabisi.

'Keep running!' he shouted. 'There's nothing to see here.' Monwabisi kept jogging right where he was.

A team of four other men, also in bright blue, came out of the other van with shovels and toolboxes. They hurriedly dug out around the water meter, then jumped into the hole with spanners and a blowtorch.

Mrs Mehlo came charging out the front door, wrapping a cloth around her waist and shouting. Monwabisi cautiously jogged forward.

A tall man with a shiny shaved head told Mrs Mehlo they were acting on the 'order of the council'. He handed her a small piece of paper. Monwabisi could hear the blowtorch cutting. He hadn't heard that sound since Metal Links. As Mrs Mehlo looked at the paper, two men lifted a water meter out of the hole and carried it towards the van. Monwabisi sprinted towards them, trying to cut them off before they reached the vehicle.

One of the guards stepped in Monwabisi's path, and pumped a round into the chamber of his shotgun. The barrel was trained on Monwabisi's chest. 'Don't come any closer,' he told Monwabisi.

Monwabisi stopped. The man holding the gun was probably younger than Oupa. How could they be turning such lighties loose in the townships? 'What's going on here?' Monwabisi asked.

'It's not your business,' said the young man.

The two men carrying the meter slid past the shotgun-toting guard. They had cut the water pipes. Not even the struggle plumbers would be able to reconnect Mrs Mehlo's sister now.

'We must stop these illegal connections,' the shiny-headed man told Mrs Mehlo. He had an unusual accent, maybe Portuguese.

'We were promised water!' shouted Mrs Mehlo. 'You want us to live like animals without even washing.'

The shiny-headed man didn't answer. The men with the shotguns walked backwards to the vans, keeping their guns at the ready.

'Let's go!' shouted the shiny-headed man. The entire Take Charge crew quickly leaped into the vans. As the doors slid shut, a flurry of stones sailed from Mrs Mehlo's sister's roof onto the windscreen of the front van.

Monwabisi saw Oupa standing atop the house picking rocks from a bucket and throwing handfuls out towards the street. Two stones hit Monwabisi on the forehead before the shots rang out. Oupa froze for a second, then dove face down on the roof and slid into the back garden. The shotgun holders ran inside the gate and fired two more rounds.

'He got away,' one of them said.

Mrs Mehlo ran towards them.

'You won't touch my son!' she shouted. Monwabisi followed her. Once again he was face to face with the young man with the shotgun.

'Lie down, both of you!' shouted the shiny-headed man from out of the van. 'Lie down or we'll shoot!'

'Voetsek, you black Boers!' a man shouted from across the street. 'Put away those guns and we'll see how brave you are.'

'Get down!' the shiny-headed man yelled again. 'I mean it!'

'Take Charge means take charge,' said the young man with the gun. 'We don't mind shooting lawbreakers.'

'We have broken no laws,' said Mrs Mehlo. She and Monwabisi stood arm in arm.

Amid the confusion, two young boys ran out from a house across the street, spread some bent nails across the road and dashed away.

James Kilgore

'Let's go,' said the shiny-headed man.

'Next time I'll shoot,' the armed man said as he tilted his shotgun towards the sky.

The nails popped two tyres as the vans made their exit. The wheels clunked down the dirt roads.

○

That evening, when Monwabisi watched the news, he saw a clip of the Mayor's press conference held the previous day. With Constantia and the other councillors standing next to him, the Mayor proclaimed that 'the city would win a victory over thugs and vandals who threaten our hard-won democracy'. In the background sat the CEO of Take Charge, Mr Mgijima, and a team of five men in those bright blue overalls. One of them was the shiny-headed man who'd been at Mrs Mehlo's sister's house.

The Mayor saluted the 'hard-toiling soldiers on the front line of service delivery' and proclaimed they had 'stopped forever the attempts to subvert local government in this country'.

Monwabisi laughed. Nothing lasted forever in South Africa, least of all trying to deny people their basic rights. Even with all his time on the Island, the Mayor seemed to have forgotten that freedom never rests.

An hour later Constantia came home. When Monwabisi told her what had happened at Mrs Mehlo's sister's house, she said she wished the Mayor had waited.

'But still,' she said, 'he had no choice. Freedom is not anarchy.'

'What is freedom, then?' Monwabisi asked.

'People are blocking the efforts of government to implement,' she said. 'Lawbreaking is not the answer.' She asked Monwabisi where Musa and Fidel had gone. There was homework to be done.

'Implement what?' said Monwabisi. 'People have no jobs, no money to pay. Does that mean they deserve no water?'

'They get a lifeline.'

'When?'

'The meter will take care of it,' she said. 'There are still some kinks in the system. We can make it work.' She went into the front yard. The boys were in the street. She chased a mangy old dog away from the gate.

Constantia came back inside and straightened some magazines on the coffee table.

'They have removed the meters,' said Monwabisi.

'That girl has been reading my *Cosmo* again,' she said. 'Look at this.' She opened the magazine to show Monwabisi the torn-out pages. 'I wanted that recipe,' she said.

'The lifelines are too little,' said Monwabisi. He stared briefly at the framed picture of Doctor Khumalo on their lounge wall. That was the Doctor at his peak in 1989. The years the Amakhosi took the Iwisa, the Ohlssons and the BP Top 8. He turned his eyes away from the Doctor. How could his wife worry about recipes at a time like this?

'I know there are problems,' she said. 'But I'm tired of negativity. This is not what freedom is about.'

Monwabisi switched on the TV. 'What would you know about freedom for the working class?' he asked. 'Let me watch my Amakhosi in peace.' He sat down on the sofa, putting his feet on the coffee table.

Constantia strode to the wall socket and pulled out the TV plug. 'History can never go backwards,' she told him. 'You are living with dead ideas. There is a saying: "The genius of the past who refuses to change becomes the fool of tomorrow."'

'Who said that?' he replied, staring at the blank TV screen as if Doctor Khumalo had somehow plugged the cord back into the wall.

'The bottom line here is that the expenditure of a

municipality must not exceed its revenue,' she said. 'There is not enough money for everyone to get water for free.'

'That is the language of consultants,' he said. 'Freedom is the only bottom line for the proletariat.'

'You just don't want to understand,' she said. 'Just like with our family. If there is not enough money coming in...' She slammed the *Cosmo* down on the coffee table and left the room.

'The prepaids will come back to haunt you!' he shouted as she went into the kitchen. 'There will be babies with no formula to drink, no clean napkins, grannies fainting from dehydration. You will see.'

Monwabisi got up and plugged the TV back in. He stood next to the outlet while he watched the match. The Doctor sailed a cross right in the front of the goal but there was no one there. How could he play without support?

He heard his wife in the kitchen mumbling something about that girl and the recipes.

Then disaster struck. The Sundowns scored on a counter to take a 2–0 lead. That was a margin even the Doctor with all his magic would struggle to overcome.

Part 4

Chapter 36

'This country's not ready for the real world,' Peter said. 'First, illegal connections; now they're digging up meters. When will South Africans realise they have to pay their bills?'

Susan folded the custard into the trifle. She should have made a melktert, but she could never get it quite like her mother's. Maybe it was the farm-fresh milk that made the difference. Anyway, the sweet curry of the bobotie and the yellow rice would make up for it. At least Peter would get the idea that South Africans could do more than put wors on the braai.

Peter sneaked up behind her and tried to dip his finger into the custard but she swatted him away. He retreated to the kitchen table. Susan started to lick the extra custard off the rubber spatula. It came from a mix, not as good as on the stove, but who had time to make custard from scratch?

'There's no free lunch in this world,' Peter said. 'It's a basic principle of economics. If you don't pay for it, it has no value.'

She stopped licking for a second and turned toward him. 'Is jy befok?'

'What the hell?'

'Is jy befok?'

She could tell he wanted a translation. She wasn't going to help him. She went back to licking the custard. He just didn't understand that sometimes Americans had no clue.

'Did you pay for your mother's love?' she asked after a few seconds.

'That's different,' he replied.

'How about street lights?'

'The logic of the market is second nature everywhere. Where else do people still wear T-shirts with a hammer and sickle on the front? Jesus.'

'The market alone is not enough,' she said. 'We're trying to get the mix right.' She turned back to the stove. 'I need a drink,' she said. 'Tonight it will be Laphroaig.'

Peter mumbled something about Adam Smith and Karl Marx that Susan ignored. South Africans lived with these contradictions all the time. She'd been overseas. Life seemed so easy in New York or London. People didn't worry about the basics. There was food everywhere in those bright packets. No one knew what it meant to use a pit latrine or defecate in a bucket, let alone understand the fact that crime in Joburg came right into the suburbs. One Provincial Cabinet Minister had his car hijacked in front of his house. The robbers took the bodyguard's guns.

'There are no easy solutions,' she said. 'Nothing pre-packaged for a post-apartheid society. We'll make our own mistakes.'

She handed him a bowl, a whisk and a sachet of heavy cream. 'Not too thick,' she said. 'Not like that American stuff that comes in plastic containers.'

'Cool Whip?'

'Ja, not like that.'

Peter scissored open the sachet and poured the cream in the bowl. He was comfortable in the kitchen. Susan had never been with a man who could go beyond spaghetti bolognaise. Peter could even do Thai food, though he complained that the noodles were hard to find in Joburg.

'You must be the only Deputy Minister whose boyfriend

whips the cream,' he said as his wrist flicked the whisk back and forth.

'Do you consider yourself my boyfriend?' she asked.

'Well, what would you call me?'

She opened a can of peach slices while she considered her answer. 'I guess boyfriend is fine,' she said.

'Then you must be my girlfriend,' he said.

He put down the bowl and stepped over to kiss her on the cheek. She smiled and drained the juice from the peach can into a glass. She wasn't sure she'd use it but it was too deliciously sweet to just throw away. If she had planned properly she'd have put it in with the jelly instead of water. Peach juice added a nice fruity twist.

Peter went back to the cream. 'The market might not be perfect,' he said, 'but it's the best we've got.'

'I need that cream,' she said. 'Are you almost done?'

He turned the bowl on its side. Nothing ran out. 'Must be done,' he said. 'Let me add a little vanilla and powdered sugar.'

'Icing sugar,' she said. 'And you should have put it in earlier. We'll end up with butter.'

'Trust me,' he said.

'We never trust Americans,' she said. 'They're too aggressive, too loud, and they only speak one language.'

He slid the bowl of whipped cream along the counter towards her. 'And don't forget that we can't live without hamburgers,' he said.

She spread the cream over the top of the jelly, then dotted the top with the peach slices. Not perfect. She would rather have had fresh strawberries than the canned peaches, but life in South Africa was always a compromise.

Peter sat down at the kitchen table and asked Susan what she thought about Fikile Siziba, the Mayor of Ukusa.

'I don't know him that well,' she said. 'He spent a few years on the Island.'

'I see him as a new type of freedom fighter,' said Peter 'He understands the realities of democracy.'

'I've never heard anyone praise him for being overly democratic,' she replied.

'Well, democratic doesn't always mean popular. South Africa needs a good dose of tough love.'

She put the trifle in the fridge and pulled out the Laphroaig. She didn't drink whisky very often, but she wasn't in the mood for one of Peter's lectures. As if Manhattan was paradise. 'What you need is a good dose of tough single-malt whisky,' she said.

'No, I'm serious,' he said. 'Tough love.'

She added a little soda water to the Laphroaig. The first sip went right to her head.

Peter embarked on an oratorical journey. He was a nice enough person and he meant well. Who could deny the brilliance of Water for Freedom? But he still had that American arrogance. When she told people in New York about informal settlements, they acted as if they'd seen it all before.

'Tough love is one of those irritating American buzzwords,' she said. 'It means nothing.'

'At least we can agree on a national anthem,' he said, 'without having to debate it for months on end.'

Susan opened a jar of maraschino cherries. She'd toss a few of them on top of the trifle. Why not?

Peter started in on the prepaid meters again, how they were the 'perfect tool' to teach the 'gospel of economics'.

As she sipped the single malt she ran through her 'to do' list for the next day. If she was lucky she might get home by midnight. And the following morning she had to catch the 6 a.m. flight to Cape Town. It just never stopped.

'People can't love a leader all the time,' said Peter. 'It's just like your parents. As a teenager you hate them, but then later on you realise they made a lot more sense than you ever thought.'

'That's your parents,' she said. 'Mine still vote for Constand Viljoen and curse the day I was born.'

She went through that 'to do' list for the next day one more time. What a kak day it was going to be. At least after another Laphroaig her mind drifted from tomorrow's diary.

Peter said he loved the bobotie. 'I've never even seen such a thing in New York,' he said.

'Is that supposed to be a compliment?'

'I didn't mean it that way.'

'No problem,' she said and kissed him on the cheek.

As she cleared the table her mind drifted back to that schedule for the following day. She could feel her eyelids growing heavy just thinking about all those meetings. Daily life now was about sitting around tables of massive egos vying for political turf. She knew it was all important and necessary, but sometimes she missed the university, where she could debate an issue without fear of repercussions for the Minister or the ruling party. Maybe she wasn't cut out for politics at this level.

Peter poured her another shot of Laphroaig. She'd had three already. She'd feel that fourth shot tomorrow morning, but sometimes she just had to cut loose and time with Peter was a good enough escape. Better than solitude anyway. He took their relationship a little too seriously, though. She wasn't sure how to handle that part, but she had more important things to worry about.

Chapter 37

SLIM AND CORLEONE were standing in front of Rocky's Five Star Café sharing a Coke and some bread as Monwabisi raced past. They waved him over. Monwabisi wondered where they'd been. He hadn't seen them for awhile. He'd heard that Slim had started a new business selling vegetables. Congratulations were in order.

There wasn't much time to talk, though. Constantia would be arriving home from her first overseas trip in just four hours. Monwabisi had a lot to discuss with her – Take Charge and how both Musa and Fidel had caught flu. He swerved to avoid a goat as he approached the two young comrades. He declined Corleone's offer of a sip of Coke. He only drank water when he ran.

'They have started removing people's meters,' said Slim. 'This is the end. We need our own organisation now.' Monwabisi kept running in place as Slim talked. He tried not to stare at the lumps behind the young man's ears. They had grown.

'We must fight them,' Monwabisi said, 'but you can't give up on the structures yet. Standing outside the house screaming is useless.' The sweat from his nose left a speckled pattern in the dirt next to Corleone's slip-slop. He slowed his pace, then stopped. These boys needed a quick lesson.

'We are serious,' said Slim. As he stuffed the rest of his bread in his mouth, a group of four Bible-carrying men laid a blanket down on the other side of the spaza shop. Three more people joined them, including an elderly man who looked like a preacher.

'Siyalidumisa igama lakho!' the elderly preacher shouted, calling out his blessing in God's name. His congregation of half a dozen began to sing the Lord's Prayer. Monwabisi jogged away slowly to escape the noise. Slim and Corleone followed. The mandrax of the masses was still finding receptive ears.

'My first year as a shop steward,' Monwabisi told the pair of youngsters, 'I challenged the bosses on every issue. If a foreman spoke rudely to a worker, I filed a grievance on his behalf. If a worker was disciplined for arriving late, I filed for victimisation.'

'You were a monster in those days,' said Slim. The prayer of the small group hummed in the background. Now Monwabisi didn't recognise the language.

'The workers lost time after time,' the former shop steward said. 'They ended up electing a very quiet man named Albert Kgomo as their shop steward instead of Monwabisi.'

The three of them wandered past a dreadlocked sax player attempting McCoy Mrubata's 'Tears of Joy'.

'This is the real South African music,' said Monwabisi. 'Not this kwaito of yours.'

'This is music for the madalas,' said Corleone. 'They can beat the rhythm with their canes.'

'You are mad,' said Monwabisi. 'This is the music of the class struggle. Listen.'

The sax player wound into his conclusion, jumping high in the air to hit the last note. Slim and Corleone shared a laughing high five. Monwabisi reached into his pocket, found a one-rand coin and dropped it into the open horn case lying on the ground. The man nodded, then launched into his own riff.

The three moved down towards the rows of vegetable stands, a world of tomatoes, onions and bananas in neat little plastic bags. Monwabisi always wondered how the sellers earned enough to survive.

'You must choose your battles,' said Monwabisi. 'And choose carefully.'

'You are telling us it's wrong to connect people's water?' asked Slim. 'To give them back life? We didn't force anyone.'

'But the council brought Take Charge,' said Monwabisi. 'You weren't prepared for that.'

An old woman stepped in front of Monwabisi, holding two plastic packets of very dark-coloured bananas. 'One rand, one rand,' she said, glancing at his gleaming trainers. 'Guaranteed to make you run faster.' Monwabisi bought one packet and kept walking with Slim and Corleone. The woman hurriedly reached down to pick up some tomatoes. 'Two rands, two rands,' she shouted, but Monwabisi didn't turn around.

'The government has turned reactionary,' said Slim. 'They are using thugs against the people.'

'But who will the people blame?' asked Monwabisi. 'That is the question.'

'The council and the Mayor,' said Slim.

'Maybe your wife,' added Corleone.

'Hayi, hayi, comrades. They will be blaming you for getting their pipes and meters taken away.'

'You are becoming soft in your old age,' said Slim. 'The time of the ANC has passed. We need a new party.'

Monwabisi shook his hands to loosen his wrists. These lighties were ruining his run with this ultra-left politics of theirs. He had to get back on the road. A chill had set in. He handed the bananas to Slim, put his right foot out and reached down to touch the toe, then did the same with the left. If a hamstring went tight, he could get a cramp.

'Look at your COSATU,' said Slim. 'Some of their affiliates now have investment companies, putting workers' dues into the stock exchange. The officials are becoming millionaires while workers remain poor.'

'Who are you to talk?' said Monwabisi. 'You are now running your own business. You have joined the capitalists.'

'I am a petty trader,' said Slim. 'Part of the survival sector selling a few vegetables with my sister.' He added, 'At least this way we will always have fresh bananas, not these rotten things of yours.' He tossed Monwabisi's packet of bananas into a nearby bin.

'I wish you luck in the capitalist jungle,' said Monwabisi. He bent down to touch his toes again. His hamstrings felt fine.

'That reminds me,' said Slim. 'I must get back to work.'

'I must run,' said Monwabisi, 'or I'll be getting cramps.'

'We can call an ambulance for you,' said Slim.

'And they'll arrive tomorrow afternoon asking for money,' said Corleone. 'This is not Northridge.'

'Your party has gone down a wrong path,' said Slim.

'Politics is like running the Comrades,' said Monwabisi. 'You can't burn yourself out in the first kilometre. There are eighty-eight more to go.'

Monwabisi skidded on a banana peel on his first stride but he caught himself. These youngsters were good-intentioned but too impatient. The unions were so different. The workers understood that things didn't change overnight, that building an organisation was a process. Premature action had serious consequences. These amakhaba wanted to be militants day and night without consolidating their base. People couldn't just start a new organisation every time theirs did something they didn't like.

As Monwabisi turned onto a side street, three barefooted boys tried to run alongside him. 'You run too fast!' they yelled as Monwabisi pulled away. His legs were getting warm again; he could feel the momentum rising.

Marx once wrote that the only thing constant in life was change. Something like that. But these changes taking place in South Africa weren't the ones Monwabisi had expected. His wife thought she could change the world by passing a few council resolutions or filling out forms from the days of the Boers. Now the lighties were calling for a new party. South Africa became more confusing by the day. When he was a shop steward he talked to the comrades and read the *Business Day*. The world made sense. Where was the working class these days? They had gone quiet.

The last four kilometres flew by. He was finally getting into stride. He had time to make up. Plus, he had to squeeze in a haircut from Mrs Sithethi before he and the boys took a taxi to the airport. He sprinted the last three hundred metres. Running was the one thing that never let him down.

○

'Ufikile umama!' screeched Musa and Fidel in unison. They ran full speed and crashed into Constantia's knees as she came through the swinging doors from customs. Yellow duty-free bags hung from her arms like ornaments on a Christmas tree. Monwabisi's charcoal suit sparkled. His haircut gave his ears an overexposed look.

Constantia had been gone two weeks. Three councillors – herself, Koosman and Jacobs – visited six cities in the US to study local government American style. The trip had been a blur of airport lounges, shopping malls, PowerPoint presentations and handshakes with strangers. She'd met black, white, Latino and Asian mayors from Miami to Seattle.

She'd brought back new running shoes for all three males in her household. Monwabisi's red Samsonite overflowed with clothes from Wal-Mart and a store in Baltimore they called the Big Box. She never thought anything could be bigger than the Pick 'n Pay Hypermarket in Norwood. She'd tried to buy a television and a VCR, but they told her they wouldn't work in South Africa, that the electricity was different. Everything seemed different in America, why not the electricity? They measured everything in miles. And it seemed like they never slept.

Constantia hugged her husband. He gave her a soft kiss on the cheek. He'd never kissed her in public before. He told her how Fidel had gotten the flu and had to stay home from school for three days.

'He vomited up everything, even water,' said Monwabisi. 'Then Musa got sick. He always threw up in the night when Portia wasn't around. Have you ever cleaned up piles of vomit?'

Monwabisi rolled the suitcase out of the airport to the taxi rank.

'Then Portia got sick,' he said as they climbed in the back seat. 'When she came back, I gave her an extra R30. We don't always appreciate what the working class does.'

Constantia told him how big the cars were in America. 'Cadillacs, Lincolns and those SUVs. Nkosi yam'. They are like a bus.'

'They had sixty-seven channels in our hotel,' she continued. 'You would have loved it. You could watch news all day. Another channel had nothing but black American music. Whitney Houston, Luther Vandross. Twenty-four hours a day.'

Riding up the Space Needle scared her and she almost missed a plane in New York. She directed the taxi driver to the wrong airport. She didn't know there were two. How could a city be so big it had two airports?

'I made a speech in Atlanta,' she said. 'I spoke about

Madiba, democracy and my husband the shop steward. I told them apartheid could have never fallen without the workers. You would have been proud.'

He seemed to be smiling, but she wasn't sure. He looked different. Maybe she was seeing him through American eyes.

'They stood up and applauded when I finished,' she said. 'Even the whites.'

'Thank God those boys got better,' said Monwabisi.

Musa told his mother about the time Monwabisi left the water running in the sink and it flooded the house.

'It was like a river,' said Fidel.

Suddenly Constantia's eyes snapped shut. Jet lag. She tried to fight it by pinching herself in the arm. Richard had told her it happened like that sometimes, that it hit you like 'ten cement trucks'.

She started to dream about the hotel room in Seattle. Richard was lying next to her. His hands were softer than a white woman's. Sometimes he massaged her feet.

'That mop was so sour,' she heard Monwabisi say as the taxi stopped near their house. 'I had to wash it out with Lysol and mop again. Smelled like a rural hospital when I was finished.'

Richard gently rolled under her and before she knew it her body was free, like she was on the dance floor. No weight of a man to press her down. She thought that the virus had stolen all of her urges. His hand flicked her nipples. She didn't know they were that sensitive. They were for milk.

When they got home, Monwabisi slipped into his new shoes. They were bright blue.

'New Balance has always been my favourite,' he said. 'Others prefer Nikes, but these are perfect for my feet.'

'I knew those were the ones you liked,' she said. The wave of jet lag had passed, taking with it the vision of Richard. After their third night together, he went chasing after some twenty-five-year-old blonde American who was researching South African political prisoners. Before the blonde went trundling off with Richard, she told Constantia she'd already interviewed fifteen people who'd done time on the Island. Constantia wondered how many of them she had slept with. Why would a man in his fifties chase after a silly young girl with a fringe?

Fidel and Musa insisted on sleeping in their gleaming white Adidas running shoes.

'Just untie them,' said Constantia, 'and sleep on top of the blankets.'

When the boys fell asleep, she slipped the new shoes off their feet. Then her husband told her something about Take Charge removing water meters. He seemed quite agitated but she was too tired to make sense of it all. He was probably just overreacting again. She'd wait until she heard the story from someone else.

In the morning Fidel told his mother she must go back to the shop in America and get a tracksuit to go with his shoes. Monwabisi came in, a trail of sweat behind him. He'd already run ten kilometres.

Constantia stood up and kissed her husband on the cheek. She hadn't tasted that salty sweat in years. She brushed the dampness off the front of the sweater she'd bought at Kohl's in Miami. Or was it Seattle?

'My feet feel as light as air in my new shoes,' he said.

'Mama, will you?' asked Fidel.

'Will I what?'

'Go back to that shop in America and get a tracksuit to go with my shoes?'

'America is very far away,' said Constantia. 'I doubt I'll get back to that shop, but if I do I'll buy it for you.'

Portia set coffee in front of them, then mopped the drops of Monwabisi's perspiration. He apologised for messing the floor.

'There were no coloureds in America,' Constantia said. 'They didn't notice the difference between Richard and myself. People who were very light in complexion kept calling me their "long-lost sister from the motherland".'

'They now call themselves African Americans,' said Monwabisi. 'Something new.'

He sat down to read an old *Business Day* as Constantia's driver hooted outside. As she got ready to leave, Monwabisi mumbled something to her about De Beers moving its world headquarters.

The driver took Constantia straight to the office. Now she'd be back to tackling the water cut-offs. Nothing in America prepared her for that. She hoped her husband had gotten it all wrong about Take Charge.

○

Two days later Constantia came home with a proposal. A teacher who had just been appointed at the nursery school where Constantia used to work was new in town and needed a place to stay. Constantia wanted to rent her a room in their house.

'It would be another R200 a month and she could help with the children,' she told Monwabisi.

'We don't need another childminder,' said Monwabisi. 'What's wrong with Portia?'

'The people at the nursery school say she's quiet, a churchgoer.'

'Let them offer her a place to stay.'

Monwabisi understood that there was financial pressure. Constantia was still the only councillor without a car. Usually she could get a driver from the car pool but sometimes she ended up travelling by taxi. She said it was embarrassing. She'd discussed the new cellphone issue with him before. She wanted one with email. All he could say was that they didn't live in Joburg. He'd sold the one Pellmar gave him for R25. Nowadays, he said, cellphones were nothing but 'Gauteng earrings'.

'We can try moving her in for a month,' said Constantia. 'If it doesn't work out, we'll find someone else. Unless of course...'

'Of course what?'

'We put up a shack in the backyard instead,' she said.

'I know you're joking now,' he said.

Monwabisi went to the kitchen. He made his own tea these days, though he had cut back. The doctor had told him the caffeine was bad for his heart. With the virus he couldn't even be a teetotaller. Why couldn't his wife just come out and say it? Their financial problems all boiled down to one thing: her unemployed husband.

The next day, when Monwabisi came home from a meeting of the Community Policing Forum, he heard the voice of a strange woman inside. She spoke Xhosa like a Zulu, only not exactly. Maybe she was a Swazi.

Constantia introduced her to Monwabisi as Madeline Moyo. She wore black canvas tennis shoes and a yellow headscarf – not the attire of South African women. He shook her hand, then went about his business. Nowadays everyone came to the house to talk to the councillor.

Monwabisi had taken to reading Lenin again. He'd gotten a copy of *Left-Wing Communism: An Infantile Disorder*. He lay on the bed and took out a red bookmark with the logo of Pellmar which he'd used to mark his place at the start of Chapter 6. He wanted to explain it to Slim. The boy was always in too much of a hurry. Lenin called such people 'infantile'. How right he was. Plus they are dangerous, leading the masses into traps.

As Monwabisi read about the errors of the Spartacist League in Germany, he heard Madeline Moyo departing.

Constantia came into the bedroom and told him that Madeline, the new nursery school teacher, would be moving in at the weekend.

'Where is she from?' he asked. He put the book down on the bed.

'She has got a South African passport,' Constantia said. 'She showed it to me.'

'The Moyos are Zimbabweans. If they're not Moyos they're Nyathis. How do we explain that we're keeping a foreigner here? People will talk about makwerekwere and all that.'

'Let them talk.'

'People always look for a scapegoat,' said Monwabisi. 'It's not Zimbabweans who are shipping our jobs overseas.' He carefully closed the Lenin book and placed it on the nightstand. 'Since when am I not consulted on such things?' he said.

'I told you about her before.'

'You informed me, but you didn't say she was a Zimbabwean or that she was moving in. You just suggested.'

'You were consulted. We need the money. Kuphela.'

'Consulting happens before a decision, not afterwards.'

'You were consulted. We can't take a vote on every issue in the house. If you have a better idea how to find the money we need for school fees, for my phone...'

His wife had crossed the line this time. It was bad enough relying on her for food and for his medicine. Now she was taking decisions unilaterally. Constantia had become the general secretary of the family. Monwabisi was nothing but a marginalised shop steward.

'You are acting like a boss now,' he said. 'The next thing I know, I'll be sacked.'

She laughed but Monwabisi wasn't smiling. He laced up his cross trainers and went to the lounge. He put his hands on the wall to get a calf stretch.

'Better to do that outdoors,' said Constantia. 'Your fingers will leave marks on the wall.'

Monwabisi didn't move. A Zimbabwean woman he'd never met was moving in and now he couldn't even do stretches in his own lounge.

He ran ten kilometres in just over forty-three minutes. He wasn't even pushing himself.

○

The following Saturday, while Constantia was at an all-day workshop on cost recovery, Madeline Moyo arrived with a beaten-up leather suitcase resting on her head.

Monwabisi imagined her father using that same suitcase thirty years earlier to carry his belongings to the mines. Madeline was a slight woman, still wearing those black canvas tennis shoes. She carried two blankets, plus a plastic bag full of books.

'I'm so sorry, mama,' said Monwabisi, 'but there's been a change of plans. My wife's mother will be moving in. I've spoken with a friend of mine who may have a room for you. He will get back to me tomorrow. Sorry.'

'It's all right,' said Madeline, setting her suitcase down. 'I just don't know where I'll go.'

Monwabisi gave Madeline a glass of water and two lemon cream biscuits and brought her a wooden chair to sit down on the front veranda.

'Take a little rest before you walk back,' he said. 'There is no hurry.'

'You have a lovely house,' she said.

She sat on the veranda for another fifteen minutes. Monwabisi helped her load the suitcase on top of her head as she got up to go.

'Be careful,' he said to her as she walked out the front

gate. 'There are some people in the township who don't like Zimbabweans. They are confused.'

'Thank you, bhuti,' she said and set off for the taxi rank.

When Constantia got home, Monwabisi told her that Madeline Moyo had come by and said she had found another place to live.

'She was very polite,' said Monwabisi. 'She apologised for the inconvenience.'

'I thought we had solved this problem of money,' said Constantia. 'Now we are back to square one.'

'We will think of something,' said Monwabisi. 'Where there is a will, there is a way.'

Chapter 38

JOANNA ORDERED A SALAD and a side plate of Italian bread. Most days she didn't even eat lunch, but she had to have something today. Peter had invited her out to Leonardo's in the Rosebank Mall, one of those places that made it hard for her to remember she was in Africa. The two of them sat in a sea of well-shaded outdoor tables while waiters in black ties served a clientele of deeply tanned, precision-groomed white people and a sprinkling of blacks. Two women at the table next to them were drinking a bottle of Chardonnay sitting in a silver ice bucket. It could have been a scene from a New York City summer.

Ordinarily Joanna didn't venture to such places, but she and Peter hadn't spoken since the launch of Water for Freedom. He assured her there was a lot to talk about. He tried to interest her in sharing a carafe of house red, but she told him she had a three o'clock meeting with some church people.

'They don't appreciate the smell of alcohol on your breath,' she said.

'I hate to drink alone.'

'You've managed before,' she said with a smile.

He ordered a beer to go with his ravioli.

'These bloody things can be annoying,' he said as he switched his phone to silent. 'Always going off at the wrong moment.'

'I'm still a holdout,' she said. 'I like the feel of a receiver against my ear.'

Peter told her Pellmar's projects in the Eastern Cape were going 'great guns'. 'From strength to strength, as they say here,' he added.

She mentioned that she'd had a letter from Slim a few days earlier.

'He doesn't seem to be doing well,' she said. 'The government needs to move faster on Aids.'

'Sorry to hear that,' said Peter.

'I'm thinking of trying to raise some money for him,' she said, 'to tide him over until the government starts providing medication.'

'They have so many problems to address,' said Peter.

Joanna was tempted to mention the rest of Slim's letter, the part where he talked about residents in Sivuyile having their water cut off because they couldn't afford to pay the bills. But she decided against it. Peter already had one ear tuned into a conversation at the next table. Two white men in suits were talking about offshore options. Besides, Slim might have been exaggerating. Joanna was sure that if she had HIV, she'd find it difficult to see anything in a positive light.

'I think I could get some UV members in the States to support him,' she said. 'I'm just not sure it's the right approach. UV doesn't like that sort of thing.'

He took a sip of beer and pulled out his chequebook.

'Maybe this will help,' he said, writing out a cheque for R500 and handing it to her. 'Always easier to make money when you have money.'

She thanked him and started in on her salad. She hadn't been trying to persuade him to make a donation. Now it felt as if she owed him something.

For the rest of the lunch, Peter talked about Pellmar. He said their brand was gaining important profile via the pilot in Sivuyile. He did admit, though, that the project had a few growing pains, that some people still didn't understand they had to pay for water.

'There's no free lunch,' he said as the waiter set the black folder in front of him with the bill inside. Joanna fumbled in her wallet for some cash.

'This one's on Pellmar,' Peter said, sliding his credit card into the folder.

As the two of them got up to leave, Peter gave her a quick hug. The days of departing kisses on the cheek had passed.

That afternoon Joanna put together a letter for UV members to raise money for Slim. She emailed a copy to the office in Washington. A few minutes later, Angela phoned.

'This goes against UV policy,' Angela said. 'We support collective action, not personalised charity.'

'Supporting his health is supporting those around him,' said Joanna. 'He's one of those dynamic individuals who can galvanise an organisation. A young man's life is at stake.' She didn't mention it to Angela, but she figured if Peter Franklin could donate R500 to save Slim, so could UV members. There was nothing wrong with that, even if it was personalised.

After a brief discussion, Angela and Joanna reached a compromise. No direct funding from UV would go to Slim, but Joanna could solicit individual contributions through her reports in the newsletter. The fundraising period would be limited to just a few months. After that Slim's fate, like that of thousands of other HIV-positive South Africans, would be in the hands of the government.

When she put down the phone, Joanna wrote Slim a letter, informing him of the fundraising drive and asking him for a photo of himself. In his response he referred to Joanna as a 'giant of international solidarity'. He included two photos and said he preferred the one where he was wrapped in the kafiyyeh.

Joanna overrode Slim's preference, choosing instead the picture where he wore a T-shirt with Madiba's smiling face on the front. Some Americans would get the wrong idea about the kafiyyeh.

She quickly put together an article that said that Slim Yanta was 'no ordinary twenty-three-year-old, not at all like the boy next door to you. He faces a range of unimaginable adversities with courage and conviction.' She added a caption to go with the photo: 'Your donation will keep this future leader of South Africa alive.'

Within a month, Joanna received over $4 000 in donations. With the exchange rate, that was more than enough to supply Slim with medication for a year. One woman from Iowa sent a cheque for $600 and a note saying it was the least she could do 'for a young man whose problems would overwhelm the strongest of souls in Des Moines'.

Once she tallied the money, Joanna told Slim to open a bank account and promised him that the money for his medication would be deposited there every month. She also bought him a cellphone. If he had any problems with his bank account or medication, he could call her.

After just two weeks of taking the tablets, Slim phoned Joanna to tell her that he felt 'strong like an ox'.

'It's like I've been born again,' he said, 'and it's all because of Comrade Joanna and the solidarity of the American people. We may not like your government, but the people we love. I owe them my life.'

Joanna reported Slim's remarks in the UV newsletter, just to reassure the members that their donations were well spent. She felt proud to have contributed to saving a life.

○

A couple of weeks later Slim phoned Joanna to tell her he had moved in with Corleone in OR Tambo.

'I thought you should know,' he said.

'What happened?'

'My uncle's neighbours discovered the virus. They said I would infect their daughters. There is no reasoning with these people.'

'Are you safe there?' she asked.

'I am very comfortable. I was afraid for what they might do to my uncle and his family.'

'I'm sure you did the right thing,' said Joanna. She was still worried. She'd driven past OR Tambo. No one would ever describe it as comfortable.

'I didn't want you to hear the story from someone else,' he said.

'I don't listen to stories,' said Joanna. She thanked him for calling. She was already trying to picture where he slept. She wondered if they had toilets in those shacks, how many people shared a bed.

'The next time I'll just send an SMS,' Slim said, 'though I'm still not quite sure how to do it. My sister can show me. These youngsters know about such things.'

'We're all still learning,' said Joanna. Slim's voice began to break up so she cut the call. Maybe she should have offered to rent a flat for Slim. Was that why he phoned? It could be that he was in real danger. She thought of calling Peter, but she didn't need money, she needed advice. She was glad she and Peter were at least on friendly terms but she couldn't count on him for support. He was too preoccupied with his projects and, as he put it, promoting the brand. She'd have to make another trip to the Eastern Cape soon and find out what was really going on.

Chapter 39

THE MAYOR HAD INVITED all the ANC councillors to his new home in Northridge for a braai. In their monthly caucus meeting he told them he'd just installed a new water feature in his back garden. A miniature version of Victoria Falls was how he described it, with a pump imported from Maryland in America that could hit 20 000 litres an hour.

He informed the councillors the braai would be a 'casual affair'. Constantia was never sure what casual meant for a woman. A man could wear shorts and sandals or running shoes. She didn't know anything about this sporty look. She was a little too old for running shoes and tracksuits and she'd never worn shorts in her entire life.

Jacobs gave her a lift. She ended up wearing a plain yellow dress Monwabisi had bought for her before she became a councillor. It would make him happy. Her yellow African-print headscarf matched the dress. Jacobs said she 'coordinated beautifully, like always'. She said something about the talk of an impending thunderstorm. She didn't know why Jacobs still bothered with the compliments.

Jacobs drove his Audi through the electric gate and parked next to Councillor Fakude's Range Rover. Constantia was breathing heavily by the time she finished hiking up the stone stairs to the front door. The Mayor's house was halfway to the sky. Zukiswa, the Mayor's wife, showed them to the pool area, where the others were sitting. Constantia would never have guessed the woman had spent four years in detention. Her shiny blue West African-print dress made her look fresh out of varsity. The only sign of wear was a mother's midriff. Two children could do that to any woman.

The Mayor circulated with the Glenfiddich, boasting that it was fifteen years old.

'Scotch is like politicians,' he said. 'Both grow better with age.'

Constantia asked for a Fanta.

Fakude told them all he'd been to Vuyani Bungu's fight the previous night in East London. 'The Beast was at his best,' he said.

Constantia excused herself and went to find Zukiswa in the kitchen. Maybe she could help prepare the food. Anything was better than listening to talk about boxing.

The kitchen felt bigger than Monwabisi and Constantia's entire house. A row of Siemens appliances adorned the gigantic black granite slab in the middle of the room, where a young girl was chopping cabbage for coleslaw. Constantia recognised a blender and an electric mixer, but she wasn't sure what the huge white cylinder did. Maybe it was like a grinding mill.

'Is there anything I can do?' asked Constantia.

'Sit down and help me finish this bottle of wine,' said Zukiswa. The Mayor's wife was sitting alone in a little breakfast nook, pouring herself a glass of white Zinfandel.

'I'm not much of a drinker,' said Constantia.

'Never too late to learn,' said Zukiswa as the young girl brought a long-stemmed glass and a bowl full of ice blocks.

'Will your husband be returning to Joburg?' the Mayor's wife asked.

'I don't think so,' said Constantia. 'He is trying to get his welding business going but it's slow. He can't seem to stay out of this politics.'

'It's a disease,' said Zukiswa.

'But we are happy to have him here after all these years,' said Constantia.

Zukiswa poured the wine for Constantia, then plopped in two ice blocks with a pair of tongs. A third one fell on the floor. The girl picked it up and deposited it in the bin.

'It's semi-sweet,' Zukiswa added. 'I hope it will do.'

While she and Zukiswa chatted, Constantia picked up bits of the men's conversation outside through an open window.

'I only need your neutrality,' she heard the Mayor say. 'What I don't need is councillors leading rebellions against government policy. It's already happening in Joburg. What a nightmare. We must leave Take Charge to do their job.'

'Sisonke,' said Fakude. 'We are all on board.'

'Drink up,' said Zukiswa, holding up the bottle. 'It must be empty this afternoon.' Then she told the girl to fetch her a tissue.

The young woman went out of the room and came back with a box of tissues.

'I didn't ask for a whole box,' Zukiswa said. 'Where did you get these from?'

'From the bedroom, m'am.'

'Then take them back there,' said Zukiswa. 'What will we do if we need a tissue in the bedroom?'

'I don't know, madam.'

'And you don't know because you don't think.'

The girl left the room.

'Izintombi zesimanje-manje,' said Zukiswa as she filled up her glass.

Constantia heard the Mayor say something about 'financial realism', but with Zukiswa's chatter she couldn't quite make it all out. The councillor excused herself to use the ladies. She might be able to hear the men better from there.

'The fourth door on the left,' said Zukiswa.

The hallway was as long as a hospital corridor. The fourth door on the left opened into a bathroom, where thick blue towels hung from gold racks. The shower head was on the end of a cord that seemed to come out of the wall. Constantia had seen them in American hotels. She figured four people could fit in the Sizibas' shower at once – maybe five.

She slid the window open gingerly, hoping no one outside would notice.

'The council has begun to understand the principles of financial management, the constraints we face,' said the Mayor.

'Too many people were just taking chances,' said Fakude. 'Acting as if government has a bottomless pool of money.'

Constantia tiptoed over and sat down on the commode.

'Take Charge is going to stop these hooligans in their tracks,' said the Mayor. 'Plus the measures I'm taking on these so-called indigents.'

'These thugs have allies in high places, even within the council,' said Fakude.

'That I doubt,' said Jacobs.

'If you sleep with the devil, eventually you grow horns,' said Fakude.

Constantia heard the back door open, followed by female footsteps moving across the brick patio. She heard Zukiswa tell the men the food was ready. What measures was the Mayor taking on indigents? She'd heard nothing.

'We will continue this discussion, gentlemen,' said the Mayor. 'As for now, there is a more important item on the agenda: meat.'

Constantia went to help Zukiswa serve the food. When the men started talking soccer, the women retreated back to the kitchen. Zukiswa told Constantia she needed the wine on the weekends to blot out Monday to Friday. She was the director of a home for Aids orphans. 'You have no idea what it's like for them,' Zukiswa said.

Constantia thought of Musa and Fidel. What if they lost their father? What if she had turned out to be positive? While Zukiswa spoke of three-year-old triplets from Aliwal who'd been left wrapped in blankets outside the front door of the home, Constantia's mind drifted back to the men's conversation in the back garden. She was the only member of council who slept with the devil. She knew she should be sympathetic to the wonderful work Zukiswa was doing, but she couldn't take her mind off Take Charge. Why was the Mayor so eager to cut these people off? With all the problems of Ukusa, it just didn't make sense.

○

The following morning Constantia received an email with the subject line 'Embargo – not for circulation until 1400h today'. The title of the document was 'Address to Northridge Rotary Club'. Constantia rarely read such things. If she read every statement the Mayor made, she'd never have time to do anything else. Besides, he never wrote his own speeches. He had a team of ghostwriters.

After she skimmed the first screen, she was ready to close the document. Then she saw the word 'indigent' and read further.

'Our council can no longer provide water to those who do not pay. The indigents will receive their lifelines but they must clear all arrears forthwith. We are tired of the persistence of this boycott mentality.'

This was what she'd heard the Mayor mention to Fakude. Ntoni must have known as well, but he'd never said anything to the branch.

'This is an attack on the freeloaders,' the Mayor's statement continued, 'meaning those who can afford to pay but are refusing to pay. Whether they refuse out of habit or because they are trying to undermine government does not matter. The impact is the same. They must be dealt with.'

How would Constantia explain this to Mrs Mehlo or Mrs Ximiya? As a councillor she thought she would be among the first to know when the Mayor changed policy. She was out of the loop. No doubt the Mayor was afraid she would tell everything to the devil she slept with.

Chapter 40

SLIM AND CORLEONE HAD called for a community meeting about the water cut-offs. They'd followed proper procedures, paying the R10 deposit for a room in Sivuyile Hall. As they arrived to set up the room for the meeting, they found the police had circled the building. When they asked one of the officers what was going on, he referred them to Sergeant Zotwana. The Sergeant stood by the front entrance, towering over all the other officers. He looked tall enough to play basketball for one of those American teams.

'In the interests of your safety,' Zotwana told Slim and Corleone, 'we are postponing your meeting indefinitely. We have had a bomb threat and until we have secured the building, it is closed to all.'

Slim surveyed the front of Sivuyile Hall more carefully. He counted a dozen men wearing plastic SAPS face shields blocking all entrances to the building. A bevy of office workers and cleaners stood next to an idling SAPS kwela-kwela in the car park. Apparently everyone had been evacuated.

'We have a democratic right to meet,' said Slim. He fished the permit to use the hall from his pocket and showed it to Zotwana. The Sergeant didn't bother to look.

'We are not denying your democratic rights,' said Zotwana, 'but we cannot allow your meeting to jeopardise the property of the municipality or the safety of the community.

We must secure the area first, search all possible places where an explosive device might be hidden.'

'How long will that take?' asked Slim, putting the permit back in his shirt pocket.

'Not long,' said Zotwana, 'provided it all goes well. Two hours, maybe three.'

'We know your tricks,' said Corleone. 'This comes from the Mayor. He wants to block people from responding to his declaration on indigents.'

'I have my orders,' said Zotwana. 'I don't know about the politics.'

Slim and Corleone backed away from the Sergeant.

'We will remain here until we have exercised our democratic rights,' Corleone said loudly. Three of the police in full riot gear stepped in unison towards Corleone. One slid his nightstick out of the loop in his belt.

Slim grabbed Corleone by the arm and moved him farther from the police.

'There is no use in fighting these people,' said Slim. 'They are lackeys of the Mayor. We must just reschedule and find another venue.'

'We can't let them intimidate us,' said Corleone.

As the two debated the issue, several people arrived for the meeting. Despite Corleone's objections, they all agreed with Slim's proposal. Waiting could turn into an all-day affair and the longer the police baked in the sun in their riot gear, the more likely they were to start trouble.

◯

Ten days later, thirty-three people gathered in the creaking pews of the Methodist church. Most of those attending brought their Bibles. Mrs Mehlo had told the Pastor the group was studying the Psalms. She brought along three of her neighbours, including the rotund Mrs Ximiya, who'd been in arrears ever since the night the Mehlos' house burnt down. She said she used up two months' water to fight the fire.

Slim directed the proceedings from a folding chair in front of the altar railing. He felt a little faint, but the turnout was encouraging.

Mrs Mehlo opened by asking God to 'deliver everyone to a day when they didn't have to choose between water and food, when they would have enough water to put out the fires in their lives'. Slim was relieved when she got to her 'amen'. Sometimes the woman got carried away, talking about everything from her unemployed son to the latest inventory in the clothing stall. Before Slim could propose adoption of the agenda, Mrs Mehlo started up again, telling everyone the council's next move would probably be to start charging people for the air they were breathing.

'May God forgive them if they do,' she added.

'Or strike them down,' said Mrs Ximiya

'The council has sold us out,' said Mrs Mehlo.

Slim reminded the people the purpose of the meeting was to address the water problem. 'There are so many issues,' he said. 'Payment of arrears, emergency water, the Mayor's declaration on indigents, the activities of Take Charge.'

As Slim finished with his list, Monwabisi came in through the door and said he wanted to render an apology.

'Apology accepted,' said Slim.

'I haven't delivered the apology yet,' said Monwabisi.

'You are late,' said Slim. 'Apology accepted. Let us move on.'

'I'm not apologising for arriving late,' he said. 'I apologise for being tricked. I have sold the community a white elephant.'

Mrs Mehlo proposed a motion to accept the apology. Slim argued that Monwabisi was not to blame, that they must maintain focus on the 'true culprits' – the Mayor and the American company that was running the show.

'Where is your wife?' Corleone asked Monwabisi.

'I don't speak for her,' Monwabisi said. 'She is free to come and go as she pleases.'

'Nothing is free in this free South Africa,' said Mrs Mehlo. The ululating drowned out the rest of what she had to say.

Slim tried to call the meeting back to order.

'Let us march to the Mayor's house and show him how we feel,' said Corleone. 'He has plenty of water there, comrades. We can bring our swimming costumes.'

Corleone's proposal brought the crowd to their feet. While they sang 'Sifuna amanzi', Mrs Mehlo paraded down the aisle mimicking a prancing beauty queen contestant in a bikini.

Once the singing subsided, Monwabisi cautioned the meeting that a demonstration at the Mayor's house could be dangerous. 'There will be twice as many police there as they used to block the hall,' he warned.

Corleone said the people must not be afraid of a few overweight goons. 'We will not be intimidated again,' he added.

'If we shout loud enough through the Mayor's front door, he is bound to listen,' said Mrs Mehlo. Her parade route in her imaginary bikini had landed her right next to Slim at the front.

Monwabisi's next comment, that people must remain level-headed, brought silence. Slim felt embarrassed for this once great hero. He hated to see a former shop steward so out of step with the people. Monwabisi was still stuck in the past. Once they marched to the Mayor's house, maybe Comrade RDP and even his wife would realise that for the first time in history, the people's voice would be heard in Northridge. This was what a democratic South Africa was all about.

Monwabisi made one last appeal for moderation. 'If the police want to arrest us,' he said, 'we must disperse. We are not strong enough to afford to have all of us in jail. Most of us can't afford water, let alone lawyers.'

Though Slim didn't agree with Monwabisi's assessment, he was too tired to resist. The meeting agreed there would be no arrests. This was just a protest to show the Mayor how serious the problem had become. 'The next time,' Slim assured the crowd, 'we will occupy the Mayor's house until he agrees to our demands.'

○

Later that night Monwabisi reported on the meeting to his wife.

'The people are calling the council members sell-outs,' he told Constantia. 'You must stand up to the Mayor.'

'He doesn't listen to me,' she said. She had to wash Musa's school jersey for the next day. Portia was already gone and Musa had spilled gravy on it at dinner.

She carried a bucket into the bathroom. 'I hope it can dry by morning,' she said. She filled the bucket about halfway, added a little Omo and a shot of Jik. 'Portia should have made him change clothes,' she said, scrubbing at the stain. 'This may not come out.'

'That party of yours, they are crossing the line,' said Monwabisi.

Constantia scrubbed with care. A jersey could stretch.

'You must quit,' he said. 'Resign.'

'We can't just resign every time something bad happens,' she said, wringing out the jersey. The water in the bucket turned very light blue. 'Too much Jik,' she said.

She draped the jersey over one rung of the drying rack. New jerseys dried fast. The old wool ones could take two or three days in winter.

'I'm walking a tightrope,' she said, 'doing what I can to keep the indigents receiving their water. It's not perfect, but if I wasn't there do you think Fakude would do the job?'

'You're missing the point,' he said. 'Even the language these days. These are not indigents. They are the oppressed masses. Don't you remember them? Besides, the Mayor wants to cut them off as well.'

Suddenly Monwabisi staggered, then reached for the kitchen wall. Constantia grabbed him by the arm.

'Just a little dizzy spell,' he said.

She led him off to the bedroom. He flopped down onto his back on top of the mattress. 'It's nothing serious,' he said. 'It just happens once in a while. I'm fine.'

Constantia turned away from her husband and squirted some lotion into her hand from a bottle on her dresser. It had a lovely coconut smell. She'd bought it in Atlanta.

'You must challenge the Mayor,' Monwabisi said, 'and his bourgeois ideology.'

'A councillor must do more than engage in debates about whether the ANC is a bourgeois organisation,' she said.

He didn't reply.

She squirted some more lotion into her hand and spread it up and down her arms. 'A councillor is not paid just to discuss,' she said. 'We must deliver something to the people.'

She waited a few seconds for Monwabisi's answer. When she heard nothing, she turned around to read the expression on his face. He was fast asleep.

Chapter 41

THE MAYOR AND HIS TWO children, Oliver and Olivia, were coming home from a birthday party at the house of one of their schoolmates. The Mayor didn't get many opportunities to do things with his children, so this was a special day. He'd stayed at the party for almost an hour, talking to the parents of other kids, drinking some very watered-down fruit punch and nibbling on a far-too-sweet chocolate cake.

Energised by a feeding frenzy of Fanta, Smarties, cake and vanilla ice cream, the back seat of the family Benz could barely contain the two youngsters. Hours of bouncing on the jumping castle hadn't tamed all that sugar. They couldn't stop singing the *Takalani Sesame* song.

Their glee evaporated as the driver turned the corner near their house. Dozens of people were standing in the street shouting and singing. The Mayor speed-dialled his wife on the home phone. She picked up on the first ring.

'They've turned off the water,' Zukiswa told him, 'and dumped rubbish across the front garden.'

There was a calmness in her voice. She hadn't started drinking yet.

'The police said they are on the way,' she said. 'Why didn't they stop this?'

'The Chief told me there were roadblocks on every access road,' said the Mayor, 'but Bush Bucks are playing today, so the Chief is not around.' He told the driver to drop him off and take his children to his wife's brother's house in Sivuyile.

The driver told him he shouldn't run the risk of confronting these hooligans. He spoke in Sesotho so the children wouldn't understand.

The Mayor said that he couldn't allow anyone to intimidate him. 'I didn't do it on the Island,' he said. 'I won't have it happen in my own house.' He looked again at this group of invaders. There was a TV camera among them.

'Tata, the people are messing our house,' said Oliver.

'Don't worry,' said the Mayor. 'I'm going to tell them to clean up the mess. When they've finished cleaning, you'll come home and watch *Antz*.'

'On the big TV?' asked Olivia.

'On the big TV,' said the Mayor. He kissed each of the children on the forehead before the driver sped off.

The Mayor adjusted his coat and made sure his shirt was properly tucked in. A youth stood near the front gate of the Sizibas' house shouting through a bullhorn.

'We are the people's voice,' said the young man. 'We will not allow our community to suffer without water while some American company rakes in profits from prepaids. Phantsi ngeeprepaid, phantsi.'

A short youngster with dreadlocks was the first to spot the Mayor. He pulled some stones and a slingshot out of his pocket and took aim. Monwabisi grabbed him from behind before the young man had a chance to shoot.

'You're playing into their hands,' Monwabisi told him.

'Let him see what it feels like to suffer,' said the young man.

'He's had his share of suffering,' said Monwabisi. 'We are here to talk.'

'You don't talk to the enemy,' said the young man.

'Sometimes you have no choice,' said Monwabisi. 'Put down the stones.'

The young man dropped the rocks on the pavement and ran up the street, calling on everyone to follow him and confront the Mayor. The crowd toyi-toyied their way towards Siziba. Several women had pinned their yellow indigent forms to their chest. Mrs Mehlo, supporting herself with a black wooden cane, had only a tiny scrap of hers taped to her hat.

Mrs Ximiya carried a banner that said, 'Indigents need water too.' Behind her were the Damanes, the first people to receive water in Sivuyile. Their placard said, 'Another cut-off victim.'

The young man with the dreads circled around the Mayor, his knees driving up to his chest while he pointed a menacing finger at this man he'd called an 'enemy'. The crowd launched into a song about the leaders with big bellies.

'Amaqabane!' shouted the Mayor. 'Let us talk. Who are your representatives, comrades?'

'Simunye,' said Slim. 'We are one.' The crowd laughed. SABC slogans of the Rainbow Nation days were ancient history.

'Comrade Mayor,' said Mrs Mehlo, 'we have come here today by the grace of God to remind you that some of us in Ukusa are still without water, some of us who stay just a block or two from where you used to live.'

'We have come to tell you our swimming pools are empty,' shouted Corleone. 'We need a refill.'

'We demand that you take back the decision that everyone must pay immediately,' said Slim. 'We have no money, we are unemployed, but still we need water. You can make us pay when you have provided us with jobs.'

A few women ululated, then Corleone began another song. 'Siziba, Siziba, Siziba,' he sang, invoking the Mayor's name. 'Ngamasimba lent'uyenzayo.'

This time it only lasted half a verse. The lyrics caught some of the women off guard. Corleone had told the Mayor he was 'up to shit'.

'Amaqabane,' said the Mayor. 'Let me assure you that no one who is truly indigent will go without water. You have my word on that.'

Mrs Ximiya yanked the indigent form off her chest and threw it at the Mayor's feet.

'Your word is useless!' shouted Mrs Mehlo. 'My ID was burnt in a house fire, now they tell me I can't be indigent.'

'Phantsi ngokuthetha!' shouted the young man in the dreadlocks. 'Down with talking. Sifuna iaction.'

The Mayor let the hecklers finish.

'Comrades,' he said, 'we must remember that we now have channels to settle such issues. We fought long and hard for them.'

As three yellow police bakkies turned the corner, a fountain of water exploded several metres in the air from the Mayor's front lawn. Two young men ran away from the broken water line with fists held high.

'Here come the proper channels,' said Corleone, glancing at the police vehicles.

A Hippo followed, then a Nyala. From the other end of the street came more bakkies. A voice from the sky boomed out a warning.

'You have two minutes to disperse,' spoke the helicopter PA. 'This is an illegal gathering.'

'Voetsek!'

'Fuck off!'

Dozens of policemen jumped out of the bakkies. The yellow SAPS lettering on their shields looked like fresh paint.

'You must disperse,' the Mayor said. Then, looking at Monwabisi, he said, 'Get this impi of yours out of here before someone gets hurt.'

Some of the youth started to toyi-toyi again. A friend of Mrs Mehlo grabbed her cane and shook it at the chopper. 'Asina amanzi!' she shouted. 'Voetsek!'

Comrade Slim ordered the group to sit with him in the middle of the street. 'They can't touch us here,' he said. 'What are they going to do, run over us with their bakkies?'

Half a dozen people sat down next to Slim. Another group toyi-toyied and kept up the refrain about the big bellies.

Mrs Mehlo rushed over to Slim. 'We agreed to disperse,' she said. 'People will be hurt.'

'Amaqabane,' said the Mayor. 'This is now your last chance.'

The youth kept toyi-toying, singing louder than ever.

'Talk some sense into them, Radebe,' the Mayor said to Monwabisi. 'You know what can happen here.'

'We will keep coming back,' said Monwabisi, 'until our victory is won.'

'Just leave immediately,' said the Mayor, 'before people get hurt. Their blood will be on your hands.'

'You have one minute to disperse,' came the booming voice from the chopper. 'You are engaged in an illegal gathering.'

Monwabisi rushed towards Slim. The young man was sitting in the road, his arms locked with the protestors on either side of him.

'We agreed to disperse,' said Monwabisi. 'People can be injured here – maybe killed. It will be on our hands.'

'I can't control what the police do,' said Slim.

Monwabisi and Slim continued their debate. Several people sitting on the road stood up and started to walk down the street.

'We are now disorganised,' one of them said. 'Our leaders are quarrelling while the enemy load their guns.'

Slim leaped to his feet and stood still for a moment, as if he was trying to find his balance.

'Amaqabane,' he said. 'We have won our victory for the moment. The Mayor has heard our demands.'

While the rest of the people walked away, Slim slumped to the ground. 'I'm tired, qabane,' he said to Monwabisi. 'I don't know what's happening to me.'

Monwabisi was suddenly aware of the odour of dirty nappies – only this was from a grown man. He lifted Slim up and helped him walk down the street. 'It must have been something I ate,' Slim said with a childish grin.

Within five minutes the street was clear save one bakkie-load of cops who remained behind to guard the Mayor's house and clean his yard. Half an hour later the Mayor's driver dropped off Oliver and Olivia, who went inside the house and watched *Antz* on the big TV.

Chapter 42

SUSAN CHECKED HER DIARY again. She had a meeting with some Germans at ten o'clock. She'd tell Dipuo to hold all calls until then. Maybe she could get a little work done on the quarterly report for the department. Tumahole had offloaded it onto her as usual. She put the tea in the microwave. Not even enough time to let it steep. Peter sat at the table reading the morning paper. He'd already had some toast.

'This is bullshit,' he said.

She glanced over his shoulder at the article. 'People Protest Water Cut-offs in the Eastern Cape,' the headline read.

A photo showed the Mayor's driveway littered with white plastic bags and empty dog-food cans. Water from a sprinkler was shooting into the sky. The writer went on to quote Monwabisi on how the prepaids were 'undermining democracy in South Africa. The rich are getting richer while the poor are getting thirsty.'

'The man was an unemployed bum before we hired him,' said Peter. 'As soon as he got the job he started shooting off his mouth.'

'Don't make too much of it,' said Susan. 'We are a protesting nation.'

'It'll probably be on national TV,' said Peter. 'Look.' He pointed to a TV cameraman in front of the Mayor's house in the photo. He opened the paper to read the rest of the article. He tapped his finger on a page-five photo of Slim Yanta leading the crowd in some chant.

'And to think I gave him money,' said Peter. 'I should have known better.'

'Calm down,' said Susan. 'Tomorrow there will be a strike in Bloemfontein, a march to the housing office in Mmabatho. It's business as usual here. Haven't you figured that out yet?' She got the cup out of the microwave, removed the tea bag and added a little milk. She hoped Peter would calm down.

'I have to go to the Eastern Cape ASAP,' he said. 'To show we are behind Siziba 100 per cent. At least in Bulgaria people knew a good thing when they had it.'

Susan sat down and scribbled a reminder in her diary about getting a researcher to evaluate the impact of a gas-fired power station in Cape Town. It was time for the nation to move away from coal. She got up and gathered her bag and briefcase.

'Can't you see how wrong this is?' said Peter. 'The Mayor spent years on Robben Island. He's a real gentleman.'

'Siziba?' she asked as she made her way towards the back door. 'C'mon, let's go.'

'Well, you know what I mean,' Peter said as he folded up the paper and stuck it in his jacket pocket. 'And that Joanna. I can't believe her.' He followed Susan out the door.

'Siziba used to donner people for disagreeing with him,' she said. 'He had to be disciplined twice by the ANC.' She headed for the car, wondering if that gas-powered plant was realistic or just another consultant's pipe dream. Peter was already off her radar.

'At least he has some spine,' Peter replied as she got into the Jetta. She waved goodbye without looking and he headed for his car. The driver reminded Susan to put on her seat belt as she pulled the draft of the quarterly report out of her bag. The drive would give her time to rework the executive summary.

She just wished Peter would stop being so critical, as if South Africans never got it right. And the way he slid into a panic over the most trivial issues was so annoying. There wasn't even a gap in her diary for the next ten days to give her a moment to think about their relationship. Sometimes she wondered if she'd end up as a sort of trophy of Peter's African adventure, her picture hanging like a kudu head over a mantelpiece in a New York flat. Relationships were hard even before she became a Deputy Minister. Now they seemed impossible.

She hoped he wouldn't go jetting off to the Eastern Cape to confront Monwabisi. She had enough fires to put out already without adding one started by her boyfriend.

Chapter 43

THE ANC'S DISCIPLINARY committee held their meetings in the small conference room in Sivuyile Hall. This time they had two cases to consider: Slim Yanta and Monwabisi Radebe. The hearing would address the actions of the two members during the demonstration at the Mayor's house.

The brick walls of the conference room held flip charts of previous users: the Rural Development Forum revisiting their strategic plan, the Communist Party's notes on the 'nature of the NDR'. A few faces from a ragged poster of the 1987 miners' strike peeked out between some lists of measurable outcomes and quantifiable outputs. A small space heater glowed in the corner but it wasn't having much effect. Constantia could see her breath.

While waiting for the urn to boil, she read the brief outline Ntoni had prepared. She and the other committee members – Nobatana, Fakude, and Nompumelelo Mpupa – would need many cups of tea to get through this day. Nobatana had wrapped himself in a brown blanket but he claimed the blood wasn't reaching his feet.

Nompumelelo sliced a chocolate cake and put some samoosas on paper plates. 'Men never think of bringing food,' she said. 'If we left it to them, we would starve.'

Constantia wasn't worrying about food. Her family's future could be in the balance.

Slim came first. He wore combat boots and a black ANC

cap slightly askew. Constantia hoped he would remove the cap as a sign of respect for the committee. Instead, as he sat down, he reversed it so the ANC logo was at the back. Fakude and Nobatana would already be put off.

'Comrade Yanta,' said Ntoni, 'the ANC is a democratic organisation. We encourage debate among our members. At the same time, we are disciplined cadre. Debate must be constructive, conducted in a dignified manner. Respect for others and the welfare of the organisation are paramount.'

Slim stared off at the brick walls, as if he was trying to find an answer to Ntoni from one of the flip charts. He hadn't even worn a jacket, just a grey jersey with a hole at the elbow.

'The charges before the committee state that you went beyond our boundaries,' said Ntoni.

Fakude read from a prepared text containing the allegation that 'Comrade Yanta' had intentionally bypassed proper party structures and knowingly promoted the destruction of the property of a member of the ANC and harassed his family members.

'We harassed no one,' said Slim. 'We were exercising our democratic rights.'

'Please, comrade,' said Ntoni. 'Your chance will come.'

'This is a kangaroo court,' said Slim.

Constantia could hear the irritation in Fakude's voice as he continued reading. He was almost shouting. She hoped the councillor could hold his temper.

'You want to punish those who protest,' said Slim once Fakude had finished, 'not those who cut off people's water. You are lost.' He took off his hat and slapped it on the table.

Nobatana raised his hand to speak.

'I have seen many cadre like yourself in my lifetime,' said the old man. 'Angry, undisciplined. When those boys from Soweto came to the Island after 1976, they were just like you.

Political struggle is a long process, comrade. Those who want change overnight are always disappointed.'

Steam began to rise from the urn.

'While we take our tea, I want you to think carefully about what Comrade Nobatana has told you,' Ntoni said to Slim.

The committee busied themselves with tea bags and sugar. Constantia used her fingernail file to slit open the box of long-life milk. Monwabisi was sitting outside in the hallway. She thought of bringing him some tea but the committee might take it wrongly. Instead she set a steaming styrofoam cup down in front of Slim. He left it sitting there, didn't even wrap his hands around the cup to keep them warm.

When the committee regrouped, Nobatana continued.

'I suggest you rethink your actions at the Mayor's house,' said the old man. 'You must engage with people, debate, discuss, think, analyse, listen, then repeat the process, not just run into the streets when something doesn't go your way.'

The young man looked down, avoiding Nobatana's gaze. Constantia read it as a gesture of respect, a good sign. Maybe he was starting to listen.

'We can forgive your actions,' said Nobatana, 'but you must be prepared to meet us halfway.'

Slim put his ANC cap back on his head, pulled it down almost over his eyes and looked straight at Ntoni.

'I believe in the spirit of no surrender,' said Slim.

'What does that mean to you?' asked Fakude.

'You have forgotten,' said Slim. 'The ones who have sold our water to the Americans have forgotten about the spirit of no surrender. I should have expected such a thing. How much does it take to buy an ANC councillor? How many trips to New York?'

Fakude rose out of his chair and moved towards Slim. Constantia jumped up and ran over to protect Slim, but Nobatana grabbed Fakude's arm before she got there. She went back to her seat and just sat with her eyes closed. The hearing was falling to pieces before it had even started.

'If the ANC were not a party of discipline,' said Fakude, 'I would thrash you, teach you a lesson.' He pounded his fist into his palm.

'Who are you to question me?' Fakude continued. 'I was in detention when you were in nappies. What have you done for the people of South Africa besides litter the Mayor's house and disrupt the meetings of our organisation?'

Ntoni tapped his spoon against the metal table.

'We must follow procedure here, comrades,' he said, 'not resort to personal attacks no matter how justified we may think they seem.'

'Sorry, Com Chair,' said Fakude. He massaged his tightly balled right fist with his left hand, then cracked his knuckles and glared at Slim.

Constantia asked for the floor. If she couldn't calm things down, the committee would become totally fed up before they even got to her husband.

'No one questions your dedication,' she said to Slim. 'We know you are seriously committed to developing this community. Do you realise that?'

'Yes, comrade,' Slim replied.

'And do you recognise that a political organisation needs some form of discipline, that every member cannot just do as they please, especially if it involves endangering other members?'

'I have endangered no one.'

'That is not my question,' said Constantia. 'I asked about the need for discipline.'

'It's completely obvious,' said Slim. He sat back in his chair and folded his arms. She could see he was starting to shiver. Young men always seemed to think they were immune to the cold. How could her husband have spent so much time with this youngster? She wasn't sure if Slim had ever shaved. Had he slept with a woman? He looked like one of those chaps from the eighties who used to fire their guns at funerals. And he had those lumps behind his ears. Maybe that's what he shared with Monwabisi. But now that her husband had the medication, he didn't have to worry.

'If it is so obvious,' said Fakude, 'why could you not follow the discipline of this organisation and avoid marching to the Mayor's house?'

'I wasn't aware that exercising my democratic rights violated the rules of the organisation.'

'And if you were aware,' said Fakude, 'would you still have embarked on this action?'

'People have no water. The Mayor needed a wake-up.'

Constantia raised her hand to speak again but Ntoni ignored her.

'That is why we have structures,' said Fakude. 'You seem to feel you are above them. You treat them with disdain.'

'My disdain is for those with big bellies, who sell our water to the Americans. Those who grew up here but have forgotten their roots.'

'Enough, comrade, enough,' said Ntoni.

Fakude asked to be excused to use the gents. The slamming of the door echoed across the room as he left.

'Has this kangaroo court finished its business?' asked Slim.

'We will deliberate and inform you of our decision in due course,' said Ntoni. 'Wait outside.'

'A luta continua!' Slim shouted as he left the room, his right fist in the air.

Constantia buried her face in her hands. Is this what her husband was going to do as well – shout slogans at the committee like a child who didn't get his way? Slim could at least be forgiven. He was young, inexperienced. Monwabisi was too old to be acting like he was still in COSAS. Constantia tried to convince the rest of the committee that Slim could still be saved.

'Besides,' she added, 'if we expel him, he might create bigger problems.'

'We can't decide on the basis of our fear of what he might become,' said Ntoni.

A sound of running shoes squeaking on the floor came from the hallway. Then something slammed against the door.

'Uthengise ilizwe!' shouted Slim. 'You have sold the nation.'

Ntoni and Nompumelelo dashed for the door. Constantia followed.

Fakude had Slim pinned against the wall, his fist poised to smash the young man's face. Nompumelelo grabbed Fakude's arm.

'You are nothing to the ANC!' shouted Fakude. 'Nothing to South Africa! We have no use for thugs and hooligans.'

Slim twisted loose from Fakude's grip. He bent down to pick up his cap.

'This is why we have structures,' said Ntoni.

'Your structures are useless,' said Slim. He walked down the hall. Just before he got ready to turn towards the door, he faced Ntoni and the others and threw his cap at them. It landed at Fakude's feet.

'He bumped me on purpose when I was walking to the loo,' said Fakude, 'then said I was a sell-out. Sometimes a young boy must be taught a lesson.'

'He's a loose cannon,' said Nobatana.

The vote was four to one in favour of expulsion. Constantia felt as if her dissenting vote was like shouting at the incoming sea.

◯

Constantia had moved to the back of the room by the time Monwabisi came in. The committee had agreed she could stay but without the right to speak. Her husband had ignored her suggestion to wear his navy-blue suit. He'd worn his colours – the red of the metalworkers. As Ntoni outlined the process of the hearing, Constantia thought about her trip to Northridge the day before. She'd gone with an estate agent to look at a house. Three bedrooms; the plot fenced and gated. The agent had told her she could qualify for a bond. She hadn't told Monwabisi. He would have called it one of her 'bourgeois fantasies'.

She took a big bite from one of the samoosas Nompumelelo had brought. The green chillies in the mince brought perspiration to her forehead.

'My disappointment is endless,' said Monwabisi. 'I never thought I would reach a point where people in Ukusa would have their water cut off and not a single official of the ANC would be prepared to lift a finger. Water cannot wait until tomorrow.'

He looked at Constantia. She turned away and took another samoosa. She'd regret it later. Hot food always stirred up her heartburn. But she had no choice. The cake was finished.

'If this were just about water,' said Fakude, 'it wouldn't be a problem. But it is a matter of undermining those elected to office, the heroes of our struggle. You should have learned discipline by now.'

Constantia wanted to interrupt Fakude. The councillor spoke as if her husband was looking for power. Monwabisi Radebe wasn't like that. He had the interests of the working class at heart. Even with a deadly virus he was thinking of others. He just wasn't thinking quite clearly.

Nobatana spoke after Fakude, noting that he had more sympathy for a lightie than for a veteran of the struggle. 'By now you should know better,' said the old man. He tightened the blanket around himself and looked away.

Ntoni asked Monwabisi if he had anything to say in his defence. The former shop steward cleared his throat, then glanced at Constantia. She hoped he would keep quiet. Whatever he had to say would be something no one wanted to hear.

'The ANC became a party of the bourgeoisie when we abandoned the RDP for GEAR,' said Monwabisi. 'Water cut-offs are a direct result. The Mayor and his neighbours have no problem of water. It is time he thought of Sivuyile. We wanted to give him a reminder. Nothing more.'

Nobatana wriggled free of the blanket so his hands could help him speak.

'I have a simple question for Comrade Monwabisi,' said Nobatana. 'If the ANC is a party of the bourgeoisie, how can you continue to remain a member?'

'That's a question I have asked myself many times,' said Monwabisi.

'On the other hand,' said Ntoni, 'why would we want members in our party who think we are the enemies of the working class?'

'My question exactly,' said Fakude.

Constantia finished the last samoosa. The peri-peri was already percolating with the greasy onions in her stomach. She thought about Musa and Fidel. How would she explain it to them if their father was expelled? They still hung on his every word when he told stories about Johannesburg, often stood in the front garden and cheered for him when he came home from a run. He was still their father, but she didn't want them following in his footsteps.

'It appears,' said Ntoni, 'you want the ANC to be a party

of the working class, something it can never be. We are a party for all democratic South Africans.'

'Of course,' said Monwabisi. 'The question is, democracy for who?'

Nobatana had an answer. He reminded the meeting how in the 1980s many elements in the ANC tried to suppress differing points of view.

'Comrade Oliver Tambo stepped forward,' said the old man, 'and kept us from going that Soviet road where dissidents end up in Siberia and don't even know why.' Nobatana then detoured back through the Stalinist purges of the 1930s, lamenting the passing of Bukharin, Tomsky, Kamenev, Zinoviev. 'Great comrades,' he called them. Constantia knew this lesson in history wasn't helping. She wished Ntoni would intervene, get Comrade Nobatana back on track. She resisted the temptation to bend over to ease the pain in her stomach. It would look as if she wasn't paying attention.

Ntoni quietly asked Nobatana to connect those 'great comrades' to the 'task at hand, the issue of Monwabisi Radebe'.

'I'm just pointing out that we don't persecute dissidents in the ANC,' he said. 'We give them proper hearings. We educate and discipline. We have no Siberia.'

'Comrade Radebe,' said Fakude, 'do you regret your actions that day at the Mayor's house?'

'No ways,' said Monwabisi. 'How can I be regret defending people who are without water?'

By a vote of four to zero, the committee expelled Monwabisi. Constantia left the room when she heard the decision and raced to the ladies. She didn't make it. The samoosas came up in the hallway, right near where Fakude had pinned Slim against the wall. Tributaries of green liquid began to spread across the floor. She couldn't believe how many onions were in those samoosas. She rushed into the ladies, took a quick drink of water and unrolled some sheets of toilet tissue. She needed a dustpan or a mop but she wasn't about to go and ask someone. How would it look for a councillor to be throwing up in the hallways? She tore a poster for a secretarial course off the wall and used it to scoop up some of the vomit. After dumping four scoops into the bin, she got another wave of nausea. Sometimes when she had to clean up after the kids at the nursery school when they got sick, she felt like throwing up herself. It was all coming back. She took a deep breath and got down on her hands and knees to wipe the floor clean with the tissue. Her hands looked different now, even to her own eyes. Carefully manicured nails didn't fit with scouring vomit off of floors. She heard some rustling inside the conference room, as if they might be coming out. She couldn't let them find her like this. She wiped faster and faster until all that remained was the stink. If anyone asked, she could blame that on someone else. Monwabisi had driven her to this, taken her backwards to those days when she was on her hands and knees cleaning up other people's messes.

She got back in the meeting room in time to watch Monwabisi circle the table and shake hands with each member of the committee.

'I respect your verdict,' said Monwabisi, 'though I disagree. I hope the ANC can find its way out of this darkness.'

'We hope one day you will see the light,' said Fakude.

Monwabisi left the room. Constantia didn't try to catch up with him.

Chapter 44

'YOU TAKE THE BOYS TO school tomorrow,' Constantia wrote on a piece of paper. She handed it to Fidel. 'Give this to your father,' she said.

Fidel walked into the lounge and delivered the note to his father. A few seconds later he returned to Constantia. 'Tata says that's okay,' Fidel told his mother.

This was the sixth day of silence in the Radebe house. To top it off, Constantia had bumped into Madeline Moyo the day after the hearing. The young Zimbabwean asked Constantia how her mother was adjusting to living in the house. As their discussion continued, Constantia figured out that Monwabisi had chased Madeline away with a lie. Things had reached a new low.

On the evening of day seven, Monwabisi appeared at the bedroom door when his wife was preparing to sleep.

'This can't continue,' he said. 'I've done nothing to you.'

Constantia removed the elastic band that gripped her extensions together, then rubbed her arms with lotion.

'You've destroyed our family,' she said. 'There are other ways to help people get their water.'

'Better to die standing than to live on my knees,' he said.

'Enough of slogans,' she said. 'They mean nothing.' Her husband was now acting like Yanta. The next thing he would be shooting his hand up in the air, shouting down with this and down with that.

He followed her as she went to check on the boys. They were curled up on their beds in deep sleep. Musa let loose a gentle snore as his parents left the room.

'You consult that small boy Yanta about all these things but not your wife,' she said. 'Who buys your food? Am I the enemy now?'

'Must I get a mandate from my wife to talk to people in the community?' he asked. He reminded her she was probably making up shopping lists for the nursery school when he was dodging bullets at train stations and on the streets of Katlehong in 1992. 'Why should I be asking you permission for anything?' he said.

'You treat me like a schoolgirl,' she said.

'You are the mother of my children.'

'I am also a cadre of the African National Congress,' she said. 'You don't see that. If you did, you wouldn't act like this. And you wouldn't have lied to me about Madeline Moyo.'

Monwabisi went silent, then flopped down on the sofa. 'You must resign,' he said.

'Resign,' she said. 'Is that all you can think of to say? Resign for what? What about our sons? Resign and do what? Will those small boys of yours buy your medicine? And now I find you are a liar on top of it all. I should have known all this the moment you came home with that virus.'

'The ANC is lost, don't you see that?' he said. 'We can make something else, an alternative.'

'No party is perfect but there is nothing else. You're not hearing me.'

'We can make something else,' he repeated.

She left the room. Once again her husband had disappeared into a world of wild ideas. He'd taught her to be 'strategic'. Now he was getting caught up in the heat of the moment. The time for this debate had passed. And he still hadn't admitted the lie about Madeline Moyo, let alone apologised.

'We can't pretend that the ANC hasn't crossed a line,' he shouted at her as she went through the front door. The night air cooled the tension. She wanted to scream at him. Was that the only way he would listen to her? She heard a car backfire in the distance. Or was it a gunshot? Cars didn't backfire these days.

Two days later he showed her his bank account balance: R18 563. More than a year of his medicine money had gone into that account and he was still running ten kilometres in less than forty-five minutes.

'I don't need those little pills,' he said. 'Just more vegetables and a clear conscience. Aids is a myth, an invention of the imperialists.'

'How many other secrets are you keeping?' she said. 'Maybe you have another family somewhere, a flock of children.'

'I was saving the money for a rainy day,' he said. 'I didn't feel right taking so much from your salary.'

She wanted to believe him but it was too late. What if Fidel or Musa had gotten sick? Would he have volunteered to pay the doctor bills? If he had all that money, he didn't really need her any more. He could buy his own medicine or choose not to. And now he was saying that Aids didn't even exist. So he thought she was a silly fool for making her family suffer to buy him tablets for a myth. What she really wanted now was to get that R18 000 back from him. It was enough to make a deposit on a house. She'd ring that estate agent in the morning. Even without that R18 000, there was no choice.

Chapter 45

'I WASTED MONEY ON those suits,' thought Mthetho as he pulled up to the Ukusa municipal offices. 'My cousin refuses to learn. Now I must clean up his mess.'

Constantia wasn't in and her cell only gave a voicemail option. Shell House – or Luthuli House, as they called it nowadays – had ordered him to talk to her. After his expulsion, Monwabisi spoke to a reporter from Radio Netherlands. He said the ANC leadership had 'abandoned the working class'. He also threw in some disparaging comments about GEAR and the World Bank's growing influence in South Africa. 'We are in danger of a coup by free-market economists' were his exact words.

The people in Joburg told Mthetho that 'Comrade Constantia must rein in her husband's efforts to achieve global notoriety'. He'd try to find her at the house.

Portia told Mthetho that Constantia was not in and Monwabisi was asleep. 'He often sleeps during the day now,' she added. 'You can wait inside while I wake him.'

Mthetho took one step into the lounge and wondered if he was in the right house. It looked as if burglars had cleaned it out. There was no sofa, nothing on the walls except a lone poster of Doctor Khumalo. The lounge suite had shrunken to a white plastic garden table and three matching chairs. Even the television was gone.

'What happened?' Mthetho asked Portia.

'Tata can tell you better,' she said.

Ten minutes later Monwabisi came out of the bedroom. He stepped slowly towards one of the plastic chairs and eased himself down into the seat with a series of grunts. He must have lost ten kilograms.

'The family is gone,' said Monwabisi. 'Two days ago.'

'Gone?'

'Moved out. She's bought a house in Northridge. She's driving a new A4.'

'Shame,' said Mthetho.

The Deputy Minister waited for the void in Monwabisi's eyes to disappear. He wasn't sure whether to talk about the expulsion or Constantia's departure. The people in Luthuli House would be relieved to know that Ukusa's only female councillor had decided to look for greener pastures.

'Where are the boys?' asked Mthetho.

'They will come on weekends,' said Monwabisi.

'I can speak to her,' said Mthetho. 'Such things blow over.'

'We are divorcing,' said Monwabisi. 'She has abandoned the working class.'

'But you are okay?' asked Mthetho.

Monwabisi looked like a startled little mouse waiting for the next footfall. Mthetho knew the symptoms.

'If you need medical assistance,' said Mthetho, 'I have some connections.' He glanced at his watch. The Danes were coming for another meeting that afternoon.

'It's all right,' said Monwabisi. 'In a couple of days I'll be fine. It's just the flu.'

'I'll let you rest,' said Mthetho. 'I must speak to your wife. We can't have your family falling apart.'

Monwabisi thanked Mthetho and apologised for not escorting him to the door.

As his driver pulled the BMW away from the house, the Deputy Minister tried to get Constantia again on her cell.

This time she picked up.

'What's wrong with my cousin?' Mthetho asked.

'He hates the prepaids too much,' she said. 'He is the most stubborn man in all of South Africa.'

'He is not well, my sister. It appears he has caught the wrong train.'

Constantia didn't reply. She knew what train Mthetho was talking about. She said she'd phone him back 'straight away', that she had some people in her car. She returned the call ten minutes later and told Mthetho the whole story of Monwabisi's HIV, right down to him hoarding her money 'like a squirrel hiding nuts'.

'He must see a doctor,' said Mthetho. 'Those three letters can make a person crazy. Dementia is not a joke.'

'My sons need their father,' she said, 'not this wild man. Talk to him, bhuti.'

'I did already,' said Mthetho. 'He won't tell me a thing.'

'All right, then,' she said. 'I'll take care of it.'

○

On the way home Constantia stopped by the house to try to talk to Monwabisi one more time.

'I was wrong,' he told her. 'This virus is real. It's time to tell the world that I'm HIV-positive. If I speak out, others will do the same.'

His decision would make life unbearable for her and the boys. Not only was her husband an ANC renegade, now he would become the public face of HIV in Sivuyile. Everyone would assume she had the virus as well. She didn't need their pity.

'I'm through with the medication,' he said. 'I won't take it until it is available to every member of the working class. No more gravy train.'

'You want to disappear?' she asked. 'Ufuna ukuba famous. What are you doing to your sons with this stubbornness of yours?'

She picked a teacup off the white plastic table and smashed it into pieces on the floor. Two chips from the handle slid all the way into the bedroom.

On her way home, she phoned Mthetho and convinced him to try talking to her husband one more time.

○

'We must cling to life with everything we have,' Mthetho told Monwabisi the next morning. The former shop steward had arisen early, before eight o'clock for once. The two sat facing each other in the white garden chairs.

'For our children, if nothing else,' added Mthetho.

'My sons understand it is better to die standing up than to live on your knees,' said Monwabisi. He tried to stand but lost his balance. He caught himself on the arm of the chair but his right knee banged on the floor.

'The worst is to die on your knees,' said Mthetho. 'You are like an old donkey that refuses to move off the railway lines even though the train is speeding towards you.'

Monwabisi found his feet but stumbled twice more before he reached the bedroom door. 'People must have their water,' he said as he staggered into the bedroom.

Mthetho had done everything he could. He needed to get back to Bhisho. On the way he listened to the old Crusaders' album *Scratch*. He and Monwabisi had played it for hours when his cousin had visited New York in the eighties. Their favourite song was 'Way Back Home'. It made them think of how wonderful South Africa would be when freedom came.

○

Fidel had sneaked off to see his father on his way home from school. The two of them lay on a single mattress on the floor, Monwabisi's new bed. The young boy rubbed his hand against his father's cheek.

'Your beard tickles my hand, tata,' he told Monwabisi. His father didn't open his eyes.

'Tata,' Fidel continued, 'Mama was crying this morning, saying you won't take your medicine. I heard her say to someone on the phone that you wanted to die.'

'I'm not going to die,' said Monwabisi. 'Your father is a fighter.' He remembered his decision. If he was going to tell all of Ukusa he was HIV-positive, he'd have to tell his sons first. For a second, Monwabisi thought he might cry. Then he caught himself. Weeping wasn't for metalworkers.

'I'm sick,' Monwabisi said. 'Have you heard of HIV?'

'The three letters?'

'Yes, I've got that disease.'

'You must take your medicine,' Fidel said, trying to reach around his father's neck to give him a hug. 'Who will teach us soccer if you are sick?'

This thin boy with short hair, long eyelashes and the graceful strides of a long-distance runner had broken down his father's will as easily as Mbulelo Botile could tear apart a schoolyard bully. Monwabisi would start taking the cocktail of pills again.

That afternoon he took his green passbook and withdrew enough money to buy a month's worth of medication. He was still going to tell everyone about his affliction, though. That was non-negotiable.

Chapter 46

THE KOMBI DROPPED Joanna right next to a row of ten porta-potties. Corleone was there to meet her. He told her residents referred to the line of toilets as the Great Wall of China. 'They say the astronauts could smell it from the moon,' he said. She wasn't sure whether to laugh.

The roads through OR Tambo weren't even as wide as the pavements in New York City. Joanna had to turn, step sideways, look up, look down to make her way through the flow of people. Every two or three steps brought a new set of aromas – burnt porridge, dirty nappies, fresh paint on a door. One conversation trailed into another, with the hooting of the taxis and the thumping of kwaito as the background refrain.

She wished she hadn't worn her nylon running shoes. Though young girls tried to keep the streets clean, the fallout from households with no running water or flush toilets was soaking through her socks. In one shack a group of women huddled around a battery-powered TV watching *Days of Our Lives*.

'Yiza,' said one of the women as Joanna passed. 'We are waiting for the madam here.'

'Did you travel well?' asked Corleone.

'Fine,' said Joanna. She didn't mention the pop-down video screen on the bus or how loudly she'd laughed at the Mr Bean movie that kept repeating. Since her incident in the taxi, she never let herself sleep on public transport.

'I hope the smoke doesn't bother you,' he said as they passed a house where a woman was cooking some meat on an imbawula. Joanna had heard stories about fires in these settlements. She imagined all the residents pouring onto this road in a panic trying to grab small children and a few belongings while trying to escape an advancing blaze.

A couple of children called out 'Umlungu!' as Joanna turned a corner. A toddler fell in front of her. Joanna stopped. The child looked up at her and cried in horror until a smiling young woman picked her up.

Joanna looked straight ahead, like she was travelling in a car with one-way windows and no one could see in.

'Smoke is no big deal,' she said. 'I've done a lot of camping.'

She felt stupid once she'd mentioned camping, as if the residents of OR Tambo rented chalets in national parks or snuggled into down sleeping bags for their vacations. They wouldn't even know what a vacation was.

'How often does the Mayor come here?' she asked.

'Only during elections,' said Corleone, 'or if there is a disaster. Maybe a flood or a fire.'

Corleone's house had two rooms. Multiple pictures of Nelson Mandela's beaming face plastered to a scrap-wood wall greeted Joanna as she got inside. 'A Better Life for All,' the lettering said below his name.

Slim lay on a thin mattress in the corner, behind a curtain fashioned from a nearly transparent bed sheet. In his letter he had told her he was 'not feeling well', and asked her to come 'if she could find the time'.

His voice was a whisper and the fading incense wasn't strong enough to overpower the odour of what Joanna figured was rotting mackerel. She could barely see his shrunken face wrapped in the red-and-white checks of the kafiyyeh.

'A freedom fighter forever,' said Corleone. He lit the candle atop the Olivine bottle next to Slim's bed. Peter Franklin's business card lay next to the bottle. The raised gold lettering beamed with each flicker of the flame. Joanna needed to phone Peter, tell him of Slim's condition.

'Now you can see the comrade,' said Corleone.

Joanna reached for Slim's hand. Streaks of white trailed around his cracking lips. He swallowed like he had a mouthful of sand.

'Water is finished,' said Corleone to Slim. 'The card is empty. Your uncle will be here at four. He promised to load the card.'

Joanna looked at her watch. Eleven thirty. Why didn't these people have water? She remembered the joy in this community that day she stood out in front of the Damanes' house. Back then, Water for Freedom seemed to have solved these problems in one fell swoop. But like everything else in South Africa, bringing water to the poorest of the poor was complicated. One fell swoop didn't solve anything here. There was always another side to the story.

A young woman came in carrying a plastic milk jug full of water. Corleone introduced her to Joanna as Slim's sister, Mandi. 'Sister' was a word with many meanings in South Africa. Joanna didn't probe.

'I have found some water,' said Mandi. 'Just fifty cents.' She picked up a glass next to Slim's bed and filled it, then brought it up to his lips. Mandi propped his head up with her hand as he drank. When he finished she wiped his mouth with the sleeve of her blouse and left.

'I'm sorry, Comrade Joanna,' said Slim. 'You've come all this way and I can't even stand to greet you. It's my back.'

'Just rest,' said Joanna.

'I've eaten your money,' he said. 'It's gone.'

'We'll talk tomorrow,' she said. She tried not to show her

anger. How would she explain this to Angela and the others? She'd promised them the money would go for medication. If he'd spent the money properly, he wouldn't be in this condition. Even a sick person had to account. Wasn't that the South African way?

'We'll find you a doctor tomorrow,' said Joanna.

'Doctors are in town,' said Corleone. 'It's far.'

'We will let you sleep,' said Joanna. She wanted to leave. She didn't know how much longer she could take the rotting mackerel smell.

As she and Corleone ducked under the curtain, Mandi returned with two little children clinging to her leg. One of them stared at Joanna's bare white legs. Mandi went to Slim. The children dashed out the door.

'Sit down, comrade,' said Corleone, pointing to a wooden chair that once had a cushioned seat. Corleone perched on a plastic milk crate while the two hunted for conversation. She didn't know the customs. Was she supposed to ask questions about a sick person? She wanted to know how long he'd been like this, when did he start to give off that odour? Maybe such issues were taboo. She kept quiet. Who was she to judge?

Corleone gave her a copy of *Sechaba*, the 'voice of the ANC'. She read it while he boiled water for tea on a hotplate. She saw Corleone passing an electric cord out through a small hole in the window. Someone outside said, 'Okay.'

One of the small children came back with a tattered copy of an old *Cosmopolitan*. She handed it to Joanna with both hands. Joanna thanked the girl. The cover showed a picture of an actress called Pamela Nomvete.

The *Sechaba* was even older, promising 'full and complete liberation of the masses through the RDP'. Joanna set it aside. She once held the RDP just a notch below the Bible. Things had changed.

Apparently many people hated Pamela Nomvete. The

article said her portrayal of an evil soap opera character called Ntsiki was so convincing that she was once slapped in the face for it by someone in a restaurant.

A woman in a black skirt came in and handed Mandi a small brown paper packet. As Mandi opened it, a smell of slightly tainted meat drifted across the room.

She asked Mandi if she could help.

'You are the guest,' said Mandi. 'You must relax.'

Joanna read an article on the best way to remove nail varnish from clothes. She'd forgotten how many different ideas women had on such topics. Emily from Ermelo said that Doom inspect spray worked 'like a charm'.

Mandi dumped mealie-meal from a small white packet into a bowl of water and stirred it with a long wooden spoon.

A few minutes later, Joanna gathered with Corleone around Slim's bed while Mandi helped him to eat.

'The meat is painful to swallow,' Slim said.

'You need food to get your strength back,' said Joanna.

'There are sores in my mouth,' he said. 'So many. Let me try later. My back hurts too much. I'm feeling cold.'

Corleone exited and came back with a brown jersey. 'It can help,' he said. 'It's wool.'

When Slim rolled over on his side, the mackerel smell was suddenly much worse. Joanna wanted to gag on her pap. She glanced at Slim's back. Two boils had come to a head. One was the size of a table-tennis ball. Mandi squeezed the bigger one. Slim yelped. Mandi caught the blend of pus and blood with a piece of newspaper before it slid onto the bed.

Joanna spit the pap back into her bowl and escaped to the other room. She stood near a small end table and looked at the photo of Pamela Nomvete on the cover of *Cosmo*. The woman gave off an air of total contempt. Slim screeched one more time and Joanna started to shake. That mackerel smell again. She wondered if the odour would get into her clothes like cigarette smoke in a bar. The sound of crumpling newspapers didn't reduce the stench.

'Much better,' said Slim. 'Now I can lie on my back.'

Corleone came into the lounge.

'We must get him to a doctor,' said Joanna.

'The comrade can't walk,' said Corleone. 'We can try a wheelbarrow.'

'I could hire a car,' said Joanna.

The two agreed. In the morning she would park the car where the taxi dropped her and wait for Corleone.

'Mandi or one of the neighbours can help me push the comrade to the taxi rank,' he said. 'It can work.'

'Here,' said Joanna, handing Corleone R20. 'In case you have to buy more food or water.'

Corleone thanked her and put the money in his shoe. Joanna wanted to say goodbye to Slim but Mandi said he had fallen asleep.

'You can see him tomorrow,' she said. 'By then he will be feeling much better.'

Corleone walked with her to the taxi rank. They didn't say much along the way. When he hugged her before she climbed into the taxi, she caught a faint whiff of the rotting mackerel smell from the shack.

Joanna phoned Peter that night. She didn't know who else to talk to.

'I'm sure he'll be all right,' said Peter. 'The medications work wonders these days.'

'Maybe they don't work the same for everyone.' Her words fell dead in the receiver. She heard Peter's fingers gliding across the keyboard in the background.

'Don't get me wrong,' he said after a few seconds. 'I hope the young man gets better, but he needs to learn that freedom comes with responsibility. He's been stirring up a lot of trouble in Sivuyile.'

'He means well,' said Joanna.

'Maybe you need to look for some new friends.'

She didn't want to admit it but he had a point. She had gotten it all wrong with Slim, trusting him the way she did with all that money. She wished she'd never even talked to him that day in the taxi. It would have made her life a whole lot less complicated. How would she ever explain all of this to the people at UV?

○

When Corleone wasn't at the taxi rank in the morning, Joanna had no idea what to do. Where did a person park a car in OR Tambo? She should have learned her lesson by now. Slim had spent her money. Why should she expect Corleone to keep an appointment? Maybe he'd taken the R20 and bought beer. A taxi hooted at her.

'Clear out, madam,' said a young man in a red shirt standing just outside her window. 'This area is for business.' She checked again to make sure the doors were locked. She had no choice. She drove back to her bed and breakfast, parked the car on the street and went to her room to have a cup of coffee. The old couple who ran the place, the Thompsons, had given her some extra packets of Ricoffy. Might as well put it to good use.

She worried that something had happened. She thought she could find her way to Corleone's shack. But was it safe? She'd had that horrible experience in a taxi, but she carried herself differently now. If it was daytime, she could manage.

She drove back to OR Tambo. This time she parked near the row of porta-potties and started walking, repeating that one-way window act from the day before.

'I've got something here for the madam!' one young man shouted through a window as she passed his shack, but she just kept going.

A few doors down a middle-aged woman dressed in the red and white of the Methodists asked Joanna who she was looking for.

'I want to see a young man named Corleone,' Joanna replied.

'I can take you there,' said the woman. 'My name is Charlene.'

She followed Charlene down the road. It all looked familiar from the day before. She doubted that a woman dressed as a Methodist could lead her astray. As they neared the final corner to Corleone's place, Joanna heard singing. Actually it was more like a group wail. When the pair turned the corner, the sound grew louder. There were lots of people crowded together in the road near Corleone's. Joanna wondered if there'd been a fire. Charlene motioned to her to wait.

'I'll find out what is happening,' she said. She shouted something in Xhosa through an open door to a woman inside. When the woman replied, Charlene said, 'Just look after her for a minute.'

Suddenly Corleone came out of the crowd. He moved towards Joanna, reaching out for her hand.

'We lost the comrade during the night,' he said. 'He has gone to the other side. We shall always remember him. It's so wonderful that you came to visit before he passed.'

Charlene got back just in time to grab Joanna as she fell. She woke up inside a nearby house with Charlene and Corleone standing over her.

'I'm sorry,' Joanna said.

'We are glad you are awake now,' said Corleone. 'To lose one comrade in a day is more than enough.'

Chapter 47

'Our government let Slim down and they are letting us down today,' said Monwabisi. He was wearing his white 'I'm Positive' T-shirt for the first time.

'Phantsi ngabelungu abamnyama, phantsi!' shouted Corleone.

As if on cue, the crowd began to chant and sing their condemnation.

'Slim never had access to the anti-retrovirals that could have saved his life,' said Monwabisi. 'Yet the government continues to deny there are more cases of HIV every day in our communities.'

Joanna stood towards the back. She'd bought a new black dress and had her hair cut for this funeral at Sivuyile Hall. Corleone told her she looked 'beautiful' when she arrived. She didn't feel beautiful now. The speeches didn't tell the whole story. Slim had the money for medication and squandered his chance. Blaming the government for everything didn't help. She wanted to repeat what Peter had told her, that freedom came with responsibility, but this was not her place to speak. Slim's kafiyyeh had been laid across the coffin, along with the South African flag.

Corleone spoke after Monwabisi. 'Slim's dream was to form this organisation,' he said, 'to ensure people received what was promised – water, housing, electricity, education, jobs. I call on everyone here to join in building

Slim's organisation, the People's Voice.'

Corleone pointed to his chest where a picture of Slim's face, wrapped in his kafiyyeh, smiled underneath the words 'Ilizwi labantu: The People's Voice'. 'Let us not allow imperialist companies like Pellmar to plunder our communities while we are silent,' he added. 'Our voices must be heard.'

Joanna didn't know what to think. This was taking it too far. The party of Mandela had brought down apartheid. It was too early to give up on them. Besides, this martyr they were honouring was a fraud, someone who got money for medication, spent it on himself and then blamed the ANC and condemned Pellmar as imperialist. Peter had his faults but he was no imperialist. Mrs Mehlo led two dozen people clad in red People's Voice T-shirts in a musical expression of their betrayal by the ANC.

'Sakunika ivoti,' they sang. 'We gave you our votes, we even gave you our breasts, now you don't know exactly what you want. Awuyaz'oyifunayo.'

Constantia Radebe was the last speaker.

'Let us use this day of dark clouds as a wake-up call,' she began. 'We have achieved this miracle of democracy, but the struggle is not yet over. I pledge to carry the concerns of our departed brother into the halls of government, into the council chambers. It is a fitting way to remember him.'

'It is too late,' cried Mrs Mehlo.

'It is never too late,' said Constantia. 'I ask you to come with me, not to lose faith, not to give up, not to surrender. We know that it is on a stormy day that we finally see the hen's tail. This is our stormy day, where we show our true colours.'

A few people clapped. Joanna wanted to join them but she feared some people might take it the wrong way. Constantia Radebe was a brave woman.

'We have already seen those tail feathers of that party of

yours,' said Corleone. 'They are not a pretty sight.'

'We don't need a new organisation,' she said. 'You cannot have two bulls in the same kraal. We need the people's voice to become louder in the ANC, to drown out those who want to use our organisation for their own selfish ends.'

Constantia paused. Out of nervous habit she tried to adjust the wedding band on her finger. It wasn't there.

'I am not the ANC,' she continued. 'The president is not the ANC. It is you, all of us. Let us not be hijacked from our goal of a better life for all, including for the Slim Yantas of tomorrow.'

She ended there, to polite applause. At least Joanna could see that someone was talking sense here. The last thing South Africa needed was another revolution.

The People's Voice cohort carried the coffin to the graveyard. Constantia and Monwabisi walked side by side but they didn't speak.

As they laid Slim into the ground, Mrs Mehlo began the first note of the traditional 'Hamba Kahle' farewell. Corleone and two other youth fired shots into the air. The chorus took diverging lyrical paths, some sticking with the traditional 'mkhonto' while Corleone and others in the red T-shirts resorted to 'PV' instead.

Oblivious to the linguistic tensions and not sure how to fit into all of this, Joanna read a quote from Che Guevara that Corleone had selected for the neatly printed programme: 'Wherever death may surprise us, let it be welcome, provided that this, our battle cry, may have reached some receptive ear and another hand may be extended to wield our weapons...'

Che's words made Joanna even more uncomfortable. The second half of the passage spoke of the 'staccato singing of the machine guns'. Just reading those words frightened her. A horde of youngsters circulated to collect the programmes and toss them into the grave. Monwabisi threw the first scoops of dirt; then Mandi and Corleone neatly folded the kafiyyeh and the flag and presented it to Slim's uncle. The shovels kept changing hands as Slim's coffin gradually receded into the earth.

A few more shots echoed across the graveyard and then Slim Yanta's mourners made their way back to his uncle's house. Joanna didn't stay long there. She made her exit while the crowd was still emptying pots of samp and beans, downing beer and cool drinks, and recalling the short but determined life of Comrade Slim.

Joanna made her way back to her bed and breakfast, changed out of her black dress, made herself a pot of tea, and sat in the garden watching squirrels diving through the network of branches in the Thompsons' backyard. She fought back the urge to cry by trying to figure out how to explain to all those UV members who had contributed money that Slim was not the hero she once thought he was. She owed them that much.

Finally she accepted the obvious: Slim had played her for a fool. She couldn't put that in a report. Then the tears came. She wasn't just crying for the loss of Slim. These were tears of confusion. She didn't know who to believe any more. There was no way to put that into a report.

Chapter 48

IN HER PRETORIA OFFICE Susan Vickers read an online account of Slim's funeral. She'd been to so many funerals in the past. As she finished reading the story she hummed 'Hamba Kahle' to herself. She remembered the youthful black comrades carrying Graeme's coffin out of Orlando Stadium. Even if Slim was misguided, Susan didn't think badly about the dead. Funerals were some of her most cherished memories, expressions of life at the moment of death. So different from the repressed white church of her youth. Who ever danced at a white funeral?

Peter visited her that night. He'd had a meeting with Minister Tumahole that afternoon.

'It's taking off,' he told her. 'Three new municipalities are targeted for the prepaids. We might have to adjust the tariffs upward a notch or two as revenue is still slightly less than projections, but it's still early days.'

He'd brought a video of *Roxanne*, the old Steve Martin movie, and a dozen red roses. She thanked him for the flowers. Nothing transformed a room like roses. Red was her favourite colour. She kissed him gently on the forehead, then put the flowers in some water. A lovely gesture, but she was still thinking about Orlando Stadium, those thousands of black youth packed against the chain-link fence around the edge of the pitch.

'*Roxanne* may be the funniest film of all time,' said Peter. 'You'll love it.'

'Not tonight,' she said. 'I've got a lot of work.' She'd seen the movie before and thought it was dreadful. She didn't fancy American comedies.

Peter watched *Roxanne* by himself in her lounge. By the time it was over, Susan had fallen asleep with a 300-page report next to her on the bed.

When they woke up the next morning, she told him the relationship wasn't working, that the worlds of 'business and government were just too different'. She knew it sounded like a foolish explanation, but it was the best way she could think of to characterise their differences without a long discussion.

'These days we are partners,' he replied. 'You should have watched that video with me last night. It would have cheered you up.'

'I don't need cheering up,' she said.

'You don't look very happy,' he said.

'We can talk about it later.'

'Right,' he said. 'I'll leave the video for you. Trust me. It's a classic.'

'Thanks,' she said as she flipped through some file folders trying to decide which ones had to go to the office.

As soon as they got outside, Susan strode quickly towards her car.

'I'll phone you when I get back from Brazil,' he said. 'I'm leaving tomorrow, early.' He held up a Portuguese phrase book and smiled. 'The Brazilians are begging for the prepaids,' he added.

'I may be out of town,' she said without turning around. 'I'll let you know.'

'Whatever,' he replied and got into his car. He switched on the CD player.

'Bon dia,' Susan heard the voice on the tape say.

'Bon dia,' Peter repeated and pulled out of the driveway.

Chapter 49
Sivuyile Hall

THE BANNER ON THE front wall proclaimed: 'No More Cut-offs: Water for Freedom.' Flyers for the event promised to expose how the ruling party had failed to deliver services, that lifelines had been turned into 'deathlines.' Joanna had arrived in Sivuyile the night before to observe for UV. She still hadn't worked up the nerve to write all those who'd donated money to Slim and tell them what had happened. Still, she didn't want her disappointments with Slim to colour her judgement. The problem of water cut-offs was becoming serious. Peter and his prepaids had not delivered the magic bullet.

Monwabisi, wearing his charcoal suit, chaired the hearing. Fidel and Musa sat on either side of him. Both sported grey ties, just like their father's. Next to Musa was Mrs Mehlo. Her arm was in a plaster. The Take Charge guards broke it when People's Voice members unsuccessfully tried to stop the seizure of Mrs Ximiya's furniture. She still owed more than R1 000 for old water bills.

Monwabisi began by noting that cut-offs, like HIV, were a 'national pandemic'. Then came the witnesses.

More than a dozen people came forward to register their complaints about the meters. One woman blamed the prepaids for the death of her baby from diarrhoea. She said her child became dehydrated in the night and by the time the kiosk opened the next morning so she could load her card, the baby had passed away. The final witness was Mr

Yanta, Slim's uncle. At age fifty-seven he still worked as a 'tea boy' at Kuper Construction. As he took his seat, a lone reporter at the back of the hall casually flipped open his notebook.

Monwabisi welcomed Mr Yanta while a young woman adjusted the microphone in front of the witness chair. The brief delay gave the old man time to catch his breath.

'Mr Yanta,' said Monwabisi, 'can you tell us how you came to have arrears with the council?'

'We were trying to bring down the Boers,' he said. 'We were boycotting our service payments.'

'And you succeeded?' asked Monwabisi. The crowd of several dozen laughed.

'We elected Mandela, then our new council,' said Mr Yanta. 'We were so happy.'

'And what did the new government do for you?'

'At first it seemed they were trying. They installed taps in our houses and we celebrated. No more long queues, no more going to vendors.'

Mr Yanta looked around. A jug of ice water was just out of his reach at the other end of the table. A young woman filled a glass and passed it to him.

'Then what happened?' asked Monwabisi.

'They gave us the cards, said we had to pay first before we could get water.'

'So you had water?'

'Not without the card. Then they told me I owed from the old days. My card stopped working.'

'How did you manage?'

'I agreed to pay so much a month,' said Mr Yanta. 'Then my nephew Slim came. He had medical bills. He was sick. I had to try to save him.'

Mr Yanta held out the glass and asked the young woman

to fill it again. He emptied it in one gulp. 'The water is so cold, Mr Chairman. The ice blocks are delicious,' he said as he put the glass down.

'I had to buy the tablets for Slim,' Mr Yanta continued. 'I was no longer affording my monthly payment to the municipality. So I went to the offices to explain.'

'And what happened there?' asked Monwabisi.

'They just kept telling me I must pay R300 a month or they wouldn't turn the card on.'

'So what did you do for water?'

'I bought from vendors. Sometimes I borrowed from neighbours, but they became fed up. Their cards went dry. Then my nephew brought his friends.'

Musa stood up and whispered something in his father's ear. Monwabisi asked Mrs Mehlo to take over. He said he had some 'urgent business' to attend to. He took Musa's hand and walked him out the front door of the hall to the bathroom.

Mr Yanta explained how Slim's friends reconnected his water, only to have the Take Charge people return and remove the meter and all the pipes.

'So you've never had water since that day?' asked Mrs Mehlo.

'I had nothing for some months. Then my nephew paid. By that time they were threatening to evict me from my house.'

'Your nephew paid?' asked Mrs Mehlo as she dabbed her brow with a pink handkerchief.

'By that time he was getting money from the American lady,' said Mr Yanta. 'I don't know how he knew her. She is here today.'

People's eyes found their way to Joanna. She sat alone in a blue jersey.

'The lady was giving him money to buy medication,' said Mr Yanta.

'So he spent the money for his medication to pay your arrears?'

'Yes.'

'God bless him,' said Mrs Mehlo, wiping her forehead again. 'I think we should say a prayer in his honour. He was a son like Jesus.'

'He said that with my big family I couldn't afford to be evicted. He said he was just one person. Then they chased him.'

Monwabisi returned with Musa.

Mr Yanta explained how Slim ended up in OR Tambo because people in the neighbourhood thought he would infect their daughters.

'He became ill there in the squatter camp,' said Mr Yanta. 'I'm not ashamed to tell everyone. Slim suffered from Aids.'

'Thetha tata, thetha!' shouted a young man in the front row.

Mr Yanta paused for a minute. His heavy breaths poured out from the speakers at the front of the hall. He looked for more water. The jug was empty.

'The day he left us I was on the way with more water,' said Mr Yanta. 'I had loaded the card during lunch hour but then I was delayed at work. The American lady had come. She helped him with food.'

No one looked at Joanna this time. A tear of shame rolled down her cheek. She didn't wipe it away. She wouldn't have to write that report after all. Why had she just assumed Slim had wasted the money when there were so many other possibilities?

'Who do you blame for what happened to your nephew?' asked Mrs Mehlo.

Monwabisi signalled Mr Yanta to wait before answering. He got up, switched off the microphone and whispered something to Mrs Mehlo. She shook her head and turned the mike back on.

'The question is fair,' she said, still looking at Monwabisi.

'There are too many people,' said Slim's uncle. 'Those Boers paid me peanuts or I would have looked after him, paid the arrears. I wouldn't have relied on a young boy to pay my bills.'

'So it was the fault of the Boers?' asked Mrs Mehlo.

'I am also to blame,' he said. 'I should have worked harder, studied more at school. I was clever.'

'Is that all, Mr Yanta?'

'Not quite. I feel the government is also to blame. They promised us water and so many things. The problem is that some of them seem to have forgotten us.'

Mr Yanta reached down and picked up a small wooden box off the floor. It was painted in the black, yellow and green of the ANC. He put it on the table and took off the top.

'This boy didn't have to die,' Mr Yanta said. He removed a photo of his nephew from the box and held it up for all to see. 'This is what we have to remember him by,' he said. 'This little box full of his things.'

He put the picture down on the table, then took the other items out of the box one by one and held them over his head. A copy of Lenin's *State and Revolution*, a cassette of Mzwakhe Mbuli's 'Resistance is Defence', a key ring with the initials RDP, the red-and-white kafiyyeh and, lastly, the business card of Peter Franklin.

'This must not happen to other young men of Sivuyile,' said Mr Yanta. He placed everything back in the wooden box and wrapped the kafiyyeh around it as a final covering. With the box under his arm he walked over to the jug of water. The young woman had just refilled it. Mr Yanta drank two full glasses.

Once Mr Yanta had finished his water, Monwabisi closed the proceedings, calling the hearings a historic occasion as important as the Truth and Reconciliation Commission.

'We salute those people who have come forward fearlessly to express their outrage,' he added.

'The government must respond!' Corleone shouted from the floor. 'Comrade Slim didn't die for nothing.'

Mrs Mehlo closed with a prayer. 'Let free water rain down on people like a storm from above,' she said. 'And please, Heavenly Father, help our leaders to see the light before it is too late. We don't know what they are thinking.'

As the crowd filed out, Monwabisi reminded everyone that the following week People's Voice would be hosting groups from other communities around the Eastern Cape who also had experienced cut-offs.

'We are mobilising the grassroots,' he said. 'Just like the 1980s.'

'Comrades,' said Corleone, 'the eighties were long ago. There is no going back.'

'We know that,' said Monwabisi, 'but we can always learn from history.'

'We are tired of hearing about history,' said Corleone. 'People don't listen to Bra Hugh any more. They are talking on cellphones, playing on computers.'

Corleone walked away, then stopped and kicked the dirt twice before he continued.

Monwabisi grabbed his sons by the hand and started for home. He had them for three whole days now while Constantia was away. A block from the house Fidel reminded him to stop at the kiosk and put money on the card.

'I almost forgot,' said Monwabisi. 'Maybe one day we won't have to worry about such things.'

'Was there a time when there were no cards?' asked Fidel.

'Let me tell you the story of how we came to have these cards,' said Monwabisi. The boys grinned and Monwabisi began to tell his very long story.